# altered

# altered

## Aubrey Coletti

ESCAPE ARTIST PRESS

ESCAPE ARTIST PRESS

ISBN 978-0615650920

*Designed and typeset by Joshua Langman · JL Typographic Design*

This book is set in Garamond Premier Pro, designed by Robert
Slimbach in 2005. This type family is a revival of the roman types
of Claude Garamond and the italic types of Robert Granjon,
designed in the mid-1500s.

For all my friends who inspired the characters —
see, you're famous now!

# author's note

*This is a work of fiction, and any relationship to actual organizations or individuals is purely coincidental. However, the school mentioned by the character Charlie Persan as being in Canton, Massachusetts is real. The Judge Rotenberg Center is a residential treatment center for students with emotional disturbances, conduct, behavior, emotional and/or psychiatric problems, and developmentally delayed students with autistic-like behaviors. The school is privately owned and has near-zero rejections and near-zero expulsions, and uses no or minimal psychotropic medication. They have been met with controversy due to their use of aversive treatment tactics, specifically their use of skin shock devices that administer electric shocks to various parts of the students' bodies.*

*There are many strict residential rehabilitation centers in the United States, alternatively known by such names as "behavior modification centers," "wilderness programs," and "emotional growth boarding schools." Often these facilities are regulated like ordinary boarding schools, even though they sometimes use more severe methods of restraint and isolation than psychiatric centers. There are often no special qualifications required of the people who oversee these facilities, nor any diagnosis required before enrollment. There have been reports of beatings, sleep deprivation, use of stress positions, emotional abuse and public humiliation. Teens are often sent to these facilities in the midst of a parental divorce, when they are suffering from or assumed to be suffering from drug use or abuse, because of depression or other severe mental illnesses, and many have lengthy histories of trauma and abuse. Justice Department reports released in 2001 comparing boot camps with traditional correctional facilities concluded that neither facility "is more effective in reducing recidivism." The National Institutes of Health released a "state of the science" consensus in late*

*2004 concluding that "get tough" treatments "do not work and there is some evidence that they may make the problem worse."*

FOR MORE INFORMATION:

"Judge Rotenberg Center — Residential Program Treating Behavior Disorders and Developmental Disabilities." judgerc.org. N.p., n.d. Web. 09 October 2007.

Kindlon, Rusty; Bandini, Susan; et al. *Observations and Findings of Out of State Program Visitation Judge Rotenberg Educational Center.* JRC Program Visitation Report, 09 June 2006. New York State Education Department. Retrieved 30 October 2007. <http://ww.boston.com/news/daily/15/school_report.pdf>.

Szalavitz, Maia. "The Trouble With Tough Love." *The Washington Post,* 29 Jan. 2006. Web. 05 October 2007.

Szalavitz, Maia. *Help At Any Cost: How the Troubled Teen Industry Cons Parents and Hurts Kids.* 375 Hudson Street, New York, New York 10014: Riverhead Books, 2006.

# altered

# prologue

*The Headmistress opened her private files and logged the date before beginning.*

```
Three days since the tests. Subject 1 shows
signs of encroaching depression, which is to
be expected after the mania during the days
leading up to the tests. Whether the answer to
her abilities lies in the extreme nature of
her mania itself, or in some coping mechanism
that has evolved to try and combat the
debilitating effects of the disease remains
to be seen.
```

*The Headmistress paused before typing again.*

```
Subject 2 remains difficult to gauge. Should
my suspicions prove correct, it will take
time to sort out how he may be used fo—
```

*"Oh, I'm sorry ..."*

*The Headmistress saved her files and closed her computer quickly. "Yes, Wendy. What is it?"*

*The chemistry teacher in the door panted. "I was in class, and we were working and ... and I really think you need to come down and see this."*

# chapter one falling

**"All we need are a few more documents from your parents and your** school."

Toni looked up at the woman who had spoken. Short and heavy, with full curves and a round face, Toni's green eyes stood out against her brown skin. She tugged nervously on one of her many curls.

"Should I be worried?" Toni asked.

The principal of J. Alter Academy, Mrs. Carter, smiled, her high heels tapping the floor as she sat at her desk. Though pearl earrings set in gold and a jet necklace adorned her ears and neck, she had the look of a business executive, stern and cool, and Toni shifted in her seat under Mrs. Carter's gaze.

"No." Mrs. Carter smiled. "The Headmistress will look over them, but I expect she has already approved you personally."

"Really?" Toni asked.

Mrs. Carter's mouth twitched, and it seemed to Toni that the woman bit her tongue as if she had misspoken. "I wouldn't worry about it. As a boarder you will be spending most of your time with your housemates. I will be your supervisor, so I will be around whenever I can to answer your questions."

Toni nodded, swallowing. *Great. I'm right under the Head Bitch-In-Charge's gaze. This should be fun.*

Mrs. Carter gave a motherly smile. "Don't worry. Moving away from your family is hard. But you'll make new friends ... Katrina and my daughter Becky are your housemates. You'll be fine."

*Will I?* Toni wondered. *Friends were what did me in last time.*

The dark circles under Joseph Valdez's eyes were mocking him. Sleep eluded him and always had. He loved sleep but rarely got more than two hours a night, and he had gotten even less on the torturous plane and bus rides here. He doubted that it would change here.

"Please God," he prayed under his breath. "Make this some kind of hallucination, some kind of bad dream. Tell me my parents didn't sign four years of my life away."

He could take only a half-minute more of himself before he turned roughly away and walked to the one window in the white tiled bathroom. He grabbed the sill and jumped up. "God this place is like a fuckin' prison," he muttered.

He dropped to the floor, turned into a stall, and sank down, running his hand over his face. The whole plane ride then bus trip here, he had been trying to work out what kind of place wanted to take him. He wasn't enough of a delinquent to warrant a serious correctional facility, and his academic record sure didn't win him any scholarships. *How come they want me?*

Joseph pulled back one of his sleeves to reveal the small black cross tattooed on his bronze wrist. He touched it and swore.

*That's the last time I let a tattoo artist give me a discount.*

Lean and lightly muscular, Joseph's insecurities constantly reminded him of the scrawny awkward boy he had been until this summer, so that he swaggered more than necessary to compensate. His short black hair spread into light side burns. Thin and angular, his face was marked by a sharp nose and delicate mouth. But the most interesting part of him was undeniably his eyes.

The color of dark amber, he closed them as he tried to breathe. Dressed in a faded blue shirt and jeans, Joseph looked down at worn white sneakers that were, aside from the contents of the backpack by the door, the only possessions he cared about.

Joseph closed his eyes and waited a second before slamming one hand against the side of the stall. It hurt. A lot.

*Great. I love my life. It's just so much fuckin' fun.*

"I told him to keep his mouth shut, he didn't listen. It'll be his own fault when she finds out —"

Joseph stood up to face the three boys who had entered.

"Hello," said the one in the center, turning his face to the side and squinting down at Joseph. He was tall and imposing enough that Joseph could only assume he was a senior. He wore his overly large black jacket with a physically imposing confidence that Joseph could never master.

"What are you doing here?"

"I'm plannin' a massacre," Joseph said dryly. "What do you think?"

"Where did they drag you in from? I didn't know we took charity cases here, but I guess we're caring like that."

The two boys behind the senior snickered, and Joseph narrowed his eyes. "If you think he's funny, you must both be in love with him."

The senior made a whole production of dramatically looking apologetic. "Oh, did I hurt your feelings? Well, I really am so, so sorry." He held out his hand. "Seth Dryer. I'm a senior, so I can help get you acquainted with our school."

"Joseph Fuck-You-Very-Much Valdez," Joseph answered. "I gotta go find my class —"

Seth stepped in front of Joseph. "I don't think I heard you right," Seth said coolly as he fingered the panther emblem on his collar. He was about a head taller than Joseph, his hair blond to Joseph's black. He had the appearance of an All-American model. Joseph, for his part, zeroed in on the markings on the boy's fine skin, and the mole beside his thin mouth. It came to him that he disliked — no, he hated, this senior.

Seth's eyes were strange. The irises were light but surrounded by a thick dark ring. He held them wide open, and Joseph felt he would be sick if he continued to look into them.

"Get the fuck outta my way," Joseph said, forcing himself to meet Seth's gaze. Seth's mouth twitched with what was almost a smile.

"Swearing isn't allowed here," Seth said, sing-song.

"That's great," Joseph said in a low voice. "I'll keep that in mind. Meanwhile, I'll leave you and your boys to your *private business*: fuck all you want when I'm gone."

"You've got some bruises on you," Seth noted casually. Without warning he kneed Joseph in the chest, knocking him off his feet. Seth laughed softly, almost giggling, as Joseph coughed painfully.

"I think we can all agree that was called for," Seth clarified for his two friends. "Swearing isn't tolerated here. You're gonna hafta get yourself a vo-cab-u-lary if you wanna express yourself," he directed at Joseph mockingly.

Seth's friends snorted, and Seth smiled cruelly at Joseph. The smile faded when Joseph started to laugh.

"What?" Seth demanded. "*What?*"

Joseph tilted his head up so his amber eyes met Seth's blue ones. "Nuthin' man, just never seen a male model try so hard to pretend he was straight. Really man it's nuthin' to me. I ain't got an issue with gay people, just fuckin' pussies who need two boys to back 'em up while they fuck with the new kid."

Joseph's next retort froze on his tongue as he watched Seth's face become ugly with rage. Joseph frowned, his eyes traveling to Seth's left hand, which touched the ring on his right. Again, Joseph was caught off guard as he was hit. He tasted blood.

"You know there's no cameras in the bathrooms," Seth said, looking around before smiling down on Joseph as the other boys gathered around him. "Isn't that nice?"


Ann bit the inside of her cheek and walked up the line to the metal detector.

"Stop," the guard said. "Earrings."

"Why? You want to wear them?" she mumbled. "I don't think they'll go with your bone structure."

The student behind her smothered a laugh.

"Hand them over," the guard insisted.

Ann rolled her eyes and took her earrings off.

"You have a nail file. I will take that," the guard stated. He removed the nail file from her coat pocket, as well as a necklace and a case of cigarettes.

"The bracelet."

Ann grasped her wrist, her eyes widening. "No. Not this."

"You knew the rules when your parents enrolled you. No jewelry or metal."

Ann shook her head. She could remember so clearly when her sister had given her the charm bracelet: she had been seven years old.

"Please," Ann asked, hating herself for begging. "C'mon, I never take this off. It was a gift."

"Now."

She had given her sister a big hug — Ann loved to give hugs — and they had poorly painted each others' faces with their mother's makeup.

"It isn't dangerous." Ann talked quickly. She was good at bargaining, good at getting out of trouble. "It's just a charm bracelet."

"Now."

"Look, I'm sorry about the comment, but please, just leave me this."

"Hand it over."

"No," Ann said. There were mutterings behind her in the line. The guard grabbed her wrist to remove it. Ann dug her nails into the sensitive flesh between his thumb and forefinger and yanked her wrist back, her blood up.

Two arms held hers down from behind and the guard removed her bracelet.

"Let go of me," she ordered, dangerously.

"You're already in trouble for talking back and resisting relinquishing items: don't make it worse for yourself."

"Sure," Ann said, pulling her arms away and walking past the detector, leaving her belongings behind.

Charlie Persan looked out the bathroom window. She noted the locks and the metal gate. The school itself clearly reinforced the message that this was a four year sentence with no chance of parole.

*You did agree to this remember. It's not as if Mommy and Daddy forced you to go to boarding school.* Charlie sighed.

'Interesting' was the word most often used to describe Charlie. Short with dark, damp-looking hair that she let run wild to her shoulders, Charlie had light skin, a small nose, and cracked lips. The only feature she liked was her dark eyes, accentuated by thick dark brows. They were the one pretty thing on her plump face.

She heard voices and froze. Slowly, she turned to the window. It was opened just enough that a breeze carried the sounds of voices to her.

"You are a saddest, Lieutenant."

"I am a what now?"

"You know! One of those people who gets turned on by pain."

"Yo, I'm straight thanks."

"No, it's a word."

"Uh — you mean a sadist, sweetie?"

"You know what, Lieutenant!"

Lieutenant laughed, and Charlie heard a light slap.

"Hey, stop playin', stop playin', damn," she heard Lieutenant say. "You punch me, I punch you see —"

"Ow, L!" the male student protested. He had a slight lisp. "You can't kid around like that! Your arms are rock hard. They're lethal weapons."

"Melvin you gotta learn to —" Lieutenant stopped. "Here he is."

"You ready to do this thing?" said a new male voice, deeper and raspier.

"We'd better do it quick if we don't want to get caught," said Melvin.

"Hey, maybe we'd get expelled," said Lieutenant. "That's a nice thought, ain't it Anton?"

"More likely we'd get sent to jail," Anton replied. "And jail they will never take me to. I'm too damn pretty. You know what they do to pretty people in jail."

"Can we hurry up and get this over with?" Melvin said nervously. "I don't know why we chose to do this in broad daylight."

"Cause it's the one time they'd never expect," Anton said as if repeating something for the second or third time. "We cut the wires and get back in the damn bathroom —"

"Then let's *do* it!" Melvin whispered fiercely.

"A'ight," Lieutenant said. "Let's go. One ... two ... three."

Charlie shivered as the lights in the bathroom buzzed fiercely, and then went out. She wondered if the voices heard her scream.

chapter two **down**

**"So what made you take the plunge?" Becky asked as she offered**
Toni a brownie.

"Feel free to just tell what you feel comfortable with," said Katrina, a tall tanned sprinter who had the room across the hall.

"They just seemed like they really wanted me here," Toni said honestly.

That was the reason she had given her parents, her teachers, and everybody else who asked why she decided to go to a new high school so far away. She didn't feel she needed to say the rest.

"Whatever your reason," Becky said, ignoring Toni's answer, "just know that whatever problems you had at your school ... you can put them behind you here."

"Who said I had problems?"

Katrina and Becky exchanged a look.

"It's okay," Katrina said soothingly. "I had issues, too. Don't think of this school as a punishment, because it's really a wonderful place."

"Why would I think of it as a punishment?"

Again, the two older girls glanced at each other. "Well, because —"

"You cannot be serious?" said Mrs. Carter suddenly.

Becky and Katrina turned to peek into the kitchen as Mrs. Carter paced with the phone to her ear.

"Well the lights are back up now, right?" the principal continued, and Toni leaned in with the other girls to hear.

"Well then we can check — yes, I'm sure it is just a power outage, but ... we need to make sure it isn't ..."

Mrs. Carter looked up, and the three girls quickly resumed eating their brownies. The principal moved further into the other room and lowered her voice.

"I'm sure it's fine," Becky said, pushing back her brown hair. "My mother always takes care of everything. You don't need to be worried."

"I never said I was worried," Toni assured.

"Good," Becky stated. "Don't be."


*An escort right to the door,* Joseph thought, as he heard the guard lock him into his new home securely. *I must really be big news.*

Joseph was looking up so he didn't see the large potted plant he bumped into.

And knocked over.

Which subsequently broke.

*Shit.* He looked around awkwardly, and then tried to stand the plant back up and turn it so the crack in the pot didn't show. He held it with his hands and then stepped back. The pot fell over.

"Yeah, so that worked," Joseph mumbled flatly and walked away.

Joseph moved into the large, dingy kitchen, feeling that he deserved water from his absent hostess, his tattered sneakers squeaking on the sunflower-plastered linoleum floor. It wasn't until he opened the fridge that a swish of blonde hair at the other end of the kitchen informed him that he was not alone.

"How the hell did you get in here?"

*Shit.* Caught.

Joseph turned and stepped backward into the fridge door, stumbling and standing up.

"Oh I'm sorry I didn't see you I was just thirsty and —" Joseph stopped when he realized he wasn't speaking to his supervisor, Sherry Nearson.

"Hey, you're not Sherry. What are you doin' here?"

The girl sat on the counter by the sink with a Pop-Tart in one hand, staring at Joseph, her one eyebrow raised. Her gaze made him feel as though *he* was the intruder, even though he held his note of introduction in his left hand.

"What am I doing here? I'm going to be living here, apparently," she drawled. "If you broke in to see if she hides cash under her bed, I'll have to disappoint you. She's found a safer place, if she has any money at all. Call her crazy, but don't call her stupid."

"I didn't call her stupid, and I didn't break in neither! I'm stayin' here, too," Joseph said. The girl folded her arms, clearly disbelieving, and they stared at each other.

She was tall, with pale skin that made her facial features stand out. She wore her blonde hair pulled back into a high ponytail and had a strong, dominating nose, delicately arched brows, and green-blue eyes that she held half-closed, giving her a furtive, shifty look. Her tight blue shirt let a stripe of her stomach show, and she leaned back against the cabinets in a way that let him know that she had a big attitude.

Joseph watched her mouth spread into a slow smirk.

"Was the sound of somethin' breaking you?"

"No." Joseph colored. "Okay, yeah. There was this plant, and me and the plant had a little disagreement, and the short of it is, the plant is lookin' a little down now," Joseph offered.

"You broke Sherry's plant?" The girl raised an eyebrow. "Actually, thanks." She brightened. "If you're even more trouble than me, I might actually slide by."

"Wow, don't you just win at bitchy," Joseph grumbled.

"Excuse me?" the girl snapped. "If you're gonna insult me, don't mumble like a coward," she threw at him.

"Don't call me a coward," Joseph warned.

"Don't call me a bitch."

"Don't act like one."

"When did I act like one?"

"Just now when I walked in!"

"Yeah well I've had a rough day, and obviously you did too since you look like you got beat up pretty good."

"Yeah, well you ... got ... crumbs in your hair!"

The girl stopped glaring at him, and then they both started snorting awkwardly, then outright laughing.

"You look much older than a freshman," Joseph said after a moment. The girl looked at him, still half laughing. "I mean, you look like you could easily be seventeen, eighteen."

"That a good thing?" she asked, her eyebrow going up again.

"Could be," he said. "You know, normally, you ask somebody's name before anything else," Joseph said pointedly.

"Oh, yeah?"

"Uh-huh."

She shrugged. "Guess I figured if you wanted to tell me your name you would have introduced yourself by now."

"You ain't exactly giving me a chance!" Joseph said. He looked at her sideways. "So are you boarding, too? Or is Sherry your aunt or somethin'?"

"No, she's not my aunt," she answered. "My house is way at the other end of town; it takes a while to get to school, so my parents decided this would be easier."

"Any other reason?" She didn't strike him as the academic type, but then, he didn't really know her.

"I had nothing to lose," she gave her reason briskly. "Ann Cost," she said, holding out her hand. "And *now* I'm asking for your name."

"Joseph Nathaniel Valdez," he gave quickly.

"Nice name," Ann said. "Better than mine, anyway."

Joseph laughed when she frowned, crossing her arms and turning away. Then she smirked. "Wonder how Sherry'll react when she finds out you tracked dirt through her dining room," she said, jerking her head toward the imprints of Joseph's sneakers left on the floor. "She has a rule about keeping things clean: the school does for supervisors, since the supervisors have to follow all their rules when they take us in."

"Well I didn't know that! Why didn't you tell me?"

"I didn't hear you come in," Ann answered.

"Liar," Joseph shot back. "You said you heard me break it. How come you didn't come down?"

"I was in the shower," Ann offered smoothly, but her eyes had that veiled, shifty look again.

"Then why ain't you wet? How come your hair is dry?"

"I dried it off."

"You're lyin," Joseph stated.

"Excuse me?" Ann leaned back. "Maybe you'll find out it's hard to hear in this house."

"Maybe I'll find out you're full of shit in this house," Joseph rebounded.

"Here you are!"

Joseph turned away from Ann to look over the woman who had elected to take him in. Sherry Nearson looked like a blonde Cher, if Cher had decided to become a part-time housewife. Long hair came down over a fringed leather vest, almost touching her tight black skirt. A pair of dark sunglasses held the hair back from her face, and in each arm she held a full bag of groceries. A pair of very wide eyes with very small pupils took in Joseph's messy appearance and then moved slowly over the dirt imprints of his shoes on the floor.

"Was it you who broke my plant?" Sherry asked. Joseph winced.

"He didn't feel like wiping his feet either," Ann added.

*Did she just* completely *throw my ass under the damn bus?* thought Joseph. *Yeah, she did.* He glared viciously at her, and she just gave a little grin.

"I'm so sorry, it was an accident, and I tried to fix it but — I didn't ... I'm sorry," he excused himself.

"Well, I guess I can let this one slide," Sherry sighed. The smirk fell off Ann's face and reappeared on Joseph's, who mimicked her eyebrow raise. "But we're all here together, so you kids can get settled in," Sherry continued, unpacking her shopping bags. "Ann's got a heavy suitcase I can't get upstairs, Joseph, so maybe you could help her —"

"That's just fine. I can carry it myself," Ann cut in.

"Oh ... okay," resumed Sherry on a lower note. "Well, since you got here first, maybe you could help Joseph find his room, and —"

"Nah, it's cool. I'll find it myself," Joseph said to Sherry, still staring at Ann. For some reason he was unable to tear his eyes away from her as she walked out of the room.

Both he and Sherry heard the sharp closing of a door upstairs. Shaking his head, Joseph went up the stairs. *It's not like she's anythin' special,* he thought, his temper uncurling as he walked upstairs. *She's only kinda hot anyway, and she's got a big fuckin' attitude and sure as hell doesn't know how to make a first impression.*

"Alright then," Sherry shouted up, as cheery as she could. "We'll just all have dinner together at seven and we can —" a second door slammed — "get ... to know each other better," her voice trailed off.


"And you are?" Ms. Lovejoy pointed at Charlie.

"Charlie Persan," Charlie said, waiting for the teacher — who was also her supervisor — to show any sign that she knew who she was. Charlie had fallen asleep as soon as she was escorted to her new house and hadn't had a chance to meet her yet. This was her fourth class of the day, and she had been excited to learn that it was her supervisor teaching.

*But she has to know who I am,* Charlie thought. *Right?*

Ms. Lovejoy just smiled and gestured to the three lines on the white board. Lines A and C were about the same length, while line B was slightly shorter. "Which lines look the most similar?" Ms. Lovejoy questioned.

"A and C," said one boy, raising his hand.

"You sound really sure," Ms. Lovejoy responded. "What if everyone else here said they thought A and B were the most similar?"

"Why would they say that?"

"This line question was put to groups where everyone was a plant but one," Ms. Lovejoy stated. "All the people in on the experiment were told to say that A and B were the most similar. And when they did, overwhelmingly, the unsuspecting person in each group agreed."

"It's the Asch Experiment," Charlie stated. Ms. Lovejoy turned to look

Charlie straight in the eyes.

The boy raised his hand again, and Ms. Lovejoy nodded at him. "How do you convince yourself your eyes are wrong?" he asked. No one answered.

"Not everybody went along with it, though, right?" a bronze-skinned boy asked.

"No," Ms. Lovejoy explained, "if just one other person said that it was A and C, then the guinea pigs stuck to their guns and agreed that it was A and C."

A girl with brown skin and a mess of curly hair raised her hand. "Not to be rude but what does this have to do with English?"

"It's our introduction to *One Flew over the Cuckoo's Nest* this semester," Ms. Lovejoy responded. "And because these things are just as important to think about as academics. Knowing how to stand up and trust your own eyes is a pretty crucial thing to know," Ms. Lovejoy said earnestly. Charlie frowned slightly. She had been here almost a day and knew that this teacher was different. For starters, she actually listened to them instead of speaking at them. *She's different. I wonder how she ended up here,* Charlie mused.

*I wonder how long she'll last.*


*Yeah, she's got the right idea,* Joseph thought, sliding into a seat beside a girl who was already fast asleep. It wasn't that he was opposed to studying, necessarily. He was just so tired, and this was the time of day when he usually took a nap.

*It's not like I'm gonna fail Spanish,* he reminded himself. *My whole dream last night was in Spanish.* He settled his head down on his desk.

It was unfortunate that he was so tired; otherwise, he might have noticed that everyone, save the girl beside him, was sitting erect and silent, waiting for Mr. Protus.

The door opened and a short beefy man walked in, dressed in a black shirt and plain khakis. He moved heavily, his combat boots rapping the hard, polished floor. He carried the list of students in his right hand. At his waist hung a pair of tags. Joseph squinted at them. They appeared to be emblazoned with faces, like driver's licenses. He couldn't be sure though. Without his glasses his eyesight wasn't very good.

Mr. Protus looked down at his clipboard. He hadn't looked at the class once.

"Detention, Ms. Jackson. Maybe you'll finally learn to sleep at night instead of in my class. You have ten seconds to lift your head."

Joseph stared at the dark-skinned girl. She didn't move.

"Nine seconds, Amina," Mr. Protus repeated without looking up.

Joseph took the chance. He leaned over and nudged Amina. "C'mon girl, get up."

"Huh?" she said, looking up.

"Apparently ... Joseph Nathaniel Valdez," Mr. Protus read off the attendance list. "Apparently Joseph wants one of my detentions too."

"What?" Joseph demanded. "I just helped wake her up. That's all. That's what you wanted, isn't it? Now you got one less detention to do. So really, you should thank me for savin' you time."

"No, it means I have two more detentions now." The bald teacher glared at Joseph. At least it looked like he was glaring. The man's brows were so low and thick they almost obscured his eyes. *Great. I'm bein' taught Spanish by a Cro-Magnon.*

"But your countdown ain't reached 'one,'" Joseph challenged. "You only got to nine, and she woke up."

"With you helping her," Mr. Protus said. "She should have woken up when I said so, Mr. Valdez."

"If she's up, she's up. Shouldn't you care that she's awake instead a' carin' whether you made your point?"

Mr. Protus stood silently for a minute, face blank. "Maybe you are right. Ms. Jackson, you've lucked out. Mr. Valdez will take your detention. I want to make it clear that detention is a one-time opportunity before real punishment. Now maybe I can teach Spanish instead of dealing with disturbances in my class."

Joseph opened his mouth to snap back at him, but Amina Jackson laid a hand on his arm and made a cutting across over her throat, shaking her head. Joseph swallowed and made himself hold his peace.

*Great. My first day and I'm already back right where I was at home. Guess nuthin' is gonna be different here.*


"Come in and sit down. No talking please, no talking," the history teacher said. Toni passed the plaid-and-khaki clad teacher, who watched as each student filed in and then shut the door firmly with the click of a lock.

Toni looked briefly around the class. Everyone here seemed to be from the town and settled in with their friends. Her eyes spotted Charlie. Toni went to sit beside her.

"Hello," Charlie greeted. "I don't think we've been introduced. I'm Charlie, you're foxy, and everyone in this room is watching us."

Toni whipped her head around. About a dozen heads that had been gazing at them turned away. Toni rotated back to Charlie's very bright eyes. The plain girl gave a friendly smile but shifted in her seat.

"Nice call," Toni said. "I guess we're today's entertainment."

"America," Mr. Alderman began, silencing them. His voice was soft and methodical. He gave the class a big smile. "The greatest country the world has ever seen. And what is it that makes this so?"

A boy in the front row raised his hand. Mr. Alderman nodded to him. "Yes?"

"Well, freedom. I mean, we're a democracy, and we've always been based on freedom and had more freedom than other countries."

"True," Mr. Alderman agreed. "But what kind of freedom? The freedom to take anything we want, go anywhere we please, or do whatever we want?"

"No," said a girl behind Toni. "Then you're, like, infringing on somebody else's freedom."

"And freedom comes with responsibility," Mr. Alderman continued. "It also comes with danger, for some people abuse freedom."

"That's what jail is for," said the boy beside Charlie.

"Yes, but can we rehabilitate these people? And if complete freedom isn't what makes our country great, then what?" He looked around the class, his blue eyes scanning faces over his spectacles. Charlie raised her hand.

"It's law," Mr. Alderman continued. "Laws are what guarantee that we have freedom and not chaos. In our republic we have laws to assure that we are free from chaos. People who start breaking laws aren't free at all —"

"Only if they get caught," Charlie remarked.

"We raise hands in this class, Ms. Persan," Mr. Alderman responded. "You would have criminals rove free?"

"I didn't say that," Charlie defended. "But sometimes laws are unjust. People broke laws when they helped slaves escape or when women registered to vote when it was illegal. Not everyone considers themselves bound by the same laws."

"That's why we have democracy," said the boy who had answered first. "So the majority rules."

"Sometimes the majority rules in favor of prejudice," Charlie countered. "For a long time the *majority* of Americans thought it was fine to own slaves. For an even longer time most people thought that women were inferior and shouldn't be allowed to participate in our democracy."

"Maybe they weren't wrong," mumbled the boy.

"Maybe you're an idiot," Charlie responded. A collective gasp went up through the room.

"Detention, Ms. Persan," Mr. Alderman remarked.

"What about him?" Charlie pointed at the boy who had spoken.

"Mr. Little was out of line," Mr. Alderman conceded. "He will be punished too. But violence should not be our first response —"

"Vi ... violence?" Charlie squeaked. "All I did was say —"

"It is a precursor to violence," Mr. Alderman cut her off. "Violence begins with small incidents — and then works up, until you do something you regret."

"Jerk," mumbled Toni under her breath.

"You can join Ms. Persan in detention this afternoon," Mr. Alderman said, now turning towards her. "Ms. White over next to Ms. Connors, and Ms. Persan over by Mr. Donovan. Now, please."

As they moved apart, Toni watched Mr. Alderman's face. When both girls had settled, he gave a sigh of contentment. His voice had never raised once.


*My first damn day and I'm in detention,* Toni grumbled inwardly, walking into the room. Mr. Alderman stood blocking her path to the desks. "Your backpack, please?"

"What?" Toni said dumbly.

"You need to give me your backpack," Mr. Alderman said. "So I can search it." He began removing it for her, and Toni pulled back. "Why? They already searched it when I came at the beginning of the day. What do you think you'll find?"

"Hopefully nothing. Why, is there something you wish to hide?"

Toni gave him her backpack.

"And your coat, please."

"You have to be joking."

"No. I also need you to empty your pockets."

Disbelieving, she did as he requested. Mr. Alderman then gestured for her to sit beside the only other student there, a tall, thin, redheaded boy. Sitting, Toni watched as the history teacher unloaded her backpack and inspected each item carefully. He put her books and notebooks with the contents of the other students back pack on the left side of the table, and her planner and lip gloss on the other.

"It makes me sad," he said. "It makes me sad to see students in Discipline on their first day here. Not surprised, but sad because it is only the first day. After today it is not tolerated.

"You are here for the infraction of using inappropriate language. Do you understand why that is such a problem?" The two students shook their heads. "It is because inappropriate language is the first step towards inappropriate action."

Toni had the urge to mime shooting herself in the head, but she resisted. She didn't want to find out that using a fake gun was the first step towards going on a shooting rampage.

Mr. Alderman plopped down a hefty packet on each student's desk entitled *School Behavioral Management Handbook.* Then he enthusiastically turned to the whiteboard and wrote *Action,* drew an arrow, and then wrote *Consequences.* He turned back, alight with fervor.

Toni desperately longed to kick him.

"If you'll open to the first page, please," Mr. Alderman said. "In 'Precursors to Harmful Behaviors.'" Toni read the behaviors: swearing, hair pulling, talking back, sexual comments, loud/inappropriate noises, spitting, gum chewing.

*Gum chewing?* Toni heard a gulp and turned to the redhead, who appeared to have swallowed something.

"When we spot these behaviors, we stop them with these." Alderman tapped *Consequences* on the board. "You are given a grace period to learn how we do things here. After this week these behaviors will not be tolerated. If you complete this week without incident, you will not suffer actual punishment. We have a simple system here: positive behaviors are rewarded, negative ones are punished. If you go a number of weeks without incident you get points to spend at our Big Reward Store or —"

"And if we mess up?" Toni interrupted.

"If you, for example, interrupt the teacher," Mr. Alderman said, "then you will have to forfeit these activities, and put up with the consequences that correspond with the action. They are in your handbook," he said. "You are dismissed. You may collect your things."


"It's very disappointing to see anyone here on their first day," stated the woman who had walked into the small, windowless room. "But we are going to try to get you back on track before the school year really begins. Okay — Joseph ... Valdez?"

"Yeah?"

The woman smiled at him. Joseph's face didn't move.

"Do you understand why you are here?" the teacher asked.

"I'm a bad, bad boy," Joseph said, shaking one finger. "Shame on me."

"Do you feel shame for your actions?"

Joseph snorted.

"You think this is funny?" the woman asked.

"If you tryna to get into my head, stop now. By now you can't find anythin' that makes sense under the rubble."

"That's very poetic. Would you like to talk about why?"

Joseph laughed again. The woman's lips tightened. "Maybe we could address why you are so angry?"

"Ma'am, don't take this the wrong way," Joseph said, eyes narrowing, "but why don't you put your shrink degree back in your purse and find a client who feels sorry enough for you to pretend you're good at this job."

The woman bit the tip of her tongue and then pulled something up from under her desk — a file. "Joseph Nathaniel Valdez." The woman opened it. "Held back in first grade. Failed every subject taken this past year. Described by his last principal and school counselor as 'going nowhere, learning nothing, and happy with his fate to amount to nothing.' His teachers summed him up as a complete and utter failure. Diagnosed with ADHD. Arrested for tagging: referred to himself as a 'street artist'. Was arrested and expelled after found guilty of setting fires on public property —"

"I never —"

"Was selected by J. Alter Academy after being rejected by every other school," the teacher raised her voice, "on the recommendation of the Head-mistress who convinced the board that he has something to offer, if he can learn to curb his temper and play by the rules."

"Then I guess you're gonna hafta expel me," Joseph challenged.

"No one gets expelled here," the woman said, almost smiling. "That would be letting you off to take your bad behaviors into the world. No, you will stay. We *can* help you Joseph."


"There are no windows here."

"Yes," stated the teacher who had put Charlie into a separate detention room from the other new students. *Divide and conquer,* Charlie thought.

"That's my favorite color," Charlie noted of the purple folder.

The teacher opened it. "Charlie, Charlie, let's see —"

"I'm only here for speaking out in class," Charlie pointed out.

"No. That's not why you're here," the teacher remarked. "You didn't come to J. Alter Academy for speaking out of turn."

"It's away from home and different."

"So you chose to come here?" the man said. "Interesting." He placed a sheet in front of Charlie which said *Behavioral Contract.*

"I'm sorry?" she asked.

"It's a personal contract saying you won't insult fellow students. There are plenty of these, for all of your different issues. At the end of the week, if you have stuck to your contract, you get some points. If not you will have to visit the Quiet Center."

Charlie stared. "What's the Quiet Center?"

"You did have a problem with saying inappropriate and awkward things at your other school, yes?" the teacher questioned, ignoring hers.

"I — would ..."

"And it was something that bothered you, yes?" the man pressed. "But you were unhappy with the medication your doctor proscribed. I believe it was ..." The teacher looked at the paper, "Haldol?"

"Says who?" Charlie countered.

"You did." He opened the file and lay it on the desk. Charlie stared at her own handwriting.

"I think that's a big reason why you wanted to come here," he guessed, looking at Charlie's paper. "We don't believe in medicating away problems. We believe in an action-reaction model. You didn't like all the stuff they gave you, did you? No. So here we believe in personal responsibility as a cure instead. Here we have to make sure of the safety of our students first. Sometimes that means keeping them safe from themselves. If you are able to obey the rules, then you are rewarded points, which can buy all sorts of things. If not — you will become quickly acquainted with the other rooms on this level."

Charlie felt something go cold inside of her. "Like the room with the table with the straps?"

"What are you talking about?" The teacher frowned.

"The room with the metal bed and the straps on it," Charlie said, eyes drifting. "And the wires and the machines and the screens ... what is it for?"

The teacher's eyes widened. "When did you see this room?"

"It's right beside us," Charlie said, eyes widening. Her head was beginning to hurt. "What are the straps for?"

The man looked around. "How — how did you see into that room? Who told you about it?"

"What happens in that room?" Charlie demanded. Her head was beginning to ache. She didn't want to know, but she had to, and the divide was hurting her brain.

The teacher clamped his mouth shut. "If you obey our rules, you'll never need to know."

# chapter three  the

## "Are you alright?"

Toni shrugged off Becky's question, watching Mrs. Carter make a casserole. "I'm going upstairs," she said, getting up and walking up the stairs.

"Don't you want dinner?" she heard Mrs. Carter ask.

"Yeah, tomorrow," Toni yelled back, pushing open the door to her room. She leaned back against the wall and focused on her breathing.

*Fuck this,* Toni thought. *I'm calling my mom and leaving. I swear I'm —*

Toni's room was neat.

Toni was not neat. She was the opposite of neat. Her room generally looked like an earthquake had hit it. *This* could not be her room. Everything was tidy. Her wardrobe was folded and color coordinated. *Color coordinated.* Her journal was out on the desk, her makeup was —

Toni rushed to her desk. She had hidden her journal in a pocket in her suitcase, along with her cell phone. Why was her journal out? Had they read it?

Toni touched its edges. It was mostly poetry and stories. But some of those stories were about ... and where was her cell phone?

Toni looked through the desk, her empty suitcase, her wardrobe. She ripped open the closet and pulled down her shirts, skirts, and pants, ripping through pockets like a raccoon. *Where is it, where is it? Not in my purse, not in my bed ... did someone take it?*

"Toni?"

Toni looked up as Becky and Katrina stepped in. "Guys, I lost my cell phone when somebody rearranged my room. Did you guys see it?"

Katrina looked at Becky then back to Toni. "Why do you need it?"

"Why the hell do you think?" Toni said. "To call my mom and tell her I'm coming home." Toni felt under her bed then looked up. "Look, I'm sorry, but I don't know why I decided to..." Toni looked up at the two. "Did one of you take my phone?"

"No," Becky said, standing very still. "My mom probably took it."

"So she needs to give it back," Toni said.

"No. She doesn't," Katrina piped up. "You're not supposed to have cell phones."

"Do you guys have cell phones?" Toni asked. "You don't have a right to take mine away! Oh, I am so getting the hell out of here."

Katrina patted Becky on the shoulder. "You can go. I'll take care of this," she said.

"You won't take care of anything," Toni challenged. "I'm going to get my phone back."

Becky stepped quickly out of the room, and Katrina locked it behind her.

"Get out of my way," Toni said firmly.

"Look," Katrina sighed. "I know exactly how you feel. I felt the same way when I found out about all the restrictions. But you haven't heard the benefits. Now —"

"I don't care," Toni said, wondering if Katrina was slow. "I want out. This is not my school —"

"This is your school," Katrina countered. "You agreed to come here, you —"

"I'm transferring," Toni said, moving to open the door. Katrina blocked her. "No. You can't transfer out of here."

"This is messed up," Toni said, backing away slightly.

"It feels like that at first," Katrina said. "It *is* strict, but you get to do all kinds of things you wouldn't anywhere else if you —"

"I don't care. I want to leave! I don't care about whatever 'things' you think make up for having no freedom. This is America. This stuff doesn't happen." Toni tried to move for the door. Katrina again stepped in her way.

"You agreed to it," Katrina said. "You and your parents, when they signed you up and you came here."

"I didn't agree to this!" Toni gestured around the room. "I didn't know I was coming to some kind of boot camp!"

"Well, then you didn't read the fine print."

Joseph let the rage wash over him, filling every pore of his body. He yearned to let it out.

The door to the room in front of him slammed shut, and he watched Ann give the finger to whomever was behind it.

"Bad day too?" he asked warily. She looked very angry. In his experience, angry women were not to be underestimated.

Ann rolled her eyes at the door, annoyed, and nodded. "Detention."

"Oh, you too?" Joseph said happily. "That's great!"

Ann raised a brow.

"I mean, I was in detention too," Joseph amended. "What were you in for?"

Ann looked slightly embarrassed. She brushed her hands over her body, and Joseph's eyes followed.

"My outfit," Ann explained. "Apparently, it is 'inappropriate and distracting' to my fellow students, corrupting their innocent minds and preventing them from learning. Whatever, if my body is more interesting than a class, is that my fault?"

Joseph nodded absently. He could see where they would have a problem with her outfit. *Her shirt is way too tight, and is she* wearing *a bra?*

"Hello?" Ann snapped her fingers to break his reverie.

"What?"

"Yes Joseph, I do have boobs," Ann said condescendingly. He wanted to smack her. He hated being patronized. "So, are you ready to have a look around?" she asked.

"Huh?"

"I'm going to sneak around and see what kinds of things they're hiding here."

"Hiding?"

Ann's eyes shifted from side to side. "You need to know your enemy," she said with a half-smile. "But we have to be careful. We got away with fighting at Sherry's house, even though it's got cameras everywhere —"

"What, what, *what*?" Joseph questioned. "Hold on. We're bein' watched at our *house*?"

"Of course." Ann shrugged carelessly. "You think they would leave Sherry alone with two delinquents like us?"

"Yo!" Joseph said loudly. "If we could've got in trouble for a fight, then why'd you pick one wit' me?"

Ann folded her arms and gave him a look that made Joseph feel two feet tall. *How the fuck does she do that?*

"Don't be a scared little boy. It wasn't gonna get us in any *real* trouble," Ann stated.

"Look girl, I am a grown-ass *man,*" Joseph said, stung. "Not a boy. Man. Man is not boy."

"Boy is cute version of man."

"I am not cute. I am — well, I'm manly-ish. Check my sideburns," Joseph pointed out. "Yo, forget that. I don't have to prove anythin' to you. And I ain't scared neither."

"Guys are cute when they *try* to act cool." Ann smiled at him condescendingly. "I'm sure with practice you'll get better at it. But right now, I am going to go and explore. You wanna come with? Or are you scared?"

"I'm thinkin'," Joseph snapped back.

"Well, I'm walkin'. If you wanna come, come," Ann said and turned and walked away.

Joseph grumbled under his breath before following after her.


Charlie shivered as she walked into the library clutching her books. Her whole mind was fuzzy, and she felt afraid, like there was horror movie music playing in the background of her mind. She paused suddenly beside a table, recognizing the voices she had heard from outside the bathroom yesterday.

"The rose was black and rotten, dead before it was grown,
That which would not live together was doomed to die alone."

"Wow L, that's so beautiful, I just got tears in my eyes."

"Shut up," Lieutenant said, shoving the boy sitting beside her.

Anton tsked. "Remember, shovin' is the beginnin' of violence."

"Hey, it's better than the one you wrote about your cat," Melvin snorted.

"Cats." Anton scowled. "They shed, they sneak around, and they scratch. Next time I see one a' them things I'm gonna find out what Filet of Cat tastes like," he said in his flat voice.

"Do you really wanna go to jail for killing a cat?" Melvin asked.

"I won't go to jail," Anton explained. "Small animal sacrifices are legal now."

Lieutenant snorted. "My cat back home is a fat trucker. Seriously. Cat sits there lookin' at me like, "Biotch, get me food." So I give him the food, he sniffs it, and then, "Nah, I want somethin' else." I'm like, 'I'm not gettin' you anythin' else. Eat what's on ya plate Mister'."

"And then what does the cat say?" Anton asked.

"Nuthin', he's a cat," Lieutenant said, and the others laughed.

"Don't faux-swear," Melvin warned.

"Hey it just slips out sometimes," Anton deadpanned. "'Sides, the 'B-word' really applies to a lotta people around here."

"Is that why you were in detention?" Lieutenant asked. "Callin' people out?"

"Hey, it's not like I try to offend people," Anton said, lifting and lowering his shoulder blades in a shrug. "I try to be everyone's friend, but people can only take me in small doses. I can't help it if I'm toxic."

"Hi!"

The three sophomores looked at Charlie as she sat down with them at the small table beside the copier machines.

"I just got back from detention," Charlie offered.

"Oh, really?" asked Anton. "What'chu do?"

"Shh, Anton." Lieutenant put a hand on his shoulder. "Yo, this is the Poetry Club, so, if you want to sit and … write with us … that's fine."

Lieutenant was muscular and fairly tall, with a slightly horsy face. She wore a pair of silver hoop earrings and a white fedora hat cocked to one side. Her skin was a dark brown, and she played absently with a pair of dog tags hanging from a chain around her neck.

Melvin, the boy with the lisp, was short and slightly heavy. He had gelled and spiked hair, a heart-shaped face, black nails, and just a hint of eyeliner.

Anton was tall and dark-skinned. He had designs that Charlie couldn't read cut into his closely shaved head and a small pointed beard coming almost imp-like down from his chin. His black eyes made the whites around them even whiter. His face was still and sullen at the moment, just watching her.

Charlie leaned forward and lowered her voice. "I know you guys cut the power cords."

The others froze.

"It's okay," Charlie said. "I want to help, I —"

"Stop," Lieutenant ordered. "Don't say another word."

# chapter four rabbit

## "Sit down."

"No."

"You can sit or stand, but you're not leaving until you hear me out," Katrina said.

"They're not gonna keep me prisoner here," Toni said. "This is illegal."

"I said the same thing when I was brought here." Katrina smiled. "You're now a part of STARE — that's J. Alter Academy's Success Through Alternative Remedial Education program."

"What is this, a reform school?"

Katrina shrugged. "Something like that. Look, I don't know why you were brought here. I can only tell you why I was."

"Brought here?" Toni frowned. "I wasn't brought here. I came."

"Sure," Katrina said, brushing her off. "I had always had ... issues growing up, and they got worse when I hit high school. One night, I vandalized the chemistry lab. The next day the boy I'd had a crush on invited me into his basement to see if I could 'help' him with something. I made more money from mixing drugs in that one night than my uncle did working five days a week. And I had always been the 'just say no' girl. Now I was cooking up crystal meth, even inventing my own drugs. I had a lot of money and a lot of friends. Well, a lot of friends and no friends. When cops started cracking down, guess who got turned in?"

Katrina shifted.

"I figured I was going to jail forever. Then one day my attorney brings in a tall, red-haired woman. She sits down and says she has a way out of jail for me — like a reform school. I agreed, even if it meant I was leaving Florida for Bumfuck, Montana."

Toni snorted.

"Yeah," Katrina laughed. "I got in here thinking, 'this will be nothing.' I started to cause trouble right away, but they knew."

"What?"

"Everything about me. God, they knew things about me I didn't know. When someone knows more about you than you do, and when they can do anything to you, you can't fight. But by then I didn't want to fight, because I realized this place was special."

"Yeah, boot camp," Toni dismissed.

Katrina shook her head. "No, it's about this *place*. Like, we didn't just learn chemistry, we did experiments that hadn't been done before. Things that blew my mind."

"Like —"

"We changed DNA," Katrina cut her off. "First with insects, then frogs."

"What?"

"It's in the water here, I think," Katrina said wonderingly. "Frogs with three legs. Plants I never saw before. Then we started making drugs for your body, your mind —"

Katrina stopped.

"What?" Toni pressed, the skin on the back of her neck prickling.

"I can't talk about that," Katrina said, tightening her lip. "But Toni — we're out in a place where stuff is changing right before our eyes. And whatever you want to learn, or be, or have, J. Alter Academy can give it to you. This place can make you over. So if they want to take away a few freedoms I was abusing anyway? I say fair trade."

"Shit," Ann whispered, turning back to face Joseph, her nose inches from his.

"What?"

"There's a hall monitor walkin' right toward us."

"Huh?" Joseph moved to look around her, but she grabbed his shirt and pulled him back.

"We can't let him see us!" she hissed.

"Well what do we do? This was your brilliant fuckin' idea!" he whispered back, staring at her.

Ann swallowed, just looking at him. Joseph blinked, and she tore herself away from his gaze. She narrowed her eyes, then winked at Joseph.

"Watch this — Oh my God, what are you *doing*? Please stop! We'll get in so much trouble!" Ann said at the top of her voice.

"What the —"

Ann put a hand over his mouth and continued. Joseph frowned. She was right next to him, but it sounded like her voice was coming from the *opposite* side of the hall. They simultaneously pressed themselves into the wall, watching each other trying not to breathe.

The hall monitor turned down the hall opposite them, and they were able to breathe again.

Joseph started chuckling, the nervous energy coming out as laughter, and Ann started giggling at his laugh.

"See?" Ann brushed off, regaining her composure. "Into danger, out of danger."

"Oh please, you was scared," Joseph laughed.

"Me? Scared? I don't even know what the word means. Come on," she said, motioning for him to follow her.

"So you can throw your voice. That's weird, but cool weird, like a ventriloquist. Have you ever thought about that? I mean being a ventriloquist —"

*Wow. Shut the fuck up, Joseph.*

"Sure. You can be the dummy I use as a puppet."

"Ouch! No need to get nasty with me. I was just tryna alert you of a potential career path," Joseph offered.

"Well you're funny, I give you that." Ann rolled her eyes, and Joseph felt annoyed. She pissed him off, yet fascinated him, and around her he either talked too much or too stupidly, or felt that his tongue was in knots.

"You know what?" Joseph mumbled.

"What? I didn't hear you. Come again?" Ann challenged.

"But you ain't even come once yet." Joseph grinned slyly at her.

"What — did you — I —" Ann was momentarily unable to come up with a comeback.

Joseph clapped his hands together and laughed triumphantly. "Ha, ha! I knew —" Joseph froze as he recognized the laughter ringing down the hall. "No, not him," he groaned.

"Who?" Ann whispered.

"I heard something," Seth said from feet away.

Joseph and Ann turned to face each other. *Shit,* they mouthed simultaneously.

"I think it's this way," Seth said again.

"And this is the part where we run," Joseph said to Ann.

"Fuck yes."

*Don't react to this.*

*Everything you wanna say, write down. They're watching us. Normally with cameras but right now they have some 'technical difficulties'.*

*Consider us your friendly neighborhood guerilla sabotage unit and the best friends you'll find here.*

*You're new like we were. You obviously got told all the same lies by your parents. When did J. Alter Academy start sending you stuff? Did you punch somebody out? Try to kill yourself? Talk to voices?*

*Welcome to J. Alter Academy's STARE program for fucked up teens like you and me. If it sounds like something out of a horror movie, it's because it is, and we're the only ones who can help you survive it.*

Charlie looked up from the paper Lieutenant had written on.

"I have just one question."

The others waited.

"Are you all insane?" Charlie finally got out.

Anton grinned. "'Course. That's why we're here. Ain't you?"


"This way, this way —" Ann pulled Joseph to the right.

"No, no, no," Joseph argued. "We should go down the stairs."

"No, then we end up with a group of people —"

"Exactly! Then we can get lost in a group!"

"But they're comin' from that direction!"

"How do you know, Joseph?"

"Ann —" Joseph growled at her, holding her back from going right. "Just trust me, okay?"

"Trust you? I think I —"

Voices could clearly be heard coming from the right. "See?" Joseph said. "I told you."

"Shut up," Ann grumbled, but followed him as they ran left and swerved down one of the two side hallways. Panting, they sped for the door — a door that then began to open.

"Reverse, shit, c'mon!" Joseph said. Skidding to a halt, he grabbed Ann by the shoulders and turned her so they could run the opposite way.

"Wait —"

"What?" Ann said, moving to turn the corner. Joseph caught her arm and pulled her against his chest.

"No, no," he whispered. "They're gonna be that way too. They can see us."

"Well if we can't go either way, how the hell do we get out?" Ann demanded.

"Um ... in here," Joseph said, turning to a small, unlabeled door.

"It's not going to be open. They lock everything here," Ann said cynically, folding her arms.

Joseph put his hand on the metal knob, and it warmed and turned.

The door opened.

"Oh, I'm sorry, what was you sayin'?" Joseph said, pushing it wide. "I guess you just gotta have the magic touch."

Ann began to reply, but the footsteps were closer now. "Quick," Joseph whispered, drawing her inside. Ann swiftly closed the door behind them.

"I don't think this is the janitor's closet."

"Really? I thought it was a bar."

"Do you have to have an answer for everything, girl?"

"I can't be in the dark," Ann said, swallowing and reaching for the lights.

"No, don't," Joseph said, trying to stop her hands as they fumbled around in the dark. His hand hit something and he swore.

"What is it?" Ann asked.

"Somethin' cut me," Joseph said, wincing.

Ann frowned in the dark. "I'll get the lights."

"No, no," Joseph said. "Wait." He reached into his pants pocket and pulled out his plastic lighter and flicked it on.

It was a knife that had cut him — a long, elegant serrated knife. "Looks like a surgeon's knife," Joseph noted. "Like somethin' on CSI or —"

"Joseph," Ann said slowly.

"What?" he answered.

Ann took the hand that held the light and lifted it higher.

"Whoa."

The room they were in was most definitely not a janitor's closet. It looked more like something out of a hospital. A metal bed with straps stood at the center of the room, surrounded by a series of computers and machines. The table with the knife on it was covered in brilliantly clean, mint condition surgical instruments.

"If this is their science lab, I will eat this knife," Joseph stated.

"Look!" Ann gasped, pointing at a door across the room. It was opening.

"Quick!" Joseph said as they both rushed to open the door they had come through. After fumbling for a few seconds, it opened and they tumbled out. They both slammed it shut and sank to the floor.

"We really need," Joseph panted, "to —"

"You really need," said a voice, "to do some explaining."

*I'm trapped. Oh my fucking God, I'm trapped. This can't be real. This can't be legal. They can't just ... take away my phone, cut me off, and trap me here.*

*Can they?*

"Toni?"

Toni looked over at Becky, who had opened the door. "Are you ready to come down?"

"I think she might feel a little better if she ate something, right?" Katrina said, reaching out to smooth Toni's hair. It took all of Toni's strength not to smack her away.

"Toni?"

The other girls waited expectantly.

"Yeah, sure," Toni said, standing up. "That might help."

Toni followed them downstairs silently.

"My mom is making —"

"Well, do you know who it is?" Mrs. Carter demanded into the phone.

The other girls hushed instantly so that they could better hear Mrs. Carter's voice coming from the kitchen.

"It isn't one of our ...?" Mrs. Carter continued. There was silence, then, "Well, stop them and bring them to —" Mrs. Carter paused.

"What do you mean, you lost them?"

Pause.

"Wait, wait, wait ... what do you mean 'disappeared'? Students do not disappear, Joe, they ... so let me get this straight, you heard them at the second floor Main Building when —"

There was silence as the girls looked at each other, waiting for the next words.

"What do you mean the cameras aren't working? I checked —"

Pause.

"But why ... because of the blackout ... sabotage ..."

Another long stop.

"What door?"

Pause.

"So open it and —"

There was another short pause.

"I'll be right down." Mrs. Carter clicked the phone off and walked into the dining room to see the three girls staring at her.

Her typically sunny and composed demeanor was gone, replaced by tight lips and a sharp tone of voice. "I'm very sorry girls, but I have to go to the school for bit. Food will have to wait. I apologize."

Katrina and Becky seemed stunned as Mrs. Carter exited rapidly.

"Oh my God, I hope it's not like last year," Katrina said nervously. "I'm so scared."

"Are you all right, Toni?"

Toni looked over at Becky and smiled. "Of course."

*Sabotage,* Toni thought. *I like the sound of that.*


The teacher folded his arms and looked at Joseph, who looked at Ann, who looked back to the teacher.

"I know this looks bad, but it's really not anything at all," Ann said. "This all started when we got lost. Right, Joseph?"

"Uh, oh, yeah," Joseph said, nodding his head. "And then all of a sudden — all of a sudden we heard this noise, right? And it sounded like a fight, so we moved away from it 'cause we wanted to tell somebody."

"Only then we saw people following us," Ann put in helpfully. "And we weren't sure if they were in the fight or whatever, so we ran and found this closet and said ..."

"'Look, it is a closet.'" Joseph gestured towards the door behind them. "'Maybe we can go inside of it'. And she said —"

"'Okay,' but then we realized hiding in a closet was pretty — '"

"Stupid," they said simultaneously.

The teacher started at them. "Were you doing anything inappropriate in the closet?"

"No," Ann said with an exaggerated scoff.

"No," Joseph sighed, disappointedly. Ann stole a look at him.

The teacher stared at them."Purposefully or not, you broke the rules and scared half the staff, making them wonder if you were ... well, you caused a problem, and you will both have to stay while I call for the principal."

"Look, we'll probably get detention, right?" Joseph asked.

The teacher stared at them, stone-faced. "I think you will find —"

"C'mon, give us a damn break," Joseph groaned. "I just fuckin' got here, and I haven't even —"

"Swearing is against the rules," the teacher stated.

"I don't like your rules." Joseph growled, his hand slipping into his pocket to find his lighter.

"Now," the teacher said to Ann. "You need to —"

Joseph didn't even try to stop it. He didn't see any other way out. He was trapped, and now he was again about to get into trouble for something that wasn't his fault. He wanted it to stop, wanted to burn the school to the ground. He wanted it to explode, to burn to ashes —

"Excuse me? Did you hear what I just said?"

The teacher was talking to him. Joseph looked up.

Then a spasm of light and heat erupted in the trash can, and Ann had to jump aside as its contents went up in flames.


*Breathe.*

"Charlie?"

"Yo, she doesn't look good," Anton said. "I think —"

"There is someone at the door."

The three sophomores turned to Charlie. "What?"

Charlie's eyes danced from one side of the room to the other. "Feet running, nervous breathing, yelling. Something is happening, *right now.*"

"Where?" Melvin asked.

"In the school. Can't you hear it?" Charlie demanded.

"Um … no," Anton said flatly. "Are you —"

The door opened and a panting teacher stepped inside. "After school activities are ended for the day," the teacher said. "The fire alarm went off in the Main Building."

The four teenagers had lined up to file out of the library when the teacher stopped them.

"Let me see those papers."

Charlie froze. "I —" She looked back at the others.

"It's cool, Charlie," Melvin said. "Hand it in."

Charlie looked down at the paper and stopped. The paper, which had been covered with writing, was now utterly blank. *How …* She stopped, and her eyes widened in realization.

*Invisible ink.*

She dumbly handed the blank sheets to the teacher. Charlie looked over at what she guessed were her new friends. They all gave her blank stares, except for Anton, whose face seemed to have changed in a way that Charlie couldn't pinpoint. He gave her a lopsided smile.

# chapter five hole

**"Joseph? Joseph, sit down!" Ann pulled Joseph down into the bus**
seat beside her and looked around nervously. They had both taken advantage
of the fire in the trashcan to run away while the teacher struggled to put it
out. Joseph could feel his heart pounding in his chest. *God, what did I do?*

"Hey." Someone poked Joseph from the other seat behind him. "Do you
know what happened?"

"I heard some kids, like, tripped a wire or something. We saw the teachers taking them away. They'll probably get in big trouble," Ann lied. "But
the security guy is watching, so I'd lean back." The student did, only to pass
along Ann's story to her friend.

"What the hell are you doin'?" Joseph whispered to her fiercely.

"What, you think we should tell the truth?" Ann raised a brow. "Maybe
if they're confused about the stories, we'll slip away."

"No, that teacher got our names, *and* they got cameras," Joseph pointed
out.

"You know what I heard?" a girl in front of them whispered to Ann. "I
heard someone tried to light the place on fire."

Joseph and Ann exchanged looks.

The other girl continued. "I hear they're still trying to put it out. We
might actually have the school close for a whole day. I wouldn't open up
the school again, because a little fire like that? It means the place is liable to
burn up and explode at any time."

"That's not true at all," Joseph said, knees up around him, ankles balanced on the seat in front of him. He played with the straps of his backpack,
looking down.

"It's like one of those cars you see flip over and burst. All those wires, all that electricity? That's why I don't have much electricity in my house, because you never know when it could go off," the girl continued.

"Cars rarely, *rarely* blow up like that," Joseph said, still not looking up, but raising his voice. "That shit only happens in the movies. And electricity ain't what sets off big fires. It's gasoline."

"You really know a lot about fires, don't you, Joseph?" Ann asked, watching him.

"You really know a lot about lying, don't you, Ann?" Joseph answered.

"No, I know about saying the right thing to get us out of a bad situation," Ann threw right back. "Thanks to me —"

"Thanks to you we're in this mess in the first place!" Joseph shot back. "You the one who had to act like a dumb blonde and go 'look around' and —"

"And you followed me. I didn't force you!" Ann said, hurt.

"You was *waitin'* for me to follow you, and I only did it 'cause I was bein' a gentleman and wasn't gonna let you walk off and hurt yourself doin' somethin' stupid," Joseph explained.

"Oh, well don't do me any more *favors* again," Ann hissed. "It's cause of you that we started off running and —"

"You little fu—"

"— all because you jumped the gun, and all of a sudden we're running —"

"Will you lemme fini—"

"And then you decide to give the guy attitude and —"

"*Will you stop and fuckin' hear me out?*" Joseph whisper-screamed at her, grabbing her and pulling her closer so he could speak into her ear without being overheard. "You gonna blame this on me when I got us outta it?"

"And how did you do that again?" Ann asked. "You had a lighter, dropped it in the trash can and set it on fire. That part I have all figured out," Ann said, arching up so she was closer to his face.

"Ain't you brilliant," Joseph mocked in a seductively nasty whisper, anger rushing through his veins like hot liquor. "But oh! Only problem is *you* were the one next to the trash can, not me."

"Why are you lying to me, Joseph?" Ann whispered slowly into his ear. "I'm blonde, but I'm not stupid. I can tell a lie when I see one. What are you so scared of, huh?"

"*Nothing!*" Joseph half-yelled, then looked around and swore inwardly. "Look, that fire just — just *happened*. Maybe it was a socket or somethin' but it had *nuthin'* to do with me! In fact — in fact I think maybe you did it. You were closer," Joseph accused clumsily, trying to shift the blame to her.

"Why are you lying? You threw the lighter into the trash can."

"Ha!" Joseph said, pulling the lighter out of his pocket. To keep it from view he placed it between where their chests were almost touching. "Then what's this here?"

"Put it away before they see it!"

"Hell no, I had to sneak this in the inside pocket of my pants to get it in!" Joseph said, clutching it possessively.

"You kept a lighter *in your pants*?" Ann laughed. "You are not smart at all, are you?"

"You don't know nuthin' about me. You known me for all of a day and a quarter, so don't act like you do." Joseph seethed.

"I don't *wanna* know you, Joseph," Ann shot back. "Loser."

"Bitch."

"Asshole."

"Maybe you should wear some fuckin' clothes once in a while?"

"Maybe next time you can hide your lighter up your —"

The guard walked up to them. Joseph caught himself and Ann a second before he heard them.

"Your stop," the guard said.


"Does anyone actually know what happened?" Charlie asked Lieutenant as they sat together on the bus.

"Maybe them two are in trouble." Lieutenant pointed at the two students being led out.

"No, they were separated 'cause they were fighting — or making out, I couldn't tell," Charlie said, frowning.

"Now they'll check the surveillance tapes to find out what really happened," Lieutenant continued, grinning. "But they won't find anything."

"Because you cut the cameras and the lights," Charlie stated, causing Lieutenant to widen her eyes in warning. Charlie clamped her mouth shut quickly. Then, holding up a finger, she took a piece of paper and wrote, *How did you do it?*

*It wasn't hard,* Lieutenant wrote back. *They got a room labeled "surveillance" so all we had to do was find the generator on that side of the floor and hope we cut the right wires.*

*Did you?* Charlie asked.

*We cut them all,* Lieutenant wrote back. *Just to make sure. The guard is coming back. Hide the paper.*

*FUCK!*

*This place is even fuckin' WORSE than home. I ain't even lasted a week, and it's ... happenin' again. Man, you got no self-control.*

*Okay. It's cool. I'll just stay here.*

*Yeah. I'll become a hermit and live in my tiny pathetic room with my tiny pathetic self the rest of my life.*

*Yeah. That'll be fun. But at least I won't hurt any —*

"Joseph?"

*You gotta be kiddin' me.*

"Joseph, can I come in?" Ann asked, knocking on his door. *I am not nervous,* she thought. *I am most absolutely not nervous.*

*Oh, God. I'm nervous.*

*I'm a loser.*

"Um ... how about ... no," whispered Joseph from inside.

"We need to talk, so just open the door!"

"Here's an idea. How about I sit here in my comfy room, and you can stand out*side* and talk."

There was a pause for a second, and then Ann forced open the door.

"What the fuck?" Joseph said, staring up at her, stunned, from where he sat on the floor.

"Keep your voice down, or Sherry will come up," Ann whispered, then swallowed. Now that she had burst into his room, she wasn't sure how she'd managed the courage to do it. Joseph sat on the floor with his knees up, leaning back on his forearms, his chest heaving up and down with building anger. She felt an insane, momentary desire to touch his chest where his heart was, and feel the beat.

"You just fuckin' broke my door down!" Joseph said, stepping up and zeroing in on her with his golden eyes.

"I didn't break your door," Ann responded, nonchalantly. "I only broke your lock."

"So I ain't got no lock now?" Joseph's voice rose, as he stepped towards her. Ann stood her ground.

"Why do you need one? It's not like you're doing anything special in here." She scoffed, rolling her eyes nastily.

*God, that's so annoying when she does that,* Joseph thought. "Maybe I am," he countered, his nose inches from her. "You don't know *anything* about me."

"I know you —" Ann began then pulled back slightly in realization. "You wanna kiss me."

"What? No, no I don't!" Joseph protested, pulling back from her, but his face colored.

"Yes, you do!" Ann laughed. That annoyed him.

"No, I don't!"

"Yeah, ya do."

"Do not."

"Don't be a baby."

"Well it ain't my fault you look sexy when you're angry!" Joseph blurted out then clamped his mouth shut. *Big. Stupid. Mouth. I hate it. I hate my big stupid mouth.*

Ann was thrown off. A second ago she had been ready to hit him, and he had been up in her face just as mad, angry enough to make her feel threatened. He was still angry, she could tell, but now he seemed more nervous, and for some reason she found it hard to remember why she was so angry at him.

She turned and closed the door, and Joseph swallowed, not exactly sure what he was feeling. Ann looked at him. "We need to talk."

Joseph put his hands in his jeans pockets and shrugged. "'Bout what?"

"What we're gonna say when they find out it's us," Ann stated. "I'm surprised they haven't caught us yet, but it's only a matter of time before that guard finds out who we are. We need to get our story straight —"

"I remember the story." Joseph cut her off brusquely. "I can stick to it."

Ann felt a bit of her sinking. Anger she could deal with, but she couldn't take being dismissed.

"Well, just to be clear," she said. "We get lost on our first day, we decide to look around, we get nervous when we hear a fight and start running. We end up in a closet where we can't see anything and we get scared, then we get out, try to explain to a guard what happened and then ...?"

Joseph realized she was looking at him. "Then what?"

"You need to tell me," Ann said with a raise of her eyebrow.

"If I say I —" Joseph swallowed. "If I say I ... started the fire ..." He swore under his breath and kicked the rug, making himself trip and fall.

Ann laughed, but when he put his head in his hands she stopped. Unsure, she moved over to him. Slowly she sank down beside him.

"You don't have to ... I'll just admit I started it. They'll send me to jail where I belong, and then I won't —" Joseph stopped and looked away.

"Hey, look at me," Ann demanded quietly. When he didn't, she used one hand to move his chin to her. While surprised at herself for doing it, she was unable to stop herself from running one finger down the scratchy, light sideburns. "I don't think we should say you did it," she explained. "I don't — I don't think they'd believe us if we told them, since I'm still not sure *how* you did it ... Tell me?"

Joseph looked at her finger and she pulled back, embarrassed and annoyed with herself. She didn't like this guy. She shouldn't do that.

"You already think I'm enough of a freak, thanks," Joseph said sorely. "I'd kinda like to have some pride left here."

"Oh please." Ann rolled her eyes. "You're talking to the girl who defines freak around here. If you're worried about what irritates people in *this town* — I mean ... I put a streak in my hair once." She pointed to her blonde hair. "And they thought I belonged to a cult."

"For real?" Joseph looked over at her.

"Yeah. I mean ..." Ann looked to the side. "It might have had something to do with the fact that I said I belonged to a cult, but ya know what? If you don't understand sarcasm, then you're gonna be a failure at life."

Joseph laughed at that, and the sound was so wheezing that Ann smirked at it a bit too. "So c'mon," she coaxed. "Tell me. Trust me, there's nothing you could say that would make me like you any — well ..."

"Any less than you already do?" Joseph smiled crookedly at her.

"Well, yeah," she responded sheepishly.

Joseph swallowed. Nobody he'd told had ever believed him. If he didn't believe it himself, why should she? What was to say she wouldn't turn and blame it all on him?

But then ... he could blame this one on her too, if she did that.

He decided to tell her half of the truth. "I kinda, used to ... start fires," Joseph said, glancing over at her then away. He couldn't do it if he was looking at her. "It was — I'd just always liked fires ... I can't really explain it, they just — fascinate me. They're beautiful, and they hurt, but we need 'em to survive ... whatever, one day I was pissed and angry and didn't know what to do, and I fuckin' found a match and lit a piece of grass outside, and it — I don't know ..." He knew he should stop, but he had never spoken of it, and now the words just came out. "It was beautiful. I couldn't stop watchin' it, and I felt like I got what a fire was, and how it worked ..." Joseph swallowed.

"But I just knew it was wrong and tried to stop but it seemed like — like ... I'd be pissed and angry and all of a sudden I'd have the lighter in my hand, and then it just started happenin' more and more. I'd be relieved at first, but then when it started happenin' too much ... But I never killed no one, not one person, and sometimes the fires would just —"

"Just what?" Ann pressed.

"Just happen." Joseph looked at her expression. "I would have lighter, or a match — or even just be near a spark and I'd get angry and ... the fire would go off. Or I'd be near one, and it would go higher, burn hotter and — '

*I'm gonna ... stop talkin'.*

Joseph turned away, cheeks burning. *Fuckin' idiot. Now she's gonna go and te—*

"I once stole my parent's car and almost drove over a cliff on purpose," Ann said rapidly, then realized what she'd said and bit her tongue. "Ow!"

"You — when?" Joseph asked, folding his arms over his knees, half covering his face so his words were muffled, and all she could see were his eyes.

"A year ago," Ann confessed. "I just ... there was some stuff and ... I stole the car one night after I'd been drinking, and just cranked it as hard as I could. I had only driven a little before, and it was such a rush. I was speeding so fast and I just felt — wild, like ... free? Ya know?"

"I know," Joseph said, still just his eyes visible. "What happened next?"

"I hydroplaned, you know, drove on water? Then I spun and hit the side of the road, and the car half went over — that's how they found me."

*Still laughing,* she remembered, but didn't say so.

Joseph just stared at her. Ann didn't like the nervous, jittery feeling she got in the pit of her stomach when he did that, so she decided to shrug it off. "Whatever. I'm a what'cha call it ... an adrenaline junkie. I think that was what my Mom said. I guess that's why I did it. Or ... I don't know."

*I don't know why I do half the things I do. I'm stupid. There — that's a reason.*

"It's just ... I wanted that feeling you get when you're doing something wrong but exciting, like when you're sneaking out at night or jumping off something just high enough to make it dangerous, and you get that feeling through your whole body ... after it's done, and you fall on your ass, you realize you're an idiot, but while you're doing it you just feel —"

"Powerful," Joseph finished her sentence with her. Ann gave a half-smile. "Yeah."

Ann couldn't believe she had told him this. She barely knew him. But he had confided in her, and he couldn't think too badly of her if he started fires. Her story was safe with him.

"So, you got caught drunk drivin' ... is that why you got sent here?" Joseph asked.

"What do you mean, 'sent here'?" Ann asked, voice sharp and angry.

"You know ... sent here to one of these watched houses to like, 'fix' you, like their tryna do to me," Joseph said.

Ann's body chilled. "I'm here because it's closer to the school, I —"

"C'mon Ann, that's not it," Joseph stated. He wasn't stupid. While he was in detention he had been piecing things together. He knew that this place was some kind of reform school — *Thanks Mom, love you too* — and he had guessed that the reason Ann had lied was that she was ashamed about being here. "It's okay," he rushed to say, "I mean, like — I'm not sayin' you deserve it or nuthin'. I'm not passin' judgment. I get why you would lie."

"Oh so, I'm a liar? I think that fuckin' counts as a judgment," Ann snapped.

Ann got up to leave, and Joseph grabbed her hand. "Wait." He stopped her. Ann glanced down at his hand like it was a bug and he pulled back. "Look, I'm sorry, okay? I just ... we're stuck in this together, whether we like each other or not, so can we at least live with each other?"

*Fantastic. Now he doesn't even like me,* Ann thought.

"Fine. We'll live with each other. I'll try if you will."

Joseph clenched his fists, irritated. She stood with folded arms, eyebrow imperiously raised. Ann blew hot then cold faster than he did, and it made him even more uncomfortable than he normally was around girls. She turned to go.

"Will you just *stop?*" he demanded, standing up. "God damn."

Arms still folded, Ann turned. "What?" she countered, the tip of her tongue coming to the side of her half open lips as she leaned slightly forward. "Do you actually have something to say?"

"I — I just ..." Joseph shuffled his feet and swallowed. He wasn't really sure what he wanted to say now that he'd begun.

Ann didn't understand guys who were so nervous. "If you wanna say something to me, just say it," she said. If he was going to insult her she wanted him to say it to her face.

"I'm sorry."

"Well, if you think that — what?"

"I'm sorry," Joseph repeated. "For freakin' out on you earlier. Callin' you names ... I was just — angry."

Ann blinked. "I'm ... oh."

"Oh?"

"Oh."

"What did you think I was gonna say?"

"Thought you were gonna call me a liar again," Ann confessed.

"I — I don't think you're a liar," Joseph stated. Ann looked disbelieving. "No, I don't," he said. "I mean, I get why you would say it. I — I don't know why I told you what I did but — you can see I'm crazier than you'll ever be," Joseph said helpfully.

"You think so?"

"Yeah," Joseph said, as if offended. "*You* was in a drunk drivin' accident. *I'm* a little pyromaniac. I beat you ten-to-one." He put up his hands and popped his shirt as if it were his collar, bragging. "I know, it's hard to accept. The jealousy may hurt but you just gotta accept it."

Ann couldn't help it — she laughed. "I'm —" she drew in a deep breath, and Joseph wondered if she was going to sneeze. "I'm sorry too," she said, "for getting us into this mess."

Joseph snorted a laugh. "Was that really that hard to say?"

Ann narrowed her eyes at him, and began to speak when —

"Ann? Joseph? Downstairs, *now*."

They exchanged a look. "Okay — we stick to the story right?" Ann said quickly.

"Yeah," Joseph said, holding up his pinky. "Deal?"

"Are you serious?" Ann grinned. Joseph blushed and growled. "Never mind. I was just —"

Ann caught his hand and hooked her pinky with his. "Deal."

Joseph stared down at their hands, then up into Ann's eyes causing her stomach to do weird things. *His hands are really fucking gentle for a guy's,* she thought, as he slowly interlaced their fingers.

*Okay, so the pinky thing? Dorky. Whatever, I'm a dork. But ... this is cool,* thought Joseph, pressing against her warm palm.

"Hello? Am I talking to a wall up there? Ann? Joseph?"

Ann broke contact first. "We need to go downstairs."

"Yeah."


Toni was angry.

No, not angry. She was furious.

*How could my parents send me here? To* this *place? To this fucking ...*

*I can't believe it. I won't. They didn't know — this school tricked them. It has to be that.*

Toni was glad that she had her own room. She couldn't stand it if the other girls were in here with her.

She should have known something was wrong. Known she wouldn't be able to come here and have any friends.

*You don't deserve normal friends. You don't deserve any friends. Your friends all wish you dead, and that was all the chance you got.*

"Well, I won't say I didn't tell you before all this ... this just confirms that we'll have to change things."

Toni tried to make out the rest of what Mrs. Carter was saying, but couldn't quite hear from her bed. Frustrated, she tried to ignore it.

No. She *needed* to know.

*The bathroom. I'll just pretend I have to go to the bathroom.*

Toni walked as quietly as she could. *If I wasn't so fat, this wouldn't be so hard.*

She made it out the door, dodged the light from the kitchen, and hid in the bathroom. Sinking down on the cold floor with the lights out, she left the door half open. She could hear more clearly now.

"How long until the cameras are back up?" Mrs. Carter said.

There was a pause.

"Well, we'll just have to deal until then ... oh, of course I have ideas. We won't have them walking around unsupervised anymore."

There was another short silence.

"I don't think you understand, Joe. An act of sabotage like this means our worst fear is realized: delinquent students working together. And that means we will have to make sure they just don't get that chance ..."

There was another pause. Toni could hear her own heart beating.

"Well, obviously the Report Box is not working. Oh, I'm not saying we should get rid of it at all. Once the students realize that everyone will lose privileges because of this, anyone who knows anything will come and tell us. Trust me, this has worked before. And we'll just have to be stricter about who they can speak to, what they can say, and who they can hang around with. And not just the students."

There was another tense silence, and Toni leaned towards the door.

"No, Joe, listen to me. This act was sophisticated. I've told you for a while I thought that some of our teachers were too lax ... Well, now I'm thinking that one of them is helping these students."

There was another pause.

"I don't *know* who, Joe, that is why I am putting into place these precautions. If these kids see teachers giving an inch, they will take a mile. So we have to make it so no one has an inch, in the interest of protecting everyone, both the students and ourselves. You know we have some very intelligent, very dangerous teenagers here."

Silence.

"That is why I am calling you, Joe. I need you to help me swing the vote and make sure the Headmistress sees reason. She may own this school, but *I* have to run it. I'm the principal. I have to make the on-the-ground decisions. Oh ... I don't mean any disrespect to her. Of course she always has the last word but — I know, I know. She will see reason."

Pause.

"Yes. See you at 2:30 tomorrow in the Conference Room."

Mrs. Carter hung up the phone and began moving upstairs. Toni had to move to make sure she wouldn't be found.

But Toni couldn't move.

*Please no. Please God no, not again.*

It was the terror first. Hot. It felt hot and tingling, but in a horrible way.

She felt sick to her stomach, like the bottom of it had given out. Her head swam — she couldn't see straight, and everything was spinning.

Next her heartbeat changed. It beat harder and quicker in her chest, hurting as the fear that was settling in her stomach spread over her body.

*I can't breathe.*

She was being smothered. She gasped but her lungs didn't fill with air. The more she tried to breathe the harder it was, and the more the panic took over.

Mrs. Carter's feet could clearly be heard coming up the stairs.

*You have to move, get up and make it look like you were going to the bathroom,* Toni told herself.

But she couldn't. It was like all the times before. She had to run, move, do something, but she couldn't. Her body wouldn't let her.

Mrs. Carter's steps came closer.

It hurt. Toni's whole body was shivering and shaking with physical, painful fear, and she could do nothing, nothing...

Mrs. Carter's steps reached the top of the stairs and paused, then torturously moved to the bathroom door.

It opened, and Mrs. Carter stepped back. "Toni," she said, quietly surprised.

"Hello, Mrs. Carter," Toni said, a little shakily. "I was just going back to bed."

"Are you all right?" Mrs. Carter asked, worried.

"I didn't feel well, but I went to the bathroom, and now I feel better," Toni stated.

"Really? You are sure you —"

"Yes, I'm fine. Just tired," Toni said, breathing out.

"Oh, all right. If you need anything I am here. Don't be afraid to ask." The older woman put a gentle hand on Toni's shoulder.

"Of course, Mrs. Carter."

# chapter six **taste**

**"Exactly. Melvin brings up a very real point." Dana raised her finger.**
Charlie drummed anxiously on her unopened copy of *One Flew Over the Cuckoo's Nest*.

"In Chief Bromden," Dana continued, "we have an example of an 'unreliable narrator.'" She wrote the term on the board. "An unreliable narrator is a narrator whose accounts are faulty, misleading, biased, or distorted. So we don't know sometimes whether or not what he is telling us is actually happening. We can tell most of the times when he is delusional. For example, Bromden isn't actually being lowered into the floor where patients aren't actually being split open into machine parts. That's all part of the fog of his mental illness."

"So wait, if he's not telling the truth, how do we know whether or not this is all in his mind?" asked one of the English students Charlie didn't know.

"Well, part of the time he is lucid," Dana clarified. "And the times when he isn't you can generally tell, like when he says that Nurse Ratched can slow time down. But why do you think Ken Kesey would have chosen a narrator like Chief Bromden?"

Toni raised her hand, and Dana nodded at her. "Because it's a really good way to bring your reader into the environment, by bringing them right into the mind of someone who is insane. Plus, it's like ... you can't just stand back and say, 'he's crazy' and dissociate from Bromden. You're right in his mind, so you almost have to feel compassion for him."

*That is what she is trying to tell us.* Charlie stared into blank space, then up at Dana. She could tell that the teacher was trying to communicate with them but wasn't free to speak to them out loud. *That is what this school is doing,* Charlie thought excitedly. *They are trying to turn us into automatons. Batons. The glue is gone, and now everything will un-stick. Time will pass quick.*

"Charlie?" Dana was calling her name.

"Charlie?" Charlie repeated while people around her giggled. She felt embarrassment. *They are laughing because I am ugly and stupid and awkward and evil,* she thought. *Very evil.*

"Do you think you could read us the passage about Bromden's dream?" Dana requested.

Charlie rubbed her hands together, pulling on her fingers. She had to be careful not to pull too hard or they would come right off. "Well, Bromden has this dream about being lowered into the ground, not really the ground, the underground, where he hears the sound —"

"No. It's a group reading. Could you just read the first two paragraphs?" Dana restated.

"Um ..." Charlie knew she couldn't read those passages, written so clearly, about all those wires and blood and hooks, so like the wires that were crawling all around the school and right into the students ...

"Charlie, have you read the book?" Dana probed.

"Yes. I have read this book, many times," Charlie said sharply, still pulling at her fingers but not too hard lest they fall off. "I've even read it backwards — even tried downwards, but not much could be inferred. Cuckoo birds."

The class laughed again, but Charlie felt like laying her head down on her desk and crying. Dana walked over to her desk and forced Charlie to look up. "If you are feeling unwell, you can just open your book and pretend to follow along," the English teacher whispered, and some of Charlie's tension faded. Dana was watching out for her. She would protect her.

"Lisa, could you read the passage?"

Lisa obliged, and Charlie tried to breathe. *If I can just focus on breathing everything will be fine. Like mediation. Sensation. I used to be able to sense scents, but then my nose went up to a dollar. Oh God.*

"If we —" Dana stopped as the loud speaker went on.

"*Attention, please,*" Mrs. Carter's voice came over the loudspeaker. "*I am disappointed to inform you that we had two incidents in our first week. This will result in some immediate changes, the first being the cancellation of homecoming —*"

The room erupted in boos and cries of protestation. Charlie bet it was happening all over the school.

"*Unless,*" the voice on the loudspeaker continued, "*we are able to locate the persons responsible for these events. That is all.*"

The room was silent, which made Charlie wonder if her ears had gone deaf. Everyone looked up to Dana, who looked even paler than she already was.

Charlie tried to close her mind and breathe as the reading began, but the squeaking of the pen on the board and the colors of everyone's clothes and her own panic and the cooling of the room and the thoughts of papers and due dates and secrets and sabotage and lies, all hit her at once.

Charlie felt a tap on her shoulder and turned. "Everything is happening at once."

"I know." Toni nodded. "It's crazy."

"Crazy?" Charlie said in a tiny voice.

"This school." Toni shook her head. She looked angry about something. To Charlie it felt like hot needles on her skin. "I hope people don't start lying and turning people in just to get homecoming back."

"A lie just to get by?"

"Are you trying to start a career as a rapper?" Toni asked skeptically. Charlie blinked.

"I had a career as an angel, but I was too ugly and tripped. Fell. Falling is flying when you're upside down. Did you trip the wires in heaven?"

Toni started to laugh but then must have noticed the look of terror on Charlie's face. Gently, she put a hand on Charlie's shoulder. "It's gonna be okay," she said, looking straight in the other girl's eyes.

"Okay?" Charlie whispered. "How can you say? Pl—" Charlie covered her own mouth.

"Just be calm," Toni said, keeping her voice soothing.

It was the tone of the voice that made Charlie nod, and the hand on her shoulder ... that was real. "Thank you," Charlie said.

Charlie felt Toni squeeze her hand, and hope cleared a little of the fog taking over her mind.

*A friend?*


Joseph kept his hood up and his head down as he moved through the crowd toward his algebra class. They would come for him soon. This message meant the school was looking for them. But the speakers had said two acts of sabotage. Were the running and the fire the two acts? Or was there something else?

He stiffened an instant before the arm went around his shoulder. "And maybe our new friend Joseph can tell us what happened?"

"Get the fuck off me," he snarled quietly, pushing Seth's arm away. The small group around him, of three of Seth's male buddies and three girls, laughed.

"See?" Seth pointed theatrically. "I try to be friends with him, and he acts like I've hit him in the face."

"You —" Joseph stopped and watched the amused, mocking look in Seth's gaze. If he admitted that Seth *had* hit him in the face ... that would just be worse for him, and they'd see him as a pussy. Joseph glanced at one of Seth's friends who had been there yesterday in the bathroom.

He made himself shrug. "I just didn't want you to make your boyfriend there jealous. See? He's already pissed. Now you gonna hafta buy him some roses."

Joseph couldn't read Seth's face, but he heard a snort of laughter from somewhere behind him. And Seth's friend was clearly angry. "He's all talk now, but he wasn't saying anything when he was running away from us on the first day like a little ... wimp."

"Wow, a 'wimp'. I'm so hurt, lemme find a tissue," Joseph said, faking tears as he rubbed his eyes with his hoodie. Then he offered part of it to Seth's friend. "Yo, you probably need it more than me. Maybe I ran, but at least I'm still able to, unlike you, who walks like Seth's dick is still up your ass."

Now he could tell they were gathering a crowd, but he didn't care. The look on the other boy's face was worth it.

"Fuck you, you little —" The boy stepped forward and Seth put a hand out over his chest.

"Don't swear, Andrew."

Joseph laughed. "Damn Andrew, he tells you how to talk? He tell you when to take a piss too? I can almost see the strings on your legs and arms. You ain't a man. You're a marionette. Oh," he said, turning to Seth. "Looks like Latino boy does have a vo-cab-u-lary after all."

"Latino boy also has a brain the size of walnut, since he doesn't realize that over seven people heard him swear and threaten me." Seth grinned, pityingly. "You just earned yourself a good hour in the lower levels where the real fun happens."

"Seth." Joseph put up his hands, and sighed dramatically. "I'm tryna break it to you gently: I. Don't. Date. Men."

Seth just continued smiling and backed up. "We'll see how cocky you are tomorrow. I'm probably gonna be a hall monitor soon. Hope you got that mouth cleaned up next time I see you."

Joseph felt the powerful urge to run at the smirking senior and beat him senseless. He needed an outlet ... a spark ...

*NO.* He wrung his hands, and then put them into his pockets where they were safe, and trudged to his class.

*Breathe.*

*I can do this. I — just have to concentrate. At least I'm not hearing ... hearing anything. Sing. No. All I have to too is ignore everything. I'm fine. I can tough it out. All I have to do is hide.*

Charlie walked toward her locker forcing herself to go slowly. She didn't want anyone to suspect that something was wrong. But it was difficult when she could hear every single separate conversation going on at the same time, as well as smell the four different main dishes from the lunch room, and see every color so brightly it made her eyes ache.

*I should have felt it coming.* In her mind's eye, Charlie could see the bottle of pills she had been eager to give up before coming here. She had been so happy with the feeling of not being drugged up. But one extreme dream, and not three days later she was —

"Excuse me?"

Charlie turned to see two girls staring at her. She shoved her backpack into the locker. "Uh-huh?"

"Hey," one of them spoke. "We know you're new here, and it's easy to connect first with the boarders, but it would actually be really helpful for everyone, if you didn't hang out with Toni, like, at this time. I know that sounds mean, but it's actually a better thing for you too."

"Right now they think boarders caused the two Incidents," said the more athletic looking girl. "And if you start hanging out with her it looks bad. It's actually recommended — I'm not sure why whoever you are boarding with didn't tell you — for you to hang out with people who have been here for a while."

"Why?" Charlie managed to force out.

The girls looked at each other. "It's just that," the first girl explained, "it's a better influence on you, and we're trying to be a good influence on her, and the two of you together —"

"You think I am a bad influence?" Charlie asked. *Of course they do. Everyone does. And you are. Evil, evil, bad ...*

"Have you told her?" Charlie asked. She could see a girl behind them stop and listen.

"We don't want to make a big thing," the shorter girl continued. "That's why we're doing it now, so as not to embarrass you and Toni because —"

"Mmm, question, Becky." Charlie and the other two girls turned to see the blonde on the other side of the hall raising her hand, as she leaned lazily against her locker. "Does this Toni know y'all are *Mean Girls*–ing her friend?"

"I'm sorry," Becky said. "Ann, at what point did we ask you for your opinion? Because I'm pretty sure you weren't invited into this conversation."

"At what point did the newbie over there," Ann said, nodding to Charlie, "ask for you to tell her who she could be friends with?"

"You probably don't know this," Becky said, looking at Ann as if she were a bug. "But a teacher is gonna separate them if they see them together, and we are actually trying to spare her the embarrassment."

Ann put up her hands apologetically as if laughing at herself. "Forgive me, Miss Teen USA. I should have known you were acting selflessly. See, I thought you were just being a nosy, overbearing bitch cornering a poor freshman, but ..." Ann rolled her eyes. "I mean the only reason I would think that is because you *are* a nosy, overbearing bitch who would corner a poor freshman. Well ... shame on me."

"Okay," Becky said calmly. "Of all the people in this town, you are the last person who should be calling anyone that name. Don't you ever get tired of antagonizing people? And speaking of shame on you, wouldn't it feel better to not be ashamed of yourself? I hope this school can help you to respect yourself more."

"Oh, you wanna talk about me and how I'm a slut, right?" Ann drawled, flashing her eyebrows at Becky. "Well let's talk about you. Let's talk ... career options. You know what you would be great at?" Ann said, walking over to Becky. "Being one of those people who goes door-to-door asking people if they've accepted Jesus and reformed themselves." Ann clasped her hands together and mimicked Becky's hair flip. "'Hi, I'm Becky Carter, and I used to be known as the blow job queen of my high school, and everyone called me a whore. But I've reclaimed my purity, and now I just walk around calling *other* people whores.'"

Katrina pulled back, and Ann's swift eyes followed her expression. "Oh, yeah." Ann nodded towards Katrina. "See, sometimes I think Ms. J. Alter Academy here forgets that other people were here before the school."

"Your problem is that you think everyone is like you and just runs around all the time," Katrina threw at Ann. "Not all of us are addicted to lying and sex."

"No, some of us are addicted to more illegal things, right Katrina?" Ann whispered dangerously.

"The difference between us and you," Becky said, drawing herself up to her full height, "is that we've worked with the school and fixed our problems, while you are proud of yours."

"No, the difference between me and you is that I take on people my own size, instead of freshmen like Midget over here." She gestured at Charlie. "Because really, where's the challenge in that?"

"You think you're grown up?" Becky said, folding her arms. "Maybe you should act like it."

"Grown women don't pick on freshmen." Ann folded her own arms.

"Come on Kat," Becky said, leading her friend away. "There's too much negativity here."

Charlie watched them walk away before turning to look over at Ann. Ann seemed very sharp, and in all honesty, Charlie was a little intimidated by her. Ann walked over and took Charlie's hand.

"Hi. I'm Ann." The other girl smiled. "Sorry about that."

"Hi. I'm the midget," Charlie said.

"I didn't mean it to be mean," Ann said. "It's just that you're, well not a midget, just ... fun-size!"

"Thank you. I think you might get in trouble what you did though," Charlie said while her mind raced on. *In trouble. I'm in trouble, but I can control myself. Self-control. Self-help books. Help to help you help yourself. Wealth. Stealth. I need stealth to avoid the demons watching ...*

Ann shrugged. "I'm already in trouble anyway. How about lunch? Food always makes me feel happier. No better way to cheer yourself up than comfort food, right?"

"Yeah." Charlie nodded. "Food is nice."

Ann shook her head, half-laughing. "C'mon then, Midget."


*What are they gonna do?*

That was the question that occupied Joseph's mind.

*Maybe it'll be nothing, like just detention or somethin',* he tried to tell himself, knowing he was wrong.

Joseph kept his head low as he exited Mr. Protus's class. The way the man's eyes followed him let Joseph know the teacher suspected him.

"Hey, Troublemaker."

Joseph spun and saw Lieutenant, who had walked up behind him. "Yo, I am a woman, and I am unarmed!" the tall girl said, hands up. "Don't shoot."

Joseph smiled. "Don't mean you ain't dangerous," he stated.

"That's right, Smart One." Lieutenant nodded appreciatively. "Well, not too smart if you keep picking fights with Joe in there."

"What about you?" Joseph countered. "You weren't much better yesterday."

"That was yesterday. First week, first offense, they go easy on you. That's over now 'cause of what happened with the fire," Lieutenant informed him, walking with him toward the cafeteria. "Anyway, this isn't the time for people like us to be makin' enemies."

"People like us? What, crazies? Or narcoleptics?" Joseph joked wryly.

"Both." Lieutenant snorted. "Anyone who doesn't warm up to them and their methods. Here they work with a carrot and a stick, you know?"

"Leading a dog?" Joseph nodded.

Lieutenant stopped and gave him a look. "What the hell kind of dogs you know that eat *carrots*? I had a ferret. That thing wouldn't eat vegetables if you lit its butt on fire."

"Did you?"

"Did I what?"

"Light its —"

"Oh," Lieutenant laughed. "You are gonna fit *right* it. Wow. Come meet the other crazies."


*I'm back in fourth grade,* Toni thought, holding her tray and staring around the crowded lunchroom. *Only way not as skinny.*

Katrina spotted her and waved for her to come over to where she sat with Becky and a number of other girls. Toni looked away from their table and tried to find Charlie. She didn't see her but spotted a boy from her English class — *Joseph* — over at a table with a few empty seats.

"Can I sit here?" Toni asked, putting down her tray.

A second, shadow-like boy and his taller, female friend looked her up and down.

"Did you just piss someone off?" the girl with the dog tags asked.

"Um ... well, I sort of — yeah. I did." Toni admitted, looking at Becky and Katrina. They did not seem pleased.

"Sit right down then," the tall girl said emphatically, shuffling aside.

"We were just talkin' 'bout how we all came to arrive at this lovely Academy. I'm Anthony, by the way," said the shadow-like boy.

"It's Anthony *today*. Tomorrow he'll want us to call him Anton," said the girl with the dog tags. "I'm Amina Jackson, but I go by Lieutenant."

"She thinks she's gonna join the army some day," Anthony deadpanned. "She actually thinks one day she's gettin' outta here."

"What's that?" Lieutenant demanded suddenly of Joseph, who looked up, startled. He had been busy under the table with something. He reached up and showed a notebook of sketches.

"Oh, okay," Lieutenant approved.

"God," Joseph said. "A man can't even put his hands under the table by his crotch and keep his dignity anymore!"

"No it's okay." Lieutenant sighed. "We just ... get sorta paranoid bout people listenin' in on us. We just wouldn't put it past the school to give people privileges to tape conversations."

"It's really smart all the things the Academy comes up with," Anthony mused. "Really, some brilliant shit."

Lieutenant gave him a look. "What?" Anthony exclaimed. "It's true. It's like they the Mafia or somethin'. If *I* was a Mafioso, this whole table would be see-through glass," Anthony indicated. "And all of y'all would be wearin' Bermuda shorts and flip flops, so no one could sneak in any weapons. *I* would have a gun, keep you all on edge. But I'm not a Mafioso." He looked down forlornly. "I'm just a broke as fuck actor." He sighed.

Lieutenant patted him on the back. "Sad times, sad times ... Hey, looks like we have more company coming."

"Oh, I know her!" Toni said, as Charlie and another girl walked over.

"Yeah, it's Charlie." Lieutenant nodded. Toni watched the other girl pull a half-dazed Charlie over and sit down.

"Hi, L," Ann said, sitting down rapidly.

"Hey, Blonde Bitch," Lieutenant said. "Haven't seen you in a minute."

Ann closed her eyes and waved to Lieutenant, resigned. "Go ahead."

"Oh no, it's cool." Lieutenant brushed her off. "I ..."

"I know you wanna say it, so just get it over with, so you won't be holding back." Ann braced herself. "Just ... get it over with."

The rest of the table watched as Lieutenant waited, then gave in. "Okay, so two blondes walk into a bar —"

Ann groaned, and Anthony rubbed his eyes.

"No, no, for real, this is a new one!" Lieutenant promised. "So there were two blondes goin' to a wild forest on a Christmas tree cuttin' trip, right? And they spend hours out there, and it gets cold, and one finally says: 'Look, just pick a damn tree, 'cause somebody already cut all the decorated ones'."

Ann narrowed her eyes, and Toni laughed with the rest of the table.

"Feel better?" Ann asked sharply.

Lieutenant took a yoga breath and smiled serenely. "Yeah, I do."

"Ann didn't seem to find them very funny," Charlie noted.

"Blonde jokes piss her off," Anthony agreed.

"Ooh, thank you very much," Joseph said, reaching over to shake Lieutenant's hand. "I'll remember that."

Ann scowled at him and folded her arms. "Blonde jokes are a form of discrimination."

Anthony, Lieutenant, Toni, and Joseph stared her down.

"Well they are," she maintained, and Joseph snorted.

"You are a lovable bitch, that's what you are," Lieutenant stated. "What'chu done today?"

"Me?" Ann said, as if shocked. "Why would you think I had done anything?"

"'Cause you look all happy and excited, which either means you hooked up wit' somebody, or you bitched somebody out," Anthony stated.

"Becky and Katrina were ganging up on Charlie. Midget here was minding her own business, then they said she can't talk to Toni, whoever that is."

"Me," Toni said.

"Well." Ann turned to her. "They said she shouldn't talk to you because you're both boarders, and a teacher would probably separate you because things are gonna get bad for boarders now."

"What right do they have to tell people who they can talk to?" Joseph asked. Ann looked at him with a slow smile. "Thank you Joseph. That's what I said."

"Well, that makes us all in trouble here," said Anthony with a winning white-toothed grin. "Ain't we lucky our school is so acceptin'?"

"I wanna get the hell outta here," Joseph said darkly. "What do they do to you if ... if you get in trouble for like ... causin' an Incident?"

Lieutenant watched him carefully. "Why do you ask?"

"Just ... wanted to know." Joseph shifted.

"Depends," Lieutenant filled in. "For things like yellin' at teachers you can get overnight suspension. Sometimes isolation, bein' locked in a room for hours or even days till you "cool down." Sometimes it's food deprivation, where they make you throw away part of the food on your tray. Sometimes sleep deprivation, where they keep you up. And of course, there's the TED room."

"Where you face the wrath of Ted?" Joseph raised a brow.

"No," Lieutenant said darkly. "For Therapeutic Electronic Device. It's somethin' they modified and shit, themselves. Feels like a pack of wasps attackin' your skin."

"Wait, wait. What the hell are you talking about?" Toni demanded.

"Keep your voice down," Lieutenant instructed. "It's a shock device for punishment. They bring you downstairs to a room that looks kinda like a dentist's office and strap you down. Then they give you however many shocks you 'deserve'. If you fight 'em, it's more shocks. The wires go everywhere, so you never know where on your body the shock will hit."

"I don't believe you," Toni stated. "There's no way in hell any school could get away with that."

"How ... bad does it hurt?" Ann asked, looking nervous.

"Depends on how many you get. Each shock is twelve seconds. If you get enough, they can burn your skin." Lieutenant frowned at Ann. "We told you this when we saw you, 'member?"

"It's one thing to hear it," Ann said, swallowing. "Another to ..." She glanced at Joseph.

"What did y'all do?" Lieutenant asked, eyes wide.

"We just —"

"Shh!" Charlie snapped. They turned to her. "Someone's listening."

"It's lunch," Lieutenant said. "There's so much noise that —"

Charlie hissed, and Lieutenant moved back. "Yo, you possessed or some-thin'? 'Cause I need to know if you gon' spin your head around and vomit on my new blouse."

Charlie whirled and indicated with her head. The others turned to see a boy two tables over quickly look away.

"Wow." Lieutenant turned to Charlie. "Sorry. Shit," she whispered, "An-thony, people are listening."

Anthony wasn't. He was watching the contents of Charlie's plate. "Pickles," he said disgustedly.

Charlie looked down and up. "Huh?"

"One day," Anthony announced, "I'm gonna take a shotgun out to these woods and shoot everything I hate." He ticked them off on his fingers. "Pickles. P Diddy CDs. Bologna."

"Bologna?" Joseph said, looking at his sandwich.

"It ain't real meat," Anthony attested, squinting at it mistrustfully. "It's rat meat."

Lieutenant whacked him quickly upside the head. "Haven't you been listenin'? They're crackin' down on us, people are listenin', and these two went and did some —"

"Yeah, I heard." Anthony nodded. "But we didn't do anything, so we ain't gonna get in trouble. And the best thing for them to do is wait it out, and hope they don't get caught."

For a moment, Lieutenant looked as though she was ready to commit murder. Then she nodded. "Okay. I get it. I get it."

"I don't," Joseph said in a half whimper, making Ann and Toni laugh.

"I want us to be friends," Charlie said suddenly. When the others turned to her, she jumped a little and looked around as if searching for the voice of the person who had spoken.

"Sure," Lieutenant said, looking at Charlie as if she were something very funny. "We can be friends."

"When everyone else hates you, you have to be," Toni stated philosophi-cally. "And I get the feeling people don't like us."

"True." Lieutenant nodded. "Unless you're one of the ones like Katrina, who becomes their little star example."

"I don't think I want that," Toni said quietly.

"I could never, ever sink low enough to be their puppet," Joseph spat.

"You know me." Ann rolled her eyes. "I can't not be trouble."

Charlie realized that everyone was looking at her, waiting for some declaration. She felt nervous. Were they thinking she was evil and bad and wanting to kick her out?

No, she felt something from another part of her mind say. No, they wanted to know she was with them, she sensed. Would she join?

"*Attention, please,*" Mrs. Carter's voice said over the loudspeaker. The lunch room fell silent. "*I regret to inform you that all after school activities have been cancelled until further notice. We will review each of the school clubs to determine which ones may remain open. This does not include sports. All students today will proceed immediately to the buses after school, in orderly fashion. Thank you.*"

With the announcement, the lunchroom erupted in chatter, some of it angry, some relieved, and all of it confused and excited. When Toni looked at Lieutenant's face she saw fear.

"She knows," Lieutenant said.

"Knows what?" Joseph questioned.

"Keep talkin' like we're like everybody else," Anthony said, and Charlie pulled back. His face had taken on a completely different cast, and he leaned forward.

Joseph felt the other boy press something into his hand. He pulled back instinctively, but when the hand insisted, he took the piece of paper.

"Don't look at it," Anthony said, not looking at Joseph. "Not yet."

Toni kept the conversation going. "Oh my God, do you think I won't be able to try out for lacrosse?" She was so convincing the others didn't know she was faking until she nudged Ann's leg to make her speak.

"I'm more about volleyball," Ann put in casually.

Charlie felt Anthony slip a piece of paper into her hand. When his hand touched hers she felt a shock and looked into his eyes.

What she saw there terrified her.

"Shit," Lieutenant said. "Look to the door."

In the doorway stood Mrs. Carter herself, along with Mr. Protus and another teacher who scanned the cafeteria as if looking for something.

"Fuck," Joseph whispered and ducked down. "Get down," he said to Ann.

"Why?" Toni asked. Charlie was hyperventilating.

"It's him," Joseph said, still bent down, pulling his hoodie up. "The damn teacher who caught us yesterday."

"We can't let them see us all together," Lieutenant stated. "They'll suspect we're up to something." She turned to Anthony, whose neck swiveled around almost like an owl's.

"Everybody, we're gonna walk out the doors like nothing happened," Anthony stated. "Okay, I'ma leave first, then Lieutenant, then two of you should leave together ..."

"I'll go with Charlie," Toni stated. Charlie nodded.

"We should split up," Ann said to Joseph. "They're looking for us," she explained to the others.

"It doesn't feel like school," Toni remarked. "This feels like we're in the CIA or something."

"Get used to it," Anthony said sharply. "Okay. Break."

Anthony picked up his tray coolly and exited.

"Time to dip." Lieutenant half-smiled and got up and managed to swagger away as if nothing had happened.

"Okay." Toni swallowed. "Okay," she said again to Charlie. "Let's go."

Charlie reached for her friend's hand before pulling away, not wanting to attract attention as they moved to attach themselves to another group. She and Toni exchanged a look, and Charlie knew they were both holding their breath as they passed Mrs. Carter and her guards.

But pass they did.

"We got away," Toni whispered.

"Yeah." Charlie nodded. "*We* did."


"Our turn, I guess," said Joseph.

"There ... there's only one door out," Ann said, breathing fast. "How are we supposed to get past them?"

"We both go with a group, so we blend in," Joseph proposed.

"Okay." Ann nodded. "Wait," she said, when he rose. "If one of us gets caught, we just stick to the story right?"

"Right."

Joseph got up and, heart pounding, found a group he could blend in with. He held his breath as he came nearer the entrance where Mrs. Carter and the security guard from yesterday stood. He pressed himself to the wall and literally couldn't breathe as he was passing them. He waited until the teacher was looking the other way and then dodged past the opening.

*Did Ann get through?*

He hadn't seen her pass. He turned back and felt his stomach lurch. The teacher was pointing her out. Joseph tried to catch her eye and wave her away.

She noticed, but it was too late.

A burly guard grabbed her right arm, and when she struggled, another held down her left. They were clearly hurting her.

"Hey!" Joseph yelled. That made the guards turn.

*Ohfuck.*

Joseph had a chance to run, and his body told him to take it. If he couldn't escape, he could at least give them a run for their money.

But what about Ann? Was he just going to leave her there, to take whatever punishment the teachers decided she deserved?

It had been her idea. He could have run, could have justified it. But he wouldn't. It wasn't in him. He didn't mind running to save his own skin, but he wouldn't let someone else take the fall for him.

So he stayed and felt the guard behind him put a hand on his shoulder. Mrs. Carter nodded, face grim. "Alright. Bring them both down to the Ground Floor."

The guard behind him grabbed his arm too roughly for Joseph's liking, and Joseph pushed back. It only earned him a more iron grip and a mark of some kind on a clipboard that Mrs. Carter was holding.

He cast a sideways glance over at Ann. Two guards were holding her arms because she kept pushing back at them, her head held high. *She's tough,* Joseph thought with admiration.

Ann felt his glance and turned, catching his eyes watching her. She was scared, but she was determined not to show it.

She nodded to him, and he responded before they were escorted into a white room with two doors on either end.

"So these are the two students who lit the fire in the second floor?" Mrs. Carter asked the teacher who had seen them.

"Yes," he responded.

"No," Ann corrected. "We did not set that fire. It just happened, and we happened to be there."

Two of the guards scoffed.

"There must've been a messed up spark plug," Joseph stated. "Maybe it was because the wires got messed up in the blackout."

Ann shot him a look that said if she could have strangled him she would have. Joseph frowned, confused. The tone of the room changed. Mrs. Carter looked at him more closely.

"You know something about the blackout then?" she said delicately.

"What?" Joseph suddenly understood what he had done. "No! I wasn't even *here* when whatever happened to set that off happened. I didn't do anythin.'"

He saw Mrs. Carter's gaze move to Ann. "She didn't do it either," Joseph said before the question was asked.

Mrs. Carter's eyes pierced his. "I got a report from a student that you swore and threatened him. Is that true, Joseph?"

"If you mean Seth, that lyin' muther—" Joseph stopped himself, but not soon enough. He had just confirmed the report and damned himself in the process. Mrs. Carter set her mouth and gave a curt nod.

"If you could escort Ms. Cost into the left room." The principal pointed to the left door. "We can speak with Mr. Valdez alone."

Ann shot Joseph a look of half-fear, half-encouragement before she was led behind the door and it clicked shut.

Joseph looked around. He could still see the right door half-open, and he squinted again, trying to see what was inside.

Mrs. Carter marked another tick on the clipboard and handed it to the teacher who had caught them. They spoke so quietly that Joseph had to strain to hear.

"*Fuck no!* Get off of me, don't you dare even think about —"

Everyone reacted to Ann's scream. There was the sound of a slap and then a punch landing.

"I thought we might have something like this." Mrs. Carter swiftly picked up the phone and dialed a button. "We need some assistance — yes. Yes."

Joseph felt the tightening on his arms, but he had expected it. Was ready for it. He twisted his lower body and slammed his knee into the guard's groin. The man screamed in pain and released his arm just long enough for Joseph to yank free and smash his fist into the guard's face.

Stumbling back, Joseph fell into the teacher who had caught them, who tried to grab his arms. Joseph thrust his elbows back into the man's chest, toppling him over.

Joseph felt the wind from the guard's arm coming just in time and swerved under it rapidly, his body fiercely, painfully alive.

More guards filed into the room, two going into the left door, where Ann could be heard still fighting, and three crowding in around Joseph.

He stood while they made a half-circle around him.

*Not this time,* he thought. *This time, I get the first move.*

He faked attacking the guard to his right and then leaped forward, jumping up to reach the man's face, catching him so off guard that he fell onto his back with Joseph's knee in his chest.

Two pairs of arms grabbed Joseph by the legs and feet and lifted him, still struggling, into the left room.

Now Joseph saw what it was the white room contained: a long, flat, almost dentist-like bed. Except that this bed was metal, and it had straps.

He struggled more when he saw it, but the men were larger and stronger, and had weight, height and muscle on him. They slammed him down, and despite his flailing had soon bound his arms and legs with the straps, tightly enough to hurt.

Joseph tried to find some way of moving when the men pulled up his shirt and began attaching little wires to his skin — all over his chest, his neck, his shoulders, arms and he felt someone beginning to work on his legs.

"Oh, there is no way this is legal. Get off!" he demanded. There was no response as the guards finished their work and stepped back. Joseph caught his breath for a moment, and his eyes drifted to Mrs. Carter, who had walked in holding the clipboard.

"You have now performed two acts of sabotage against the school, threatened a student, and assaulted a teacher," the principal recited.

"Is this where I'm s'posed to apologize?" Joseph half-whispered.

Mrs. Carter handed the clipboard to someone so far left he couldn't see, and Joseph realized his neck was bound too. There was a hint of movement beyond his line of sight.

"*Fuck!*"

It hit his chest like a cluster of burning pins, and he had to scream with surprise and pain.

Twelve seconds, that was what Lieutenant had said. It felt longer. The next one hit his leg, and he let out another scream.

They came in fast succession, and since the electrodes were all over his body, he couldn't predict where they would hit next. He bit his lip, determined not to give them the satisfaction of hearing him scream. He fastened his eyes on Mrs. Carter and stared her down.

The pain was like being attacked by a horde of wasps. He could faintly hear something to his side. It took him a minute to make what it was.

"21 ... 22 ... 23 ... 24 ... 25 ... 26 ... 27 ..." The teacher counted off the shocks, as they forced something between Joseph's lips to silence his screaming.

# chapter seven the

**"Careful ... the guard is pacing,"** Charlie whispered. **"We have to** wait until he passes to talk."

Toni nodded, shifting in her bus seat. She cast a glance over at Lieutenant who was sitting further up front. She didn't look back. Careful. That was what they all needed to be.

The bus guard began walking in the other direction. They waited until he was just out of earshot.

"They can't do this," Toni alleged. "There has to be some law against it. Shocking your own students? There is no other place that does this, at least not in America!"

"Actually there is," Charlie said dismally. "I lived near it in Massachusetts. They use electric shock devices there too. And there's tons of schools and centers and camps that use isolation, observation, stress positions, all sorts of things. They can get away with it if our parents give permission, and ours clearly did."

"But why?" Toni whispered. "Why are they treating us like prisoners, worse than prisoners? Why would our parents agree to that?"

"Simple," Charlie said grimly. "They think we're dangerous enough that it warrants it."

"But we're not —" Toni stopped, and they both were silent as the guard walked down their end, paused, and then turned to walk back to the front of the bus.

"But we *aren't* dangerous," Toni whispered fiercely. Charlie was silent. "Are we?"

"I couldn't hurt a fly," Charlie stated. "Literally — I can't even stand bugs being killed. So I can't see myself as dangerous. But I can see why they think we might be."

"Why?" Toni demanded.

"Didn't you say that Katrina said we're here in a program for *troubled special teens*?" Charlie pointed out. "Troubled. Meaning we caused problems back home or *had* problems. Clearly, there's a reason why they wanted each of us here. And they did want us," Charlie said surely. "Three people from the school came in to persuade my mom and dad, and my therapist, to have me come here. *And* someone made this school seem great to me. I ..." Charlie paused then looked down. "You saw. I have —" The guard passed and then waited.

"I have some mental ... stuff going on," Charlie said effusively. "Stuff my doctors and therapist didn't know how to deal with. So I guess they decided they didn't wanna try and ..." Charlie swallowed. "Sent me here."

Toni instinctively reached out and took Charlie's hand. "I have panic attacks," Toni said comfortingly. "It feels like shit. I've even managed to successfully humiliate myself in front of my whole school while doing a project once, so score one for Toni!"

Charlie gave a hesitant laugh, then her hand traveled up Toni's sleeve and rolled over her arm. Charlie ran her fingers over the image of a broken heart carved there. "Is that why you did this?"

Toni fought the urge to yank her arm back. "Yes," she lied.

Charlie looked up, and Toni had the uncomfortable feeling that the other girl could tell she was lying. The guard passed again.

"But why here?" Toni picked up. "And what do we do if they decide we've been bad and they wanna shock us?"

A visible shiver went through Charlie's whole body and her grip on Toni's hand clenched. Toni glanced again at Lieutenant. "Oh! The —" The guard passed again. "The papers!"

"Oh right," Charlie remembered, taking out the little piece Anton had given her from her pocket. They both unfolded their little scraps and —

"What?" They said in unison. They glanced at each other, and then compared their blank little sheets. "There's nothing," Toni said, flipping it over. "Nothing at all. Asshole." She glanced at the back of Anthony's head. "He was just messing with us."

Charlie frowned flipping over the little black square. No. No there couldn't be nothing. She wouldn't believe it. There had to be ...

"Do you have a pen?" Charlie asked quickly.

"A pen?" Toni swiftly began rummaging through her backpack. "Um ... here," she said, and handed it to Charlie.

Charlie clicked it on, and scribbled over one side of the paper until it was full of lines.

They waited. The guard passed.

"Nothing," Toni said, and then leaned back dejectedly. Charlie pursed her lips and twisted the paper in her hands. "Well, I guess that —"

She stopped. "Look," she whispered to Toni. "It's —"

"Hide it," Toni said as the guard passed. He lingered for a moment, finally moving away. Charlie spread the paper out with trembling fingers.

On the side she hadn't written on there was a message in blue ink.

*After 12 St. lights go out. Sneak out D's bathroom window, to left side of P. field. See you there. P.S. — Beware dogs.*

Charlie handed the pen to Toni. "Do yours," she urged. They waited until the guard passed again and Toni scribbled ferociously on her square until the message became clear.

*After 12, st. lights go out. If you can find a way to sneak out a window, come to left side of P. field. PS — Beware the Bitch.*

Charlie and Toni slowly looked up at each other.

"We are so in over our heads," Toni said.

"Yeah. Pretty much."


*I can't believe this.*

*I hate this fuckin' school.*

*I hate my fuckin' life.*

*I hate myself.*

Joseph drew relentlessly on the page — it was his third page of drawings. What else could he do? He could hardly trash his room — then he'd just get it worse. "At least I fought," he mumbled, his anger fading as it seeped out of his hand and onto the paper. His breathing became rhythmic as the drawing took shape and he concentrated, fully enveloped in it. Lost in it.

It took four soft knocks to rouse him from his work.

*Oh great — my lovely supervisor.*

Joseph ignored the knocks for as long as he could before standing and opening the door.

"Oh."

"Hey," Ann said with a weak smile.

"I ... thought you were Sherry," Joseph said stupidly. "Not that you look like her!" he corrected hurriedly. "Or that you are like her, or ..." Ann raised a brow, and Joseph stopped babbling and motioned for her to enter.

"Watch that floor board. It creaks," he warned, taking Ann's hand to help her over it. "Last time I don't think I introduced you to all the intricacies and wonders in my room. Here, I'll give you the tour. Here we have my closet." He pointed. "And over here we got a desk." Joseph indicated. "It has a special place in my heart, 'cause I banged myself into it the first day. And here is a chair." He pointed. "Which you sit in like so." He sat to demonstrate. "And here —"

"What's in here?" She grabbed his backpack.

"Oh, no!" Joseph tried in vain to grab it back. "Gimme it!"

"Nope," Ann said, pulling it away from him and defiantly opening it. Ann bit the tip of her tongue as she drew out a series of drawings paper-clipped together.

"Did you draw this?" She held up the picture, which slightly resembled Joseph, only with great dark angel wings.

Joseph looked down sheepishly. "Yeah."

Ann looked down again. "It's beautiful," she whispered.

"You think so?" Joseph looked up.

Ann turned and met his glittering eyes. Whenever the light caught them they seemed to be on fire. "Yeah," she answered. "What is it?"

"Some sketches. Back home I was a street artist. I would put stuff like this on walls and buildings at night. Never thought up a name, but I would put lots of angels up."

"Isn't that illegal?" Ann asked.

"Yeah." Joseph sighed, shaking his head. "But it's not graffiti or gang signs or nuthin'. It's art. I mean, if you take somethin' disgustin' or ugly or horrible: blood, death, pain, depression, shit people go through, and put it down on walls or paper or whatever, and make it somethin' beautiful where people can see it, it doesn't have ... power over you anymore. It's not gonna jump up and attack someone or catch on fire." Joseph swallowed. "It's contained."

"Well at least you have something special about you," Ann said, running a finger down the side of a wing.

"You're the toughest woman I ever met," Joseph confessed, watching her sideways. "That's somethin' different. Somethin' to be proud of."

"You wouldn't think that if you saw my room," Ann said wryly.

"Well then let's go see it." Joseph stood up.

"Joseph, no!" Ann panicked. She didn't want him in her room. She had said too much about herself as is. Her room ... would go too far. "I said no, you can't see my room, it's — it's off limits and —"

"I'm goin', I'm goin'," Joseph teased, sing-song. He did a little jig.

"If you dare," Ann threatened, but Joseph just grinned wickedly and ran out of his room toward hers.

"Do you want to be the first person to discover what death by acrylic nails feels like?" Ann whispered. Joseph turned the knob.

"If you —"

"Joseph? Ann? What's going on up there?"

Both froze, then Joseph dashed inside her room and shut the door.

*Ooh, you bad boy.* Ann ran after him, opening the door and then closing it behind against Sherry.

"Now you're gonna know what pain feels like," Ann said to Joseph, who just wiggled his eyebrows again. "You —"

"Ann?" Sherry hollered. They heard her footsteps on the stairs.

Ann grabbed Joseph by the collar and pushed him under her bed.

"I'm not here," Joseph mouthed.

"Nah, really?" Ann mouthed back.

The door started to open, and Ann used her foot to shove Joseph further under the bed, before toppling into it and pulling up the covers.

"Ann?" Sherry opened the door.

"Umm." Ann turned over. "What is it?"

"Were you talking to Joseph?" Sherry asked suspiciously. She moved strangely, as if she wasn't quite balanced. Ann smelled the familiar odor of cheap liquor.

"He was talking to himself," Ann said. "I told him to shut up, but he kept blabbering about X-Men or something —"

Ann felt a bump from under her bed. "Ouch!"

"What was that?" Sherry asked.

"I hurt all over," Ann said frankly. "From ... today."

"Well I am sorry you chose to bring that on yourself," Sherry said. "Go to sleep."

After her feet descended the stairs, Joseph rolled out from under the bed.

"Thanks a lot," he said sarcastically. "Now she thinks I'm some crazed fanboy with no life."

"And that is different from reality ... how?"

"You know what?" Joseph growled, grabbing something on her bed to throw at her. "You — what is this?"

"Jos—"

Joseph turned on her desk light. "A penguin?"

Ann colored. "They're cute. I'm allowed cute things. I'm a girl. Now put it down!"

Joseph put his hands around the penguin's neck. "Any sudden moves and Fluffy gets it!"

"You —" Ann grabbed for him and pulled at his arm, her nails raking down his sleeve.

"*Fuck!*" Joseph swore.

"What?"

Joseph pulled up his sleeve.

"It's a burn," Ann said quietly. "If they shock you in the same place too many times you get them."

"You have any?" Joseph asked. Ann pulled down her shirt to show a glistening red one over her collarbone.

"I have somethin' for that," he said, and snuck into his room, grabbing the bottle of aloe vera cream and sneaking back to Ann's room carefully.

"Here," he said softly, giving it to her. "Rub that on it, and it'll fade in a few hours." Ann winced as she put it on. Joseph's eyes watched her hand move slowly over the nape of her neck. Part of him wanted to offer to do it himself, but the part that didn't want to get bitch-slapped said no. Ann's eye shifted over him, and he colored red under his bronze skin. He looked down at the bottle.

"There ain't a lot in there," Joseph noted. "You got other burns?"

"A few on my legs," Ann admitted.

"Then you use it all," Joseph ordered.

"What? What about you?" Ann said. She didn't like the idea of being the weak one here. "Here." She handed the bottle to him.

"Nah." Joseph waved it away. "Ladies first. 'Sides, I'm used to burns. They don't bother me."

Ann put the cream down. "If you can tough it out, I can too."

"That's stupid, Ann."

"You're being stupid. Look, I've lived through worse. We can share."

"Will you fuckin' just put it on?" Joseph demanded. *Damn, she's stubborn.*

Ann tried to hand the bottle back to him. "I'm not gonna have you be in pain all night. It's not fair, so stop being macho and take it."

"No." Joseph put his hands in his pockets. He knew he didn't have to take care of the burns. They would heal themselves. His hands were bunching into fists in his jacket around something. Frowning, he pulled out a piece of paper.

"It's Anthony's message," Joseph noted, then snorted. "But it's not. It's blank."

"No it isn't," Ann said, grabbing it from him.

"Hey!" Joseph complained. "You always grabbin' stuff from me."

Ann took a pen from her desk. "Melvin showed me this before. Anton is brilliant. Once he realized they couldn't use phones or email or anything, he created an invisible ink from info he found on the computer. They use it to tell when they are gonna meet ..." Ann turned to show Joseph the other side. "... at Panther Field."

Toni felt like smashing the face of the clock in her room and forcing the hand to move to twelve. The wait was killing her.

She got out of bed restlessly, went to the window, and looked down. She would have to cling to her window sill, then grab for the drain pipe at the side of the house and slide down.

*You can do it,* Toni told herself over her beating heart. *You can do it ...*

She tried to open the window. It wouldn't budge.

Toni felt for the locks. Finding them, she tried to open the window. It stayed locked.

*Of course,* she thought despairingly. *They're so careful about keeping you locked up — would they really leave a window for you to crawl out of?*

Toni clenched her fists. There had to be a way out. She had to be out there at twelve.

*Think girl, think! You're not stupid. You've done this before ...*

Toni quietly rushed into the bathroom and turned on the faucet. Carefully, she sprinkled water over her face, arms, and collarbone, and composed herself.

*This could easily go very badly,* she thought as she knocked on Mrs. Carter's bedroom door.

"Yes?" the woman said sleepily.

"I'm sorry to wake you," Toni said penitently, "but I'm just so hot in my room. I'm sweating and I'd just really love a breeze to cool me off ... do you think you could help me crack a window?"

Mrs. Carter looked at her carefully. "We have the windows closed for a reason, Toni."

"I'm sure," Toni said. "And I don't want to make a big deal about it, and it's okay if you can't ... but I'm just hot, and I'm homesick, and usually I would have the sounds of birds and crickets to get me to sleep, and I miss it, and I'm so homesick ..."

*Turn on the waterworks now.* Toni forced a few tears out. "I'm sorry. I'm just so nervous and ... and I —"

"Calm down, honey," Mrs. Carter said kindly. "I'll see what I can do."

Toni made herself smile. "Thank you so much."

Mrs. Carter came into Toni's room and stood by the window. Toni watched as she pulled out a key to unlock the closed window just enough so that a breeze moved in.

"Thank you," Toni said again. "That's perfect."

"We just don't want anyone jumping out of those windows," Mrs. Carter stated. "It's happened before."

Toni looked down. "It's so high! Didn't they break a leg?"

"Some of them did," Mrs. Carter answered ominously.

*Yeah, right.* "Thank you again, Mrs. Carter."

"No problem, Toni," Mrs. Carter said and walked out. "Goodnight."

"Goodnight."

Toni waited. An hour later she heard Mrs. Carter's footsteps and lay still as the woman opened the door to check on her. Satisfied that Toni was still in her bed, the principal went back to bed. Toni didn't have to worry about staying awake: her nerves kept her up until the street lights went out.

*Here goes nothing.* Toni got out of her bed, carefully stuffing it with pillows and covering it with a comforter. Then she felt under the crack in the window and pulled up.

The window moved and Toni strained, managing to shove it up. She did away with the flimsy screen and put one foot out into the night air.

*Bad idea,* she realized, and pulled herself back in. *Okay ...*

Toni turned backwards and put one foot out the window, clinging with one hand to the sill. Hesitantly, she put out her next foot and almost slipped.

She managed to stay quiet as she dug her nails into the sill, shimmied to the right, and reached for the drain pipe.

It was inches beyond her hand.

"Damnit," Toni whispered, looking down. *Great. I knew it would come to this.*

Toni took a deep breath and let go.


Charlie could feel the woods breathing.

She walked with her hands out, her feet making no sound on the ground despite the twigs and leaves underfoot. She let her eyes go out of focus since they were of no use in the pitch black, letting her skin pick up any movement.

Her hearing was her most acute sense now. Any movement — from chipmunks under foot, to birds overhead — she heard. If she concentrated, she could hear the sounds of the bugs in the ground under her feet.

*Now I just need to hear Toni.*

Charlie was keeping to the woods on the wild side of Wendell Parkway, but when her feet found concrete, she knew she was on the road toward the school.

Charlie put her ear to the ground and listened. There it was — vibration, up ahead. She kept low to the road, her hands out, until she could just make out the figure's movement.

Toni was standing, feeling lost, until she felt hands around her mouth. She pulled in a breath to scream.

"Don't. It's me. I didn't want to startle you."

"Shit," she said to Charlie, who gestured to her ear.

"Whisper right into my ear. We don't want the sound to carry."

"It won't carry," Toni whispered back. "We're too quiet."

"I can hear the dog sleeping on the porch down the road," Charlie answered. "Don't you think he might hear us too?"

"How is that possible?" Toni breathed heavily.

Charlie shrugged; Toni could feel it under her hand. "We all have senses. We just don't pay attention to them much."

"Yeah, but that's like ... impossible," Toni said skeptically.

"No," Charlie replied. "Some ... people like me ... sometimes our senses get very sharp." *Before we go psychotic.* "It's all in the brain. I have unusual chemistry."

"Can your chemistry find our way to Panther Field?"

"It can try."


"Will you stop making so much noise?" Ann hissed when Joseph pulled at the locked window sill.

"You are so —" Joseph shook his head and looked out the window. "There's gotta be a way to open this."

"We could steal the key from Sherry," Ann postulated. "She looks like she's pretty boozed up to me." *Kinda like my mom on a typical Saturday night.*

"Yeah," Joseph said absently, staring at the glass window. *Glass ... how is glass made? Well glass is made with fire ... which means glass melts ...*

"I got an idea," Joseph said, pulling out his lighter. "Glass melts," he said intently, pressing the lighter's flame to the edge of the window. "So if we melt the edges we can pull out the window and then melt it back when we come back in."

"But doesn't the fire have to be, like, a thousand degrees?" Ann asked.

The glass began to warp and pool. Ann kept very still and watched Joseph. His golden eyes focused on the window as he drew a square around the edges.

Ann stared as the glass melted. *But that's ... not possible,* she thought, almost afraid to breathe.

Joseph finished melting the edges and carefully pressed the window. The glass pane began to fall forward, and he caught the edges and pulled it back and put it down. "See?" he said with a small smile.

"Joseph, your hands!" Ann cried, and took his left hand and turned it over. She squinted at his palm, looking for the burn mark that should have been there.

Joseph's chest fell. *Great man. Now she's gonna run screamin' from you 'cause you're a freak.*

Ann ran her fingers over his palm and Joseph shivered.

"Am I hurting?" Ann asked, still looking down.

"Not —" Joseph swallowed. "Not at all."

Ann looked up at him, and the side of her mouth spread into a devious, crooked grin. "There's more to you than a pretty face, isn't there, Mr. Tiger Eyes?"

"I'm —" Joseph stumbled. She didn't seem scared at all. "My face is pretty?"

"Yup. You'd make a gorgeous drag queen," Ann said, looking out the window.

"Girl, I am all man, but you won't find out unless you start bein' nicer to me," Joseph warned.

Ann turned to him. "Take off your belt."

"Do what now?"

"Give. Me. Your. Belt," Ann enunciated.

"Am I gonna hafta cry rape here?" Joseph narrowed his eyes.

"You wish," Ann shot back. "I need your belt so I can lower you down so you don't break your neck."

"Why would you lower me?" Joseph demanded. "I'm —"

"So what if you're the guy?" Ann cut off. "I can lower you down. I'm not as weak as I look."

"Okay, He-Woman," Joseph grumbled.

"Are you calling me manly?"

"You're actin' like it," Joseph said smartly.

"Well someone has to here," Ann said as Joseph climbed out the window.

"I don't know if I trust you with that belt," Joseph said, his eyes and the top of his head the only thing visible.

"I won't drop you." Ann rolled her eyes.

"Oh good," Joseph said, descending the belt. "So these two blondes buy a copy machine —"

Ann loosened her hands on the rope.

"Hey!"

"I didn't drop you." Ann rolled her eyes. "Yet."

"Mm-hmm." She heard Joseph sigh. "Sneaking out of your house ain't as peaceful as it was in the old days."

Ann snorted, and Joseph let go and dropped to the ground. "Joseph!"

"I'm fine," Joseph called up, wearing a smart-alec grin. "Don't worry your little head too much 'bout me, baby."

Ann grumbled something about cocky guys who should do painful things to themselves with their own belts. "How far away is the drainpipe?"

"Just fall. I'll catch you," Joseph promised.

"No, no. I can reach." Ann grabbed for the pipe.

"You are the most stubborn woman alive," Joseph informed her.

"No, I'm one of four," Ann quipped back, still reaching.

"Ann —"

"I can do it," she snapped, focusing on reaching the pipe. *You can do it bitch, just a few more inches ... there we go baby —*

Ann grabbed the edges of the pipe with one hand and tried to move her other hand to it. She almost had it when she fell.

Ann bit back a scream before she braced herself to hit the ground.

Joseph grunted and stumbled, and Ann grabbed for his neck.

"This doesn't feel like ground," she said, breathing heavily, her hands still reactively clutching Joseph's shoulder. His hands held her behind her back and knees.

"See?" He smiled. "I told you I'd catch you."

For once Ann had nothing to say.

A dog barked behind them.

"We have to go," Ann said, looking pointedly at her legs.

"Yeah," Joseph said, a little embarrassedly putting her legs on the ground.

"I know my way from here," Ann said, all business. *I almost hurt myself. That's why my heart is beating so fast.* She took his hand. "C'mon."


"Damn," Anton said. "They all here."

"No backin' out now," Lieutenant mumbled.

"So here we are," Joseph said. "Is there gonna be an orgy, or should we all go home?"

Anton stepped forward, eyes moving from Toni to Charlie to Joseph to Ann. "You all here at the Academy for a reason. I think it's good if we all say why."

Toni stepped back, Charlie cringed like a wild animal, and Ann and Joseph started protesting.

"Why should we —"

"Yo man, our reasons are our own and —"

"I got brought here in handcuffs after my friend tried to kill my parents," Anton said in his flat, low voice. "He had told me that he planned to do it after I told him ... how they treated me. But I said no, and I thought he would listen to me. He didn't, and when he got caught, he said I helped. So my parents sent me here."

There was silence.

"So?" Anton said, shrugging his shoulder. "Care to add anything?"

"My parents sent me here." Lieutenant stepped forward. "Said they couldn't deal with my moods. My mom's boyfriend made most of the decision. Good fuckin' riddance. I wasn't livin' there then anyway. I made my own money, livin' with my sister."

"You had a job at thirteen?" Joseph said skeptically.

"Fourteen," Lieutenant informed. "No matter what your age, when they bring you here you start as a freshman. I was doin' good at my school too, until this."

"So how did they make you come here?" Toni asked.

"Oh, they had to drag me." Lieutenant nodded. "I heard cops and I ran; I wasn't even doin' anything and I ran, which didn't make them like me much."

Melvin realized after a second that everyone was looking at him. "What?" He wrapped his arms around himself. "I was born here. Oh, you mean how did I get mixed up with these hooligans?" Melvin walked into the circle. "I've been here since before this school was started. Then we weren't your sweet little American town. We had kids going off and drinking and doing drugs and starting fights, 'cause what the hell else was there to do? We actually got an offer from MTV to film a reality show here, it was that bad. So when our lovely Headmistress came into town with money and said she would fix up the school, everyone jumped." Melvin clearly enjoyed telling the story.

"So she starts with the new school and manages to get everyone to clean up their act. Then gets the parents to agree to let it be a 'behavior modification school.' She started the STARE Program to bring troubled kids like you dolls *in* and 'reform' you. I came in last year, and I was so used to no one fighting back that when I realized these people" — he jerked his head at Lieutenant and Anton — "were actually crazy enough to do it, I had to join."

"Why so eager?" Joseph questioned. "Wouldn't it have been easier, you know, to just go with it?"

"It's not easier when you're the town queer," Melvin said sharply. "My neck was already out on the block."

There was a pause where the three veterans seemed to be waiting.

"I was already here," Ann put in finally. "My parents sent me into this STARE thing. It's not all bad. At least I'm away from them."

Ann paused and then pushed Joseph when he didn't speak.

"Ow! Damn, woman!" Joseph looked up and around. "So," he cleared his throat. "Hi, my name is Joseph." He paused, and gestured for a response.

"Hi Joseph," everyone echoed.

"Good, we got a little issue with the energy level here, but I'll let it slide," he said generously. "Okay, so my story is that I have this tendency to maybe light fires a little bit. I also did graffiti on places —"

"Tagging?" Lieutenant guessed.

"*No,*" Joseph said sounding supremely offended. "I did street art. One day a fire spread, and they linked it to me. I was gonna get expelled, but instead they sent me here."

"Alright, so now that I feel so much safer knowin' we got a pyromaniac here, what about you?" Lieutenant nodded at Charlie.

Charlie was unnaturally still.

"Midget?" Ann asked Charlie gently. "You don't have to be worried here. You're not gonna scare any of us away."

"I had to come here," Charlie said softly. "Or I would have had to go to a hospital."

"Bulimia?" Toni guessed.

"No, why?" Charlie asked.

"No reason," Toni covered. "Why? Where?"

"McLean Hospital," Charlie said, looking down. "I have ... well, they can't define it yet, because I'm too young but ... and I'm not violent — I think but —" Charlie swallowed, looking up. "My mind isn't really — right. I — I got sent here after I turned on all the lights, broke every mirror in the house and pushed over our TV."

"How come?" Joseph asked. "I mean ... if you have a reason ..."

"Well ..." Charlie's brow furrowed as she remembered. "I ... turned on all the lights so that demons couldn't sneak up on me, broke the mirrors so they couldn't get in, and pushed over the TV so Brian Williams would stop sending me messages."

"Oh," Ann managed. "Toni?"

Toni didn't dare move. "I'm not supposed to be here."

"Welcome to the club, darlin'," Anton said.

"No, no!" Toni pointed a finger at him, at all of them. "No, how can you be so calm? You all ... I mean, after what you've been through ... and then coming here and they can *shock* you? And you all just —"

Anton turned to Lieutenant. "She sounds like you last year."

"You, you're laughing, and cracking jokes?" Toni squeaked. "How can you do that?"

"It's called *coping,* sweetie," Lieutenant said. "I did just what you doin' right now, all last year. But freakin' out, breakin' rules is not the way to be, trust me. You learn to stay calm."

"But I ..." Toni felt like she couldn't breathe again. "I don't — I shouldn't be here."

"We all feel —"

"No, but I didn't do anything!" Toni practically screamed. The others looked nervously around, but there was no response to the noise. "I didn't," Toni continued. "I didn't try to kill anyone or, or act crazy. I just shoplifted a bit with my friends, and drank a little bit in the woods and — and —"

*The woods.*

Toni collapsed to the ground. Charlie knelt down beside her. "No, I'm okay," Toni said. "I just ... need a minute."

"Well, we only got a little time left," Anton said. "You probably got by now that we ain't really good little school boys and girls. This school brought you all here 'cause they think we're dangerous, and that means they treat us like we are. Well if they're gonna blame me for it, I'ma be more danger than they can handle. You people interested?"

Toni could hear her rapid breathing in the silence that followed.

"You already know I am," Ann said, before looking over at Joseph, who nodded.

"Yeah," he said surely, turning to Lieutenant and Anton. "This whole place is wrong. No place should have this much power over people's lives. I was gonna fight it solo, but workin' together might be better."

"What about you, Midget?" Ann asked Charlie. "In or out?"

"I'm afraid," Charlie said. "But — you all don't — don't think I'm crazy."

"Course we do," Anton said. "We're just all crazy too, so you fit right in."

"So I do." Charlie nodded. "Toni?"

"How bad is it if we get caught?" Toni asked.

"Bad," Melvin supplied. "But it'll be bad either way. They once sent me for some shock therapy after I laughed in a school meeting. A whole half hour."

"I'm scared," Toni admitted. "I think you're all a few sandwiches short of a picnic."

"Few tacos short of a combination plate," Joseph added helpfully.

"Few Taliban short of a jihad," Charlie pitched in brightly.

"Oh, too soon." Anton shook his head, while Lieutenant snorted with laughter.

"They took my cell phone and touched my clothes," Toni said decidedly after a minute. "So now I am royally pissed ... and since I fucked myself over by even coming here, I might as well stick my hand in too."

"Well, now that we've all shared and bonded," Joseph said pointedly. "What does our little clan plan on doin' as our first official mission?"

"Well," Charlie said, with a dark smile. "I have a few ideas."

# chapter eight mushrooms

**Charlie took a deep breath. This could make or break her. If Mrs.**
Carter sensed something was wrong their whole plan would fail.

Charlie watched as the principal opened the drawer. It was now or never. "Mrs. Carter?"

The principal turned to face Charlie. "Yes?"

"I'm just feeling nervous." Charlie sighed, putting herself between the principal and her desk. "With all this new material, and the new school, I was just wondering —"

Mrs. Carter put up her hand. "I really cannot discuss personal feelings with students. Perhaps you've done that with other teachers, but that is not how we operate here. Now," Mrs. Carter said in a more kindly tone. "If you have issues with your ability to keep up with the course work, we can certainly set you up for extra help."

"Thank you," Charlie said, left hand coming back to her side. "That's what I was asking."

"Good. I will schedule a time. But Ms. Persan," Mrs. Carter said. "Please don't make a habit of approaching teachers alone. File a request with the student office. It will be better for everyone involved."

Charlie watched the heels click out of the room. Then she turned to examine the gold key in her palm.


Joseph glanced around the corner to the end of the hall. Ann's eyes followed Seth as he exited the classroom. She motioned to Joseph and pointed at herself. Joseph shook his head. He would do this. Ann shrugged with a skeptical smile.

"Yo man, watch where you're goin'," Joseph said as he turned the corner and purposefully bumped into Seth as he walked by, knocking his backpack and books out of his arms.

"Most people have eyes," Seth drawled, bending down to pick up his things. "How 'bout you use them?"

"Whatever," Joseph said under his breath, picking up one of Seth's books. It flipped open.

"Give me that." The senior snarled, yanking it away. *Damn.* Joseph put up his hands. "I was just gonna hand it back to you," Joseph defended.

"How stupid do you think I am?" Seth whispered, his eyes watching Joseph. Joseph had no doubt that if the other boy had had a knife, he would have stabbed Joseph dead and walked away without a second thought.

"Whatever," Joseph repeated and walked away, rounding the corner and leaning against the wall beside Ann. She shook her head.

"What?" he whispered.

"You," she said. "Men in general."

"Now we lost our chance — he's goin' into his next class," Joseph grumbled.

Ann just gave him a pitying look. "Watch and learn," she whispered into his ear before whirling around to walk backwards away from Joseph.

"Oh my God, you are so funny it's unbelievable, Jess," she laughed. "We so have to — ooff!"

She tripped into Seth, who spilled his papers again. "Oh God, I'm so sorry," she apologized. "Here lemme help you."

"No, it's fine," Seth said, picking up his things.

"No, really," Ann said, bending down to help his collect his papers. "I'm a klutz. I should've been watching where I was going."

"It's okay, it's just this is just the second time it's happened," Seth said.

Ann looked up and brushed a piece of hair away from her face. Her eyes watched Seth's face until he glanced up. "What?" he asked.

"Nothing." Ann looked down, smiling shyly. "Nothing, it's just ..." She looked up from under her lashes. "I just see you all the time on the football field when I walk home."

"Oh yeah?" Seth leaned on one knee. "Where do you live?"

"Right by here, on Highbrow Street," Ann lied easily.

"Oh yeah?" Seth grinned. "What number?"

"Number 18," Ann said, as if deeply flattered. Joseph felt the overwhelming urge to drop heavy things on Seth's head.

"Maybe I'll come see you sometime," Seth whispered. Ann giggled a little. "Maybe you will," Ann said, handing Seth back his notebook slowly.

"I gotta go to class," Seth said, standing up. Ann smiled at him until the door was closed. Then she sauntered over to Joseph.

"Looks like he forgot something," she said, pulling a piece of paper out of her sleeve. Joseph noted Seth's handwriting then looked away. "Yeah. Great."

"Aw. Is someone jealous it wasn't him who tricked his nemesis?" Ann crooned then laughed.

"Jealous? No." *Yes.* "I just hate him. Seems like you was havin' fun." Joseph looked down the stairs.

"Yeah, I was," Ann said, turning his face towards hers. "What's the deal? We tricked him and got what we needed."

"Oh well you sure turned that trick," Joseph said, looking at her. Ann pulled back, as if he had slapped her, his comment hitting her right in the gut.

"Do you know what I was thinking of the whole time I was looking at him?" Ann said, dropping the flirty attitude entirely.

"What?"

"How much fun it would be to shove his cocky head in the elevator door," Ann said wryly.

Joseph snorted. "That sounds like fun. I personally was thinkin' of smashin' open the emergency glass and usin' the fire extinguisher to break his skull."

"Tripping down the stairs is classic," Ann considered. "But I think Charlie's idea is best."

"No doubt."


"Should we all be sitting together?" Toni asked.

"They still don't have the cameras back up," Charlie informed them.

"How do you know?" Toni asked.

"I heard," Charlie said simply.

"They could be trickin' us," Lieutenant said, not looking up. She had nearly a dozen papers and books all spread out and was switching from Spanish to English to poetry in rapid succession. "They've done it before — pretend that the computers or the metal detectors or cameras are down to see who acts out. Sometimes they bait people, to see if they act out. Then they punish them."

"That's so stupid. What's the point of that?" Toni asked.

"The idea is that if you're really 'behaviorally well,'" Anton supplied, "you wouldn't act out anyways. Like a test."

"That's so ... twisted," Toni said, shaking her head.

"You surprised?" Anton asked.

"It wasn't a trick," Charlie said firmly. "If it was a trick, they would have said it when students were near. There were no students around when they said it."

"Except you," Toni pointed out.

"No," Charlie said, looking at the table. "I was down the hall, beyond their sight."

"Then how did you hear?" asked Lieutenant, finally looking up.

"I have good hearing," Charlie said, glancing at them. "I just ... I know, okay?" Charlie watched Lieutenant, whose hand was still working even as she looked up.

"We have company." Anton nodded to where Ann and Joseph were coming over, laughing about something.

"Hey," Ann said, sliding into her seat. "Having fun today?"

"Fun?" Toni squeaked. "In this school? Fun doesn't seem to be on their agenda."

"Oh, come on," Ann said, with a lift of her eyebrows at Toni. "We're making our own fun, aren't we?" she said to the other girl. "Did everyone a ... complete their schoolwork for the day?"

"Not here," Anton warned. "What if they're listening?"

"No one is," Charlie said, playing with her peas. "They're all talking at their own tables." Charlie looked up and around. "I have it."

"Good work, Garden Gnome," Ann congratulated, clapping the other girl's hand.

"That's not a very nice nickname," Toni said. Ann's face fell. "I think it's cute."

"It's okay," Charlie said. "I like it."

"Well if you are going to call her Garden Gnome," Toni said. "You should shorten it to G squared. That's how you know the KKK was dumb. They should have just called themselves K cubed."

"*That's* how we know the KKK was dumb?" Lieutenant asked.

"Gorgeous, you do know you have five different things you're working on at one moment, right?" Ann said, looking at her friend. "Your brain is going to explode."

"No it won't," Lieutenant said, one hand writing a report for History, the other a paper for English. "The ideas are coming and I have to get them down."

"You all — what's it called ..." Anton started.

"Manic? So what?" Lieutenant said, writing more agitatedly. "We all messed up here, right?"

"How many classes are you taking?" Joseph asked.

"As many as I can," Lieutenant answered. "Maybe then I won't be a complete pariah when I get out."

"A..."

"Pariah," Lieutenant said. "Someone who is scorned and isolated and rejected."

"So us," Ann said lightly.

"Yeah," Lieutenant said, scowling. "You know I was an honors student in my old high school? I stayed in my sister's apartment, she was gon' give it to me when I got out? I had two part-time jobs, you know? *And* my dog, and my cat, and my ferret, and my birds … I was at a good school, I was gonna go to a *good* college, and now it's all fucked up cause now I'm *HERE*." Lieutenant's fury was visibly mounting. "I promised myself, I promised myself I'd have more than this," she said, her face twisting, as if she didn't know whether to cry or scream. "I *promised* myself I'd *be* more than this, and now it's all slippin' away. Nah, nah, fuck that. It's gone." She threw down her pencil and gestured with her hands. "Gone!"

Joseph pulled back as Lieutenant's tray hit his shirt, her drink spilling all over him.

"Oh, lemme get that," Ann said, grabbing some napkins and cleaning it up. "We're not supposed to get stuff on us. They can call you out on it."

"Th-thanks," Joseph said to Ann, her hands roving over his chest. Right now he was very thankful that Lieutenant's juice had spilled on him.

Charlie looked over at Lieutenant, who was staring straight ahead, breathing. "L?" Anton said, touching her shoulder. "You a'ight?"

Lieutenant nodded. "Yeah — yeah. Sorry for — for pushin' it."

"But you didn't."

The group turned to Charlie. "You didn't push it. Your hands never touched the tray."

"Well my hands were moving, and the breeze from 'em did it," Lieutenant said.

"No it didn't." Toni shook her head. "I saw. You moved your hands, and the tray flew across the table."

"So what?" Lieutenant said.

"L," Ann said, her eyes on her friend's. "You don't have to be afraid here. We're all freaks, one way or another. No one is gonna judge you."

"Oh that's rich comin' from you," Lieutenant said sharply. "You keep your business private, and I'll keep mine."

"Your private business just spilled all over Joseph's shirt," Ann responded. "I think it's a little late for secrets."

"You wanna talk secrets girl, I'll go," Lieutenant warned. "You know how well I know you."

Ann looked around the table, lips pursed. Lieutenant was as stubborn as she was. *If I push, she'll push back, and none of my 'talents' are as interesting as everyone else's.* "I'm going to get milk," Ann announced suddenly.

Joseph watched her get up and hurry away.

"And they say I'm bipolar." Lieutenant shook her head.

"She isn't goin' to get knives, is she?" Joseph asked, a little worriedly.

"No." Anton shook his head, a friendly smile on his face. "She likes you."

"Lord have mercy," Lieutenant mumbled. Charlie was staring at Anton. "What?" he asked.

"Nothing." Charlie shook her head. "You are Anton, right?"

"No, I'm Anthony." He grinned. Lieutenant snorted.

"Seriously." Charlie looked at Lieutenant. "You don't have to hide from us. I hear voices. You're not going to scare me."

"And we all saw," Toni supplied.

Lieutenant rubbed her pencil between her fingers. "It happens when I get manic. You know what that means?"

"You get crazy?" Joseph supplied.

"Hyper," Charlie corrected.

"Yeah." Lieutenant nodded. "I get ... my mind starts fillin' with so many thoughts I can't get em down fast enough. I stay up all night. I can do a million things ... everything's faster, stronger ... I'm high. Anyway, sometimes, if I focus and get agitated when I'm like that I —" Lieutenant gestured to the tray.

"Telekenisis," Charlie said.

"After it happens I come down a little bit," Lieutenant explained. "Its like — energy building up so much it spills out."

"Makes sense," Toni said as Ann sat down beside her with her milk. "Well it makes sense to me."

There was a burst of laughter from the table next to them. Toni turned to see a number of other girls at it looking at her. "What?" Toni asked.

"Nothing," said a little redhead. She gave Toni an up and down with her eyes and then a dismissive hair jerk.

"If you wanna say something," Toni said, losing it. "Say it, Pipsqueak."

The girls at the table twittered. "At least I am Pipsqueak," said the redhead audibly to her friends. "And not cow."

Toni couldn't speak and turned away. *I should make a comeback, she thought tell her off ... but ...*

*But she's right.*

Ann watched Toni's face fall. She knew that feeling, when someone tore you down for their own amusement. *Not to my friend you don't,* she thought furiously.

She swirled her chair to face the other table. "Hey, you," she called. She whistled sharply, getting their attention. "Over here. Yeah — you. How about before you start talking about my friend, who happens to be beautiful, you go look in a mirror? And then you can go and get some plastic surgery to go with that jealousy."

"Why would she be jealous of your friend?" one of the redhead's friends said scathingly. "What is there to be jealous of? Ever hear of Weight Watchers?"

"Ever hear of boobs?" Ann countered. "They're what my friend has and what *you* would need to actually fill the bra you're wearing. So why don't you leave cleavage to the big girls and leave your training bra at home?"

Ann blew a kiss at the girls shocked faces and turned back to smile at her friends. "There we go."

"Ladies and gentlemen, Ann Cost," Lieutenant announced. "The Official Bitch of J. Alter Academy."

"Official bitch of this whole town," Ann corrected.

"You really enjoy the whole bad girl thing, don't you?" Toni noted.

Ann smiled cutely. "Every town needs one, so I guess I took the job. People are gonna think of me that way, whatever I do. Might as well get a little fun in. But listen, Toni — fuck them. You know that voice, telling you you're ugly? It's wrong. You're beautiful. Those girls aren't worth anything. The redhead thinks because her sister is a beauty, she will be too. And Lauren thinks because some guys like her, she walks on water." Ann glanced disdainfully at the table. "I'm not sure why, since she is pretty boring. She must have beer flavored nipples or something."

Joseph cackled, and Lieutenant snorted.

"She's right though," Toni said bleakly.

"About what?" Charlie asked.

"I do need to lose some weight." Toni nodded.

"Why?" Lieutenant asked. "You got a chest, an ass ... the whole damn nine yards."

"Yeah, a fat ass," Toni said darkly.

"So what?" Charlie repeated. "At least you have curves. I have none, and I have a pudgy stomach."

"Oh, everyone has that," Ann attested, pulling up her shirt.

"Whoa." Lieutenant put up her hands. "I aint fallin' in this trap. I'm tired of people saying my thighs are too big."

"See?" Ann pointed. "Everyone's got that little bit."

Joseph looked at Anthony. Anthony looked at Joseph. Joseph and Anthony picked up their trays.

"Okay, so we're goin'."

"Yeah."

"Come back here," Ann said, pulling Joseph back into his seat. "We're just saying."

"Y'all are just talkin' crazy, is what you doin'," Joseph said. "Toni, you ain't fat, you're thick. Charlie, you're cute. Lieutenant, your thighs ain't big, and you ..." Joseph turned to Ann. "You know you're beautiful, so shut up. Damn." Joseph shook his head, looking at Anthony. "Women."

Ann looked away, blushing, then spotted their last member.

"Harken, the fairy cometh," she said, as Melvin sped over.

"Lunch is almost over," Lieutenant said. "You missed me bein' manic and Ann bein' a bitch."

"So just a normal lunch," Melvin said. "Look." He leaned in. "I know what to use. The homecoming banner. They unroll it tomorrow, when the whole school is watching, to kick off spirit week."

"But if they are holding back homecoming, won't they not unroll it?" Toni asked. Melvin shook his head. "I heard Mr. Protus and Mrs. Carter talking. They're doing it tomorrow. It's like a push for people to turn in the ones who blew the cameras."

"So we gotta do it before they turn us in," Lieutenant said.

"Tonight, then," Anton whispered. "We got the key?"

"Yes," said Charlie.

"The writing?"

"Got it," Ann confirmed.

"A'ight then," Anton said. "Break."

# chapter nine take

**"Where the fuck are they?"** Lieutenant muttered, glancing over the massive outline of the school, profiled in moonlight. "It ain't safe to just hold the gate open all night."

"Maybe they couldn't figure out how to get over? Maybe they got caught," Melvin said nervously.

"No," Lieutenant said. "I told Charlie to come at the low point under the fence on the right side of Panther Field. She said she could steal a dinner knife from Dana to cut it. Ann and Joseph are supposed to come from the other side, over the fence."

"Over the barbed wire?" Melvin exclaimed.

"No. Ann will know how to get in. That girl got more ways of escapin' and gettin' in and outta places than a convict. Put that chick in Alcatraz, she'd be out in a minute," Lieutenant assured.

"What if they —" Melvin looked at Anton. "You know ... decided to turn on us?"

"They won't," Anton said firmly.

"But how do you —"

"I just know, okay?" Anton said sharply. Melvin backed down. "See?" Anton noticed after a second. "There they are."

Ann and Joseph walked up, followed by the shorter shadows of Charlie and Toni.

"You got the key?" Lieutenant asked. Charlie jangled it in front of her.

"We gotta sneak 'round to the back door of the gym," Anton stated.

"Be careful, there might be guards around," Lieutenant said.

"Everybody follow L," Anton said, with a sideways grin. "She's all about the guerilla warfare shit."

"Can y'all see my hand?" Lieutenant held up her arm. They nodded. "Well, that's good and bad. That means they can see us, if we get too close. We're gonna keep low to the ground. If I put up my hand like this —" Lieutenant made a fist. "It means it's cool to move. If I do this —" She bent her elbow down. "It means get down and *do not move.*"

"Yes sir," Ann said with a grin.

"That's ma'am to you."


The security guard rubbed his hands together — it was getting colder in the year. If only the damn lights and cameras hadn't gone out, he wouldn't be here on security.

"Fuckin' delinquent kids," he muttered. "Should treat 'em like adults when they pull this shit, and send 'em to juvie."

He frowned as something moved in the bushes. Probably a rabbit or something. He just wanted to get home and get warm. He shined his flashlight over the area. The movement stopped.

Suspicious, he moved his flashlight away and waited. Four minutes ... five ... and there it was. A figure rose from the bushes and crept towards one of the school's gym doors.

The guard began to move forward to apprehend the trespasser when another shadow followed, and another.

He waited for them to descend the stairs to the side gym door — one of them jumping over the rail — before turning on his walkie.

"Yeah, this is Anderson, on patrol at the south side of the school. You're gonna wanna send some fellas over here."


"And ... we're in." Joseph grinned.

"Nice work, Charlie," Ann congratulated with a wink.

"Let's do this fast and get out," Toni said worriedly.

"Hey," Ann said with a rogue smile. "We just broke into J. Alter Academy. We bad." She bumped her hip into Toni's.

"Ann," Melvin called. "Come over here."

"Right there, sexy," Ann said, running over.

"Wow," Toni said, looking around. The gym was massive. Huge stands on either side didn't stop it from being one of the biggest basketball arenas she had ever seen. Looking up Toni saw a balcony at the opposite end by the basketball hoop.

"So they can always watch what's going on," Charlie said aloud. Toni jumped and turned to the other girl. "That hallway is placed so they can look over the rails down at whatever's happening. Which means it must be really hard to monitor this whole gym, even with cameras."

"Guys," Anton hissed. "Come over here."

Lieutenant pushed them, and they ran to where Ann and Melvin were inspecting the lock on the closet that held the school's homecoming banner. "The key doesn't work," Ann said.

"Step aside, Baby Doll," said Melvin, brushing her away. He rubbed his hands together. "Bless 'em," he instructed, and Ann kissed his hands, and the two pieces of metal he held in them.

"What's he doin'?" Joseph whispered to Ann.

"Lock pick, handsome," said Melvin. The door opened. "Who's the king?" he asked.

"Don't you mean who's the queen?" Ann said with a flick of her tongue. Melvin turned around with a lovable smirk to show the 'pick'. "Two paper clips put together. They're not as smart as they think if they give us this stuff we can use."

"Let's get this done right quick," Lieutenant said, and she and Ann pulled out the rolled up banner and laid it on the gym floor.

"Go to town." Lieutenant gestured to Joseph, who pulled cans of spray paint from his coat. "Yo, Ann," he reminded.

"Oh, yeah." Ann pulled off the small backpack and took out the rest of his things. "As quick as you can."

"Give the artist his space, a'ight?" Joseph said. They moved back as he worked.

"I never expected to be doing this at high school," Toni said flatly, looking ahead. "Partying, cliques, drunken regrets that end up on YouTube sure, but breaking into the school to tag a banner?"

"It's not tagging," Joseph said, not looking up from his work. "It's art."

"Make sure your handwriting looks like his," Ann reminded.

"We need to get outta here," Anton said, head swiveling around. "They might be doin' checks."

"I'm almost done," Joseph said from the floor. "Just gimme a minute."

"So we go out the way we came in, right?" Toni asked.

"Yeah, yeah." Anton nodded. "Just —"

"People are coming," Charlie said sharply.

"What?"

"I can hear them," Charlie said, agitated. "Footsteps. Breathing. They're getting closer."

"Okay," Toni said. "Maybe you just —"

"They came in this way," said a new voice from outside the gym. "They came in through the gym side door."

Everyone froze at that voice.

"Shit, we have to get out," Lieutenant said.

"But they know where we came in," Charlie said, panicky. "We can't go out that way, and there are voices coming from the main entrance too."

"We're trapped," Melvin whispered. Toni was looking around.

"We'll have to run, have someone distract them, then break for it," Ann said.

"No," Toni said. "I have an idea."


"They went in here," the guard said, flashing his light at the back entrance to the gym.

"Check it," Mrs. Carter ordered. Another teacher ran down.

"It's locked," he called back.

"Search the room," Mrs. Carter ordered. "Every bit. Behind the stands, by the volleyball nets, anywhere they could be hiding."

The guards fanned out and shone their flashlights around the stands. "Nothing," one guard said.

"Did you check behind them?" Mrs. Carter demanded.

"Yes," he said. "All of them. No go."

"Search under them," Mrs. Carter barked.

"Still nothing," the other called.

"They must have run out," said the second guard.

"No," Mrs. Carter said.

The guard tried again. "Maybe they ran out the way they came —"

"No," Mrs. Carter silenced, looking around. "No, they are still here."

Her eyes drifted to the closet to her right. "That," she said. "Open it."

The guards moved over to the storage closet.

"Oh my God, you guys, I think they're here. Let's run this way!"

The teacher whirled at the voice. "It came from out there," he said, pointing inside the school.

"Oh no, I think they found us. Let's go up to the third floor!" Ann's voice exclaimed again.

"Quick. Everybody out," Mrs. Carter ordered, quickly sprinting after the rest of her team as the door banged shut behind them.

The silence of the gym was broken by something falling from under the bleachers.

"You're making too much noise," Melvin chastised. "You'll bring them back in!"

"I couldn't help it," Charlie defended, crawling out from under them. "I couldn't hang onto that position a second more. When they shone that flashlight I thought they would see us, but they passed right under us."

"Because we were holding ourselves up by the steel frame," Melvin said, glancing up. They were back to whispering now. "Good idea, Ann."

"No ... problem." Ann grunted. She and Joseph were leaning against the basketball hoop board, holding onto the pole that held it over the gym. She started to slip off, and Joseph caught her around the waist.

"Thanks," Ann said, breathing hard. *That's the second time my voice-throwing talent came in handy. Maybe I have a future yet.*

"No problem," he whispered back. "But won't they be able to like, identify your voice now?"

"Hey guys," Charlie whispered. "You can come out now."

Anton, Lieutenant and Toni snuck out of the closet. "Shit, when she said open the closet, I thought we was done." Lieutenant breathed. "Thanks, Ann."

"Thank Toni," Ann said, wincing against a pain in her shoulder. "She had the hiding idea."

"Now we need a getting out idea," Anton said, looking around. "The back door? Way we came in?"

"They'll be watchin' it," Lieutenant shot down. "Mrs. Carter's like a damn fox. She'll be too smart for that. They'll be tryna see how we got in."

"So how do we get out?" Anton snapped.

"There's only one way, isn't there?" Charlie said. "Through the school. Do the doors open from the inside?"

"They should," Melvin said.

"We should split up," Toni said. "That way if they catch some of us, they might not catch us all."

"And if anyone does get caught, we make the pledge right?" Anton said to Lieutenant.

"What pledge?" Charlie asked.

"One caught, you go down for the team," Anton said. "Don't nobody list anyone else, if they ask."

"Done deal," Ann said, as if it should be obvious.

"Obviously," Joseph scoffed.

Toni and Charlie nodded.

"Charlie, you go with Melvin. He knows more of the school. Ann —"

"I think I know a way out for us already," Joseph said.

"Fine. Toni, you, me, and L go through the door. Melvin and Charlie wait and go after," Anton said. There were noises from outside. "Well y'all heard me. Why you still standin'? Break!"


"So what was your idea?" Ann asked Joseph, gripping the board harder.

"Just hold on for a second," Joseph said and swallowed, looking up at the hall above them. It was railed off ... if he could just reach it —

"Oh you are not —"

"I'ma jump," Joseph said. *You can do this, just concentrate baby.*

Joseph launched himself up, and his hands found the rail. He tightened, and one hand slipped, so that he was hanging by one arm.

"Shit," Ann swore. "Just come back. Gimme your hand."

"No," Joseph said, and gritted his teeth. Muscles screaming, he pulled himself up with his right arm and managed to grab the rail. Feet scraping the side of the wall, he balanced on the edge and leaped over the guard rail. He turned to Ann. "Come on."

"What, jump?" she asked.

"Yeah, I'll catch you," Joseph promised.

Ann looked nervous for a moment, eyes darting around. "Ann —"

"Okay, okay," she said harshly. Focusing on his eyes, she steeled herself and leaped like a cat, landing with her feet on the edge and sliding back almost immediately.

"Fuck!"

"I got you, I got you. Don't move. Hold on."

Joseph grabbed her around the waist and pulled her against the rail. Breathing hard, Ann looked down and realized how high up they actually were.

"Don't look down," Joseph instructed. Ann turned to face him. "C'mon." Joseph took her by the shoulders and pulled her over the rail.

Sweating now from fear and exertion, they stumbled back against the wall. Ann tried to think, leaning against his pounding chest.

"That way," she decided, pointing down the hall. "I think there's a door."

Grabbing his hand, she yanked him after her, and they sped down the hall.


Charlie and Melvin sped down the main hall, and every step hit Charlie's ears like a gunshot.

"Stop!" Charlie grabbed Melvin by the shirt, and they fell on the ground.

"What the —"

"They're coming this way," Charlie said intensely. "Quick — where can we hide?"

"Uh ..." Melvin raced over to a classroom door and yanked the knob. "Locked."

"Well open it!" Charlie practically screamed.

"Okay, okay! Calm down, Doll," Melvin said back, pulling out the lock picks.

Charlie could hear the voices of people coming closer. "Hurry, hurry," she begged Melvin. All of her senses were heightened now, so that the anger and fear and fury and noises and shifting lights all assaulted her poor, broken mind at once.

"I got it —"

"They're this way," Mrs. Carter said clearly as Charlie and Melvin ran into the classroom.

There were a few desks, no closets, and one whiteboard.

No place to hide.

The guard led his two companions around the corner and heard a smash come from the just opened classroom.

"The window!" he guessed, hurtling inside, seeing only the smashed glass. "Come on!" he urged his two companions, who followed suite.

One guard looked at the ground and found the globe that had been used. "They used this."

"Wait," the first guard realized. "This hole isn't big enough for them to have crawled out of."

The men whirled around, but it was too late. The classroom door slammed shut and locked before they could see the two students who had been behind the door the entire time.

Toni and Lieutenant followed Anton, who led them down a back staircase and into a side corridor by a bathroom.

"Where are we ... going?" panted Toni to Lieutenant.

"Like I know?" Lieutenant answered. "I'm followin' him!"

"This way," Anton said surely, turning a corner.

"I ain't have no idea where we goin' now," Lieutenant said.

"I do, I —"

"You might as well turn yourselves in," yelled a voice from somewhere near. "We'll find you one way or another. Running just makes it worse on yourself."

Toni and Lieutenant sped up and smacked into Anton, who had stilled.

"What the fuck!?" Lieutenant said. "You —"

Anton was breathing hard, his face filled with open horror. He whirled around, staring up and down the halls.

"Where are we?" he demanded of the two girls.

"Where are we?" Lieutenant squeaked. "You tell us! You was leadin' us!"

"No, I wasn't!" The boy shook his head. It struck Toni that for the first time since she had seen him, he looked like a boy. A very confused, very lost boy.

"Hell, no." Lieutenant snarled. "You cannot pull this shit — you got us into this, now you get us out!"

"I don't know where I am," he said, shaking his head again and again, looking as if he might cry. His voice sounded small and young. "I don't know wh —"

"If you don't get us outta this, we might as well be dead." Lieutenant hissed dangerously, hands grabbing his shirt.

Anton grimaced. He pushed her off of him. "Don't do that," he said in a low voice. "If you want me to help you, you show me some fuckin' respect, hear?"

"I do, man," Lieutenant said, stunned. "I —"

Anton looked up as the sounds of the voices came closer. "This way," he said, running off down the hallway.

Toni looked at Lieutenant, who shook her head helplessly, eyes wide.

"We better follow him," Toni said, lurching to her feet.

"We betta pray, is what we betta fuckin' do," Lieutenant mumbled.


Mr. Protus led the security guard who had discovered the break-in down an upper hall. "I know I heard something," he whispered.

"Mr. Protus, I don't think —"

"There!" He pointed, as two unidentifiable figures slammed a door behind them.


Ann and Joseph slammed the door to the little side staircase they had just come up. Someone had spotted them, and they could hear him puffing up the stairs.

"Where do we go now?" Joseph panted.

"I ..." Ann gasped, looking around. There was one hall ahead of them and a huge winding staircase to the right. "We could go down the stairs, but there are a million of them," Ann said, heart beating so fast it sounded like rain in her chest. "Or we could go down that hall."

"Hall," Joseph said, and Ann nodded.

"If we go from there," Ann whispered, since there wasn't breath to do more, "then we can —"

"Ahead! You two, stop!"

Joseph grabbed Ann by the arm and yanked her in the opposite direction.

"I say stairs," he said, voice high.

"I second."

The two freshmen hurtled down the stairs. They could hear their pursuers closing in fast behind them. The stairs swirled down, on and on.

"They're gonna catch us at this fuckin' rate," Joseph whispered furiously.

"What better idea you got — jumping off?" Ann spat, then stopped. She moved to the edge of the banister and looked down. Between the stairs was an opening that fell straight to the ground. She looked up at Joseph, a bit of hair falling over her pale face as she raised a brow.

"You're insane," he said.

"And what does that make you?"



"We're catching them!" Mr. Protus yelled behind him, jumping a few steps to see the two figures. He was almost close enough to make out who they were.

"Just give up," he yelled clearly, seeing them stopped at the edge of the banister. "You'll just —"

"Mr. Protus," interrupted the guard loudly. "I think they're going to —"

Mr. Protus's triumphant look faded as the two students leaped over the edge and fell from sight.



Charlie and Melvin forced open the main school entrance and stumbled out onto the grass.

"Across this way." Charlie groaned, her ankle aching. "We can get out how I got in. I still have my knife."

"That's always good to hear." Melvin moaned, picking himself up and running after Charlie.

They sped over Panther Field, skidding and dropping to the ground when a flashlight illuminated the grass.

"We just have to make it to the barbed wire," Charlie whispered.

"I don't think they can see us now," Melvin whispered back.

"They can't see us unless we stand up," Charlie deduced.

"Crawl?" Melvin guessed. Charlie nodded and they crawled on elbows and knees to the edge of the fence.

"Ow!" Melvin said, pulling away from the wire. "Put that knife to work, Baby Doll," Melvin urged. Charlie took it out and started to saw her way through the wire, cutting at the bottom so they could bend it up. But the knife bent back in her hand. No ... it bent back at her hand.

"What?" Melvin asked when she stopped, eyes wide as saucers.

"The knife ... it's bending back towards me ... it's aiming at me," Charlie said, beginning to panic.

"No, no it isn't honey," Melvin said, slowly.

"Yes, it *is*." Charlie squeaked. "I can feel ... oh God, take it away, I'm not supposed to use knives ... take it ..." Charlie could see it so clearly. The knife was reaching for her.

"Gimme it," Melvin said. "Let it go, girl," he said gently, prying her fingers away. "It's okay."

Charlie tried to fight her terrified heart, looking away as Melvin cut his way under the wire.

"Come on," he said, pulling up the fence. "Hey, Charlie," he said, seeing that her eyes were closed.

"I can't ... I'm ... I see it ..." she babbled.

"Charlie." Melvin put his hands on her shoulders and looked into her eyes. "It is okay," he said as calmly as he could manage. "You are fine, and nothing is gonna hurt you, I promise. But we have to go, Baby Doll. Now."

Charlie nodded. Melvin grimaced, bending the wire back. Charlie snuck under, feeling the brutal spikes scratch her back.

"I'm out," she said.

"Good, help me please?" Melvin asked. Charlie nodded and held the wire for him as he crawled out from under.

"We're up for some drama now," Melvin said before they ran into the night.


"We can't get out through the gate. We can't get out under the wire. And we can't get out over the wire." Joseph breathed, pressed against the wall on the outside of the school. "So what do we do?"

Ann stole a glance around the corner and took stock of the barrier to the gate. Two security guards — they must have recruited more — and flashlights. "We can't get past them unless we throw a diversion," Ann said. "But I don't see how that would work, or what we would use."

"Maybe if we wait, Anton and Lieutenant, or Charlie and Melvin, will come out, and we can work wit' em," Joseph proposed.

"I don't think we can wait that long," Ann said. "Mrs. Carter will have told all the supervisors and parents to look for missing kids by then." Ann slid to the ground, covering up her head. *Think Ann, think!*

Joseph turned to look at the barbed wire fence. They needed to get rid of it, to break it or cut it. But he had no tools, no —

"Yes I do."

"Huh?" Ann looked up. Joseph's eyes roved over the fence. He felt in his pocket for his trusty plastic lighter. There it was. *Metal heats. Thin metal heats quickly. Then metal can be bent.*

"Joseph —"

"I can get us outta here," Joseph said quickly. Ann's eyes widened. "You —"

Joseph pulled her by the arm over to the fence. "I'ma heat the wire, like I heated the glass, and then break through," Joseph explained. Ann stared. "What?" Joseph asked.

"Can you ... control it like that?" she asked.

Joseph's breath caught. He didn't know if he could control it: even melting the edges of the glass drained him and gave him a headache, he had to concentrate so hard. It was like a strain from lifting something huge and heavy, only not with his body.

"I'll do it," Joseph said surely. *If I say I can do it, I'll do it.*

Joseph turned and took out his lighter. He pressed it to the wire, cutting his hand. Wincing, he ignored it. *Just a little bit of blood, man. Be a soldier.* The wire began to turn a reddish color, and Joseph moved to the next bit. He bit his lip, focusing on making a wide enough circle for them to step through.

"They're coming," Ann said, trying to keep the panic out of her voice, steeling herself for a fight if they got caught.

Joseph heard her words, and sped up, his anger and fear helping him to work faster.

"Joseph, I don't mean to be a backseat pyro, but they are kinda looking our way." Ann gave a very, very nervous laugh. "So, you know, whatever I can do to speed things up, just give the word."

"You could kiss me."

"Come again?" Ann asked, for a second surprised out of her panic.

"You asked to help. I need to be as hot as possible here, so I can think of a couple things you could do," Joseph said. He pulled away and kicked the wire. It broke at some of the heated edges, but held.

"Fuckin' thing." Joseph snarled and kicked it again.

"May I?" Ann asked. Joseph stepped back and held out his hands, gentleman-like. Ann ferociously kicked the wire. Joseph grinned.

He helped her slam on the wire until it broke. "Aright, let's go," Joseph said, and Ann scrambled over the wire, swearing as her feet caught before she pulled herself out.

"Come on. I know a fast way back," Ann said, before realizing Joseph wasn't beside her. "Joseph?"

"Fuck —" The wire had snagged Joseph's jeans, tripping him and clinging to him, holding him down. "Fuck — you go," he ordered. "Before they catch both of us."

"Yeah right, like I'm gonna leave you here," Ann said, rolling her eyes. She got down to untangle him, and Joseph shoved her away.

"Would you just go?" he demanded. "I can get myself out."

"What the fuck kind of girl do you think I am?" Ann said angrily, shoving him. "You think I'm gonna leave your ass here, so you can add more bruises to your collection?" she ranted, pulling away the wires from his clothes and skin. "You think I'd just leave you here, to take all the punishment, just to save my own worthless skin?" she continued, dragging on his shirt to get him on his feet.

"Come on," she said, kicking the last of the barbed wire off of him, holding onto his shirt when he tried to move, and staring him down. "And Joseph?" she said, narrowing her eyes. "Don't shove me again."

"I was tryna help you," Joseph explained.

"Yeah, yeah, playing the hero," Ann said, looking away from his eyes. He had that look that made her nervous again. "Men," she grumbled.

Joseph laughed as they ran into the cover of darkness.


"Lock the school," Mrs. Carter ordered.

"What?" Mr. Protus asked.

"Let me repeat. Lock. The. School," she enunciated.

"Wh—"

"Because they are clearly in there, and if we stop them from getting out we will catch them," Mrs. Carter said icily. "We do have that ability, don't we? We have the power put into effect a lockdown?"

"Oh." Mr. Protus began slowly. "But ... we're trying to gather enough power to fix the generator and have the cameras up, and if we put the school in lockdown, it will set us back —"

"I don't care," Mrs. Carter cut in, her anger evident only in the tension in her controlled voice. "I want those responsible caught tonight so we can resolve this."

"Yes, Mrs. Principal."

Lieutenant and Toni ran towards the door when the speakers in the school turned on.

"*Attention: this is a lockdown drill. Please remain in your classrooms with your teachers. If you are not in a classroom, please make your way to the nearest one. Attention, this is a ...*"

"*Fuck!*" Lieutenant swore, skidding to a stop.

"Does this mean —" Toni began.

"We're locked in," Lieutenant spat. "Fuck it. We're caught."

"*No!*" Both Toni and Lieutenant jumped at Anton's voice. "No," he said again, looking to them. "No we ain't."

"But we —"

"Follow me," Anton instructed.

"There are still people in here too," Toni warned. "They —"

"I know that," Anton said. Toni was at breaking point and ready to scream at him, but she didn't really have the chance. They followed Anton, the audible sound of their pursuers behind them.

"How high are we going here?" Toni asked as casually as she could. Something told her making Anton angry right now was not the best way to go.

"Ant—"

"Don't —" Anton stopped. "Don't ask questions. I'll get us out, but y'all can't ask questions, okay?"

Lieutenant looked ready to strangle her friend. Finally they reached a flat landing with a one-way hall and a window on either end.

"Fuck it. Now we at a dead end," Lieutenant accused.

Anton was looking out the window.

"Oh no," Lieutenant breathed. "We are not —"

Toni ran over beside the older boy. The window showed that they were on a higher part of J. Alter Academy. A foot below them was a lower part of the roof, and if they walked over it —

"We can jump onto the top of the delivery truck, and use that to jump over the wire," Toni realized.

"That'd be fuckin' great, if we could open the window," Lieutenant said, arms crossed.

"You can, can't you?" Toni asked.

"I can what now?" Lieutenant pulled back. "Sweetness, who have you gotten me confused with? I might look like Serena, but even that bitch can't break through plate glass."

"But you can with your — you know," Toni said, and moved her hands.

"I — *Oh!* No, no, nuh nuh no." Lieutenant shook her head, backing away. "I can't. I ain't ... I can't control that shit. I don't even know if it's real, or if I'm just crazy."

"Come on, L," Anton pleaded, his face softening. "Help us."

Lieutenant shook her head. "I want to, but I can't."

"Lieutenant," Toni pleaded. "Just *try*."

"Even if I did, it wouldn't be strong enough to ... it's even weaker than my hands, and it only happens when —"

"Please, will you just —"

"Fuck it!"

Anton smashed his arm hard into the window. Lieutenant and Toni stepped back as he hit the glass again and again.

"He's breaking through," Toni breathed.

Anton kicked the glass, shattering it wide enough for them to get through, and turned back to them.

"Well, c'mon!" he said, gesturing for them. Neither of the girls moved until they heard footsteps on the stairs.

Anton helped Lieutenant and then Toni through the crack, before slipping easily through, himself.


The group of three men stood silent as Mrs. Carter walked toward the broken window, heels clicking on the floor.

The principal stared out over the lower level of the roof to the area beyond. There was no one in sight.

"They can't have gotten far," she said after a long silence, finally allowing the others to breathe. "Call all of the monitors and parents. Tell them to check the beds for missing students." The others stared at the window.

"Well, *now*!" she snapped. "As quickly as possible, please?"

Mrs. Carter smoothed her hair and reached into her pocketbook for her cell phone.

She dialed and waited for the click.

"Yes, Evelyn?"

Mrs. Carter bit her tongue before beginning. This didn't have to be a rout for her. This only proved her point that more effort was needed. "Hello, Sophia. I am sorry to disturb you, but we had a ... an incident tonight. Involving the school. And some of our ... yes, your ... select students."


Dana answered the ringing phone sleepily. "Yes?"

"We have just had a break in at the Academy."

"A break in? What —"

"We require you to check on your boarder immediately. This break in was almost certainly the work of students. We need to make sure your student was not among them."

"Yes. Of course. Sure."

Dana hung up the phone and breathed.

Then she walked past Charlie's room and very slowly made her way downstairs to the kitchen. There, for the first time in six years, she fixed herself a drink.


"How the hell did they break into the school?" Sherry demanded over the phone. "I thought you people had security?"

"Ms. Nearson, we need you to check up on your two boarders immediately. If they are involved —"

"Yeah, yeah, yeah, I'm walking up right now," Sherry confirmed, and forced open the door to Ann's room.

She walked over to the lump of blankets and roughly poked it. "Hey, what's the issue?" Ann grumbled, the tip of her head and eyes peeking out from under the blanket. "Do you normally go poking people around at night?"

"I need to check on you," Sherry stated.

"Well, great. I feel very checked." Ann snuggled back under the blankets.

Sherry didn't answer but moved into Joseph's bedroom.

"Close the door," he moaned. "I'm tryna sleep here. Go way, 'fore I cry rape."

"You do that," Sherry said, closing his door. "No trouble here," she said into the phone.


"Melvin! *Melvin!*"

Melvin's mother stamped her way up the stairs to her son's room and, ignoring the "Danger: Contagious Fag" sign on the door, burst inside.

"What are you doing?"

Melvin looked up and flashed the light pen at his mother. "I'm reading. It's this thing with words and eyes and paper that you do? I hear it makes you smarter."

"Don't give me that lip, young man."

"Oh, so I'm a young man now," Melvin said sarcastically. "So much better than 'self-indulgent little boy' like usual."

"For this act of defiance, you will be severely punished," Mrs. Stavos informed him.

Melvin looked at her like she had grown a third head and gasped in indignation. "I'm reading a book not snorting coke!"

"Keep going. See how bad it gets for you, young man."


Mrs. Carter sighed, trudging back into her home, and sat down at the table.

*I cannot believe this happened. I cannot believe the destructiveness of these students went this far.*

*Well, I know how I will deal with it.*

Mrs. Carter ascended the stairs to her bedroom. Tomorrow would be a long day.

She stopped.

*The window.*

She moved to Toni's room and opened the door. The little bit of window was open — perhaps an inch wider.

Mrs. Carter moved slowly toward the bed. There was a lump there, but that could easily be done with pillows and sheets.

She ripped back the sheets in one swipe.

Mrs. Carter smiled.

"What is it?" Toni asked foggily.

"You'll find out in the morning," Mrs. Carter assured. "Best now to get some sleep."

# chapter ten the

**"What's wrong, Mom?" Becky asked.**

"Nothing," Mrs. Carter said with a thin-lipped smile. "I just need you girls to be nice and neat when you go to school."

"Did something happen last night?" Toni asked. Mrs. Carter looked at her sharply. *Idiot — find a way out of it!*

"I mean," Toni said. "You said last night when you came into my room that ... something was —"

"There was an Incident," Mrs. Carter said, and Katrina and Becky gasped. Toni made herself gasp, too. "What?"

"A break-in," Mrs. Carter said gravely. "A very severe break-in. But you don't have to be afraid. We will deal with it immediately to make sure everyone is safe."

"Are you gonna catch the people who did it?" Katrina asked.

"Of course," Mrs. Carter said firmly. "We always do. But it is very sad because everyone is going to be paying for these student's cruelty and irresponsibility."

*Oh that's smart,* Toni thought, her heart chilling. *That's goddamn brilliant. Make everyone pay, and your students will turn on anyone they can find who might have done it. Or worse,* Toni thought suddenly. *They'll all turn on everyone.*

"Sleep well?" Ann asked out of the side of her mouth.

Joseph turned to stare at her like she was crazy, and saw the twitch of her lips. He propped his feet up on the bus seat as usual. "Yeah, I'm fantastic," he said, staring ahead. "I'm so fabulous, I'm just seein' trees and butterflies and rainbows and happy things. I'm so fabulous, I just wanna give the whole world a great big, squishy hug," he said in a tiny voice.

Ann snorted.

Joseph watched her. Whenever he made her laugh, she was easy to talk with after.

"Yo." Joseph dropped his voice. He swallowed, looked around, then stared her straight in the eyes. "I just wanna say ... thank you. For not leavin' me when I fell. For stayin' and just ... I really owe you."

Ann felt very unnerved whenever she looked straight in his eyes. For some reason she couldn't make herself break his gaze. "Oh please." She brushed it off. "You don't owe me anything."

"Yeah, I do." Joseph nodded, his eyes slanting. "You coulda run off, and I wouldn't a' blamed you, but you stayed and uh ... that was really brave."

Ann realized her sweater was really heavy and hot. Why had she worn it anyway? She heard herself laugh nervously. "Oh, I'm not brave." Ann smiled, pushing a bit of her hair aside. It just wouldn't stay behind her ear. "I'm just stubborn and ... tough, I guess."

"I noticed," Joseph laughed. Ann decided she liked his laugh.

"Yeah, well ... sorry you're stuck with me," Ann said, the side of her lips twisting up.

"You don't have to apologize," Joseph said softly, and Ann looked up into his eyes again. "I mean —" Joseph stumbled. "I don't mind bein' stuck wit'chu."

Ann nodded, not really sure what to say here. Or if she had breath to say it.

"Look, I just wanted to say ... thanks for having my back," Joseph finished. "And I promise to, you know, have yours too. To ... you know, I meant to not ... run when you need help. To be there to ... you know what?" Joseph laughed at himself. "I'ma just quit while I'm ahead."

Ann grinned and then swallowed, feeling a rush of nervousness push through her stomach.

"Ann? Are you ..." Joseph ventured. "Are you okay?"

Ann turned back to him with a smile. "Yeah," she said lightly. "Just feeling ..."

"Scared?" Joseph guessed. She nodded. "Yeah," he said, leaning his head back, and Ann wondered how his face managed to be masculine with such long lashes.

"Ann?" Joseph asked, looking up. "Do you ever feel like half of the world is against you and doesn't want you to be anything but gone?"

Ann looked down, and half-smiled at something not very funny. "All the time," she said softly.

"What do you do?" Joseph whispered, rolling his head to the side to look at her.

Ann leaned to the side to whisper back. "I just ... refuse. I say no ... and whether they hate me or not is their choice. But me? I'm not going away."

"What if ... they say they would want you if you just change this, or fix up that?" Joseph said with a little bitterness. "When they say they would love you if you just ... weren't so you?"

"I just refuse to let them in. I say no," Ann said slowly. "I don't ... let them fool me into fading away into something that's not me."

Joseph nodded. "Yeah."

Charlie stopped at the hallway right outside her English class. *I can do this,* she told herself. She could feel the fog coming in like a thief. A thief to steal her mind. *Well I won't let it get it. Yet. Fuck,* she thought, almost letting out a sob. All the stress of last night had undone the lock on the door she kept her demons behind, and now they roamed all throughout her brain. The beauty and excitement of her heightened senses was slowly sapped away as she realized everything she saw could be nothing but her own broken brain playing cruelly with her limited concept of reality.

"I am not sure why you are putting up such a fight."

*Because I won't be lost in my own head, that's why!*

"These new measures are for your safety as much as the students', Ms. Lovejoy. I would expect that you would want that."

Mrs. Carter's voice sounded real enough to Charlie.

"Yes, I understand Mrs. Principal, but not allowing staff members and teachers to speak to each other?"

That was Dana's voice. Charlie relaxed and listened.

"That is not what I am saying," Mrs. Carter said in clipped tones. "You are perfectly welcome to discuss matters pertaining to the immediate or future needs of the students, or academic work. Anything pertaining to your job. I am simply stopping idle, useless chatter, such as questions about personal lives, or opinions. Those things can be sent via email if you feel they are necessary for the school to know."

"So we're not allowed to talk about a Red Sox game we saw the other night, you're saying?" Dana said, irritated.

"Why would you be discussing a game when you have classes to teach?" Mrs. Carter added silkily. "I don't think you realize, Ms. Lovejoy, that if we take our eyes off of these students for a second, they will hurt themselves and others. Just like last night."

"I don't remember hearing anyone was hurt last night," Dana said with an edge.

"Not yet," Mrs. Carter said. "Because we were there and stopped them from causing anymore problems. Security had to stay up all night combing the place for bombs."

"So you think the answer to that is to practically prevent them from breathing in class?" Dana asked disdainfully.

"These students got into our not-too-shabbily guarded Academy and smashed windows, broke locks, and even burned part of our fence. These are not innocent, normal children, Ms. Lovejoy," Mrs. Carter said with infinite contempt. "They are destructive, irresponsible adolescents, with severe problems that they are fighting our efforts to fix. The more leeway they have, the worse it will be, so we will give them none."

"You can't control them fast enough to stop them from doing some things you don't want them to do. There's always the time lapse between when you see the behavior and the punishment, and if they feel threatened their behavior will just escalate," Dana warned.

"That won't be a problem very soon because we'll be able to have an instant reaction to problem behaviors. Now —" Mrs. Carter paused. "Are you able to follow our Academy's guidelines? Or do you want to take it up with the Headmistress?"

There was a pause, wherein Charlie waited for Dana to defend them. "No," Dana said. "No problem."

Charlie pulled back and pretended to be reading something when Mrs. Carter walked out. Charlie held her breath when the woman paused in front of her.

Charlie breathed out after the heels clicked off down the other end of the hall, and she stuffed the book into her bag. She walked in to see a messy-haired Dana pacing her classroom.

"You're early," Dana said, rubbing her clothes again and again as if she had a tick.

"What was Mrs. Carter doing here?" Charlie asked.

"I'm —" Dana coughed into her hand. "Not allowed to discuss that with you."

"What are you allowed to discuss with us?" Charlie asked, feeling anger build in her.

"Please take a seat, Charlie," Dana said, looking away.

Charlie opened her mouth to say more, but students were coming in. She sat between Toni and Joseph. Toni motioned for Melvin to sit with them, but he gave a little shake of his head no and glanced at Dana. Their teacher was scribbling on the board.

*interrupting the teacher*
*speaking to other students/whispering*
*fidgeting*
*making noises*
*speaking without raising hands*
*not maintaining a neat appearance*

"These are some of the behaviors," Dana said in an almost dead voice, "which are no longer to be tolerated in class. Due to the Incident that you will hear about in assembly today, we are in state of school-wide lockdown until we catch those responsible. This means no talking in class or in the hallways, and that you will be escorted by a teacher to all of your classes. Associating is allowed — if earned — in the Big Rewards Store with your friends."

"But this —"

"Hand, Toni."

Toni raised her hand.

"Yes?"

"But how fair is it to punish the whole school for what just a few people did?" Toni asked, and others nodded and voiced their agreement.

"No talking," Dana said loudly. "We are a community," Dana said tiredly, as if reciting something she was bored with. "And the actions of a few affect us all."

Students began to speak up. "I said quiet!" Dana snapped, and everyone backed off. They hadn't seen her like this. Her face looked apologetic as she said, "Please — let's open our books and go over the lesson?"

Charlie bit her lip and tried to make herself concentrate, but her heart was sinking. Dana hadn't stood up for her, for anyone. Dana was her supervisor. She was supposed to protect her. Was she going to just let this happen? *No, no, people don't just stand by when kids are shocked,* Charlie thought. *That kind of stuff doesn't happen in America. Dana must just be waiting to go tell a journalist or something, so this place can get shut down.*

"Yes, Joseph." Dana nodded at his outstretched hand.

"Somethin's been buggin' me," Joseph said, leaning forward on his elbows. "All these people here ... half the people in the institution in this *Cuckoo's Nest* book ... they signed themselves in. Why would they sign themselves in to get beat down and told what to do and have all their freedom taken away?"

"Well, many of these characters have been convinced that they are sick by the outside world, many are mentally ill, and both groups are ostracized by outside society," Dana answered.

"But they clearly hate it," Joseph said, squinting his eyes. "They keep sayin' they hate Ms. Ratched, but they won't leave. They hate the place, but they won't fight it. They don't fight until McMurphy comes and stands up to her. Then they're all happy to fight, but the minute it gets rough, half of 'em back down."

"Do you have an actual question?" Dana asked, narrowing her eyes.

"Why is there only one person who's willin' to stand up?" Joseph asked, raising his voice. "All of the other sheep in the sch— in the asylum or whatever — all of 'em just stay there, even though they're miserable, even though they *know* they're not actin' like men — they still just let this woman walk all over them."

"Perhaps because they're scared," Dana explained. "Perhaps because they have no hope and no idea of a way that could be different. Perhaps because they're too beaten down ..."

"If you're beaten down, then the only place you got to go is up," Joseph argued, raising his voice louder. "If you got nothin' to lose, you have everything to gain, and at least in fighting, you can know you ain't worthless like they want you to believe."

*He's not just talking about the book anymore,* Charlie realized. *And everyone in this room knows it.*

"You're forgetting that they do, in fact, rise up in the end," Dana reminded him. "Most of them do leave the hospital."

"Yeah, after McMurphy dies," Joseph shot back. "After he dies or as good as dies fightin' for them, *then* they decide, 'Oh, maybe we should try and act like we're actually men now.'"

"Was McMurphy really fighting for the others in the hospital?" Dana questioned. "Or was he just following a personal vendetta of his own? Or just playing the rebel, and causing trouble?"

"He was definitely —"

Charlie and Toni put their hands on Joseph's arms to reign him in.

*Let it go Joseph,* Charlie thought at him as hard as she could. *We don't need more trouble right now, when we still don't know what cards the Academy is going to play.*


"We shouldn't all sit together," Anton said, eating his green beans with a grimace.

"This may be our last chance," Charlie said, as Joseph and Ann settled themselves at the table. Melvin and Toni were looking something over. They looked up at her.

"I heard Mrs. Carter talking about it to Dana," Charlie informed. "Things are gonna get worse. She said that they're gonna have 'an instant reaction to problem behaviors,' whatever that means, soon. And if they're making us earn the privilege of talking to each other in their stupid store, do you really think they're gonna let us talk freely at lunch?"

There was silence for a minute, then Toni spoke up. "We're gonna need a new way to meet. I don't think Panther Field will work for a while."

"I know a way," Ann said. "If we make our way past the old train tracks you cross over to get to the woods, we can meet there. There's a nice place we can use. I'll show everyone."

"We shouldn't go out for a while though," Lieutenant said. Where everyone else had to fake hiding their sleepiness, she was still as wide awake as anything, her words going fast, her hands faster, as she wrote with one hand and drew with the other. "They'll suspect us, just cause we new, and we're 'the delinquents.'"

"Sounds like a band," Toni said lightly. Lieutenant nodded, trying to eat while working. "Why aren't you tired?" Toni asked. "Do you ever sleep?"

"Sleep?" Lieutenant looked up as if the question was ridiculous. "What do you mean, 'sleep'? I'ma a damn vampire on cocaine, I don't sleep."

"A vampire?" Anton looked at her.

"Yes, vampire," Lieutenant said. "You know, fangs, blood, 'von, two, tree, ah ah ah,'" she laughed.

"Did you just imitate the Count?" Charlie asked.

"Von, two, tree, ah ah ah," Lieutenant continued, cackling.

"And it all comes down to *Sesame Street*," Joseph said. "Wow. Well, with that being said —"

"*Attention students. Due to the recent Incident, lunch tables will be assigned seating until further notice. Each three days tables will be rotated. Your lunch seating arrangements will be posted at the doors to the cafeteria each day. Failure to follow these simple directions will result in immediate consequences. Thank you.*"

"There are those immediate consequences again," Charlie whispered darkly.

"And you know they ain't gonna seat us together," Joseph said, glancing over his shoulder. "Those two guards been watchin' us since we sat down. And Seth keeps starin' at us."

Lieutenant shivered. "That boy is creepy as all hell. You look in them eyes, and it's like Hannibal the Cannibal starin' back. I keep lookin' over at his lunch to see if he got fava beans and a human liver."

"He acts like he's the king of this town." Melvin rolled his eyes then slowly grinned. "But he's got a little secret he keeps in his closet."

"What?" Joseph asked.

"He's always been able to charm his way into anything," Melvin shared. "He tries to cover up the fact that he was getting a little too friendly with his guys out in the woods. He's blackmailed them into not telling."

"He's gay?" Joseph stuttered.

"No," Melvin said disdainfully. "He does anything with genitals. I even heard he did *animals*. But he ends up getting away with anything he does. It's fucking ridiculous." Melvin threw down his fork. Anton looked down, cracking his knuckles.

"He's actually in the STARE Program," Lieutenant supplied. "But he's made it so no one really knows. The mutherfucker is crazy as us. He just know how to hide it."

"You think they know it's us?" Toni asked, her lips barely moving, looking over at the guard.

"No, we'd be in the dungeon already," Ann said wryly.

"We're just gonna hafta trust that our plan works," Anton said, stirring his food. "If it works out, it won't be us taking any of the blame."


"Do you know why they invented gym?" Toni posed to Charlie.

"Um ... so teachers could watch us get hit in the head with balls?"

"No," Toni said. "I mean, obviously that's part of it, but ... no. It's so every boy can let out their aggression in 'healthy' ways, and every girl can stand around and feel like a deformed hamster in a stupid uniform next to the girl next to her."

"Not every girl," Charlie said. "Not if you're pretty."

"Even if," Toni said firmly. "Find me a teenage girl who's happy about her body, and we'll call the CIA to carry her off for dissection, because she's not human."

"But you're pretty," Charlie said abruptly then colored.

"You say pretty, I see fat slob."

"Well now I see delusional."

"Of course," Toni agreed readily. "It's called body dysmorphia. Lots of girls have it."

"I see one I think doesn't." Charlie brightened as Ann sauntered over.

"Hey, babe," she said, planting a kiss on Charlie's cheek and bumping her hip with Toni's. "What are we talkin' about?"

"Body dysmorphia and why girls hate gym," Charlie supplied. "Toni was evaluating herself."

"We need to make the Therapist loosen up," Ann said to Charlie while looking at Toni. Her eyes traveled to the other students gathered for gym.

"Look," Ann whispered, "Something's starting already."

The students made a half-circle with their backs to the teacher. Most were just talking, but two students were looking nervously around.

"How did that get in here? Put it away!"

"I was just listening to it —"

"Well —"

"Is that an iPod?" Ann asked. Toni and Charlie tried to hold her back, but she just shook them off and walked over to the girl holding the little red music player. "Come on." Ann smiled. "Let's hear something."

The girl shook her head, and Ann pouted. "Pwease?"

"Do it," said the boy beside her and pressed it, turning on a song.

"Oh, yeah." Ann laughed, starting to wind her hips.

"Oh, Lord." Toni groaned.

Ann grinned, winding her body all the way down to sweep the floor, her eyes skimming the crowd. "Oh, I see you," she said, pointing to one girl who was half-heartedly moving her body. "Come on out here."

The girl shook her head, but Ann's excitement was infectious, and soon the girl was out bumping and grinding along with her. The other students were now into it, clapping and urging the girls on.

"What the hell you doing?" Toni demanded of Ann.

"Letting off steam, sweetie," Ann said innocently. "We need it. For therapy."

"What in the hell do you think you are doing?"

The gym teacher pushed his way through the half-circle, and the commotion immediately stopped.

"They're just dancing," Toni said. "It's no big deal."

"Really? Dancing?" the teacher, a man who looked like he spent way too much time in the gym, said sharply. "It looked more like you were having sex with each other in front of a crowd."

The girl Ann had pulled into the circle looked down as if trying to disappear, when the teacher looked around. "Whose iPod was playing?" the teacher barked. The girl whose iPod it was trembled visibly, looking as if she was about to cry. Ann's eyes darted from the girl to the teacher as her friends stepped away from her. He started to move toward the girl.

"It was mine," Ann said quickly, turning the attention back to her. *That's right, ignore her. I'm the one you wanna punish.* "I was just trying to get everyone jazzed up for your 'super-fun' class. And it's not like we were hurting anyone," Ann said defensively, her hand going to her hip. "We were having 'fun.' It's this thing some people do, you know? But maybe you're just sore because you can't dance with that stick up your ass."

"Dancing?" the gym teacher said nastily. "Really? I'm sorry, but I don't consider what strippers do on poles and bars to really be considered *dancing* or to be appropriate for my class."

The group twittered, and Ann's lips spread into a little smile. "No, what we were doing was normal high school dancing," she said sweetly. "This," she drawled, unbuttoning and pulling off her sweater to gasps all around. "This is, I think, more what you were thinking about." She flashed her eyes at the teacher as she rolled her shoulders and twisted her waist, licking her lips.

"Stop this, *right now,*" the gym teacher said, horrified. Ann ignored him, winking at one boy while grinding down to the floor.

"That's it," the teacher said, moving to grab her arm. Ann slapped him away to more gasps and jumped up on one of the stacks of mats.

"Or maybe you want the full effect?" she announced loudly, daring the teacher to try and touch her. She clapped and bounced to the beat, flicking her tongue at the gym teacher as she danced as exotically as if she was on a bar.

"She has good rhythm," Toni judged. "What?" she said when Charlie stared. "I'm just sayin'!"

*Shit,* Charlie thought as two guards walked in. *Get down,* she mouthed to Ann.

"Oh, wow, two big handsome men all for me," Ann said, fluttering her eyes and putting her hands together. "How sweet."

"Time to go see Mrs. Carter, Ms. Cost," the teacher stated.

"Oh, yeah?" Ann said dangerously, looking at the two guards. One nodded to the other, and they came over towards the mat. One reached for her ankle, and she kicked him away. More gasps.

"Don't touch me." She spat, eyes flashing viciously. "I can move myself, thanks."

Ann jumped down and put back on her defiant smile as she strode up to the gym teacher. "Have fun controlling them all now," she said quietly.

"Once your bad influence is removed, I don't think we'll have a problem," he said back.

Ann didn't answer, just scowled at him. The guards moved to her side, and as she was walked out she turned and blew a kiss to Charlie and Toni.


"Everyone wait here while I open this door," the algebra teacher instructed her class. Joseph leaned back against the wall, pulling his hoodie over his face.

"I'm just nervous, man, about homecoming. If we —"

"Why would you be nervous? You're not going. Your face will scare any girls away from us."

Joseph's hackles went up instantly at the sound of Seth's voice.

"Why do you have to say stuff like that Seth?"

"Why does it bother you so much? Not man enough to handle it? Or are you —"

Seth's voice stopped, and Joseph felt a hand pull up his hood. "Peek-a-boo," said a voice paired with ice blue eyes.

"Get off me," Joseph said in a low voice, pulling himself away. Seth just laughed, as if Joseph's anger was funny.

"I don't know why you're always so angry all the time, when all I'm trying to do is make friends," Seth said earnestly.

"Make friends?" Joseph smiled bitterly. "I'm surprised you have any. What, your 'bros' don't mind bein' treated like dogs?"

"How do you know how I treat my friends?" Seth asked, his voice soft.

"I just saw you." Joseph gestured with his arm. "I just heard you treatin' em like dirt."

"That's just us joking," Seth said, his voice smooth and persuasive. "You come in here, and you act like you have this chip on your shoulder and just spit in the faces of everyone here when we were the only school that took you in after you failed everywhere else."

*Failure.* The word cut Joseph to the quick, right under his skin. He wanted to hit Seth, to kill him. He would ... no, he realized, holding in his temper. *I have a better way.* "I may be a failure, but at least I'm not a hypocrite," Joseph drawled.

"What do you mean?" Seth pulled back.

Joseph shrugged, a half-smile on his face. "I just meant that you act a lot like you're the big man of this school and seem to have an issue with me comin' in from the outside, but maybe it's cause you just don't like bein' reminded of why you in the STARE program as well," he said out loud enough for those around to here.

"You're lying." Seth spat. His friend looked confused.

"Am I?" Joseph said swiftly. "Check his files if you don't believe me. What your boys don't know? Or can't they talk because then you'll tell their little secret?"

"No one knows what you're talking about, and no one cares," Seth hissed.

"No one cares? Why? 'Cause it's my word against Mr. All-American Boy? Do they know Mr. All American boy sneaks out at night to have 'fun' with his bros? I mean, that's just hearsay but ..."

*That did it,* Joseph thought with fierce joy.

Seth closed in on Joseph, giving him the full power of his eyes. This time, instead of looking away — although there was still a cold uneasy feeling in the pit of his stomach — Joseph met his gaze, pulling himself up to his full height.

"You just make yourself sound bad when you lie like that," Seth said. "Who's gonna believe you?" he said, stepping back and spreading his arms. "The whole school knows me. You're just some gang-banging piece of scum that got dragged in here for pity."

"You wanna see what I can do I'll show you muth —"

"What the hell is going on?" the algebra teacher said. "Joseph — what are you doing?"

"Me?" Joseph looked at Seth and just shook his head with a little laugh. "I'm just tryna increase the flow of knowledge around the school, you know? Make the world a more open place." He looked up at Seth, meeting those eyes again. "Get everything out in the open."



"Is this really necessary?" Ann asked, looking down at the handcuffs.

"After your attack on Wednesday?" Mrs. Carter said, leaning back in her desk chair. "Yes, I am afraid it is."

"What would you do if three guys came to strap you down to a desk and give you shocks?" Ann asked.

"I know what I wouldn't do," Mrs. Carter said, leaning slightly forward. "I wouldn't give one of them a broken jaw, one a sprained wrist, and the other a bloody nose."

Despite her efforts, Ann smiled. "I did all that? I guess I just don't know my own strength."

"No one here is amused by these antics," Mrs. Carter said.

"Well, I'm amused," Ann lipped back. "And I'm someone."

"Hmm." Mrs. Carter smiled tightly. "Well, maybe we'll be able to change your mind. Do you think you two gentlemen could handle her for a moment while I confer with our guest?" she asked the guards by Ann. They nodded, and Mrs. Carter walked out of the room to speak to a third man in the hallway.

Ann twiddled her thumbs and looked absently around the room. "So what do you guys do to relax?" she asked the stone-faced man beside her. "Pool parties, board games?"

He did not respond. "Right." Ann looked down. "Just me then."

She frowned. The edge of a paper was hanging out of a file. She could read just a bit of it, including the name on the form: Joseph Nathaniel Valdez.

Glancing at the two guards, who seemed to be looking straight ahead, she managed to slide the form out and found another under it, embossed with the name Amina Jackson.

Ann began to read.

Toni seated herself on a chair behind Charlie. Across the row she could see Lieutenant, and in the back somewhere was Anton. Melvin was to her side and Joseph somewhere she couldn't see.

*That may be the most fucked up thing here,* Toni thought. *That you have to hide who you're friends with.*

Toni looked around the assembly. There was the general sound of whispering, but Toni couldn't locate any of the whisperers.

To her side she saw movement and turned to see Ann seated down in the back with a security guard inches from her. Toni caught her eyes and gave an encouraging smile.

Ann kept looking downward, and Toni finally got the hint.

Ann's hand was open. Written on it in marker were the words, *I'm on Shun.*

*What?* Toni mouthed.

Ann reached into her pocket and scribbled more on her hand, then held it down. Toni squinted.

*No talk.*

Ann rubbed it out and scribbled:

*You pay too.*

Toni nodded. *I get it: we can't talk to her, and if we do, we get in trouble.*

Ann held out her other hand.

*Have big news.*

"What?" Toni hissed. "Ann —"

"I have some bad news to report."

Toni turned with the rest of the school to look to the principal, who stood at the podium. "Last night, certain of our students managed to break into our Academy. They vandalized the building, breaking windows, cutting our fence, and ruining the gate to our school. This was the work of a number of students who decided that for their anger and destructive desire, the whole Academy should suffer. Because of their attack we will have to tighten our security. As you've heard, talking in class or in the hallways is no longer allowed. If you wish to socialize with your friends, you can earn the right, through good behavior, to use the Big Reward Store. Lunch tables will be assigned. We are choosing now which after school activities we can allow to reopen. And for those who still cannot learn to obey simple rules, we have new measures that will eliminate this behavior before it —"

Toni sat straighter in her seat. Behind Mrs. Carter, two men were working to unveil the homecoming banner. Toni made herself not look at anyone else and tried to keep her face blank, as if she didn't know what was going to happen.

"This school is a community," Mrs. Carter continued. "And in the Academy —"

A school-wide gasp went up as the banner came down. Mrs. Carter demanded silence before finally looking behind her.

It was written in red and black, the colors making the message seem almost demonic. The words were big enough for even the back row to read.

Whose Academy is this?

Is it for the ones who grew up here, lived here, are still here?

Or is it for the psychotic freaks rotting us from the inside? Should we be punished for what they do?

Make our teachers and our parents KNOW whose school this is.

Take it back.

# chapter eleven blue

## This was your idea. Don't back out now.

Toni swallowed, playing with her food. She glanced up at Mrs. Carter, trying to figure out the right way of asking without getting the principal suspicious.

"Mrs. Carter?" Toni asked politely.

"Yes?" Mrs. Carter said, looking across the table at her.

"I've kinda been having trouble sleeping," Toni said carefully. "I mean — I always have, but now with moving here it's even worse, and I'm worried about my grades slipping."

"Have you tried counting sheep?" Mrs. Carter suggested, cutting up a piece of chicken.

"Everything," Toni stated. "I do all of the herbal teas, meditating ... nothing." Toni kept her gaze steady. "Do you have any Benadryl or anything like that? Those are the only things that used to help me sleep."

Mrs. Carter continued cutting her chicken. "We do not believe in medicating away problems here. That can have unhealthy effects."

"Yes, but Benadryl doesn't cause addiction," Katrina pointed out. "It's a mild sedative."

"We don't have any," Mrs. Carter said flatly. "And I don't believe they would be beneficial."

*Damn!*

Toni clenched her fists under the table as Mrs. Carter told them to put away the dishes.

"Mrs. Carter can be a little harsh about medication because it's one of the rules," Katrina whispered to Toni as she helped her do the dishes. "She means well, but she doesn't know what it's like ..." Katrina trailed off and waited for Becky to leave the kitchen, then moved closer to Toni's ear. "I have some stuff I developed myself for a chemistry class."

"You made sleep meds in a chemistry class?" Toni said under her breath.

"I told you it was a special place here," Katrina answered. "I still have some I kept. I wasn't supposed to, but I figured since I made it, it's mine."

"Are you offering?" Toni asked.

"If you don't say I have it. And if ..." Katrina looked around, "and if you won't tell when I see my boyfriend from time to time."

Toni kept her eyes down. This was unexpected. *Do I take the chance she might be trying to lead me into a trap?*

*Well if I don't knock Mrs. Principal out somehow, I won't be able to go to the meeting tonight,* Toni thought quickly. *I need something to slip into her tea.*

"Done, deal," Toni said.

"Meet me outside of your room in five."


"Don't you two both need to do homework?" Sherry asked, narrowing her eyes at the two teenagers sitting together at her dining room table.

"We are," Ann said innocently.

"Can't you do that at separate tables so you aren't distracting each other?" Sherry suggested. "Ann, you're on Shun. You shouldn't be speaking to him at all."

"She's not speaking. She's helping me," Joseph said earnestly.

"Oh, really?" Sherry asked.

"Yes," Ann said, eyes wide. "With his math."

"Right," Sherry said, looking from one teen to the other. "Don't make any noise. I'll be in the other room." She walked out, glancing over her shoulder.

Joseph pushed his notebook at her. "Okay, how do you do this problem?"

"How the hell should I know?" Ann snorted.

"Ha!" Joseph cried, pointing at her. "See, you're as dumb as me."

"No." Ann laughed. "I'm not that dumb. That would take work."

"Hey, fuck you." Joseph frowned.

"Excuse you!" Ann dumped her glass of water on his head. "There, now your mouth is all washed out."

She laughed as Joseph shook his head like a dog, pouting. "You —" He growled, narrowing his eyes at her. "You —"

Ann just gave a big smile and then ran out of the room.

*Oh ho, so you think you can run from me, do you?* Joseph thought, racing after her.

"You are going to pay for that," he warned her, following her into the kitchen.

Ann smiled devilishly, hands behind her back. "I think not."

"Oh, yeah?"

Joseph found a can of Reddi-wip and advanced on her.

*Ha — now you got no way out, Little Miss Devious.*

Ann let him get a little closer then whipped out the sink sprayer. Too late, Joseph noticed the water was on. He yelped as Ann aimed and fired the water at him, soaking his face. Joseph tried to move forward but slipped on the water and fell down as if falling into a chair. Ann continued to spray until he rolled over to his side and covered his head.

"Joseph?" She stopped spraying and moved forward. He didn't budge.

"Joseph?" she asked, kneeling down beside him. "You okay?"

He didn't move.

"You're not hurt," Ann attested. "I watched you fall. Now look up. I'll poke you!" she warned.

"Go 'way," Joseph mumbled.

"Nope," Ann said and started to poke him.

"Nooo," Joseph whined.

"Poke, poke, poke, poke," Ann said happily.

"Stopp ittt."

"Poke, poke, poke, poke," Ann continued.

"You better stop pokin' me girl. Look at you, teasin' an injured man. Better stop 'fore you get in big, big trouble and —"

"Pokey, pokedy, poke, poke —"

*Grr.*

"Poke, poke, boy you have a chubbly ass."

"I do so *not* have a chubbly ass!"

"You do so *do* have one," Ann asserted, poking it and then continuing over to his face. "Poke, poke." She peered at his face. Joseph cracked an eye. "Poke —"

"Ha!" Joseph shot up and unleashed a spray of whipped cream from the can straight into her face.

"Hey!"

Ann pushed Joseph, still laughing, onto his back.

"You bastard!" she said, trying to rub the stuff off her face. "I just did water. This will stain my clothes!"

"You want me to lick it off?" Joseph offered, still laughing.

"*No.*"

"Come on —"

"Joseph —"

"Please — just a taste —"

"You are like a fuckin' child. Ann says *no.*"

"Ann tastes *yum.*"

Ann shrieked with laughter as Joseph licked away the whipped cream, even licking it off her face.

"You're like a dog," she accused.

"*Roof!*" Joseph barked.

"What the *hell* is this?"

Both teenagers turned to stare guiltily at Sherry.

"You are both disgusting," she said. "Joseph — get the hell off her! Ann, get upstairs and try and clean yourself off."

Ann picked herself up and walked upstairs, stealing a glance down at Joseph. She didn't want to leave him to have to deal with any punishment alone.

*Stupid bitch. We weren't* hurting *each other. I was about to push him off anyway.*

*Wasn't I?*

Nastily, she decided to trudge into Sherry's bathroom, staining the place with whipped cream.

She turned on the sink faucet and looked at herself in the mirror.

*I'm covered. Remind me to spill something stainable on Joseph's clothes.*

Ann gazed around Sherry's bathroom. She hadn't been allowed in here before.

She froze. *I haven't looked in here yet.*

Ann quickly closed the door and then opened the medicine cabinet. The plan everyone had agreed upon had been to slip something into each of their supervisor's drinks so they could sneak out. Melvin had some of his sleep medication stored away and had lent it to Lieutenant and Anton, but there wasn't enough for everyone else. Charlie didn't need it — there was a tacit understanding that Dana wouldn't stop her or do the new room checks. Ann had said she and Joseph didn't need it because Sherry drank and was likely to fall flat out, but she couldn't be sure. But if they could find something to slip her ...

*I know she uses stuff,* Ann thought, closing the medicine cabinet and looking in the drawers under the sink. *Everyone's heard she has problems, and she can say whatever she wants about being "reformed," everyone knows she still uses.*

"Ann?" Sherry's voice sounded up the stairs. "What's taking so long?"

"It's a lot of stuff to wash off," Ann cried back, closing the cabinet doors and looking in the closet.

"I'm coming up to help," Sherry said.

"That's okay!" Ann closed the cabinet. No go.

"What is taking so long?"

"I'm going to the bathroom!" Ann made up.

She heard Sherry's feet up the stairs. She moved toward the toilet and on a whim, glanced behind it.

Jackpot.

"Ann?" Sherry walked across her room as Ann desperately rummaged through bottles of pills, looking for anything that would cause drowsiness.

"Ann?" Sherry banged on the door. "Ann, why are you using my bathroom? Ann, would you —"

Ann opened the door and stepped out. "Sorry, just used the first one available."

Sherry glared at her. "Well, get out!"

Ann nodded, hands in her pockets, as she walked away.


*What if they don't come?*

Charlie looked around her. It was pitch black and every noise was too loud. She had finally been able to find the described meeting spot, past the train tracks on the edge of the woods.

A stick cracked and Charlie dropped to the ground, unmoving. The figure stepped out slowly. She closed her eyes, terrified. What if their plans had been found out, and they had been tracked here? The whole school must be on high alert for something like this. She held her breath, desperately wondering if she should run.

*Please, I need to see, I need to see ... please I need to see ...*

"Toni?"

"Charlie?" Toni stepped forward, hands outstretched. "It's cloudy out, there's no moon, and I can't —"

"I can see."

"I can't either, but — wait did you just say you can see?" Toni asked.

"Yes," Charlie said, voice low and excited. "Now I can." Her head whipped to the side at the sounds of people approaching. Toni stepped back.

"It's okay," Charlie said. "It's just Ann and —"

"And me," said Joseph. "Who's here?"

"Toni, Charlie, and now you," said Charlie. "Wait —"

"Why didn't you guys use the fuckin' signal?" Anton said.

"Oh," Toni said. "I forgot."

"I can't see anything, I don't know about you guys," Melvin said. "L?"

A small light illuminated everyone's faces for a second before going out.

"I stole a penlight from my supervisor's desk," Lieutenant informed. "Can't use it around here. It's too close."

"Well, then let's get where we can," Anton offered. "Ann?"

"Follow me," Ann said.

The group trekked out a little further until they came to the edge of a field.

"We should crawl across here, to be safe," Anton said.

"Nah, if anyone's out here they already know," Joseph pointed out.

"See that?" Ann pointed across the field. "It's an abandoned house. Kids used to use it for parties. After the Academy came in people got too scared to run out here."

"Won't they check here, though?" Lieutenant asked. "With all the sweeps and searches they've been doin' lookin' for the vandals?"

"Us you mean," Toni murmured.

"No," Charlie said, almost dreamily. "There's no one here but us and a few animals."

Even in the dark, Charlie could tell they were looking at her. "I have good instincts, okay?"

"Then let's make a run for it," Melvin said. "Just go."

They ran across the field as fast as they could and followed Ann into the rotting house.

"See?" she said proudly, spreading her arms. "This way we can meet even during the winter."

"Yeah, and freeze to death," Lieutenant said, wrapping her arms around herself.

"We could light a fire," Joseph said, taking out his lighter.

"No!" Anton and Lieutenant said simultaneously.

"They'll see that," Melvin explained, sitting down on the floor. "Ouch." He groan-laughed.

"What?" Toni asked, kneeling beside him.

Still laughing, Melvin moved over. "A nail went up my ass. *Don't* say it." He pointed at Lieutenant, who just grinned.

"A'ight," Anton said, sitting down. "Let's get to business."

"You said you had news." Toni pointed to Ann, who settled herself between Joseph and Charlie.

"Yeah," she said, looking down. "It's from when I was in the principal's office on Friday."

"You was in the principal's office Friday?" Joseph asked.

"Don't ask," Charlie and Toni warned.

Ann glared at them. "I found them on her desk when I was in there. Court orders."

"For what?" Joseph asked.

"For us," Ann said, looking around. "Everyone here except Toni is going to be fitted with electrodes, permanently."

"Wh-what do you mean 'permanently'?" Lieutenant demanded.

"It means we are going to have electrodes always attached to us," Charlie said. The focus turned to her, but she was looking down. "It means we'll have them attached to our skin, we'll have to wear them 24/7." She looked up. "It's happened at other places before that use skin shock, where they make students wear the electrodes on them at all times, even when they shower. I guess our teachers will have a device that sets off the shock so that they can do it at any time," Charlie explained, her voice fading with every word. "I ... I don't know ... how I can ... I mean, I knew it happened, but I never thought ... it would to me."

Ann put an arm over Charlie's shoulder to draw the shivering girl closer.

"They can't, though," Joseph said, shaking his head. "That — that can't be legal."

"If they have a court order it is," Lieutenant said, blinking. "Shit — how the fuck are we supposed to get away with anythin'? How are we supposed to *move*?"

"We don't let 'em put them on us," Joseph said determinedly. "That's what we do."

"Oh, because that worked out last time?" Ann said wryly.

"No," Anton said, sinking down. "We — we need another way ..." His voice drifted off and his face went blank.

"I don't get it," Toni said. "What do they want from us?"

"They wanna control us," Melvin supplied. "It's —"

"No, no, no!" Toni waved his comment away. "It's not that. There's something else. Why do they want us here? Money?"

"Yeah," Lieutenant said. "You know how much this school costs? My parents don't have much money, but the Academy took all my financial aid from my other school, plus some aid from the state. It adds up."

"But why?" Toni repeated. "Why us? Think about it. Look, you know Katrina? She said she was brought here because the school was 'special'. She said they did experiments here. She *made* the pills I used to put Mrs. Carter to sleep. She said that a woman came to her when she was in *jail* to recruit her."

"So?" Joseph asked.

"So," Toni said. "They came to my parents to persuade them — they did the same for Charlie. They hunted us down. They *wanted* us. There's tons of kids with problems in the country. So why us?" Toni looked around. "What do we have in common?"

"We're crazy?" Ann offered.

"Exactly," Toni said. "We have issues but ..." Toni looked at Charlie. "Charlie, you said you could see me in the dark."

"Um ..."

"And your senses aren't normal," Toni continued.

"My brain is messed up," Charlie said, looking uncomfortable.

"Yeah, but you're practically psychic." Toni plowed on. She turned to Lieutenant. "You."

"Me?"

"You moved a tray without your hands," Toni said excitedly. "You're telekinetic."

"You're saying they want us 'cause we're what — mutants?" Lieutenant asked, looking disbelieving.

"Come on, don't say you haven't thought of it," Toni said.

"Joseph's been getting us outta the house by burning the edges of the glass window then remelting it in," Ann spoke up. "*And* he burned the wire with his lighter. And he set fire to a trash can when he wasn't near it. He can like ... control the fire."

"I can't control it," Joseph said sharply. "Stuff with fire just ... just happens okay? Ain't like I can hold out my hand and shoot fire or nothin' like that, as much as I would like to be able to."

"But it's something," Toni said. "That's three. What about Anton?"

"Every time he's near something electrical, it messes up," Melvin explained. "That's how he got the gate open to the school."

Toni looked to Anton, who just grinned. "I like the idea of havin' powers," he said easily. "Anthony likes."

"Okay, so there it is," Toni said. "They want us here to ... I don't know, study us. Lieutenant's telekinetic, Joseph's pyrokinetic, Charlie's psychic and Ant—"

"No, no, *no!*" Charlie yelled. "I ... I am not psychic okay? No powers, no abilites ... no. You ... my brain isn't talented. It's *broken* okay? That's crazy stuff, crazy, and I won't believe it and go insane and ..."

"Calm down, Gnome," Ann soothed. "The Therapist is just thinking aloud."

"But doesn't it make sense?" Toni asked, looking around. "Are we the only boarders here?"

"Pretty much," Melvin said. "Other than Katrina."

"Katrina basically said they wanted her for her brains in chemistry," Toni thought aloud. "You guys, in any of your classes did they ever try to test you, like, test your abilities?"

"No." Lieutenant shook her head. "They never … " she trailed off. "Wait … Anton? Anton?" Lieutenant turned to her friend and pushed him. "Anthony?"

"Hey," Anthony said, and pushed his full bottom lip out and made it tremble as he gave her puppy dog eyes. "You pushed me."

"You 'member that time they took us for physicals?" Lieutenant asked him.

"No," Anthony said.

"What?" Lieutenant pinched him.

"Ow, woman! You and Ann there. Violent." He shook his head at Joseph.

"You don't remember?" Lieutenant repeated then shook her head. "Don't answer, you wouldn't, you and your damn amnesia. Anyway, we had our physicals, and they put us under … it was, like, nine when they started and then put us under, sayin' it was for an X-ray. We woke up like, seven hours later. They musta been doin' somethin' to us when we were under. Maybe they were studyin' us." Lieutenant rubbed her temples. "Listen to me, talkin' like this. Next thing I'm gon' be talkin' 'bout aliens."

"But that was all they did?" Toni asked.

"Yup," Lieutenant said. "Other than try to shock us into oblivion."

"Well, maybe that's it," Charlie put in. "That's why you guys haven't seen anything else, or been taught anything. First they want you to be well behaved before they —"

"What?" Anthony snorted. "Teach us to play Quidditch?"

"Seriously," Toni pleaded. "I think that this might be it. You guys are special and —"

"Sweetie, I'm bipolar," Lieutenant cut off. "A.K.A crazy. Y'all ain't seen me really crazy. I start thinkin' I'm up with the planets, or I get violent … I'm specially loco, but not 'gifted.'" Lieutenant sneered.

"It doesn't matter whether you are or aren't," Toni argued. "It just matters whether they think you are. Look, maybe you aren't gifted, even though I think you are all just in denial, but whatever. Maybe they just think that you guys have *something* worth studying."

Toni sighed at everyone's expressions and leaned back. "I'm just saying."

"So what about you?" Anthony asked. "Why you here? We never did hear."

Toni swallowed. "I don't have anything special. Well, unless you count managing my friend's psychological health. I did manage to keep one of my friends from killing himself. He has lots of issues. He calls himself my brother from another mother, but I call him my gerbil. I have to fix his issues and pet him like a gerbil."

Anthony laughed out loud. "Maybe that's why you here. We definitely need a therapist."

"And we need a plan," Toni said, looking around the circle. "We know what their plan is now. So, what do we do about it?"

"I might have some ideas," Charlie offered.

"I got a few myself," Joseph said. "I don't see this move from them as an issue. It just says they're afraid of us. That's an advantage."

"They underestimated us," Ann agreed, "and the best part is they think that it's not the boarders but the non-boarders who vandalized the school. Now the whole school knows they're not invincible."

"If you think about it," Melvin said, "right now we're their biggest fear. We should make them fear us a little bit more."

Lieutenant glanced at Anthony, then she broke into a grin. "Yeaahhh." She laughed. "Yeah."

# chapter twelve pill

**"The Board thought that we would be better served reading *Romeo***
*and Juliet*. They thought that it was more appropriate for your age group,"
Dana answered Joseph.

"Really?" Joseph asked. "'Cause it just seems weird to pull out a book
they already approved, ya know?"

Dana glanced up and sideways before looking back at Joseph. "Well,
that was a board decision."

"But ain't you on the board? I mean, it is *your* class. *You* are the English
teacher," Joseph pressed.

"I really don't want to discuss this," Dana said with another nervous glance.

Joseph leaned almost lazily back in his chair. "It's just, I mean damn, I was
really gettin' to like that book. I enjoyed readin' somethin' where everyone
could identify with the characters and their situation. Oh, wait —" Joseph
stopped, with a little mock laugh. "I forgot. That's why they banned it."

Under the desk, Toni kicked his heel. *Drop it,* she thought at him.

"Joseph, I think you should stop so we can begin," Dana said, eyes flicking
to the upper corner of the room again. Charlie's gaze followed her to where
the cameras were perched.

Joseph shifted in his seat and felt the wires under his shirt grind against
his skin. "Why can't we just call it what it is? What, they think we're so
stupid we can't see what's goin' on?"

"Joseph —"

"I mean, I'm not angry, even though they've decided that they can treat
us like we're lab rats they can do anythin' to and pretend we don't see what's
goin' on," Joseph said, his voice gaining steam. He had the attention of the

class now. "Everyone here can see what the Academy is tryna do."

"Joseph, you are the only one causing trouble," Dana said, looking desperate now.

"You're right." Joseph nodded. "Maybe they don't. Maybe they needa see it," Joseph pulled his shirt to gasps, revealing the wires and electrodes attached to his skin. "Maybe they won't know until they feel it on thems—"

Dana closed her eyes as she pressed the button on the device behind her back, and Joseph doubled over in pain. "Fuck!" he swore, and bit back his next swear as the second shock came. The class watched in silence as Joseph recovered his breathing and looked up from the desk with a small, bitter smile.

"Wow, Mrs. Lovejoy. I didn't think you had it in you."


"You are an idiot," Toni hissed with contempt at Joseph as they were led by a security guard to their next class. The Academy had hired several more in the past weeks.

"What?" Joseph said, surprised. "I'm tryna get people to come to our side! And it was workin', too. Did you see some of their faces? They know they could be next, so they'll hafta help."

"That's no use if you alienate the one teacher we have as an ally!" Charlie whispered out of the side of her mouth.

"What do you mean?" Joseph whispered, a little guiltily.

"You know what I mean," Charlie said. "Dana gave you every chance to get out of being shocked, and you didn't take it. You knew she was letting you off easy, and you pushed her into doing it."

"If she didn't wanna do it, she coulda quit," Joseph said. "'Sides, I gotta build up a tolerance somehow. Even though these hurt even worse than being burned. They upped the pain for this TED didn't they?"

"Must have. I heard them call it the TED-5," Toni said. Charlie just shivered.

"Skipped right over one, two, three, and four, I see. How am I s'posed to keep myself well-behaved when I have burn marks all over my back? Anyway, you don't need me for anythin' above ground," Joseph whispered. "You —"

"Shh," Charlie warned. "The cameras are back up, and I wouldn't put it past them to put in hidden mikes. Barely anyone else is whispering."

"They're all too scared they'll have these put on," Charlie whispered, resisting the urge to touch her wires. Dana was looking, and any attempt to pull them off meant a painful shock.

"I tell you what gets me through the day," said Joseph with a small smile, looking across the room. "Knowin' we ain't the only ones wit' em on." He looked at Seth.

"Don't anger him," Toni said out of the side of her mouth. After almost a month they had become adept at speaking almost without moving their lips. "We don't want him getting suspicious. Besides, I doubt you want him mad at you."

"I'm not scared of him," Joseph said, looking across the hall.

"You should be," Charlie whispered.

Before they could answer, Dana stepped between them. "Split up," she ordered.

Charlie and Toni glanced at each other then accusingly at Joseph. Dana had been the only one who turned a blind eye when they whispered to each other.

Joseph swallowed and nodded, moving away. Charlie proceeded just as quickly, but Toni moved a little slower.

She was the only one not hooked up to a TED device. Everyone had decided this was an advantage. It meant she had the most freedom.

*So I have to take all the big risks. Irony is a bitch.*

"Charlie Persan ... yes, you do have enough points to go to the Big Reward Store." Mr. Sanders nodded, looking at her file.

"It's like when I used to go to Sylvan for tutoring ,and they had a points system. I was bad at reading, that's why I went, but I didn't care about the points then because their prizes were always stupid, and I should really stop talking now, right?"

Mr. Sanders nodded at Charlie, and she instead walked through the door into the Big Rewards Store.

*Well, you can't say that they lie about this.*

The Big Reward Store was exactly that: big, and filled with rewards. It was the size of three rooms and stocked with everything from novels to Gucci purses. It even had an arcade.

Charlie's eyes scanned the room and caught Lieutenant's gaze. The other girl was standing by an aisle of books. Her slight of hand was so good that if Charlie hadn't known what to watch for, she wouldn't have seen her spill a little bit out of the water bottle she carried every few steps.

"Not again."

Charlie moved casually over to the arcade, where there was a chorus of groans as another game experienced technical difficulties.

"What did you do this time, Anthony?" asked one of the three guards monitoring the store.

"Nuthin'," Anthony said, holding up his hands innocently. "I just tried playin' it, and out it goes. I wouldn't mess with it. I wanted to make it to the next level!"

"Alright, alright, move over," said the guard. Anthony walked over to lean against a wall beside Charlie.

"How you doin' today, Tiny?"

"Good," Charlie said, wetting her lips nervously. "So it's friendly Anthony today?"

"Yeah," Anthony said slowly, looking sideways at her. He broke into another wide grin. "You ain't enjoyin' the marvelous bounty of the store. You wouldn't want to *miss* anythin.'"

"The only thing I like here is being able to actually talk to my friends," Charlie said quietly. "What kind of school doesn't want you to have friends?"

"This one. One where it's better for them if we all hate each other." Anthony shrugged, watching Melvin. He too was moving around the stacks of store items with a bottle.

"He's gonna buy something, right?" Charlie said out of the corner of her mouth. "So it doesn't look suspicious?"

"Yeah," Anthony said. He snorted as Melvin winked at them, picking up a purse and parading up and down the aisle.

"I keep waiting for him to break into song." Charlie snorted.

"*Five hundred twenty-five thousand six hundred minutes!*" Anthony sang, making Charlie laugh again.

"*Rent* is my life," Charlie decided. "Only without the drugs and sex and songs and everything that makes it fun. *Rent* in high school!"

"More like *Rent* in prison," Anthony stated.

"That would be called *Rape! The Musical!*"

"You would take it there," Anthony said. "No, I like *Rent*. The one problem I have is that it glamorizes bein' poor. It's like, 'We're poor and we all have AIDS, but fuck it, let's sing!' Nuh-uh." Anthony shook his head. "Poor is not fun. Poor is, 'You like this bar?' 'Yeah!' 'Good, you gon' clean the bathroom!'"

Charlie smiled awkwardly. "I'll believe you 'cause I don't really know myself."

"Well, trust me, Tiny," Anthony said as Lieutenant sat on the chair next to them.

"You finished?" Anthony asked under his breath.

"Yeah," Lieutenant said just as softly, opening the book she had just purchased with her good behavior points. "Melvin's almost done. What about the lights? Can you be sure they'll go out?"

"Do I ever fail?"

"Sometimes, so make sure this ain't one of 'em. You go over to play some more on the games and look innocent," Lieutenant said, leaning back in her chair.

"Look at you, orderin' me around like you a lieutenant or somethin'," Anthony said sarcastically. He nodded to Charlie and walked over to the store to look at jewelry.

"One minute he's relaxed and funny and friendly, and the next he's all business and sarcastic and sullen," Charlie mused. "He changes so fast."

"That's called men, sweetie." Lieutenant snorted, then laughed. "Yo — look at me talkin' 'bout mood changes."

"No, you stay *you*. He changes completely," Charlie said.

"Yo, real talk?" Lieutenant turned to her. "Don't try to figure him out. I tried for my first year here. He just crazy. This one." Lieutenant pointed at Melvin as he walked over. "This one you don't need to figure out because it's pretty easy to see."

"Thanks, Army of One." Melvin rolled his eyes, before kissing Lieutenant's cheek in apology. "Hey you," he said to Charlie. "Yeah you. Come over here and we'll find something pretty for you to get."

"Oh no." Charlie shook her head as Melvin pulled her over to the clothes section. "I can't ... I'm good with just —"

"One thousand and one hoodies?" Melvin raised a brow.

"Could you be any gayer?"

Melvin didn't answer, just licked his lips at Charlie and started to dance with her.

"No," Charlie whispered with laughter. "They'll see on the cameras."

"Good. My parents will be so happy I'm dancing with a girl," Melvin said bitterly. "Come on, let's make you pretty."

"That's impossible," Charlie said flatly. "Even if I injected myself so full of Botox I looked like a Barbie doll I'd still be ugly."

"You're not ugly," Melvin said, his face falling in sympathy.

"That's sweet," Charlie brushed off.

"No, really," Melvin said. "I do think you're pretty."

Charlie smiled, sensing he really might believe that. "To each his own."

"Oh, don't be one of those damn girls. C'mere," he said, pulling her into a hug. Charlie stiffened, then relaxed. She closed her eyes for a minute. "You're nice and squishy," she remarked.

"Oh, thanks." Melvin groaned. "Tell that to the fat boy."

"Now who's being one of those damn girls?" Charlie laughed. Her eyes moved up and she noticed the clock. "Do you think we'll be able to pull it off?" She breathed the words into his ear.

"We got it all along the aisles. They're soaked. Next part is Joseph and Toni's turn," Melvin whispered back before they broke the hug.

Charlie nodded and together they left the store.


"You do not have enough points to go into the store," Mr. Sanders told Joseph flatly. "Especially with your latest episodes."

"No brownie points for me." Joseph pouted mockingly.

"Sit down, Mr. Valdez," Mr. Sanders said firmly.

"Whatever." Joseph breathed, before going over to the wall nearest the door and leaning against it, one knee up on the wall.

Adrenaline coursed through his veins. This whole idea was insane. It was likely they would all be caught.

*It's so fuckin' stupid ... it is so fuckin' stupid, its fuckin' brilliant,* Joseph thought with a small laugh.

"What's so funny?" asked the girl who sat near him. She was clearly upset, watching her friends file in and out of the store. As she was meant to be. The purpose of having them watch was to encourage them to want to alter their behavior.

"Nuthin'." Joseph shrugged it off. He was excited now. He felt in his pocket for his lighter.

*This could happen. We could actually pull this off. It all depends on Toni, now.*


"Seth?"

Seth looked down at Toni. "Yeah?"

"We're not supposed to talk in the halls," hissed one of his friends.

"Shut up," Seth ordered. "What is it?"

"I was just wondering ... if it's true. That you broke into the school, I mean," Toni asked carefully, watching his face.

Seth's face went stony, but then he gave her a half-grin. "Yeah, it's true. I did that. If they're gonna punish me for it, I might as well own up to it."

"Oh, wow," Toni responded, covering up her shock at his lie. She moved closer to him. His pocket hung just out of reach. "That's so ... ballsy."

Seth smirked. "I guess so," he bragged.

"Well I was just wondering," Toni said, fumbling over her words. She felt guilty for doing this to him again. "If you —"

*Here goes,* she thought as she bumped into him, dropping the apparatus in his pocket. "Oh, sorry," she said. "I'm just clumsy." She didn't have to force herself to blush. She was embarrassed enough.

"I'll just ... yeah." She turned away, walking up to the desk.

"Toni White," Mr Sanders said, pulling her status up on the computer. "Let's see —"

Toni glanced swiftly over at Joseph and blinked once. He touched his index finger to his nose lightly.

"You can go in," Mr. Sanders said to her. She nodded and moved quickly past Joseph into the store.

She glanced over at Lieutenant, who scratched her neck. Toni picked her nails. Lieutenant exited the store.

Anthony got off the video game just as the screen fizzled out. His eyes caught Toni's for a second, and she picked at her nails again.

Slyly, Anthony pulled out one of his wires which fizzled with electricity, as Seth walked in.

Toni moved away from the aisles of the store to one of the couches, pulling out a book. She kept her eyes down as the sound of sizzling electricity built up nearby.

The other students and guards looked around as something short-circuited with a blast. A video game emitted a puff of smoke with a bang. The other students near it jumped back just in time as the lights went out.

Toni felt someone bump into her as screams filled the room. It was utterly dark.

That is, until with a whooshing sound, a fire ignited all along the aisle of the store. It gained speed quickly, almost as if half the contents of the store had been doused with gasoline.

The two girls nearest the blaze shrieked and sped out of the store. There was a rush on the door as the two security guards tried to evacuate everyone.

Toni felt fear as the fire swept up its prey faster and it began to move away from the aisles and toward the carpet in the other room.

Toni tried to move and realized she couldn't. Her legs felt like lead, and it was as if someone had replaced the blood in her veins with ice water.

One of the security guards grabbed her by the arm and dragged her out of the door, pushing her through before smashing open the glass and pulling out the fire extinguisher. Toni felt a hand pulling her away from the door and sitting her down.

"You okay?" Anthony asked, watching her intently. "You froze up in there."

Toni tried desperately to catch her breath.

"Yo," Anthony cried. "I think she's havin' an attack or somethin'."

"Come on," said Mr. Sanders taking them both by the arms. Toni realized they were the only ones left in the waiting room. "Let's go."

Toni let herself be dragged away from the noise of the guard and his fire extinguisher, still fighting their blaze.

"How did they do it?"

"Mrs. Principal, we don't know for sure that this was arson," said Officer Mills. "Apparently you had a problem with your arcade area, and the electricity there short-circuited and somehow the lights blew out. Now that might have led to —"

"Nothing was wrong with our arcade, Officer Mills," Mrs. Carter said definitively. She pulled on a pair of leather gloves.

"Mrs. Carter," Officer Mills began again. "To get past all the security you got up — a bunch of teenagers? I doubt they would be able to set a fire without your seeing it."

"You do not know my students, officer."

Officer Mills watched, annoyed, as the principal patrolled the burned wreckage of the store's aisles.

"This is hundreds of dollars worth of damage right here," Mrs. Carter informed him, picking up and dropping a ruined Gucci purse.

"I think that entails an investigation," Officer Mills began. "I —"

"That would be wonderful," Mrs. Carter interrupted, running her gloved fingers over a shelf. "But there are some ground rules. I need to be informed when and where you intend to investigate, and I would like for you to clear with me at what places and times you wish to do so."

"I can accommodate you, but I can't have too many restrictions on an investigation," Officer Mills informed.

"Oh, I assure you, you will have our full cooperation," Mrs. Carter stated. "But we will not be pressing criminal charges should you find these perpetrators."

"I am sorry, but by law —" Officer Mills sputtered.

"Well ,perhaps we will not need your help at all," Mrs. Carter said coolly, sniffing her gloved fingers. "Baking grease," she said, holding up her hand to Officer Mills. "Lots of it and still fairly wet, which means the students who placed it here must have done so fairly recently."

"Mrs. Principal?" A teacher walked into the room, stepping over the yellow tape. "We've found him."

"Only one him?" Mrs. Carter said, walking out. "Excuse me, officer."

"No, I'll come," Officer Mills said, hiding his irritation.

"This was not the work of only one student," Mrs. Carter said to the teacher. "This had to have been done by more than one student. Though how they got through our new security, I'd like to know."

"Well, we found the person who must have set it off," the other woman said, stopping in front of two guards who supervised the tall, handsome blonde in cuffs.

"We found these in his pockets," said one of the guards, holding out a dark stone and small piece of metal.

"Flint and tinder," Mrs. Carter observed. "Rather old-fashioned, Seth."

Seth looked up, his handsome face ugly with hate. "I didn't do this." He snarled. "I was set up."

"You walk into the room, the lights go out, and a fire erupts," Mrs. Carter said in a silky, dangerous voice. "This after you broke into the school and vandalized our banner. That doesn't look very innocent."

"I don't know what happened. Someone put that in my pocket," Seth hissed. "It wasn't me."

"Oh, I know you didn't act alone," Mrs. Carter said. "What I need are the names of the others."

"I didn't —"

"It would be helpful for you to tell us," Mrs. Carter hinted.

Seth bit his tongue, thinking.

"And the next Academy Asshole Award goes to ..." Anthony announced with a flawless British accent, miming opening an envelope, "Melvin Stavos and Amina Jackson, alias Lieutenant, for spraying flammable fluids all over the Store. People, let's clap!"

Anton, Toni, Charlie, Joseph, and Ann clapped as Melvin and Lieutenant stepped up to accept their nonexistent award. They had gathered in the dilapidated abandoned house to celebrate.

"I didn't prepare a speech," Lieutenant stated. "But I —"

"Poem!" Melvin clapped.

"May — no," Lieutenant responded.

"Po-em, po-em," Melvin chanted, getting the others to join.

"Once there was a white girl we'll call Smurf," Lieutenant said. "Who thought we should show all our worth. So we set the Store on fire. And we blamed Seth Dryer ... And oh how we showed 'em, how much we own 'em ... and y'all are bitches for makin' me do this damn poem," Lieutenant finished. "Melvin?"

"Uh ..." Melvin took a surprised Lieutenant by the waist, dipped her and kissed her full on the mouth. "Happy now, Mom? Do I get back in the inheritance for this, bitch? Thank you, I'm done." He cackled, sitting down as Lieutenant swatted him.

"What did it feel like?" Anthony cackled.

"Wet," Melvin answered, gagging.

"A'ight, a'ight, settle down," Anthony said, now with the voice of a preacher. "Brothers and sisters —"

"Will you pick a damn voice to use and stick with it?" Lieutenant demanded.

"Brothers and sisters, the Lord tells us to turn the other cheek," Anthony said, sticking his butt in Lieutenant's face. "And our next Academy Award goes to Joseph for setting a blaze that puts the fear of God into our hellbound classmates."

"You a bigger clown than me," Joseph said as Anthony stood up.

"God will forgive you for that my son," Anthony said with a straight face, making the sign of the cross.

"As for me," Joseph said, using a high girlish voice. "I just wanna thank a few people — my mom, my enemies, 'cause they just made me stronger ... uh, the girl who turned me down in fifth grade ... the boy who turned me down in sixth grade ..."

"I am revoking your man license, right now," Anthony intoned.

"Anthony, Anthony," Ann said. "It has long since been lost."

Joseph glared at Ann, and Anthony pointed at her. "Your turn."

"Okay, so I wanna keep this short, so I'll just thank Sherry," Ann said. "And by Sherry, I mean the booze, because if that Shania Twain wannabe hadn't been soaked in the stuff we woulda never been able to steal her baking grease, so ..." Ann blew a kiss. "Thanks, Sherry!"

"And up next is Charlie," Anthony said. "The evil mastermind of this whole thing."

"I would like to say I'm glad nobody got hurt," Charlie said. "And I really hope we don't get caught. Thanks!"

"Way to bring us down," Joseph said.

"I'm next, right?" Toni said.

"Yeah." Anthony nodded.

"Well I wanna say I also hope we don't get caught. And I feel kinda bad for Seth. I mean we set him up, and here we are laughing about it while he takes the blame."

"I'm laughin' be*cause* he's takin' the blame." Joseph shrugged.

"Don't feel sorry for him," Anthony said darkly.

"That asshole?" Lieutenant scoffed.

"He is evil incarnate," Melvin stated.

"Isn't this what everyone thinks about us?" Toni pointed out. "When I asked him, he said he was the one who vandalized the school. He admitted to it. He bragged about it! Maybe we should try working with him."

"No!" Both Joseph and Anthony said at the same time.

"Don't you start," Anthony ordered blackly. "Don't you start feelin' sorry for him. He don't feel sorry for nobody. He'll take your pity and use it against you. People like him don't care about you ... don't care about anyone. I know. People like him ..." Anthony's face was scaring Toni. "You know I heard about him killin' frogs out by the lake? Just for fun — just cause he could. That's what he said. Just cause he could. Sorry for him? No." Anthony growled. "No."

Toni swallowed. "Look ... fine. Fine. But now you guys have to admit that I was right about what you all can do, right? Anthony managed to screw up all of the electrical wires in the place to make the lights go out, and you can't even explain it," she said to Anthony. "And Joseph." Toni pointed at him. "Joseph managed to set a fire in the room —"

"I was close." Joseph shifted.

"You were a foot away. How'd you manage to make a fire go off?" Toni argued. "You can cause fire."

"No, I gotta start it like any normal person, 'swhy I need my lighter," Joseph argued.

"Whatever," Toni said. "You can still make it happen near you without touching it, and make them grow. And Charlie." Toni rounded on her. "Charlie was the one who thought this all up and who also has the habit of saying what everyone is thinking before they do."

"So?" Charlie said.

"I don't get you guys," Toni said, annoyed. "I would kill to be able to do the things you all can do."

"Oh, yeah." Lieutenant scoffed. "You'd just love to get kicked outta your house. You'd just love to work for four weeks to have some money, then wake up one day not knowin' why you bought half the shit you did, and spend the next eight weeks feelin' like you dead inside — oh, yeah, I'd kill for that."

"And you might," Joseph said, eyes withdrawn, his voice flat. "If not yourself, then maybe someone else. Not meanin' too, but just by accident — an accident you caused. I can't help people, I can't heal people, and I can't even create somethin.' All I can do is lose. Lose people, lose things, lose ... just lose."

"You don't want any of what we got," Anthony said, leaning against the wall. "Definitely not me. It's just a bunch of things that happen around me, and I'm not even there half the time."

"I think you're all being too harsh on her," Ann spoke up. "She's here too, remember, which means she's got problems, whatever they are. She just doesn't have anything good to make up for it. Like me — I'm not anything special, I can't fly or shoot webs from my hands. What about Melvin? He doesn't have anything to make up for his parents and their shit, you know?"

"Maybe his problems ain't as bad," Joseph shot back.

"Oh, now you wanna say —"

"Can we just stop this?" Charlie shrieked. "What's the point? Who gives a shit whose problems are bigger? We're all here aren't we? We're all fucked up, but we'll be a hell of a lot more fucked if we start tearing each other apart. Duh."

There was a silence, and then Joseph snorted. Ann raised an eyebrow. "Duh?"

Charlie opened and closed her mouth, then began laughing.

"Like, so duh," Anthony said.

"Oh my God, so Valley Girl," Toni said in her Valley Girl voice.

"And the Smurf has spoken." Joseph chuckled. Ann threw back her head and laughed.

"Wow." Melvin shook his head, "You wanna know something funny?"

"Is it actually gon' be funny?" Lieutenant asked lazily.

"Hey, fuck you." Melvin shoved her. "You know, right now? I actually feel normal."

"You're right," Lieutenant said. "That is funny."

# chapter thirteen meet

### "Mom? Did you hear —"

"Yes, I heard you," Mrs. Carter said shortly. "And yes, we will still be going to school today."

"But ... after what happened —"

"*It will not happen again!*"

Becky backed down. Toni kept her eyes on her food.

Mrs. Carter regained her composure. "We will simply have to restrict the movements of our school community even more, for everyone's safety."

"But ..." Toni couldn't help herself. "If you restrict everyone, won't that make more people want to rebel against the school?"

There was a silence.

*Damn it Toni White, why didn't you just prance out of your room naked this morning and sing a song about how you set the fire, moron!*

Mrs. Carter looked at Toni full on and said firmly, "The ones who choose to do so will only hurt themselves more in the process. They'll only succeed in making the rest of the school angry at them for bringing these new restrictions upon everyone."

Toni nodded and tried to look reassured.

"Come on then," Mrs. Carter said stiffly. "Time for the bus."


*Most important fact to know about Ann,* Joseph reminded himself. *Do not, do* not *make her angry in the mornin'.*

"Maybe you could fuck yourself with it," Ann said to Joseph, shoving the knife at him.

*Yeah ... never make her mad in the mornin'. She's like a hurricane of bitch in the mornin'.*

"I thought you already did that. I wouldn't wanna trespass," Joseph shot back.

"What the hell is that supposed to mean?" Ann whispered furiously. They had to make sure Sherry didn't hear.

"Means your reputation precedes you," Joseph mumbled. "And maybe if you didn't piss Sherry off by always tryna get past the dress code, she wouldn't have gotten suspicious and moved the sleepin' pills."

"You're blaming this on me?" Ann scoffed. "This is your fault and you know it."

"Is not!"

*Okay — so maybe it had somethin' to do with my comment to Sherry yesterday that sleepin' wouldn't be so difficult for her if she wasn't drunk all the time,* Joseph grumbled to himself. *Still —*

"Still, you ain't have to be so damn vicious whenever I make a mistake. Everyone makes them!"

"Yeah, and our mistakes cost a lot more," Ann said, scowling at him. Joseph glared back. They had a strange pattern of one good day where they were friends alternating with a day of fighting. Right now was not one of the better days. He was pissed, and she was furious.

*Damn she's beautiful when she's mad.*

Joseph looked down at his food. *This would be so much simpler if she was a bitch twenty-four seven. But when she lets her guard down she's actually funny, interestin' and — wait for it — sweet.* She had even begun sneaking into his room at night to talk.

"We have to go looking for them again, you know," she said in a low voice.

"I know," Joseph said shortly. "Despite what you seem to think, I actually have a brain. Sometimes I even have ideas!"

"You think you're so funny," Ann said. "I'm glad you amuse yourself."

"Amuse you too sometimes," Joseph said under his breath.

"Right," Ann said, rolling her eyes.

"Maybe if you was less of a bitch to me, I wouldn't have to —"

"Maybe if you didn't always call me na —"

"What are you two doing?" Sherry asked, coming downstairs. Her hair was badly done and her makeup a bit smudged.

"We're eating," Joseph said, picking up his toast, taking a bite, and giving a thumbs up. "Breakfast is healthy and nutritious."

"Don't give me that attitude," Sherry said sharply. "I am not a moron. I know what breakfast is."

"Really? 'Cause for most people, breakfast is somethin' you eat, not somethin' you drink from a glass bottle." Joseph attacked before thinking.

Sherry's eyes widened. "You liar!"

Joseph doubled over in pain, gripping the edge of the table.

"Hey," Ann said, walking over to Sherry. "You didn't have to shock him for saying the truth."

Sherry's hand moved and Ann took the shock, eyes still defiant. "Aren't you a big woman," Ann said softly.

"I don't need to justify myself to you. I am a grown woman," Sherry said, pulling herself up.

"Then act like one," Ann challenged before picking up her backpack. "Oh listen, there's the bus."

Joseph almost laughed at Ann's gutsiness. Sherry was so stunned she didn't even try to shock them again, and Ann grabbed Joseph by the shoulder to pull him towards the bus.


"Charlie?"

Charlie held her eyes closed then opened them slowly. *Why is everyone whispering so damn loud? And why doesn't he get angry at* them?

"Ms. Persan?" Mr. Alderman repeated. "Do you have an answer to the question?"

The girl beside her was whispering on about something about someone she liked but couldn't let anyone find out about. Charlie couldn't really make much out — just the emotions of crush and the excitement at something being forbidden.

"Charlie Persan," Mr. Alderman said sternly. "I will ask you again: in what year was the Treaty of Paris signed?"

*Shit, shit, shit,* Charlie thought. Dates were the only things in history she was bad at. "I ... just give me a minute ..."

She tried to think through the babble from the girl next to her.

"Ms. Persan?" Charlie heard the impatience in his voice, and she wanted to avoid a shock.

"I know that it was in seventeen ... seventeen ..." Charlie's fingers curled. The date was on the tip of her tongue, if only the girl beside her —

"Will you shut up about your precious forbidden crush?" Charlie exploded. "Nobody cares!"

She stopped at the look on the girls face. There was silence in the class. Even Mr. Alderman seemed to have forgotten that here he was supposed to shock her.

"Brad? You like Brad?" mumbled an unidentifiable voice.

The girl beside Charlie colored but kept staring at Charlie as if she had grown three heads. Charlie swallowed and looked around. This dead silence was even worse than a shock. Why were they so silent?

"Oh." Charlie breathed out, looking at the girl. "You weren't talking, were you?"

The girl shook her head.

Toni glanced across the lunch table at Charlie, who looked down as Seth placed his tray down.

"Hey," whispered one girl. Toni looked up. She too was avoiding Seth's gaze. "Yeah?"

"No, sorry I was talking to your friend," the girl said. Charlie looked up through her hair.

*It's really messy,* Toni noticed. *And I gotta admit Charlie smells like she hasn't had a good shower in a while.*

"What?" Charlie asked, nervously.

"I'm in your history class," the girl said. Charlie nodded, no recognition in her eyes.

"How ... how did you know about Felicia and Brad? I thought I was the only one she told."

"I ... she was whispering about him," Charlie stuttered.

"Um ... I was right next to her and I didn't hear," the girl said. Charlie shrugged and looked away.

"Are you like ... psychic?" the girl asked.

Charlie took a deep breath and then met the other girl's eyes. "Hopefully."

"Can you tell what I'm thinking right now?" the girl asked with a smile.

Charlie opened and closed her mouth and then turned to Toni. Toni gave an encouraging look.

*Why not?* Charlie thought. *If I'm crazy ... well, I already know how that will turn out. But if not? If she's right? I have nothing to lose.*

Charlie turned back to the girl and stared into her eyes. The girl played along, although she giggled nervously.

"All I'm getting is a ... pink feeling," Charlie said clumsily.

"Um ... that is *not* what I was thinking," the girl giggled.

"No, wait ..." Charlie shook her head. *It feels so funny. Kinda like what I feel when I look at ...* "Oh!" Charlie realized. "You're in love for the first time," she said happily. That was why she thought of pink. She didn't know what in love felt like, but pink always said love to her.

"I'm ... well I ..." The girl's forehead creased, and she pulled back.

"Are you?" asked the boy across from her. The girl didn't answer.

"Do me," the boy said, and Charlie felt a sense of elation as if she was in a hot air balloon going up for the first time. She looked into his open brown eyes for a minute. Nothing seemed to come except frustration.

She pulled back. "You're annoyed at something," Charlie pronounced. "That's all I'm getting."

The boy leaned back. "Hey, that's cool."

"Just a good guess," said Seth, his face a mask of boredom.

Charlie's face fell.

"Leave her alone," Toni defended.

"Alright then," Seth said, leaning forward. "Try reading me, *Madame Persan*."

Charlie swallowed. "Come on, you can do it," Toni whispered. Charlie shivered. She didn't want to meet those eyes.

"See, she's afraid because she knows she's faking it," Seth pronounced.

Something in Charlie rebelled, and she looked up. Seth grinned and met her gaze.

Every muscle, sense, and pore in her body screamed for Charlie to run. Her fragile mind started disintegrating at the edges. She wanted to look away, but forced herself to stay and see.

"Nothing," Charlie whispered.

"See?" Seth scoffed. "I told you she couldn't —"

"No." Charlie cut him off. "I said nothing. I see nothing. No fear. No pain. No love, no caring. No dreams, no wishes, no plans. But there is ... um, the need to win."

"Win what?" Toni asked.

"Win ... just win," Charlie said, still staring at the senior's face in disbelieving horror. "Just ... to win and dominate."

"So you're saying I'm a winner," Seth stated, but his eyes narrowed like the gaze of some predator not sure if it should attack.

"No." Charlie shook her head. "No, I'm saying you are empty. Hollow. There's ... the stuff that should be there — all the feelings that should be there — just *isn't*. All I get is boredom. Boredom more than anything else."

"I think you're just making this shit up," Seth said, and there was a soft gasp at his swearing. "You didn't get this much from everyone else."

"That's because there was too much in there to see. I just got whatever was most overwhelming," Charlie answered. "But in you ... there isn't. Your mind is just —"

"You tryna say I'm stupid?" Seth said, voice relaxed, eyes lethal.

"No, no." Charlie shook her head. "It isn't that there aren't thoughts, but ... I can't ... I can't tell what you are thinking like it's a sentence, because people," she struggled to explain it. "People don't usually think in sentences. They think in feelings or pictures or just knowledge. But in you I don't ... I don't like —" Charlie shivered again. "All I get is scary and cold," she said, and looked down.

"Scary and cold," Seth mocked. "Please, you're just some sick little girl who's gonna end up in a hospital for the rest of your life because she thinks Satan's coming to get her."

Seth's remark was so close to the truth that Charlie flinched. She felt like crying but faced Seth again with whatever courage she could muster.

"You'll probably end up just fine, huh? But even if I die, I have something that you don't. You got looks, and smarts, and even if it was you who set the fire and vandalized the school, you'll still have followers huh? But you won't have friends. You won't have any love. I know what you are and every person here, even the stupidest, we all have something you won't ever have. You'll just go through life, always bored, always needing another thrill."

"I think you're jealous, little girl." Seth snarled softly. "Because I'm a winner, and you're a head case."

"And you'll keep on winning," Charlie said, with a strength she didn't know she had. If she backed down she knew those eyes would overwhelm her. "You might win being the president, you might win being rich, you might become the leader of the world — but then you'll just need another something to win, another thrill. You can't run away from your boredom and your emptiness any more than I can run away from my crazy. So no," Charlie said, trying to get all the words out before her courage fled, "you aren't better than me. And I think I win."

"You." Seth pointed at her. "Are a fuckin' lunatic. And I think all of you should run away before this one starts to think that the table is a bomb and trashes the place. Fuckin' schizo," he hissed, throwing her greatest fear in her face as he got up, grabbed his stuff, and stamped away.

"If people are asking us to help fight the school, then they know we're doing it. We're fucked," Lieutenant whispered.

"I don't think so," Toni responded, sitting beside her at the bus. They had to keep their voices down. No one was supposed to talk during school except at the lunch table. Even then, aides would patrol up and down the tables, listening in on conversations. "It just means they think that because we're boarders we'll fight back."

"Still —" Lieutenant paused, waiting for the guard to move away. "Still," she began again, "how do we know we can trust them?"

"We don't," Toni said. "But if they're willing to put themselves out there and ask us —"

"It's probably a trick," Lieutenant whispered. "Yo, Mrs. Carter ain't stupid. She'll get people to pretend they wanna fight to see who takes the bait, and then she'll catch 'em. She's been doin' that with teachers. She'll have one try to start a conversation about somethin' like a game or their hair, and if the teacher don't say, "I can't talk about that," they get busted. I heard it happen to Ms. Lovejoy."

"So how are we supposed to know if they really wanna join?" Toni asked.

"Maybe a sign," Lieutenant said.

"What do you mean?" Toni asked.

"Like, put out a sign that's a symbol of us, but not one that they can link to us," Lieutenant explained. "But —"

"But one that shows you have to commit yourself first," Toni caught on. "So that —"

"Shh," Lieutenant warned. "I think he's looking."

*Who invented algebra? Why is it important to be able to put numbers on a god-damn checkerboard? Did someone actually find this shit* fun*? They couldn't have just played charades like a normal bored human being with no beer on hand?*

Ann threw her math book across the room into the door and rolled onto her back.

*What are you supposed to do to control your temper? Count to one hundred? More math. Yeah, that'll relax me.*

There were two knocks on her door.

"Who's there?" Ann asked.

"Jesus."

"Jesus who?"

"Jesus Christ. What other Jesus is there?"

Ann snorted and got up and opened the door for Joseph. "Jesus?" she asked with a half smile.

"Nah." Joseph shook his head. "Not exactly. I couldn't live up to the whole savin' the world thing. Well ... that would be fun, actually."

"Being crucified would be un-fun," Ann pointed out.

"Even that I could live wit'," Joseph said with sincerity. "But the no sex thing? I couldn't keep myself celibate even if God was my father. Can you *imagine* masturbating with God as your father in the other room?"

They both cracked up helplessly, Joseph shaking his head to rid himself of the thought.

"We're goin' to hell," Joseph stated.

"Yup," Ann said happily. "We're not supposed to be talking you know," she reminded, listening for Sherry.

"I know," Joseph said, shifting from one foot to the other in her doorway. It was a nervous tick he had. Ann couldn't stop a smile.

"Joseph, what is it?" she asked, trying to relax him. "Whatever it is, you can say it."

Joseph cleared his throat. "It might annoy you," Joseph warned. "But please just hear me out first. If after, you feel the need to bitch slap me, uh … don't? Please?"

Ann nodded, half frowning.

Joseph closed his eyes as if prepping, then pulled out a piece of paper and a pair of glasses.

"Ten reasons why you should go out wit' me," Joseph began. "Number one — I'm funny. I make you laugh. This is a good quality in a boyfriend because it makes dating them amusing.Reason number two, I have good conversation. I will talk about almost anything."

"Like about chick flicks?" Ann asked.

"If you … really, really want to," Joseph said with difficulty.

"Clothes shopping?"

"Ann —"

"PMS?"

"Will you let me finish my list?" Joseph asked. "Reason four is we have a lot in common. Reason five is I shower a lot. Reason number six is goin' out wit' me would show your patriotism as an American …"

"Is this a joke?" Ann asked blandly.

"No!" Joseph said. "I just … I — I wanted to find a cool way of askin' you out, but I didn't have a lot of time, and I thought this would be funny and … yeah."

"You wanna go out with me?" Ann asked, blinking.

"Yeah," Joseph answered, swallowing.

"Where … would we go?" she asked. "Out, I mean?"

Joseph brightened. "That … is still a work in progress, considerin' the whole …" He held up his arms and gestured to their respective wires. "You know …"

"Ann! Joseph!" Sherry shrieked from the bottom floor. "Dinner!"

"But how are we supposed to meet with them if we don't know if we can trust them?" Anton asked swiftly. They had to keep this meeting short. It had taken them a while to all get to the abandoned house safely. The Academy was watching their every move now, waiting for a mistake.

"Maybe we don't have to."

The group turned to Ann. Toni, Melvin, Anton, and Lieutenant had all seen people who seemed to be hinting that they wanted to join their mini rebellion.

"What do you mean?" Toni asked.

"What if we show them that they don't need to meet us at all — just join and work themselves?" In response to the looks she was getting, Ann tried to explain. "You know, in grassroots stuff? People there do their own thing. They're all fighting for the same thing, but they don't answer to anyone. What if that's how we do it? What if we give them a sign that all you need to do to be part of us is fight against the school? That way, all of us are protected if someone gets caught. If they get caught they can't turn us in, and if we get caught we won't know who is helping us."

"I get it," Charlie said. "It's the way a guerilla army fights. With no actual leaders, even if someone gets caught, the fight goes on."

"But what if they don't understand that they have to act on their own?" Anton asked.

"Or get too scared of acting by themselves?" Lieutenant questioned.

"If we don't want them feelin' alone," Joseph said slowly, "we should make it clear that there are other people in this wit' 'em. Like, that it's a movement. Not only will that get more people, it'll terrify Mrs. Carter and the whole Academy, so they'll be runnin' around tryna find the leader when there isn't any."

"So?" Ann said, looking at Lieutenant and Anton. "Do I pass? Is this a good idea?"

"I like it," Anton said with his crooked grin. "Lieutenant? What'chu think?"

"I think Ann just got promoted to Captain," Lieutenant said, clapping her hand to Ann's and pulling their fingers apart.

Ann grinned. "But how will we get other people to know to show that they're part of our ... rebellion, or whatever it is?"

"They'll need a symbol," Joseph said. "And I can do that."

## "Does anyone know what the answer is?"

Joseph raised his hand slowly. Ms. Donelle looked at him coldly, but answered. "Yes?"

"I can try it," Joseph offered. Donelle gestured for him to approach the board.

Joseph located the right marker. He picked it up and focused on the spot where Ann had written with it two problems ago. He frowned as he wrote and no imprint was made.

"This one doesn't work," he said.

"Then throw it away and use another," Ms. Donelle instructed.

Joseph threw out the marker and picked up another. This time with his left hand, he began working.

*She didn't notice — I think. Please say she didn't notice ...*

"Just get rid of it if it doesn't work," Mr. Alderman said impatiently, holding out his hand for the marker. Toni gave it to him, a shiver running down her spine as he took it. She felt a surge of relief as it went into the trash can.

"Yes, that is right," Mr. Alderman said as Toni wrote with the untainted marker. "Very good. Now just erase that and we can move on."

"No, that is not the answer," Ms. Donelle said briskly.

Joseph gritted his teeth against his classmate's suppressed snickers.

*Right — I don't understand what a curve has to do with numbers. Sorry*

*I spend my time over shit that matters.*

Joseph sat down as Ms. Donelle called another student to the board. He began to erase the problem Joseph had drawn.

"So," Ms. Donelle began to explain. "When you have to graph a parabola which —"

"Ms. Donelle!" one girl interrupted.

"We raise hands in class, Ellen," Ms. Donelle said. "Detention."

"But — look!" The girl pointed at the board.

Ms. Donelle turned as the boy pulled away from the whiteboard. The class gasped at the half-revealed image.

"What did you do?" Ms. Donelle demanded.

"I — I was just erasing," the student stuttered as Ms. Donelle snatched the eraser and rubbed it furiously over the board.

To her visible anger, the more she erased the clearer the message became.

*Stand up, hit back.*
*Act alone — we all are behind you.*
*Fight before there's no one to fight for you.*


Mr. Alderman stopped reading off the board. "There are copies of this message on the whiteboards of five classrooms."

"What is the uh ... the symbol thing?" Mr. Protus gestured to the large red symbol on the board. It showed an inverted A with some kind of knife plunged through it.

"I would think that's obvious," Mrs. Carter said in a clipped voice. "The inverted A is for Alter Academy. The sword means down with the Academy."

"It showed up every time after an eraser was used," Mr. Alderman informed them. "Also, all the classes reported using defective markers at one point."

"But how the — how did they do it all in plain sight, without us seeing?" Mr. Protus sputtered.

"That is obvious," Mrs. Carter said swiftly. "The defective markers had some kind of invisible ink on them that could only be activated after other markers and the eraser had been used over them. Pretty ingenious. I would like to know how our students managed to develop the method without us seeing."

"Too ingenious. There's no way students could have thought of all this," Mr. Alderman stated.

"Are you suggesting we suspect our teachers, or our aides?" Mrs. Carter insinuated silkily. The others in the room stiffened.

"I think we should pick up all the students who used the defective markers," Ms. Donelle said.

"That would be half our students," Dana interjected. "Almost all of my students used the defective marker at least once."

"You can see it in the random strokes around the message," Mrs. Carter pointed out. "Clearly some of the students who used it knew what they were writing, while others just tried them once, saw it didn't work, and used another."

Mrs. Carter moved closer to the board. "Look at the handwriting. Besides being messy, each line is different. This message wasn't written by just one student — at least two different students wrote this one, line by line." She smiled tightly. "Brilliant, actually. Even if we take samples of handwriting from the whole school, we might not find them. This took time. Time and patience."

"So how are we supposed to catch them?" Ms. Donelle said.

"I don't know, but we have to or there will be more," the principal warned. "This isn't just a group of students bragging about their defiance. This ..." She tapped the inverted A. "This is a call to school wide rebellion."


"Were you in a gang?"

"No."

"But didn't you get arrested for being in a gang?"

"No, I was arrested for graffiti."

"But isn't that what gangs do?"

Joseph considered stabbing himself out with his fork — but then the girl across from him at the lunch table would just ask him if he had ever stabbed someone in a gang.

"I didn't do taggin', which is what gangs do. I was doin' art. I just used a bigger canvas than most people, and the city didn't really appreciate that," Joseph explained.

"But ... I heard you set fires," the girl said. "Did your gang tell you to do that?"

"I wasn't in a gang!"

The girl just looked skeptical, and Joseph gave up. If she wanted to believe he was some gangbanger, she could go ahead.

*No gang would be stupid enough to take me,* Joseph thought, echoing his father's words.

*Stupid enough? I coulda burned down the whole damn city,* Joseph rebelled darkly. *When he lit that fire I shoulda made it burn* him *to the ground.*

"Okay, if you didn't like, kill someone, or weren't in a gang, then why are you here?" asked the girl.

Joseph looked up into her eyes and gave a smile that made her pull back.

"Because I'm crazy," he said in a low voice. "Why else?"


"So we haven't seen you in a while," Becky said.

"You saw me this morning," Toni said flatly. "If that's long time no see for you —"

"Do you really think we haven't noticed who you're hanging out with?" Katrina put in.

*Both of the Stepford girls at one table,* Toni thought dryly. *Lucky me.*

"I don't know what you're talking about," Toni answered. "I've been being a good little girl this whole time, doing my work, watching the school going up in flames. I thought I would be safer here than at home, but I guess not."

Becky's eyes narrowed. "You know what's happening and who's doing it don't you?"

"Me?" Toni said. "Sure. I suspect either the Joker or Bad Santa."

Katrina shook her head. "Whoever's doing this is just making it harder on the other boarders."

"Why do you say that?" Toni asked. "All the signs point to this being from the non-boarders here."

"My mother says she doesn't trust signs. She trusts her own mind," Becky said, looking hard at Toni. "And she knows that whoever is doing this is just making it harder for themselves and everyone else. She has all the time in the world. Whoever it is, they're stuck here, they can't get out. People have tried escaping before, and she always catches them. Besides, she says she's already solved part of the puzzle, and that all of these people are just making themselves hated before they walk into her trap."

"Really?" said Toni, hiding her shiver. "Because it sounds to me like she'll have more and more people to trap. It seems like this whole thing is growing — that more and more people are joining. What happens if the whole school rises up?"

Becky pursed her lips. "You know what I think?"

"What?"

"I think that you sympathize — and I'm wondering if you might be one of the ones whose been doing this stuff," Becky said, the threat clear in her voice.

"You know what I think, Becky?" Toni said.

"What?"

"I think you're afraid."

"Well, I think that they're just bringing us down with them."

Charlie just watched as her table talked. She didn't trust herself to speak. She knew if she opened her mouth the truth might come tumbling out.

"Hey, Gnome," said a voice to her side. "Mind if I sit?"

Charlie slid over as Ann sat down beside her with a grin. Charlie couldn't help but smile back.

"Well, that symbol creeps me out," said one girl. "It's like a Satanic sign, like a horn, or a pentacle, or something."

"The pentacle isn't Satanic," Charlie said without thinking. "It's a Neo-Pagan sign and Pagans don't believe in the devil."

"Yeah but they worship trees and other gods and stuff," snorted one boy. "They don't believe in God."

"No," Charlie corrected again. "They believe that the Divine is seen in many ways, which are present in all people, creatures, and living things. They see God as something positive, all-incorporating, and greater than anyone could imagine."

"But do they believe in Jesus?" asked a girl.

"It's like ..." Charlie thought for a minute than said, "It's like ... the Divine, or God, is seen as something present in any positive spirituality. It's as if all the different religions are each like a path. They are all different, but they're all going to the same place. And the Divine is like a diamond — one person could pray to Jesus, another to Allah, another to Buddha, another to the Goddess — and they are all just different faces of the one."

"Right..." One boy scoffed, but one of the girls looked interested.

"I'm not explaining it right," Charlie sighed. "It's like — filtered light. If light hits a stained glass window, you are going to see blue light from one square, red from another, but all pure light is just white light. Has anyone seen *Star Wars*?"

"Now you lost me," Toni said.

"In *Star Wars* they talk about the Force: an unknowable, all inclusive essence that runs through us, penetrates us, is the source of all life, and contains all things within it. You can't really describe it, but it's something you can feel. We create gods to put this — whatever you call it — into terms we understand. So when you pray to God, or Jesus, or the Goddess, that is how you see the Divine, and how it appears to you."

"But don't pagans believe in magic?" asked one girl.

Charlie shifted uncomfortably. "Some."

"And do you?"

Charlie looked down. "I used to."

"Is that why you have wires on you?" said one girl.

"She has wires on her," Ann said lazily, "because the people who run this place are sick, twisted, and want her to think she's crazy."

"I think people who burn down half a building are pretty crazy," the girl who had questioned Charlie said. "Those people are criminals."

"Criminals?" Ann laughed. "Sweetie, if you take anyone and shock them, lock them up, and don't even let them speak, they become a 'criminal.'"

"Don't call me sweetie," the girl said.

Ann leaned forward. "Or what?" she asked softly.

"Are you threatening me?" the girl asked.

"No, *sweetie,*" Ann said, leaning back. "I wouldn't waste my time on you."

"See, this is why half the people here don't like you," the girl shot back.

"Good — the feeling is mutual," Ann said dryly.

"Seth keeps staring over here," said one boy. Charlie's head whipped up, and the blonde senior found and held her eyes.

Charlie felt as if her body had been doused with ice water. Her breathing turned fast, like a rabbit that has been spotted by a wolf. Charlie felt her stomach give out.

And then something else gave out. Her mind began to feel like a melting ice cube, and then as if that melted water was evaporating. Her mind was no longer quite there. The 'her' that was Charlie began to fall apart, as if her self was sand being swirled by wind. Thoughts and feelings and sights flitted by, but nothing saw them. There was no one viewing them, because Charlie was no longer together. Time wasn't flowing. It had no structure. It was random. Everything was shattered.

*Shattered.*

Charlie slowly came back together, but the world wasn't the same. Everything seemed as if she was looking through a plastic screen. It was cold, unreal, unfamiliar. Terror flooded her body, but she couldn't scream.

But Charlie could move, and move she did, getting up quickly and hurrying out of the cafeteria.

"She doesn't look too good," said one boy.

"Maybe she's going out to hug a tree," said the girl.

Ann waited only a moment before she got up and went after Charlie.

"Are they supposed to do that?"

"Who cares?" said the girl. "If they get in trouble, it's their fault."


"I ain't had chocolate in four damn weeks," Lieutenant said, frowning at her tray.

"It's banned," Melvin said grimly. "There's a bunch of stuff not on the menu anymore. I think anything with caffeine or anything too fatty is banned."

"Well I need chocolate," Lieutenant said stubbornly. "Helps my mood like ... be happier. I need chocolate, burgers, McDonalds, barbeque and triple-fried-southern-style anythin'."

"Well I don't," Melvin stated. "I can't gain any weight, or they'll put me on restriction. They're making me keep a food diary and all that crap. I don't even want to eat this," he said, pushing away his tray.

"Then don't," Lieutenant said, putting her head down on her tray.

"I can't! If I don't finish everything, they'll make me eat it mashed up with liver powder on it," Melvin stated.

"I hate this place," Lieutenant said.

"Don't say that," Melvin said, glancing at the others at their table.

"I don't care," Lieutenant said through her hands. "I don't care about anything."

"L," Melvin said, pushing her. "C'mon, get up."

"No. I'm tired, man," she said in a flat voice. "I should have stayed in bed. I tried, but my supervisor shocked me."

"L —"

"Please take your head off the table," said an aide who walked up beside Lieutenant.

"No thanks," was Lieutenant's muffled answer.

The shock elicited only a physical reaction — Lieutenant contracted, but didn't move her head.

"Get up," said the aide.

"Gimme a minute to think about that," Lieutenant said and was hit with another shock.

Melvin reached over and pulled her up by the shoulders, and got hit with a shock of his own.

"I was *helping* her," Melvin defended. The aide just hit him with another shock. Melvin stared daggers at the aide who watched them for a moment before walking away.

"And they wonder why we're depressed," Melvin said in a dead voice.

"This is what no chocolate does to the world," Lieutenant pronounced.


Ann walked into the girls' bathroom and looked around the empty white walls. "Charlie?"

There was no answer, but Ann listened for a second until she heard a sniffle. She looked under the stalls but saw no feet. "I know you're in here."

"We're not supposed to be talking," came the soft answer.

"What are you, on the walls like a spider?" Ann asked, looking under the stalls again.

"I'm sitting on the seat. Please — you'll get in trouble if they see us on the cameras."

"Yeah, well I need my trouble fix," Ann said locating which stall Charlie was in and walking into the next one. There were no cameras in the stalls. Ann pulled down the seat and sat with her knees up on the toilet. "You gonna tell me what's wrong?"

"I can't," Charlie whispered. "I can't ... I just ..."

"Charlie, nothing you say is gonna scare me," Ann said to the next stall. "Hit me."

"They're right," Charlie said so softly that Ann had to press her ear to the stall door to hear. "I am crazy. I — I should be in a hospital. I deserve these wires."

"Now that is bullshit," Ann declared. "You aren't crazy, remember? You're psychic. We decided this and —"

"No, no, *no*," Charlie said. The desperation in her voice made Ann's throat close up. "I ... I am crazy. My mind — I just went to *pieces*."

"Everybody does at one point, Gnome."

"No — not like other people. I ... my head was all in pieces," Charlie said, barely able to get the words out through her tears. "I wasn't there anymore, and I was — my brain isn't special, it's shattered. And I made Seth mad at me, and now ... now I'm a danger to everyone because I'm bad and —"

"If you don't stop saying that, I am going to be forced to shove your head down the toilet," Ann warned. "You do *not* deserve these wires. God, of *all* the people in this school you are the *last* person who deserves any of this. The rest of us are dangerous — *you* couldn't hurt someone if they were murdering you. If your brain has a problem you should be getting medicine and therapy and big cheesy teddy bears and gift certificates to Disney World, not shocks and liver powder."

Charlie laughed clumsily through her tears. "It's just ... this wouldn't be happening if I fought it harder. I wish I was tough like you."

"Oh please." Ann groaned with a smile, rubbing away the betraying drops under her eyes. "I'm not that tough — I'm just bitter and trigger happy. You don't want to be like me."

"It would be better than being like me," Charlie said. "At least you're not a head case."

"Oh I'm certifiable," Ann said. "I'm fucked six ways from Sunday, and I'm a major bitch. But Charlie, if there's something wrong with your head, it doesn't mean there's something wrong with *you*. You're a good person.

Not like the rest of us."

"I'd love to be one of 'the rest of us' though," Charlie admitted, leaning her head against the stall wall.

"Yeah," Ann said softly, leaning her head on the stall wall as well. "Me too."

There was a silence for a long minute, and then Ann gave a half-smile. "I think we need to get back now."

"I missed lunch," Charlie said forlornly. "Oh, lunch. Eatable, tasty lunch."

"You want my apple?" Ann offered.

"Sure."

Ann tossed it over the wall, and Charlie caught it. "Thanks."

"Welcome."

Ann looked down at the floor when Charlie opened her door and squinted.

"Is there water on the floor, or am I seeing things?" Charlie asked.

"No," Ann said, walking out and hearing the splashes. "You're not. Unless I am too, which is possible but —"

They walked out of the girls' bathroom, following the water to its source under the door of the boys' bathroom.

"Uh ... do we get in trouble for looking in there?" Charlie asked.

"We'll get in more for walking away from a problem," Ann said. They looked at each other and nodded before pulling the door open.


Toni flinched when she felt another paper clip hit her shoulder.

*Just ignore it, just —*

Another clip hit her, and she turned her head with a glare as Melvin flicked his eyes to the door. Their photography teacher was on the phone, and her eyes were widening with each second.

The class noticed when she walked out, leaving the aides in charge.

Someone threw a paper clip at one of them, and the aide stood up.

"Who threw that?" he demanded. The class stayed silent.

Everyone hated the aides. Even those who despised the boarders hated the new recruits. Toni understood why. It seemed like all of the aides were hired because they had never had any power in their lives, and now that they did they were going to abuse it throughly.

"Did you hear what happened?" whispered one girl. The aide looked around, but she had stopped talking and no one was turning her in.

"Someone flooded the boys' bathroom," said another voice. "And drew the sign on the walls as well."

"Stop talking," the aide demanded.

Toni glanced at Melvin who shook his head imperceptibly. *We didn't do this,* Toni realized. *This was someone else. Which means our plan is working.*


"They caught him, you know," the girl in the bus seat in front of Charlie whispered. Charlie listened carefully.

"I know," the girl's friend whispered back. "They found him with the cameras. They're still trying to find out how he did it."

"I just don't get why he would. I mean, he's not even a boarder."

"I heard he said like, right to Mrs. Carter's face, 'If you treat people like they're bad that's how they act' or something."

"Oh my God, what did she do?"

"She took him downstairs."

"They're not gonna put like, the wires on him right? I mean — he's just normal. He's Gregg. He's not crazy! They couldn't do that to a non-boarder right?"

"I don't know."

"Hey," ordered the guard patrolling the bus. "No talking."

Charlie pulled back, her mind working furiously.


"I want you both to stay here. Do not speak or interact, because there *are* cameras here," Sherry ordered before walking upstairs.

"Great. The only place we get to be private is in the bathroom," Ann mumbled darkly.

*Of course, that's how we get away with stealing her pills and sneaking out. And how that Gregg kid managed to flood the school bathroom.*

*I'd really love to send him flowers for a job well done, but since he's probably being shocked senseless, I don't know if it would help.*

"I needa do somethin," Joseph said.

"She didn't say anything about the radio," Ann pointed out. "Perfect." She happily turned up the country station.

"Yo, we've been tortured all day. I wanted a break now," Joseph pleaded.

Ann scowled, and changed the channel to some slow R&B song.

"C'mon then." Joseph grinned. "Dance for me."

"Uh-uh," Ann said, backing away. "Just cause you're cute you think you can make me embarrass myself."

"You can't pull that shyness on me," Joseph said. "You ain't shy."

"Well, I would rather not dance on *film,*" she said significantly, looking around, "unless I'm gettin' paid."

"C'mon," Joseph said, still laughing. He pulled her over so she was backed against his front and he wrapped his arms around her waist. "I'll pay you."

"Yeah?"

"Sure, in pennies," Joseph said brightly.

"Meanie."

"Yup!" Joseph said, moving her waist against his. "But I'm so charmin' and lovable."

"If you say so," Ann said and laughed when he picked her up and dropped her onto her feet again. "I *do*," Joseph said. "Which means I'm right, so dance girl."

"Bossy," Ann said, moving slowly against him.

"Yup!"

Ann rolled against him, and Joseph swallowed hard, his hands finding her waist. Ann was abruptly aware of how very, very warm his skin was, and she felt herself relax into his arms.

Joseph bit his lip, very conscious of where her body touched his. He moved, hesitantly, closer to her cheek, the scent of her making his skin burn.

"Ann," he whispered, almost pleading, and she let her head fall back onto his shoulder so she could stare into his insanely amber eyes. Ann knew she had a comment she was going to make here, but for her life she couldn't remember it.

Joseph's hands found hers, and he interlaced their fingers before moving so that his mouth was inches from hers. *I don't care — I'm goin' for broke here, and if I get slapped, so be it.*

"They'll see," Ann whispered, the tip of his nose brushing hers, her knees practically giving out.

"Let 'em." Joseph breathed back before kissing her softly.

Ann stiffened, her breath catching. He kissed her carefully, almost as if he was afraid of doing it wrong. Ann kept her eyes open. She always did this. It meant she was in control of the situation which was the only way she could stand to have it. She watched the way his head turned, the way he concentrated, the way he tried to make it perfect. A wave of heat hit her hard and, before she knew it, her eyes fell closed and with a tiny moan she opened her mouth.

Joseph felt the kiss turn, and he buried his hands in her hair as the kiss got faster, harder, more heated. He groaned as they stumbled against each other, backing up until he had Ann pressed into the fridge. His tongue stole into her hot mouth, and she pulled at his shirt. He pressed himself up against her as her nails found the sensitive skin at the back of his shoulders, urging him on.

A door slammed, and they shot apart instantly, so fast that Joseph bumped into the counter and winced.

*Shit, shit, shit,* Ann thought as Sherry came down the stairs.

*Ohfuck,* Joseph swore inwardly, pulling himself up and brushing his clothes down.

"What were you two doing?" Sherry demanded, her sharp eyes moving from one person to the other.

"Nothing," they said simultaneously. All three looked to the radio.

"We don't know how that happened," Joseph said. "It just turned on."

"Like that." Ann snapped her fingers.

"Maybe it's broken."

"Maybe the house is haunted."

"You do know," Sherry said airily, "that if you're caught fooling around, as boarders you get separated, and it's a three week shun for each of you?"

Ann nodded and Joseph followed.

"Good," Sherry said flatly. "Because if I find you been messing around, you'll be begging to be let out of this house."

*Now is your chance Toni. Do it.*

Toni moved over to slip the ground-up pill into Mrs. Carter's boiling tea water.

"Do you feel safe here?"

Toni pulled her hand back as Mrs. Carter turned around. "What?"

Mrs. Carter looked up from her seat at the kitchen table. The woman was dressed in a pink, spotted bathrobe. Her hair was down, and she wore no makeup. "Do you feel like you are safe at this school?"

Toni couldn't speak for a second. *Well let's see. Here I can be shocked, force fed, locked up, deprived of most of my rights — sure, I feel safe.*

Mrs. Carter sighed. "I can see the answer. I know." She looked off, eyes distant. "I know. You know that was the whole reason for starting this school. Kids were running around, causing every kind of trouble there was, getting beat up, drunk — it was awful, uncontrollable. People said it had to be something in the water. But with the Academy we put some structure in and it cleaned up. Kids could feel safe again, could live up to their real potential. And now —" Mrs. Carter stopped, and Toni wondered for one horrified, stunned moment if the woman would cry. "And now here we are, with fires and fights ... now how can they feel safe?" Mrs. Carter sighed. "Now we have to hit down harder, and I hate it."

Toni didn't say anything. She found herself swallowing hard, and focusing on the absurd slippers the woman was wearing — pink and fluffy slippers.

"Well," Mrs. Carter said, taking a deep breath. "Eventually we'll fix this, just as we fixed it before. And not just for the ones who aren't guilty." She shook her head absently, as if seeing into the near future. "For the ones doing this, too. Because to cause hurt like this, they must really be hurting."

Mrs. Carter looked up with a little shake and a wan smile. "You must be tired, Toni. You should go to bed."

"Yes," Toni said quietly. "I am. I will."


"What are we doing here?" Toni asked.

"Please don't tell me you gettin' amnesia, too." Lieutenant groaned, lying on her back. Joseph held up his lighter so they could see each other.

"We are in an old house," Joseph began slowly, "that Ann found so we —"

"No, no." Toni shook her head. "I mean — with our sabotage. Are we just trying to ruin the Academy?"

"We're starting a revolution," Charlie said, eyes glinting in the firelight.

"So that the school gets shut down?" Toni asked.

"Would that be possible?" Ann asked.

"Could be," Anton said. "I mean, it's probably the only way we ever gettin' out."

"Unless we escape," Lieutenant said. "And we tried that before."

"What happened?" Joseph asked.

"They caught us," Anton stated. "We actually made it into the woods, but they brought us back. Nowhere for us to go anyway — no money, even if we made it to another town."

"But we can beat this from the inside," Melvin said. "I mean, people are already joining us. People who aren't even boarders are joining. Gregg — he isn't messed up at all."

"Do you think they'll hook him up, too?" Joseph asked, gesturing to the wires.

"If they do it could either help us or break us," Charlie said, eyes roving around the circle. "It could show people that they have to join us — or make them all too scared to join us."

"How do we make it so that they turn wit' us?" Anton asked.

"We have to keep fighting," Charlie explained. "And we have to make it clear that we're not fighting the students. We're fighting the school."

"We gotta be careful," Melvin said. "They're gonna come down harder than ever on us with this."

"What do we do then?" Joseph asked. "Any ideas?"

"We wait," Charlie said. "We wait for them to make the next move. If they hit hard over everyone equally, it will turn more people against the school." Charlie gave a sinister smile. "Isn't it lucky that they think it's the non-boarders doing all this?"

"You planned this from the beginning didn't you?" Toni asked, and Charlie just shrugged with a smile.

"Kinda ironic," Joseph said, watching everyone around the circle. "You know, how they send us here to fix our behavior and stop us before we become criminals — and here we go, becomin' their worst fear."

"We're not ... proving them right, right?" Toni asked.

"What do you mean?" Ann asked.

"I just ... aren't we proving them right?" Toni asked. "By doing all this they think we're dangerous and crazy. Don't we prove them right by doing it?"

"You sayin' it's wrong to fight back against people shockin' us and treatin' us like we're in prison?" Anton asked.

"No, I'm just saying we shouldn't give them reason to do this to us," Toni argued.

"No," Charlie said. "We have to make sure that people see us as fighting for them. I say we wait until the Academy plays their hand before we make our move. If they hit everyone with more restrictions, then when we fight it makes us look like the heroes. Does that answer your question?" she asked Toni.

"Yeah." Toni nodded, even though the answer was no.

# chapter fifteen mad

**Toni was walking to history when Lieutenant gave her the sign. Just** two taps on her thigh — nothing that could be seen as suspicious.

*So they gave him the wires after all.*

Toni walked into her class. Charlie looked up from her seat on the other side of the room. Toni blinked once.

Charlie blinked back, and Toni looked down before an aide could see anything suspicious.

*They just made their biggest mistake. They played their hand.*

*Our turn.*


Joseph kept his head down and focused on the food he was supposed to be eating.

*All natural, no chemicals, special diet ... in other words, disgusting.*

*God I miss Wendy's.*

There were a few muffled sounds of disapproval from a table full of girls, and Joseph looked up as Ann strode past. He knew he wasn't the only one watching, and the thought brought the sick taste of jealousy to his mouth, making his food even less appealing.

The girls sneering at the table were giving Ann especially nasty looks. Ann stopped and blew a kiss to all of them before turning and walking away, the hand bent behind her back flashing her middle finger. Joseph laughed, and she caught his eye and winked before turning quickly away.

*The school didn't catch us kissin', which means Sherry is definitely tryna hide her little problem from them,* he thought, poking his fork at whatever vegetable it was that he was supposed to be eating.

There was movement, and a boy sat down at their table. Joseph glanced at Gregg, the boy who flooded the bathroom, as he settled himself, wincing at what Joseph knew were wires under his clothes.

*This place doesn't even feel like the real world anymore. It's more of a game. Just one where you only get to play once.*


Charlie shivered as she walked into the bathroom, the aide who had escorted her there staying outside.

*How am I supposed to go to the bathroom when I know they're watching?*

She looked into the mirrors above the sink for a second. She knew she should write the feeling off. *Paranoid delusion. One of the most common: the belief that others are watching you, and/or monitoring your thoughts,* she recalled, just as she had read it in the textbook.

*But —*

*This isn't a delusion,* she thought firmly. *No — because it makes sense. Gregg vandalized the bathroom. The one place they didn't have cameras. So now they put them up, because they can't take any chances.*

Charlie looked at herself in the mirror. Her hair was messily brushed and her face was pale, making the dark shadows under her eyes even easier to see. She frowned as she pulled a bit of asparagus out of her teeth. *Have I brushed this morning? How often are you supposed to brush? Once a day? Twice? Only on weekends?*

*Loss of basic self-care skills: the first sign of —*

Charlie rushed into the stall and knelt down on the floor, putting her head between her legs.

*No, no, it's not happening ... I'm psychic, not schizo, everybody thinks so. I'm — I'm —*

*Breathe.*

Charlie closed her eyes, shutting out all vision. The sound of her heart beating in her ears was deafening — or was that supposed to be the blood rushing there? She couldn't remember. She just knew everything was becoming louder — the drip from the leaky faucet, the sound of her own rapid breathing, the rustle of her clothes. If she could just focus, if she could just calm herself ...

"She's here."

*Oh no. Not Voices.*

"Well then, let her in."

*That's Mrs. Carter. When did Mrs. Carter become one of the voices my head?*

"But —" someone, a male, answered. "Do you think we should tell her what's been — ?"

"Have you never met the Headmistress, John? You can't lie to that woman. It's been tried and it always fails."

Charlie didn't open her eyes, but something in her head clicked.

*Mrs. Carter's office is just next door.*


"We didn't expect you in until —"

"Yes, well you seem very good at not expecting things," the Headmistress said bluntly, striding into the principal's office.

"We're hitting back in every way we can," Mrs. Carter said, her voice registering mild annoyance as her superior walked around her office, picking up and putting down things, not facing her square on.

"You seem to be hitting back very hard," the Headmistress noted, picking up a paperweight.

"It's aversive therapy," Mrs. Carter said, crossing her arms.

"And what are you using as the positive reinforcement?" the tall woman asked lightly, tossing and deftly catching the globe. "Now that these problem students have burned the Big Reward Store?"

"That will be back up in just a few days," Mr. Alderman assured.

"But how many students will feel safe enough to go back in?" the Headmistress asked. "An interesting choice, to hit the place we use as a reward for those students who obey our rules. A clever way to make it easier to disobey."

"Hold on — let's not give too much credit here," Mr. Alderman interjected. "These aren't guerilla warriors. These are angry, self-destructive teens that are causing trouble any way they can."

The Headmistress caught Mr. Alderman's eyes and just held them for a minute. "I give credit where credit is due, Mr. Alderman," she said. "As of now, they seem to have the upper hand. We still haven't caught the students who have been doing this."

"We have one student under suspicion," Mrs. Carter defended. "And we found the latest perpetrator."

"Yes." The Headmistress nodded, flipping casually through Mrs. Carter's files. "Gregg Hayman and Seth Dryer ... hmm." The Headmistress paused. "Funny. I had thought Seth to be more content since we gave him so many privileges. He's smart enough to pull this off, and certainly the adrenaline rush and the dismissive attitude towards societal norms would appeal to him, but ... he is far too clever to do something so erratic when he could have power so much more easily by playing along."

Mr. Alderman gave a little laugh. "What is that, women's intuition?"

Again the Headmistress fixed him with a quick glance, and again he shut up, bristling inside. The only thing he enjoyed about this meeting was seeing someone take Mrs. Carter down a few rungs.

"I am a behavioral scientist, Mr. Alderman," she informed. "We know more about Seth Dryer than he knows about himself simply by scientific method. It's not psychic, it's psychology. I am simply noting the pieces that don't fit. For example, this." The Headmistress tossed out Gregg's file. "Gregg was not much of one to act out until now. Not even one of our boarder students."

"We think this is not a boarder problem," Mrs. Carter offered. "That was what Seth wrote on the banner, even though he insists he didn't."

"Still?" The Headmistress looked interested. "Even after he has lost all his influence and had to deal with all of the consequences?"

"He says he was framed," Mrs. Carter said, standing up very straight. "No matter what, he sticks to the story. Of course, our students usually lie."

"And we treat them accordingly," the Headmistress said.

"Are you saying you want us to abandon our methods?" Mrs. Carter's voice rose. "Stop the use of aversive stimuli? Ease up?"

"You think we should increase these tactics?" the Headmistress asked.

"It would stop any chance they have to cause this destruction," Mrs. Carter said emphatically. "It would protect all the students — including the ones who are attacking our school."

"Has it ever occurred to you that expanding the use of these tactics," the Headmistress posed, "might encourage more students to join this little uprising?"

"If they are presented with the choice of fighting or the choice of avoiding punishment," Mrs. Carter stated, "any sane student would choose not to deal with the consequences."

"Mrs. Carter, we are dealing with teenagers," the Headmistress said with a hint of a smile. "Whoever gave you the idea they were sane misinformed you."

"If you approve these increased aversives, and we aren't the only school which uses them," Mrs. Carter spoke quickly, "I am certain we can nip this before it goes any further. Look, we are dealing with students who have broken through security, who have burned down wire —"

The Headmistress froze and then turned, finally meeting the principal's eyes. "Where? Show me."


Toni's photography class was in mini rebellion.

"What makes you think you can tell us what to do?" said one girl to one of the aides the minute the teacher left the classroom.

"You need to be quiet," the aide said.

"Or what?" asked another student. "You gonna hit me?"

"I'll report you," the aide said, walking over menacingly.

"Oh, so you're gonna shock us like you did Gregg? What gives you the right?"

"I'm in charge right now —" the aide sputtered.

"Did you even graduate high school?"

The other aide picked up the phone to call the office, and someone threw a shoe at him to cheers.

*Holy shit,* Toni thought. *This cannot be happening — everyone here will get so screwed.*

*It's awesome.*

"Hey — who threw that? Was it you?" the aide practically screamed, still dialing in for help. The other grabbed the kid by the shoulders, and he struggled to get away as the aide dragged him to the doors.

"Let him go!" someone yelled.

"They're taking him away like Gregg!" said one girl.

*Oh I get it,* Toni realized. *These are Gregg's friends. That's why they're doing this.*

The boy being pulled away didn't seem too worried about what was going to happen to him when he was brought down to Discipline. Instead, he encouraged his friends to chant 'Gregg' and kicked at the phone the other aide was using to call for security. He missed and hit the light switch so hard it yanked out of the wall, plunging the room into chaotic darkness.

Toni felt something soft hit her and heard one of the aides calling for a light. The only light Toni could see came from the screen of the absent teacher's computer.

*The computer.*

The idea hit Toni so fast she didn't stop to consider how ridiculous and dangerous it was. She just ran — or more accurately, bumbled — over to the teacher's desk, swiftly opening her email.

"Someone turn on the light! Quick — open the door!"

Toni typed as fast as her fingers would go, her left foot tapping anxiously as she finished the message and clicked 'Send All.'

"Here — here!"

Mr. Harris, the photography teacher, burst into the room along with three security guards who immediately located the three main problem students, pulled them out roughly, and barked for the other students to form a line. Seeing that the fun was over, the class followed the teacher out silently now.

"What did you do?" Melvin's whisper rose hairs on the back of Toni's neck.

"You'll see," she answered, before forming her face into a liar's mask.

"They cut the wires under the fence in two areas," Mrs. Carter explained as the Headmistress touched the edges of the melted wire. "Another group jumped out of a smashed window onto a truck near the wire, and over the barrier. But this ..."

"The edges have been melted," the Headmistress noted. "And then kicked down."

"That part we can't figure out," Mr. Alderman explained. "How did they burn the edges? A flamethrower?"

"Something like," the Headmistress said with a small smile. "You said they smashed a window? One of our windows?" She smiled again. "They must be very strong."

"They must have used something — must have been carrying something," Mr. Alderman said. "But we didn't find any shards, only some bits of blood, as if someone had used their arms, but...that's not possible. No one could be strong enough to break through that glass, not a student."

"Many things are possible, John," the Headmistress said, turning to look at him. "They simply haven't been cataloged and put in our science books yet. They —"

Mrs. Carter's phone rang and she placed it to her ear. "Yes?"

"There was another Incident."

The principal's eyes flashed to the Headmistress and back down. "Where? How?"

"In the photography room," Mr. Harris explained over the phone. "I left the room, and the aides were unable to control the students. We have the problem students isolated but ... well one of them kicked the lights out, and while they were down and I was out of the room, I guess ... my computer ..."

"Get to the point, Mr. Harris."

"Check your email."

Mrs. Carter looked up. "We — we all seem to have an email."

The teachers ran through their phones, and Mrs. Carter quickly pulled up her email on her Blackberry.

"Oh God," Ms. Donelle whispered. "Did you see —"

"I have it right in front of me, Kerry," Mrs. Carter said sharply, before reading it aloud.

```
The more you try and control us, the more we
won't be controlled.
Give us the right to be treated like you.
And you won't catch us, because we're
everyone.
```

"There's that 'us' again," Mr. Alderman noted as Mrs. Carter passed her Blackberry to the Headmistress. "'Us' who?"

"'Us' the students," the Headmistress said, her hands running over the screen. "Mrs. Principal," she said suddenly, meeting the other woman's eyes. "I assume you have some ideas on how to handle this?"

"Yes —"

"Then you have my full confidence and approval — but be careful," the Headmistress warned. "We are running a behavior modification program here — not a prison."

Mrs. Carter nodded.

"We can find out who did this," Mr. Alderman said confidently. "We won't be outsmarted by a bunch of teenagers."

"You *have* been outsmarted by a bunch of teenagers," the Headmistress said curtly. "They are clearly as smart as most of you and smarter than some of you. We won't win because we are cleverer, we will win because we are older, more experienced, and adult. These are clever ... *talented* adolescents — but they are adolescents. Young, proud, courageous, impulsive, passionate, and easily swayed and turned, especially against each other."

The Headmistress nodded at the silent circle and began walking off.

"Where are you going?" Mrs. Carter asked, surprised.

The Headmistress kept moving. "I am going to have a chat with someone who will help in doing what we have to."

"Which is?"

"Catch them, Evelyn. Nothing changes until we catch them."

# chapter sixteen hatter

"**Mom?**" Becky asked carefully. "**Can I ... can I ask you a question**
without you getting mad?"

Toni and Katrina froze, waiting for Mrs. Carter's response.

"Of course, Becky," Mrs. Carter said. "You can always ask. If I can't
answer, I will tell you."

"They say — everyone is saying," Becky began, eyes moving nervously.
"That Seth is the head of this whole 'rebellion' thing. I just — is it true? And
— didn't you catch him? Won't you be able to end it now?"

Mrs. Carter slowly placed down her fork and crossed her hands on the
table. "We found out that it is Seth's handwriting on the banner, and Seth
had confessed to both acts of sabotage against the school. We've —" Mrs.
Carter cleared her throat. "He has refused to tell us who the others are, or
what they are planning next. We don't think he will be able to do anything
since he is so closely watched, but he and Gregg seem to have become martyrs
for some reason." Mrs. Carter's upper lip twitched. "We are worried because
they are attracting so many 'followers' who seem to be able to sneak away
as if they are ghosts—"

The principal stopped abruptly. "You don't have to worry." Mrs. Carter
bit lightly on her tongue. "We have it under control."


Ann padded quietly through the sleeping Sherry's room to her bathroom,
hoping the extra doses of Valium the woman had taken would hold. She also
hoped she wouldn't be waiting alone in the bathroom all night.

*It was just a stupid fight. We have them all the time. And he doesn't really have any right to be mad, since he started it.*

*Okay.*

*So maybe I started it — but still! I —*

*Fuck.*

*I hope he's there.*

Ann bit her lip and pushed open the bathroom door. No one.

*Great. I fucked up — like always.*

A breeze ran over her face as she turned to go —

"Ann?"

She turned back to see Joseph's silhouette in the window and gave a slow smile. "Hey."

"Hey," Joseph said back, just staring for a moment. "You ... comin' out?"

"No, I was gonna go wake up Sherry and see if we could go out and do shots," Ann said weakly. Joseph half-smiled, and Ann moved across the room. Joseph took hold pof both of her arms and helped her out of the window.

"Careful — the edges of the top are still hot where I melted 'em," he said softly. Ann ducked her head down as she moved her legs through. Her skin flushed when her body pressed up against him and they stumbled out a bit, forcing Joseph to grab her waist. They fell back onto the roof.

There came a sound from Sherry's bed and they both froze, the cold night air whipping at their black clothes.

Sherry turned over and quieted. They breathed out.

"This is better than some borin' restaurant, right?" Joseph grinned as she lay half on him.

"Oh, yeah. Better than dancing or drinking too," Ann said, sticking her tongue out at him before getting up. They both slid lower on the slanted garage roof. This had been Joseph's idea. Two weeks before he had made a big presentation of covering her eyes and sneaking her out onto the garage roof for their first date. Since then they had been coming here almost every night. Ann liked it. It struck her as romantic, which made her annoyed at herself.

"When we get back to New York," Joseph said, leaning back on the tar, "we will go out."

"Oh yeah?" Ann asked, leaning back too. "Where will we go?"

"I know an awesome place in the Bronx — it's not underage, but I got a friend who can get me in." Joseph glanced over at her with his smart-ass smile. "You'll hafta get in on your looks."

"Great date *you* are," Ann said, narrowing her eyes. "What am I supposed to do? Open my shirt for the guy?"

"NO," Joseph said, loud enough that Ann hit him lightly. "Not that," he grumbled, and Ann could feel the tension there. She didn't really wanna go back to that stupid fight on the bus. "So what'll we do once we get inside?"

"Once I've snuck you inside," Joseph continued. "Then we'll get drinks — beer for me —"

"Tequila for me!" Ann said brightly.

"No tequila for you," Joseph said and gave his soft wheezing laugh when she pushed him.

"Why not?" Ann said, pouting.

"Because jail ain't a fun date, and if you start drinkin' I got the feelin' that's where we'll end up," Joseph said.

Ann laughed, she couldn't help it. They had been doing this now for four weeks. They slipped through the house dressed in all black into Sherry's bathroom and out onto the garage roof so they could talk, laugh, and kiss as best they could without falling off and killing themselves.

"I'm sorry," Joseph said after a moment of silence. "For ... what I said —" He swallowed. "You know —"

Ann nodded. They had had a fight earlier in the day. As usual it was something minor. They were both supposed to put the dishes away and clean up, but Joseph was shirking his half — or at least, that was how Ann saw it. Joseph thought differently. Ann stated that he was lazy and useless. Joseph said she just wanted a reason to be a bitch, and from there it became a rundown of each other's faults with lots of harsh language thrown in.

It ended up escalating so much so that Sherry had to separate them. The fact that their supervisor didn't report them further confirmed his suspicions, that Sherry was as afraid of being caught doing something wrong as they were.

"I just don't get why you got so mad to begin with," Joseph said. "You don't even care about doing the dishes. You don't mind it like I do."

"Yeah, but then you gave that crap about 'It's a woman's job to clean,'" Ann pointed out.

"I was *kiddin',* Ann. It's called sarcasm. Plus, I was just tryna get you mad," Joseph admitted.

"Why do you do that?" Ann said. "It's so annoying, Joseph!"

"See?" Joseph laughed, pointing at her face. "You get all cute when you get pissed. So really, it's your fault. If you didn't look cute mad, I wouldn't get you mad."

"Grr."

"I'm sorry," Joseph repeated. "But you get me mad on purpose sometimes too. Admit it."

"Me? Never at all." Ann sniffed.

"Liar, li-ar!"

"Never, Ne-ver!"

"Liar." Joseph scooted over to her. "Liar." He rolled her toward him. "Liar," he whispered to her.

Ann pinched his nose. "You aren't really sorry," Ann said, her eyes narrowing. "You just think if you say sorry when I'm up here, you'll get to kiss me."

"No," Joseph said. "Maybe I just met you up here to talk. Maybe I don't want to kiss you."

"Fine," Ann said, leaning back. "You can move over there."

"Maybe I will," Joseph said moving back away from her. Ann just smiled and arched up her back with a little moan, stretching herself like a cat.

Joseph glanced over at her and swallowed but then looked decidedly up. "Nice stars," he noted.

"They're gorgeous," Ann purred and saw him shift. She grinned.

*He-he. I like this game. I always win.*

Joseph looked carefully up. They would do this, tease each other, turn each other on to see who would last longer. Ann usually won.

*Well this time I'ma win, girl.*

Joseph looked up at the sky and busied himself counting stars. One, two, three ... those looked like a belt, those looked like a star, those looked like a woman's figure —

*Dammit.*

"It's pretty warm for November isn't it?" Ann asked lightly.

"It's thirty degrees out."

"Warm for me," Ann said as she took off her coat slowly, eyes closed, so that it pulled up a little bit of her shirt and showed her bare stomach. She shook out her hair, letting it fall over her shoulders, and turned over to smile invitingly at Joseph.

Joseph pushed the hair out of her face as he launched over and caught her mouth, bearing her down on her coat as their tongues met in each other's mouths.

Ann arched up against him, making him groan. "I win," she said brightly.

"I'm on top, so I say *I* win," Joseph shot back, just laughing when she shoved him, her hands running up under his shirt over his abs, making his breath catch. Ann loved it when his eyes rolled up just a little.

He leaned down and kissed her neck, biting and sucking on her, and it was her turn to moan, pulling him down closer so she could feel his heart beating in his chest against hers. She tugged on his shirt to pull his mouth back to hers, and Joseph grinned. "Someone's hot tonight."

"So?" Ann said, raking her nails gently up his back, making him groan helplessly.

"Love — love when you do that," he managed to moan. "No fair."

"Yes fair," Ann said, dragging her lips up his neck to kiss his chin and work her way to his mouth. He pushed his tongue inside slowly, tasting her fully. She gasped into his mouth when he pressed down against her, and she kissed him back harder.

It took them both a minute to realize they were slipping.

"Shit!" Joseph yelped, grabbing for the pipe on the upper roof to keep from falling. Ann tried to dig her nails into the shingles, screeching in pain as she slipped faster.

Joseph grabbed her wrist with his free hand, and Ann dug her nails into his skin, making him swear again as he pulled her up.

"What?"

They both stared at each other as they heard Sherry get up.

*She'll see,* Joseph realized, staring around wildly. *She'll —*

*Wait.*

Joseph pulled Ann up beside him and then reached up and put his hands on the upper roof. Pushing off, he leapt onto the upper roof, then reached down to help Ann up.

Ann grabbed the edge of the roof with one arm and flipped herself up.

"Showoff," Joseph grumbled.

"At least I have some talents," she whispered back.

"Whoa."

"What?" Ann asked. Joseph was looking away, and she snapped her fingers to get his attention. "Earth to —"

"C'mere." Joseph grabbed her hand, and together they stood up shakily. "Look," Joseph whispered, turning Ann's shoulders so she was staring out.

"Oh, God."

From their vantage point they could see everything: not only the town, and the school, but the forests outside, a glistening streak of silver that was a river, and even beyond —

"Yo, there's another town." Joseph pointed, wobbling. Ann grabbed his hands, and he held onto her arms.

"We must be able to see for miles," Ann said. Everything looked so small, like a play town, something they could reach down and touch. They stood in silence for a moment, just watching.

"It's like," Joseph mused quietly, "like we're a million miles away from everything ... almost feels like we could step out and walk over the air and nothin' could stop us."

"Yeah." Ann leaned back against him, balancing as they stared out. "Um ... Joseph?"

"Uh-huh?"

"How do we get down?"

"Jump," Joseph said. "We slide to the edge, hang off, and just let go. And pray. We do lots of praying."

"Great, nothing too easy," Ann said sarcastically, looking at Joseph.

"You ready?" Joseph asked, and she nodded, nervous. He wet his lips. "Okay. One ... two ... three."


"I think the Headmistress knows," Charlie said.

"Nah." Lieutenant shook her head. "If she knew, we'd all be in Discipline, strapped down and restrained and shocked till we couldn't move. She don't know."

"How did you even hear her?" Anthony asked. He had informed them it was Anthony tonight.

"Mrs. Carter's office is on the other side of the second floor girls' bathrooms," Charlie explained.

"Yeah, but there's still a wall between the two," Melvin pointed out.

"I just heard, okay?" Charlie said, voice rising.

"We believe you, Charlie," Ann soothed from where she was leaning on Joseph. "We're just not sure what to do with it."

"What is her real name?" Charlie asked, curious. "Or is 'Headmistress' her official name, like Madonna?"

"Don't know," Melvin explained. "She doesn't show up too much. She leaves stuff to Mrs. Carter mostly."

"She was there when I was brought in," Lieutenant revealed. "I remember kinda what she looks like. Tall, red hair, coulda been in her thirties ... I don't know. I wasn't exactly able to see clearly."

"How come?" Joseph asked.

"Because about five minutes after I was pulled in, they stuck a needle in my arm, and I knew no more," Lieutenant said, leaning back on her elbows. "I was out for a whole week, then I woke up strapped down in a white room with padded walls. It was like some horror movie shit."

"I hate horror movies." Charlie shivered.

"I love horror movies!" Joseph and Ann said together. "I love serial killer ones," Joseph said. "Hello, Clarice," he whispered in a Hannibal Lector voice to Ann who just pinched his nose so that it sounded squeaky instead of scary.

"I like how the girl is always the one to survive at the end," Ann said serenely, still pinching his nose. "Just like in real life."

"D'ats dot dru," Joseph tried to say.

"Yo, have you ever noticed how in horror movies sex always gets in there right before somebody gets merked?" Anthony noted. "Like, they'll always have a mad arousin' scene right before somebody gets their head diced like a tomato? Kills all my sex drive. Once I went to see *Texas Chain Saw Massacre* wit' my sister and they had this guy get picked up and put on a meat hook, and I'm like, 'You — you know we can ... we can go if you want.' And my sister's like 'What? It's just gettin' to the good part!' And I'm like — oh. Okay." Anthony whimpered, pretending to sink down in a chair.

"I thought you weren't scared of anything?" Lieutenant asked.

"Everybody's scared of somethin'," Anthony defended. "I'm scared a' lots of things. Death, blood, spiders —"

"When I was twelve I had a tarantula named Spot!" Charlie said brightly, and Anthony jumped about a foot in the air and shook himself.

"Spot?" Toni said, raising a brow.

"I think it's a good name for a tarantula," Charlie said stubbornly.

"It's cute," Ann affirmed, and Charlie grinned.

"You think a tarantula's cute?" Joseph said, eyes widening.

"What's wrong with thinking a tarantula's cute?" Ann said. "I think you're cute, don't I?"

Joseph's lower lip popped out. His head dropped and he got up to walk away.

"Aww, you made him feel sad," Lieutenant laughed.

"Guys," Charlie began.

"Joseph, stop sulking," Ann ordered.

Joseph just walked over into a corner and stood without facing back. "I'm not sulkin', I just don't wanna be round people who think I'm ugly," he fake whined.

"Guys —" Charlie said louder, trying to get their attention.

"I don't think you're ugly, you —" Ann stood up and pulled him back by the arms.

"No!" Joseph stood, folding his arms as she tried to move him, laughing. "What, you gonna pick me up?"

Ann narrowed her eyes. "No." Swiftly she yanked his legs out from under him and then pulled him back so they both fell clumsily down. "Ha! I win!"

"Ow," Joseph moaned. "My head — you want me to wake up wit' amnesia like Anthony?"

"Sure, then you won't remember to act silly," Ann said, pulling Joseph so that his head was in her lap, and yanking down his hood so it covered his eyes. She kissed his lips. "There. That looks sexy."

"Really?" Melvin asked dubiously.

"I can't see," said the voice under the hood.

"Yes, very sexy. Can I borrow him?" Toni asked.

"No!" Ann pouted, clutching his head. "My sexy."

"Sexy is dyin' of asphyxiation," the hood groaned.

"Sexy is not allowed to talk," Ann said.

"Oh, yeah?" Joseph said, flipping her over so he was on top. "Yo, we're gonna have a five minute commercial break here," Joseph said as Ann tried lazily to push him off. "So y'all can just ... go pick flowers or something."

"Guys," Toni said, loudly over everyone's laughter. "I heard something. When I was at dinner Becky asked Mrs. Carter if it was true that Seth was leading all this. And Mrs. Carter as good as said yes, and she said that he and Gregg were like martyrs for the whole school."

"Right." Melvin snorted. "Martyr. Right. To be a martyr you have to have a heart first. Seth couldn't be a martyr if Jesus beat him over the head with his cross."

"I take offense at that."

Seth grinned as he leaned on the open door. "But I think I can forgive you."

Anthony, Lieutenant, Joseph and Ann jumped to their feet. Melvin froze, and Toni stared at Charlie.

"I tried to tell you," Charlie whimpered.

"Get out," Joseph growled. "Yo, you guys run out the back."

"Relax. We come in peace," Seth laughed, holding up two fingers.

"We?" Toni whispered.

Seth grinned over at her. "You — didn't know you would be here."

"How did *you* know to be here?" Lieutenant demanded. Seth winked. "Little birdie told me."

"We're caught." Melvin choked. "The Academy knows."

"No, actually, they don't," said a voice from outside the door. Seth gestured like an announcer as another boy — Gregg — stepped inside.

"We do, but that's it," Gregg said.

"How did you guys find out?" Anthony demanded, his face darkening.

"I told you," Seth said, looking long at Anthony. "A little birdie said."

"What the fuck do you want?" Joseph growled.

Seth walked closer to Joseph, his eyes boring into the shorter boy's fiercely before he stopped and laughed. "Chill man," Seth said in his smooth, mocking voice. "I'm here to help."

"We're good, thanks," Ann said, arms crossed. Seth's eyes flicked over to her. "Maybe you're forgetting, but I'm *already* helping you," he said, his low voice almost hissing. "Since it's *my* handwriting on the banner, and *me* who got charged with the fire, and *me*," Seth's voice rose, "who everyone thinks is the head of your little rebellion. Well ..." Seth shrugged, looking around.

"If I'm gonna be taking all of the blame, I want some of the damn fun."

Charlie moved over to Lieutenant, who caught her eye. Charlie shook her head.

"No," Lieutenant said. "It doesn't work like that. We set it up so no one was supposed to know who the other people doin' sabotage were so if we get caught no one can turn someone else in."

"You guys are meeting all together," Gregg said. "Isn't that breaking that rule?"

Seth tilted his head and moved to the right — Charlie scurried left. Seth looked over Lieutenant's head, and Charlie leaned down. Seth bent over. "You," he said with another smile. "I shoulda known you'd be here."

"You don't really want to help," Charlie said, back pressed against the rotting wall.

"You reading my mind again?" Seth whispered. He leaned forward a little more. "Boo!"

Charlie shivered.

"No, *Madame* is wrong," Seth said, drawing himself up. "I do want to help." His face became harsh with anger. "The Academy fucked me over. I played by all their damn rules and then when I get framed they don't believe me, and I get *this*." He spread his arms to show all the wires along his arms, chest and back. "So fine. I never liked rules much anyway. Now I want some payback, so what's the plan, friends?"

The room was quiet, and Seth rolled his eyes. "Don't tell me you don't *have* one?"

"Safer that way," Anthony said. "That way if they catch us —"

"They won't know the plan," Seth cut him off. "What do you think you're doing then? What's your motive?"

Again there was silence, then —

"Revolution," Ann said.

Seth half-grinned. "Right. And then what? If the whole school rebels, what do you think will happen? It'll shut down, and you'll all get sent back home?" His voice was sweetly mocking. "You really think that'll happen just because the students break some windows? And now, with the Headmistress here?" Seth scoffed. "No. The only way to make sure you get free of this school is to make sure there is no school."

"What are you sayin'?" Lieutenant asked sharply.

"You know what I'm saying," Seth said softly. "Take the school down to ground zero."

"No." Anthony shook his head. "No way. It won't work, for one thing. Two, it might kill people, and we ain't murderers. Three, if it *did* and we got sent back, it'd be in handcuffs."

Seth laughed outright. "Man, you think they'd send you to jail after everything you've seen? Where you could testify against them? No, no they're not gonna send you home with evidence against them. They're not gonna send you away from here. But if their time is spent picking up the pieces here? You'll have a chance to run away."

Seth watched the group exchange looks and gestures.

"We can't hurt anyone," Toni said, throat constricting.

"We won't do it when people are in there," Seth said, voice harsh with disdain. "We'll just do enough damage that they won't have a school to keep us in."

"That's a terrible plan," Joseph said. "If we do that then it'll definitely get us caught, and then they'll fuckin' kill us. Plus, the whole school ain't gonna join against 'em, and that's what we need if we're gonna bring this place down."

"You want the whole school with you?" Seth said. "I can do that in a week. But this is the plan that will work."

"Maybe we have our own plans," Melvin said.

"Maybe you should have thought of that before you brought my name into this!" Seth yelled, making Charlie jump.

"Look," Seth said, seemingly calming himself. "I wanna screw over this school as much as the rest of you — whether you trust me or not, which you don't, I can tell by your faces — you kinda have to deal with me now. I know enough that I could turn you in and get all my privileges back if I wanted to." Seth looked around again. "I think the fact that I haven't should at least earn me some trust."

"Fine. We'll work with you, but it doesn't mean we have to follow your plan," Anthony said.

"My plan," Seth countered, "will work. That's all that should matter. I've lived here for a long time. I know how to break their rules without getting caught, I know how to make it so they don't find out, and I know how to rip something apart till it's nothing but fuckin' shreds." Seth spat out the last word, and waited. "So?"

"You think you can have everyone on our side?" Lieutenant asked, disbelieving.

"I can have anyone I want on my side," Seth said. He took the silence for agreement and clapped his hands. "We're all gonna be great friends. I can just tell!"


Toni felt Seth nudge her forward.

"Do it," he whispered under his breath.

Toni swallowed and raised her hand.

"Yes?" Mrs. Waters said.

"May I go to the bathroom?"

Mrs. Waters nodded, and Toni tried look as innocent as possible. She walked down the side hall to the bathroom and noticed the door labeled *Supplies* propped half-open. Seth had done his part. Now it was her turn.

"I can't believe we're actually listenin' to this fuckin' bastard," Lieutenant said to Anton as they moved down the side hall. Someone a classroom over swore as his computer crashed.

"Keep your voice down, L. They can still hear us, even if the cameras is down," Anton warned.

"You sure they'll go down?" Lieutenant asked. "How you makin' sure?"

"I don't know, okay?" Anton whispered back sharply. "But they ain't figured out a way to make technical things stop messin' up around me yet. I'll bet that right now all them cameras just seein' static."

"Well let's just hurry up and get this shit done with," Lieutenant growled.

"Glad to see you ain't depressed anymore," Anton shot back. "Now you're just bitchy."

"I don't trust Seth. He's a liar, he hates us, and he got no reason to help us. What if he turns us over to the principal?"

"He's helpin' us now, right?" Anton said, leaning against the wall and glancing down the hall. He could see the movement of Mrs. Waters' hands as she taught.

"How did he find us?" Lieutenant asked, as Anton leaned further over. "Either he just tracked us and found out, in which case anybody can find us—or one of us told." He wasn't looking at her. "Anton!"

"Quiet," he ordered. "I gotta concentrate."

Joseph slid into a seat beside Gregg, his eyes fixed downwards. He was still boiling with anger that —

"Well, look who is at my table." Seth grinned. "My friends."

"Friends? You need to go look up the word," Joseph muttered darkly, staring up at Seth. "I'll lend you a dictionary."

"Oh so you've been *reading*?" Seth whispered back while Gregg looked around. The three of them were alone at the table. "How's that been working out for you?"

Joseph shook his head. "There are so many things you don't know man, you define ignorant."

"Now that's where you're wrong *muchacho*," Seth said back then stopped.

"Look, we're all working together here, right? As students, I mean," he said, looking swiftly around. The aides were busy elsewhere. "Let's just man up and put our differences aside so we can at least acknowledge were on the same side, right?" Seth held out his hand.

Joseph stared at it for a second. "Yeah." He nodded, shaking the senior's hand. "I can do that."

*See how I can put my own issues aside and be a man, even wit' this igno-rant bitch?*

"Great," Seth said happily. "Now we're all friends. I like this. This works for me."

Gregg was leaning over, staring across the hall.

"Your head's almost in your soup," Joseph pointed out.

Gregg nodded.

"What'cha lookin' at?" Seth asked, staring over. "Oh," he laughed. "I see."

Joseph frowned and traced Gregg's point of view. Ann was walking through the cafeteria looking for her assigned table.

"She's really not a bad person like they say," Gregg said, still watching her.

"Oh, she is." Seth patted Gregg on the back. "But in a very good way. She's the only really wild bitch we got here."

"Excuse me," Joseph interrupted.

"Yeah?" Seth asked.

"That would be my girlfriend you're talkin' about," he said sharply. "I would appreciate you *not* sayin' shit like that, thanks."

Seth coughed into his hand, and Gregg nodded slowly.

"Okay," Seth chuckled, shaking his head. "You're new, so I guess we can't totally blame you for thinking that, but she has you snowed. Man." Seth glanced over at where Ann was sitting, with a laugh. "Her?" He pointed. "Girlfriend? Well, I guess that depends on how you define 'girlfriend,' if you know what I mean."

"No," Joseph said slowly. "I don't know what you mean."

Seth sighed. "Ann ... she's wild," he said, almost with admiration. "She's not your average school slut."

"Shut the fuck up," Joseph snapped. "You don't know anythin' but rumors man, so stop gossipin' like a little girl."

"Calm down." Seth put his hands up. "I was just repeating what's known around here. You're new, and I don't think it's fair if you get played."

"Listen, bitch," Joseph growled. "First off, you say another word about Ann, and I don't care how many times they gotta shock me, you'll have your major organs punctured by every fork on this table. Second," Joseph continued, "it ain't like ... it's a real relationship, okay? She's my girl, not just some chick I'm fuckin', so you back off." He pointed at Gregg. "And you." He pointed to Seth. "At least *try* for an expression that don't make you look like a rapist?"

Seth just smiled pityingly. "Hey, you know what, maybe you're right. Maybe she does consider you a boyfriend. It would make sense — something different, dangerous, piss off her parents. I'm sure there are plenty of girls here who would totally go for you. Not too bad looking, nice accent, and the fact that they don't have to worry about it being long term."

"What the hell you talkin' bout?" Joseph narrowed his eyes.

"Come on man," Seth said, with a wry smile. "You know what I mean. You're *different* — if she dates a Latino boy, it makes her even more wild and bad and edgy, and she never has to worry about bringing you home to meet her parents, because she never plans on doing that. I mean, it's not like she ever plans on marrying you." Seth scoffed.

"How do you know?" Joseph snapped back. "As a matter of fact we do plan on bein' together fore — a long time."

"Forever?" Seth laughed outright. "Look, even normal girls that age don't want to be tied down forever. You think *Ann* is gonna give up her freedom to one man? No." Seth shook his head. "She's staying with you as long as it's dangerous, until she gets bored, and then she's gone."

"You're a liar," Joseph snarled.

Seth shrugged. "Don't need to believe me. Ask her. Ask her if she ever plans on introducing you to the family, or if you're just her back door boy."

Joseph turned away from the smirking senior's eyes to watch Ann tilt her head back and laugh at something. Joseph swallowed.


"Toni White."

Toni took a deep breath and stepped through the metal detector.

"Stop."

Toni felt her stomach convulse as she stepped to the side and handed her backpack over. The security guard emptied its contents and spread them out. Toni glanced back. Lieutenant had frozen. Seth's eyes were fixed on the backpack.

The guard ran the detector over each item. Toni stopped breathing when he paused.

"This." The security guard held up a nail file. "I'm gonna have to confiscate this."

Toni bowed her head as he stuffed the rest of the contents back inside and waved her through. She knew she would pay for that tomorrow.

Toni glanced behind her, eyes catching Lieutenant's. She nodded and the other girl responded in kind. Behind her, Seth winked.

## chapter seventeen face

**Toni sat down beside Charlie, her eyes following Seth's tall blonde** head. He gave her a sleek smile before sitting beside Melvin.

"He's plotting something," Charlie said, voice low.

"We're all plotting something," Toni reminded her.

Charlie gave a shudder as if she had seen a bug. "He's different. He's ... he's not a good person."

"Who says who is a good person?" Toni argued. "You? People aren't one dimensional, Charlie. Not everyone comes in a neat little box."

Charlie's eyes widened as she stared at Toni. "God. You think he's your friend, don't you?"

"He *is* my friend," Toni said firmly. "He's all of our friends."

"He's *nobody's* —"

Seth turned, and Charlie whipped her head away. "Is he still looking?"

"No, he's back talking to Melvin. Charlie, calm down," Toni tried to soothe.

"He's not your friend, Toni," Charlie said, almost pleading. "I know. I can see it in his *eyes*. I'm not making this up. His kind doesn't have any friends, people don't mean *any*thing to him. He's evil and —"

"Are you listening to yourself?" Toni demanded. "You sound — well, I mean honestly, you sound —"

"What?" Charlie spat. "I sound what?"

"Crazy."

Charlie's stomach convulsed as if she'd been punched. She looked away.

"I'm — I'm sorry," Toni apologized. "I didn't ... I didn't mean it like that. You're not crazy."

"Then what am I?" Charlie asked in a flat, toneless voice after a long moment of silence. She turned her head drearily back to Toni. "What are you?" Her eyes flicked over to Seth. "What's he?" Charlie turned back. "We're something. Crazy's a good enough word for it, I guess."

Charlie smiled. It was an ugly one, strained and unnatural.


"Hey, baby," Ann whispered with a smile, sitting beside Joseph on the bus.

Joseph sat down and put his knees up. "Hey."

"What's wrong?" Ann asked, face falling.

"Nuthin'." Joseph shrugged. "I just ... I'm just wonderin' what we're doin' here, you know?"

"On the bus?" she asked, confused.

"No." Joseph shook his head. "Just, you know ... us. Together. What are we?"

Ann leaned in. "What? What are you talking about? Are you ... are you mad at me?" Joseph looked away. "What? Joseph, *look* at me!"

Joseph looked up, then over at her. "Am I ever gonna meet your parents?" Ann pulled back. "My *parents*?"

"Yeah," Joseph said shortly. "Your parents. You know ... they got hot and heavy one night and forgot to use a condom and made you? Am I ever gonna meet 'em?"

Ann laughed uneasily. "Why would you want to meet my parents *now*?"

"I didn't say this minute, I just mean, in the foreseeable future will I meet Momma and Poppa Cost?"

"Not if you're lucky," Ann half-laughed, and Joseph bit his lower lip and turned away.

"What is this?" Ann asked, blindsided. "Why do you want to meet my parents? What, you gonna ask for my hand in marriage or something?" she giggled.

"Maybe," Joseph shot back. "I mean, no, but I'd like to think the possibility is open."

Ann drew in a shaky breath, and her eyes narrowed. "Who have you been talking to?"

"No one," Joseph snapped. "Everyone. I've just been ... hearing stuff and —"

Ann's eyes snapped wide open. "Oh no. You cannot start ... what we have is between us Joseph, between us, no one else and —"

"Clearly," Joseph laughed bitterly. "Since you don't wanna tell anyone we're together."

"We *can't* tell anyone we're together Joseph," Ann said, getting angry.

"If we do —"

"Sure, sure we can't now," Joseph cut her off. "But even if we could you wouldn't want to because —"

"Hey!" the security guard said sharply, and they both jumped as a shock hit each of them. "No talking."


Seth whistled for a few minutes under his breath, while Melvin decidedly ignored him, before placing his arm around the shorter boy's shoulder. "So how's life, Fag?"

"Screw you."

"No thanks, but maybe in another life."

"Do you ever get tired of being the world's biggest prick?" Melvin asked casually, watching the guard, who was preoccupied with Ann and Joseph.

"Look, I'm just saying to your face what everyone else says behind your back," Seth said, putting up his hands. "I don't have anything against you as a person, but you had to know coming out in this town was a big mistake."

"Oh that's right," Melvin drawled. "I coulda just done like you did — collect all your little boy bitches and take them out into the woods to fuck behind everyone's backs."

"You don't know what you're talking about," Seth said, eyes shifting downward.

"But I do," Melvin said. "Don't even come and talk to me about being gay — pussy."

"I'm not gay." Seth snarled softly. "And you can't prove that I've done anything."

"Only because they're all too scared to talk," Melvin said bitterly. "Well I'm not — and I know a few things I could use on you if you push me."

"Oh, yeah?" Seth widened his eyes with a grin. "You think?" He leaned over to whisper right into Melvin's ear. "You try and it'll be the death of you. Not that anyone would cry if you died. You have no life here anyway, and you know it. Even if anyone did know, they'll never admit it, and you'll never get outta this town unless ..." Seth leaned back lazily, "You play along with me."

"I'd rather rot." Melvin spat.

Seth's eyes bored into Melvin's. "Then have fun six feet under."


"He's a fucker."

"Yeah, but now he's our fucker."

"He's still a little bitch," Lieutenant growl-whispered. "And he's ruinin' everythin'."

"I don't know," Anton whispered back. "His plan could work ... but I think we should make escape plans now."

"I just wanna know how the fucker found out where we were," Lieutenant said. "It means our place ain't safe no more."

Anton frowned. "It's my fault. I shoulda seen that comin'. And I should be able to see what'll happen next."

"It's not you." Lieutenant shook her head. "You couldn't have seen this comin'."

"I saw everythin' before now," Anton said darkly, holding his head. "I saw the freshmen comin', I saw how to get 'em in, but now I can't —" He gritted his teeth. "If anythin' happens it's my fault."

"No it isn't —"

"Yeah, it is." Anton half-smiled. "It's my job. I brought us together. I started it, and I need to be the one to finish it."

"Well, we're all in it now," Lieutenant whispered back. "We'll all finish it."


*Think of* something, *Toni!*

Toni watched Mrs. Carter unload the cabinet and spotted her prize.

*I have it.*

"Mrs. Carter?"

"Yes?" The woman turned around. She moved slowly, as if she'd just woken from a deep sleep and was prone to fall over any minute.

"I just ... the bar that holds up the clothes in my closet broke. I'm just wondering if I could borrow some duct tape to repair it."

*Please buy it — please.*

"Oh, I'll come and fix it," Mrs. Carter said haltingly, almost as if she'd had a stroke.

"No, no. I can do it," Toni said, trying not to rush and seem too worried. "I don't wanna stress you. I've done it plenty of times. I can fix it. All I need is duct tape and determination."

Mrs. Carter nodded slowly — *what's wrong with her?* — and handed Toni the duct tape. "Well, I don't think you can do much damage with duct tape."

*That's what you think.*

Suddenly Toni was cold with revelation. The slow movements, the halting voice ... it had all begun slowly, accumulatively since —

*Since I started slipping her Katrina's pills.*

Toni swallowed and looked down at the tape. She'd gotten what she wanted, what they needed. Mrs. Carter effectively tortured them.

*So why do I feel like the villain here?*

"It doesn't even matter, *Joseph*!"

"Yes, it does, *Annabelle*!"

"Why?" Ann whispered furiously. "Why do you wanna know all about me now?"

"I thought I *did* know all about you. I told you all about me!" Joseph fired back. "I say I wanna meet your family, and suddenly it's like I asked you to jump off a cliff wit' me!"

"That I would do in a heartbeat, but this is —" Ann dug her nails into her palms.

"Because you don't want them to know about me," Joseph stated flatly. "Admit it —"

"I —"

"Admit it!"

"Of course I don't!" Ann yelled.

"'Cause you're fuckin' ashamed of me, ain't you?"

"No! I — would you introduce me to your parents?" Ann shot back.

"Sure, if I could, but one of 'em's mentally gone, and the other —"

"Ha!" Ann pointed at him. "You'll never be able to, so you're safe!"

"Safe from what?" Joseph spat. "What's wrong wit' you tellin' me why I can't meet 'em? Is it because of who I am? Because you don't want 'em to know you're datin' someone like me?"

"No, Joseph, it's not you. It's —" Ann bit her lip, blood welling over.

"Then tell me why?" Joseph asked, his eyes boring into her. "Tell me why you had to come here, why you left. Why you *really* came here. Don't even try to say you already told me. I know there's more you hidin' from —"

"What about you?" Ann flipped. "Why did you come here? How come you never talk about *your* family? We've talked about everything else right?" she said, spreading her arms.

"I —"

"What about you, huh? What's your big secret, you —"

"They didn't want me, okay?" Joseph yelled. "My father burned my whole room before I left right in front of me, and my mother was away when I left. I never knew how long she'd be gone, or if she left for good, a'ight?" Joseph heaved, hating her for making him admit that aloud. "So what about you, Ann?"

"Your mother wasn't —"

"Answer the question!"

"I just want to know —"

"Why did you run away, huh Ann?" Joseph demanded, cutting off her protests. "Why'd you run? Was it the car accident, or the drinkin'? Or was it somethin' else? Was it when they heard the reputation you got around town, huh?" he added in a lower drawl. "Was it because they were ashamed of you?"

"You fuckin' son of a —"

"Yeah, insult me and dodge the question, Ann. Why'd you run away? Did you run around and —"

"My mom wanted me out, okay?" Ann shrieked. "She wanted me out, my stepdad wanted me out, and that was just fine, because I wanted out!" She swallowed hard, painfully. "I needed out. I had to get away. I didn't wanna come here, but I had to get out. I got out, but my little sister is still stuck there, and I'm a cunt for leaving her there. I know it, alright?" Ann bit her tongue, but her face still twisted with the tears sneaking through. "I'm the world's biggest bitch because I'm here while she's still there, and even covered in wires here is still better than here. So there," Ann said in a small voice. "There's my sob story."

"I'm — I didn't —"

"What the hell was that?" Sherry stomped into the room. "I can't stand you two. I swear, I'm getting one of you transferred. Both of you upstairs, and if you speak again I — I'll —"

"Are you high?" Joseph frowned.

"No!" Sherry shrieked, shocking him clumsily, as if she couldn't quite find the button.

"You." Ann hissed. "If you didn't have that thing I would have you on the ground in five seconds."

Sherry gasped and pressed the button again and again and again.


Charlie moved on cat-feet through the house and down the stairs. There was nothing suspicious about what she was going to get, but it would be better if she wasn't seen —

*Shit.*

Charlie pulled back from the kitchen, but Dana raised her head.

"Oh, don't be shy Charlie. Come in and have a drink with me," Dana called.

"I'm —" Charlie peeked around the corner. "I'm underage. Plus, you could get in trouble for that."

"Not anymore." Dana smiled wanly. "I'm no longer a teacher at J. Alter Academy."

"Oh, no," Charlie said, coming into the light.

Dana waved the comment away and motioned for her to sit down. "It's fine. I've hated this job for a long while. Once they started to bring in all these new measures ..." Dana sighed. "I knew I couldn't do this when it meant practically torturing kids. I knew it for a while, and I'm ashamed that I didn't stop earlier."

"Is that why they fired you?" Charlie asked hesitantly. "Because you stood up for us?"

Dana nodded. "Too little, too late though. They barely listened when I began my speech — yes, I wrote a speech — trying to persuade them how insane this all is. They just reminded me how dangerous you all were, and then told me I could clear out my desk."

"Well, I'm sad you're leaving," Charlie said honestly. "Really sad, but at least now you can find a good, not prison-like job."

Dana snorted. "Oh, Charlie. I wish. But when you leave the Academy, you *leave*. Teaching —" Dana drew in a breath. "I love teaching — God, so much — but it's over for me now. I won't get another job after this."

"But — someone will —"

Dana shook her head. "Not even at a public school with a dozen vacancies a million miles away. They made that clear. I can't speak out against the school either," Dana said, not facing Charlie. "No one will listen. They made sure of that in my contract, and from what I've seen …"

"Ms. Lovejoy," Charlie said.

"Dana."

"Dana." Charlie put her hand over her teacher's. "You have to speak up. You have to so this place will get shut down, and if you do —" The woman was shaking her head. "Please all of us — once people know —"

"There's nothing new about what they're doing here," Dana said. "It's all perfectly legal."

"But it *hurts* us," Charlie emphasized.

"And you hurt each other." Dana smiled bitterly. "Or at least they think you do, or will, and it's all the same thing to them."

"Ms. Lovejoy," Charlie began slowly.

"Dana," the woman insisted.

"Dana," Charlie repeated, looking around.

"I pulled out the cameras," Dana informed her. "My last act of rebellion."

"Take me with you," Charlie pleaded. "Not today, but in two weeks. I'll — me and my friends, we need a way out. None of us wanna stay. If you can wait just over the left side of town —"

Dana was shaking her head. "If I kidnap you —"

"You'll be *saving* us!" Charlie corrected. "We all want out, we *need* out and —"

"Your parents will —"

"Fuck our parents!" Charlie said, making Dana jump. "They dumped us here. They obviously aren't any good. No one needs to know. If you wait for two weeks and they all think you left they won't suspect. You won't have to take care of us, just scatter us around different cities. We can all live alone if we have each other."

"I don't think —"

"Think about it," Charlie interrupted. "Please." Charlie sunk to her knees.

"Oh God, Charlie, please don't —"

"Please, please," Charlie begged. "Help us."

"I'll ..." Dana could not have looked more uncomfortable. "Fine, fine, I will, if you'll just get up and stop this."

Charlie got up, eyes sparkling.

"Oh, don't cry," Dana pleaded.

"Don't worry." Charlie smiled. "These are happy tears."


Ann moved past Sherry, the other woman fast asleep. Ann felt a violent urge to triple-dose her next time, so the woman wouldn't wake up at all.

*If they've got cameras, how come they can't see how she's a fuckin' drunk druggie who isn't fit to run her own life, let alone ours?*

Ann managed to pull herself past the woman and into the bathroom. The window pane was out, melted at the edges, but —

"Joseph?"

He didn't answer, and Ann swallowed. *He probably doesn't wanna talk to me anyway. Can't see why he wanted to in the first place.* She turned and started to walk back out.

"I'm out here."

Ann stopped. "Joseph?" She walked back over to the window and looked out. Joseph was lying on his back, hands behind his head.

"Do you want to be alone?" Ann whispered.

"No you — you can come out, if you want."

Ann nodded and started to crawl through. Joseph started to get up to help her.

"No, its fine," she said softly, sliding down to lie just a little away from him. Joseph nodded, looking up again.

There was a silence. Ann closed her eyes and took a deep breath. "I — didn't mean to. I get not wanting to talk about it. I just ... if you want to, you know I'm here —"

"It wasn't my father who surprised me," Joseph said. "I knew he didn't want me. He was just ... never there. He worked, and he paid money, but — I can barely remember him bein' around, 'cept for a few times to visit Mom. Then when I got older, he started to try and take an *interest* in me," Joseph said scathingly. "Right. He basically looked at me and decided he hated what he saw. Like I didn't already have enough people tellin' me I'm a failure, and an idiot, and a freak. I remember — after ... the fires, my father bursts into my room and starts yellin'. "They come up and ask me if my son's in a gang," Joseph imitated. "'I said, 'My son? No gang would be pathetic enough to take his worthless ass.' No gang would be pathetic enough to take you, and you're too stupid to get better than a D in school. So — you can't be a respectable workin' man, and you can't be a respectable criminal, so what are you?" Joseph half-laughed. "I said, 'I'm an artist. Maybe I won't make any money, but at least I won't have to kiss ass so I can have the privilege of bein' stuck in a dead-end job like a slave all my life.'"

Joseph swallowed.

"He started ripping down all the pictures I had and pilin' em up. Rippin' down other shit too — my clothes, comics, posters ... just piled em up, sayin' 'So you like fire?' I tried to stop him, but he —" Joseph set his jaw. "He kicked me into the stair banister. Then he took my lighter and lit it up. Almost everything ... it was huge, and when everything was done, he sprayed the fire extinguisher, and handed me back my lighter. 'That's what fire does,' he said."

Ann drew in a breath. "What did your mother say?"

"My mom ..." Joseph rubbed the tattoo on his wrist. "She was out. She — sometimes she would do that. One time she said she was goin' back to school and was outta the city for two months. She actually got in somewhere, I guess. Didn't find out till the call from the Health Department sayin' to come and take her home from the hospital, 'cause she'd had a nervous breakdown." Joseph closed his eyes and bit his lip before continuing. "She would start a job and get fired, or get money from Dad and spend it all. She took care of me, she bought me clothes, and made food when she was there, and she — I know she loved me. She just ... didn't really know how to take care of herself. And sometimes she — she would get a certain way and think things that wasn't real," Joseph explained, forcing himself to get the words out. "She would think that people were out to get her when they weren't. Or that there was conspiracies goin' on ..." Joseph trailed off.

"Oh, God," Ann whispered, and Joseph turned to look at her with his incredible amber eyes. "What about you? Why did you have to leave?"

Ann felt herself shaking, and didn't understand why she couldn't look away, or why she started talking.

"We grew up outside of town, and we never — me and my sister — knew our father. He moved away." Ann shook her head. "He was probably the smart one. So my mom worked, but we never had a lot of money, and we knew it. We were always complaining about it. Well, I guess we got what we asked for when she married Rick." Ann clenched her fists. "I can almost forgive him for what he — did to us, how he ... but I will never, *never* forgive him for what he did to Mom."

"What'd he do?" Joseph asked.

Ann looked at him. "He changed her. Before it was the three of us against the world, and she loved us and we knew it, and she only drank when she thought we were asleep and couldn't see. It was something that made us sad, but everyone in our family did it. But once *he* came in it was up from two nights heavy a week to three ... then four ... then every week. And it changed her," Ann barely whispered. "She got angry easier ... more and more angry, and then she started to crack. We all have tempers in our family — maybe you noticed — but she started to ... she would throw dishes, and you had to duck. She would hit, and you weren't supposed to cry. Once ... our grandmother was over, and she's really heavy and I think Mom hated to see that that's what she was starting to look like. My mom ... it was a party there was alcohol, and she got angry at my Gran for something. There was tea water boiling. My mom picked it up and threw it all over Gran's face." Ann's breath hitched. "Gran didn't move. She couldn't, she was so scalded. And I went into the bathroom and threw up."

"So ... why did she want you out?" Joseph asked.

"I told her, said I hated Rick, and I started mouthing off to him and saying why — saying I hated him. And he said he wanted me out, and she just went right along with him." Ann's voice dripped with bitterness. "She does whatever he says. Even if they fight, she goes along with him because she *loves* him. You know, because it's not like she has children or anything."

"I'm sorry," Joseph said, looking at her.

"Yeah," Ann said quietly, staring at the stars. "Me too."

There was another silence, and then Joseph huffed a small laugh. "I know — I should hate her. I should hate him especially but she's my mom and he's ... I hate them but —" Joseph's chest rose and fell. "I still want them to love me." Joseph laughed, his voice rich with self-loathing. "I'm pathetic."

"No you're not," Ann said. "They're our parents, Joseph. They're sup-posed to."

"I don't want to be my father," Joseph confessed.

"I don't want to be my mom. I'm fuckin' petrified of it."

"Then we won't be," Joseph said defiantly.

"No? Don't kids from fucked up families always end up like their parents?" Ann asked ruefully.

"No." Joseph shook his head, his jaw set, and Ann knew that expression. It meant his mind was made up. "Let's try not — no. No, let's promise not to."

"Okay," Ann said, reaching out her hand. Joseph took it, linking their fingers, and Ann felt the warmth of his palm and a shot of energy that warmed her whole body.

Joseph ran his eyes over her whole body and back to her face. *She's even beautiful nervous.*

"Are you gonna kiss me?" Ann asked, raising a brow. "Or are you just gonna lay there and —"

Joseph swallowed up her response in his kiss, and Ann wrapped her arms around him as he pulled her up against his body. His skin wasn't just warm to Ann now — it was scalding. Joseph moved from her mouth to her neck, and his hands snaked under her shirt. She gasped when one gently rubbed her nipple, and the other slid smoothly down her stomach. Need hit her hard. Her hands pulled his waist to hers, and she was rewarded with his groan.

"Wait." Ann breathed heavily when he started to undo her bra. "We ... we have to go meet everyone."

"Damn it," Joseph swore. *But I really want her.* "You — you're right." *Shut up dick.* "We should go." *I hate my sensible self.*


"Don't run — it's me."

Toni stilled and waited for Charlie to come to her side.

"You get the sugar?" Toni asked.

"Yes. Dana's been fired, but that's a good thing, because she's our way out," Charlie whispered, as they walked through the woods.

"Huh?" Toni said, tripping. "Shit."

"Be careful."

"How come you don't trip?" Toni grumbled.

"I can see," Charlie said, taking Toni's hand and moving forward. "Look, let's just hurry and get there so we can tell everybody. Did you get the duct tape?"

"Yeah," Toni answered.

"What is it?" Charlie huffed as they ran across the field.

"Did I say something was up?" Toni asked harshly.

"No," Charlie said, more timidly. "But you — well I could tell —"

"Well maybe you're wrong," Toni panted, as they reached the house. "But I'm —"

"Look Charlie, sometimes your feelings are just random feelings, okay?" Toni cut her off. "They — what's going on in there?"

Toni didn't wait for Charlie as she walked inside the dimly lit old house, and immediately noticed —

"New member," Seth announced, gesturing to the new addition, a pretty brown-haired girl. "I promised," he reminded Anton and Lieutenant who sat looking less than pleased. "I promised I would get the whole school to come join us. This is just the beginning."

"We didn't mean for you to bring all these people here," Anton corrected.

"We meant for everyone to join, not to know who else is," Lieutenant said darkly.

"I won't turn on you guys," said the new girl. "I mean — if I did we'd all get in trouble right? And —"

"Whoa, what's happenin' here? When did we become a country club?" Joseph asked, walking hand-in-hand with Ann. His eyes landed on the girl he recognized as the one who had asked him about being in a gang.

"You lied you know," she said to him, grinning a little.

"I did what now?"

"You said you weren't in a gang," the pretty brunette reminded him. "This looks like a gang to me."

"No, we're a book club," Ann said, and the girl frowned, not knowing she was being mocked.

"This is Gina." Seth gestured. "She wants to help."

"I know what you're doing," Gina asserted. "And I hate the school too."

"You never showed it," Melvin said.

"Well. no one was ever fighting like this — all organized," Gina said. "We never thought we had a shot."

"So." Seth clapped. "Did everyone bring their things?"

"Remind me again what we need sugar for?" Joseph said once all the apparatus, including metal pieces scrounged from Gina and Gregg's garage, were all spread out.

Seth ripped off a piece of tape. "The sugar, mixed with the chlorate Toni got from Mrs. Waters is what makes the bombs go boom. The tape works as the fuse."

"And how are we supposed to sneak them in past the metal detectors?" Gina asked.

"We're not gonna be putting them in during the day," Ann said, eyes rolled upward in annoyance. "Then people could get hurt. We're gonna put them in at night."

Charlie came up behind them and tapped Joseph and Ann on the shoulders. "Can I talk to you guys?"

Charlie led them into the next crumbling room with Lieutenant, Anton and Melvin. "Toni already knows," Charlie began. "Dana's been fired."

"Shit — the one good teacher we had," Anton swore.

"Sad times." Lieutenant shook her head.

"Oh, but it's good for us," Charlie explained. "She's our way out. She's gonna make it look like she drove away at the end of this week — but in fact she's gonna wait for us over on the outskirts of the town. She said near Per-Pres —"

"Prescott Street," Ann said. "My house is near there."

"Good," Charlie said. "So two weeks from now — after the bombs have gone off — we follow Ann and get in Dana's car. She said she has enough money to give some of us plane tickets, and the rest of us bus rides. That way, if they catch her later, we'll be long gone."

"Damn, Charlie." Anton grinned. "You think on your feet." Charlie beamed.

"But why wait?" Melvin asked, looking for the first time this week as if he was alive. "Why not run off sooner?"

"Well, we do have to give her some time to pretend she's gone," Charlie said. "Otherwise they'll know it's her. But we could go before the bombs are set," Charlie proposed, dropping her voice. "Seth would never need to know."

"If we leave before it's done, he'll turn us in," Lieutenant reasoned. "We need a head start, 'cause they can have people after us in less than twenty-four hours. But if we blow the school, they'll have their hands full for a while before they can come chasin' us."

"I know," Charlie said, glancing back. "But...I get the real strong feeling we shouldn't trust Seth."

"Of course we shouldn't," Ann said. "He'll probably turn us in once the bombs go off and say it was all us. But if we run, he won't be able to."

"Maybe that's what he's expectin'," Joseph said. "I mean, if we run it's proof of our guilt."

"He's got us, and he knows it," Melvin said despairingly. "No matter what we do we're trapped. Unless we turn him in, and he knows we won't do that."

"Because unlike him, we have consciences," Charlie whispered. "But that's why I'm telling just us this, so we have one up on him now. He doesn't know about our ride, and all we have to do is get outta state somewhere — a bunch of teens in cities across the country? Even if they send the FBI after us we should be able to get away."

"We'll have to split up," Anton said. "At least some of us."

"We should travel in two's though," Ann said, grabbing Joseph's hand. "I mean, who's gonna just make it on their own?"

"I'll travel with Anton," Lieutenant said. "Charlie and Toni —"

"No," Anton said. "I should go alone. That way there's two for each."

"But some of us might not be able to make it," Ann said, looking at

Charlie. "I mean — you two girls — Charlie, do you have anywhere other than home you can go?"

Charlie shook her head. "They'd all turn me over to my parents. I'll have to see if Toni has anywhere to run to."

"We can work this out later," Anton said. "They're watching us."

"We need some wood for a fire," Gregg said as he worked on the first bomb. "I need to heat this."

"I'll go get it," Seth offered, standing up.

"No," Joseph said, rising as well. "I will."

"Do you still not trust me?" Seth asked.

"Nah, I just think I can blend in better than you. Don't want anyone to spot the albino," Joseph said, turning to go out.

Seth narrowed his eyes as Joseph walked out and then drifted over to sit beside Ann. "Hello."

"Goodbye." Ann waved.

"Don't be like that," Seth said leaning back against the wall. "I like you."

"Wow, the feeling is so not mutual," Ann said looking away. Seth just laughed. "The attitude, that's part of it. But the other part is how alike we are."

"Bullshit."

"No." Seth shook his head. "We're both clever, attractive, we break the mold ... we get what we want."

"Except that I have a heart in my chest, and you have a shriveled up plum in yours," Ann shot back. Seth just raised an eyebrow and looked out the door. "Really? Did someone finally tame the wildcat?"

"Okay first, I did not ask for that ridiculous nickname. Two, Joseph didn't *tame* me," Ann said sharply, turning to look at the senior. "He — we I — like each other, okay? Which is something you would know nothing about," she finished.

"Hmm." Seth smiled. "I never thought you would settle down so quickly ... you know go from being the party girl who does what she wants to being the good girlfriend. I mean ..." Seth clapped. "Bravo. Eventually people settle down and have a family and plan a life, but most people like to play the field, have fun, live and be young while they can before they tie themselves to another person. Your mother is probably real proud."

"My mother would hate Joseph," Ann snapped.

"But I'm sure she would be proud you put aside the whole bad girl thing to shack up with a guy and be his girlfriend. No more Wild Ann."

"Joseph doesn't want a bland girlfriend," Ann argued. "He's not gonna ask me to not be *me*."

"He was really upset when Gregg said you were beautiful," Seth said slyly. "He didn't want anyone looking at you. Not that that's huge. Most men don't want their girls dressing too sexy or flirting. But you know they say Latino men are the most controlling —"

"You would buy that racist bullshit," Ann said. Seth just shrugged. "Hey most men aren't too different.No guy is gonna want his girl going crazy and running around — welcome to what it means to be *involved*. I'll probably be the only one," Seth said getting up, "but I'll miss the old Ann Cost, the one who didn't take shit from anyone and took what she wanted without caring if people hated it. It was nice not being the only one who was free around here. Anyway ..." Seth shrugged and walked over to talk to Gregg.

"So how long until these are done?" Joseph asked, holding his lighter up and watching them finish the first pipe bomb.

"Well, obviously until two weeks later," Seth said, looking up. "Or we wouldn't need that time to get it ready."

Joseph fought the urge to duct tape Seth's mouth shut as the senior moved past him.

Charlie's eyes widened when the senior smiled at her, and she tried to move away.

"You don't have to run," he said, still smiling as he boxed her into a corner. "We're on the same side here."

"Yeah," Charlie said, avoiding his eyes.

"What, you won't face me now?"

"I already know what I'll see," Charlie mumbled.

"Oh, yeah?" Seth folded his arms. "What's that?"

Charlie slowly raised her head and looked straight at him. "Why are you all ready to blow this place up?" she asked. "You're a senior. You'll get out at the end of the year anyway, but we still have four more years."

Seth smiled as if she had just handed him candy. "Uh-oh. Don't tell me that your friends haven't told you yet?"

"Told us what?" Charlie asked. Seth turned and hollered over to where Anton and Lieutenant stood. "Hey, you never told your friends about what it means to be committed in? About how long you stay?"

"What's he talking about?" Joseph asked.

There was silence, and Charlie glanced at Melvin, who seemed to be trying to say something. "What?"

"You don't ... unless you —" Melvin sighed, closed his eyes, and then looked at all of the other freshmen. "If you're a boarder, they have the rights on how long to keep you. If you're in the STARE Program, it's the Academy that decides when you're well enough to go, unless your parents pull you out."

"But they have to let you out when you're eighteen," Toni said.

Melvin shook his head. "No. It's like in a hospital. When you're committed, they can keep you as long as they see that you aren't ready to leave. It's a court order."

"So — so we could be here all our *lives*?" Joseph yelled.

"If they say so," Anton said darkly. "Right now? They own us."

"No." Charlie began hyperventilating. "No — they can't. They ... they couldn't ..." But even as she said it, she knew it was true. The silence in the old house was constrained and vicious.

Joseph was the first to break it. "Muther*fucker*!" he screamed, and the fire erupted violently. Everyone fell back, including Joseph whose eyes stared at the cold, fallen lighter on the dark floor.

"Why didn't you tell us this?" Toni accused Anton, while Gregg, Gina, and even Seth, stared in shock at Joseph.

"'Cause it don't matter," Anton said.

"It *does* matter!" Toni practically screamed. "Why are you guys fighting like this if it just means they'll keep you longer?"

"So you think we should just lie down and take this?" Anton said, getting up in her face. "Just lie down and let 'em do experiments and shit to us? Let 'em shock us just cause we talk in class? You just gonna lie down and take that?"

"If you did they'd let you *go*," Toni argued back.

"No they won't," Charlie said, voice harsh. "No ... no they wanted us here because there's something different about us — Toni was right about that. They want us here, you think they'll just let us go because we play nice? No," Charlie said. "No, they'll keep us here until they're done with us."

Toni opened her mouth to argue, and found she had no breath.

*Not again.*

"What's ... what's happening to her?" Ann asked, getting down beside the heavier girl.

"Panic attack, I think," Anton answered. "She's had 'em before."

"What do we do?" Joseph demanded as Toni's face began to pale.

"Wait?" Lieutenant offered. Charlie touched Toni's hand, and the other girl grabbed onto it so tightly that Charlie winced. "It's okay," Charlie said, staring at Toni, whose eyes were clearly terrified. "It's okay. We're here. We're all here."

"Yeah," Ann confirmed. "You — you'll be fine."

Charlie felt Toni's grip on her hand loosen as Toni slowly regained her breath, and she looked up at Anton.

Anton was glaring across the room at Seth, and Charlie could feel the hatred between them like heat off a bonfire.

"We gotta get outta here," Charlie whispered, looking around. "Before we really are as crazy as they think."

# chapter eighteen the

## "Have you seen the tape, Toni?"

Toni swallowed hard. "No ... I thought I put it back in the cupboard?"

Mrs. Carter rummaged around and then shook her head. "No. It isn't there."

"I could have sworn I put it back ... "

Mrs. Carter looked at her sternly. "In our community we believe in responsibility. You cannot borrow things unless you put them back."

Toni nodded.

"After school I want you to look for the tape, and come back down when you have it," Mrs. Carter instructed. Toni knew that wasn't going to happen.

"Yes, Mrs. Carter."

"And I —" Mrs. Carter stepped forward and then wobbled. Toni shot to her feet and helped catch the woman. "Thank you, Toni." She breathed heavily.

"Are you alright?"

"Yes — I've just been feeling dizzy ... tired lately, and having headaches. Almost as if I'd been drinking too much, except I don't drink and ..." Mrs. Carter shook herself and took a breath before drawing herself up. "Thank you, Toni. I can handle it now."

Toni just nodded, backing away slowly.

"S— sure, Mrs. Carter."


Joseph walked onto the bus, and his eyes scanned for Ann. Usually she would wait for him and they would walk there together, but today she was out before he was even up. He frowned, eyes narrowing, as he saw the blonde hair and walked over.

"May I sit here, ma'am?"

Ann nodded quickly. "Yeah. Of course."

Joseph sat down beside her and put his feet up as she looked out the window. "What's wrong?"

"Did I say something was wrong?"

"No," Joseph said, eyes narrowing. "Where were you last night? I waited for you on the roof."

"I was tired," Ann said shortly.

"But I passed your room, and you wasn't there either," Joseph said, and she finally looked at him straight on — or rather, she looked slightly at him, not meeting his eyes. "You were looking in my room?"

"It was just once," Joseph said, looking down guiltily. Then he sighed. "Okay — it was more than once, but you look really cute when you sleep. I'm not creepin' really," Joseph said earnestly. "I'm an artist. We just appreciate beauty."

Ann smiled, then trembled and looked away. "I know. I was just ... I needed to be alone."

Joseph nodded. "Yeah. I understand that. So ..." He glanced at her sideways. "Am I gonna see you tonight?"

"Oh, sure," Ann agreed, eyes wide. "Definitely."

"Ann, I just wanted to say ... you know I ..."

"You what?" Ann frowned.

"Nuthin'." Joseph bit his lip, staring at her. "Nuthin', Ann."


"You aren't going to really trust him, are you?"

"But there is nothing she can do. She will be paralyzed."

"You are very evil and bad."

"You are Chosen. You are filled with great power."

"Charlie, why are you ignoring us?"

"Charlie, are you afraid? You should be."

"You really need to listen to us, Charlie."

"No I don't!"

Mr. Alderman looked up and the class turned to her. Charlie felt the shock hit her arm, and the spasm disoriented her so that the room seemed to be moving sideways.

"Ms. Persan?" Mr. Alderman said in his dry, logical voice. "What were you screaming for?"

"Everyone was ..." Charlie looked around at the room. "Nothing. I didn't know the answer on the last test. Kept thinking — thinking I did, but don't. I don't. Didn't know. The answer. I —" Charlie held her breath. "Nothing."

*Only two more days,* Toni thought, staring at her lunch plate. *Only two more days. We have only one more pipe bomb to make —*

*Oh, God. We're making pipe bombs. It's like fucking Columbine.*

Charlie sat down across from Toni and gave a little wave. Then another wave. Then she grabbed her hand and forced it down.

"Are you alright?" Toni whispered. The other girls at the table glared at them for talking, but Toni ignored them.

"Fine, yes." Charlie nodded. "I'm — no." She shook her head. "Not fine."

"Go to the nurse's," one of the girls mumbled.

"Shut up," Toni said, and the girls gasped again. "Oh, please. Charlie ... everything's gonna be okay."

"Yeah." Charlie nodded, her eyes saying no. She glanced over at the table Joseph sat at with Seth.

"Bad combo," Charlie remarked.

"Yeah, there's a lot of testosterone goin' on at that table." Toni nodded. "Seth is definitely the alpha male though."

"Seth is a spider," Charlie said, looking over at the back of his head. "Spinning, weaving. Perceiving you know. It's a question of points. Points of view, points of reasoning, points of reckoning ..."

"Charlie," Toni warned softly as the other girls stared. Charlie blanched, and immediately got up and dumped her tray before rushing out.

"What's wrong with her?" asked one girl.

"I don't know," Toni said.


"That's the fifth time you've looked over at Ann," Seth noted, watching Joseph. "Is there something wrong?"

"No," Joseph said. "I'm not allowed to look at her?"

"You can do a lot more than that," laughed one of the boys at the table quietly. The silence rule at lunch was one everyone had learned how to break, since the aides couldn't be everywhere at once.

"What are you talking about?" Joseph asked slowly.

The boy raised his eyebrows. "Her? She's pretty much officially the town slut."

"What the fuck are you talkin' about?" Joseph snapped.

"Whoa!" The other boy raised his hands. "I'm just saying. It's common knowledge about her."

"She's my *girlfriend,*" Joseph sounded out harshly.

"Not according to Gregg," said Seth.

"What do you mean?" Joseph looked to him. Seth sighed.

"I didn't want to be the one to tell you, but ... Gregg says she came onto him strong and he couldn't help it," Seth informed Joseph.

"What — when? When did he say that?" Joseph demanded.

"Told me on the bus," Seth said gently. "I hate to break it to you man, but it's probably good for you to understand this now before you get too attached." Seth laughed a little to himself. "Sorry."

Joseph clenched his fists hard then shot up from the table and stormed away.

"Damn. He took that hard," the other boy at the table remarked as his friend sat down.

Seth shrugged, smiling. "Love's a bitch."


Ann slammed the stall door shut hard and sat down.

*Goddammit.*

*God.* Damn. *It.*

"I am such an idiot," she moaned aloud.

"Idiot. Fool. Fool's gold is like winning the battle and losing the war. Before. It's all a question of keeping score."

"Is that you, Gnome?" Ann asked.

"Yes," Charlie said, voice shaking.

"You all in pieces again?"

"Yes," Charlie answered. "My head doesn't make any sense, and I am talking not right. I don't want to get taken downstairs."

"I won't let them do that," Ann promised. "I'll beat them all down before I let them do anything like that."

"You'd get in trouble," Charlie said.

"I'd deserve it," Ann said darkly.

"Trouble with your boyfriend?" Charlie guessed.

Ann didn't bother asking how Charlie knew. "It's all my fault. All of it. Things were good, and I fucked it up by messing around with Gregg. I didn't even really want him," Ann said disgustedly. "He's cute, but I wasn't even attracted to him."

"Then why cheat?" Charlie asked.

"I — I —" Ann swallowed. "I was *scared.* I ... I wanted to go wild and be free and not tied down. I kept hearing almost this voice saying 'If you stay, you'll be like your mother, old before she's even thirty and tied down and never able to be herself because she's with a man' ... and I just had to run. So I did — right to into Gregg."

"How did you feel?"

"At first?" Ann admitted. "Powerful. In control. It was me seducing a guy on *my* fucking terms, and that's how I always feel. But after — after I just felt sick and all I could think about was Joseph, and would he find out and now I know he will, because even with a practical gag order on the school, it'll still get around and then he'll fucking run."

"Are you crying?" Charlie asked.

"No!" Ann whimpered.

"It's okay," Charlie crooned.

"No, it's *not* okay!" Ann said through her stuffy nose. "I completely fucked up, and now he'll just hate me, and I don't want that," she realized. "He — I can talk to him about anything, he can make me *laugh* so hard I forget where we are and what we're going through, and even when we're fighting sometimes I just wanna kiss him and ... I can cry in front of him and not be ashamed. And for one second there —" Ann laughed through her salty tears. "For a minute I actually thought he might ... when he looks at me sometimes I think he — he —"

"You're in *high school*, Ann," Charlie said. "We're allowed to make mistakes, and plenty of grown-ups who are married cheat and fix it. You know what you need to do, right?"

"Buy him a fruit basket?" Ann joked without humor.

"Sort of. Apologize, Ann," Charlie urged softly. "Tell him before he can hear it from anyone else. Yes, he'll get mad and rant. He's a guy, that's how they take these things. But he'll forgive you and —"

"No," Ann said, wiping her eyes. "He'll be too angry. Besides, it was only a few months we were officially together and look what I do? I'm a shit girlfriend. I can't do this. I'm not built for this whole commitment thing. I'm fourteen. I'm not ready to be all tied up and ... it's better if we just end it now."

"Loving someone doesn't have to mean giving up your freedom," Charlie said softly. "Just because you love him doesn't mean you have to lose yourself."

"Did I say I loved him?" Ann snapped. "He's never said he loved me either."

"No," Charlie said, surprisingly not backing down. "But anyone with eyes can see the way he looks at you."

"Yeah, like he wants to fuck me." Ann snorted, then sniffed.

"Like you're the only one in the room," Charlie said quietly. "Like he doesn't want to look away. Like he couldn't if he tried."

"You sound better," Ann changed the subject. "Not in pieces anymore."

"No, now nothing looks real," Charlie whispered. "Like ... everything has been replaced with copies." Charlie didn't even notice herself sink to her knees. "Like — like everything is fake — a trick. Nobody is really who they say they are, everything is replaced with a plastic imitation. I ... I can't explain ..."

Ann knelt down in the next stall, looking at the other girl put her head to the floor. "I'm real Charlie."

"You don't sound real," Charlie moaned. "You ... everything is fake. You ... you're an impostor, not the real Ann."

"Charlie —" Ann reached out and took the girls hand. "Look at me."

Charlie tilted her head under the stall to look at the blonde.

"I am right here," Ann whispered, looking straight in Charlie's eyes. "I am real. *This*," she touched their clasped hands. "This is real. You are not crazy," Ann promised. "Not now. Not yet."

"I am crazy. I'll live and die crazy and alone," Charlie pronounced desperately.

"No," Ann whispered. "Not alone."


"But why not?" Lieutenant argued.

"Because those are the rules. You will need to get your makeup like everyone else," the security guard insisted.

Anton's hand was almost where it needed to be. "But I played by all the rules. Just 'cause some bi — fools blew up the Store, I gotta have ashy skin? Do you know what it's like for a woman to be deprived of her lotion for two weeks?" Lieutenant asked, holding the guards eyes. "Ever *heard* of ashy?"

"The answer is no," he repeated.

Anton was almost finished. They had worked all day to get into this camera blind spot. He just needed a few more seconds. "Look, all I want you to do is tell somebody about my —"

"You file a complaint just like any other student, on the computer," the guard warned dangerously. "Now go through the detector like any other student."

"All I want is my make —"

Lieutenant doubled over with the shock.

"Now go out the detector," the guard instructed.

Wincing in pain, she nodded. "Yes, sir. Damn," she whispered as Anton fell in behind her.

"You get it?" she mouthed.

Anton touched the wallet now residing in his backpack. "Yes ma'am."


Toni felt a brief shock and turned around.

"What happened to you?"

Charlie just shuddered, and Ann whispered, "They saw us talking in the bathroom and thought we were doing things. So of course, the evil lesbians had to be punished with shocks. I don't think Charlie took it well."

"Charlie?" Toni whispered, taking the other girls hand and sitting her down. "Charlie?"

Charlie took in a shaky breath and turned to Toni, her expression almost hazy.

"If we get caught," she mouthed, so the guard not pacing wouldn't hear, "we will be very, very dead."


Ann looked over the heads of those on the bus and saw Joseph's. She moved to sit beside him.

*No one is supposed to talk, so he might not know. And if he doesn't know now, it won't matter, 'cause we'll be gone soon, and it'll never come up.*

Ann put on her sweetest get-out-of-trouble smile and moved down to the seat.

"Oh — hey," Gina said, waving at her a little bit.

"Hey, Joseph," Ann said, ignoring the other girl. "I — thought we were you know ..."

"Oh yeah," Joseph said, his eyes hooded. "Well ... you were late, and Gina was here so ... but you can sit next to Lieutenant over there."

Ann opened her mouth to speak but nothing came out.

"The guard is looking at you," Gina warned. "You're gonna get in trouble."

I'm *gonna get in trouble?*

"Listen you —"

"Seat, here, now, with me." Lieutenant pulled Ann so that she sat with a thud.

"What was that?" Ann hissed. "I was in the middle of —"

"Yeah I know. You was gonna pull out your earrings and throw down with Ms. Smiles over there," Lieutenant said. "But you can't."

"Why not?"

"Because we're on a bus patrolled by a guard who can press a button and shock you stupid?" Lieutenant reminded. "Also you can't fight with Gina. We need her. You can't go beat her face bloody."

"Why not?"

"Let me re-it-er-ate for you," Lieutenant sounded out. "We —" She looked around for the guard. "We're tryna blow up and break outta here we don't need you causin' a fuckin' scene! We need to be professional here, like we're an army unit —"

"Oh, cut the bullshit," Ann said. "We're a bunch of fuckin' teenagers who are trying to run away from school. It's a crazy school, but it doesn't make us special or adult or anything."

"Well speak for yourself," Lieutenant drawled. "I hadda grow up pretty fast in —"

"Yeah, I've heard the superwoman story before," Ann said scathingly. "Well not all of us are as brilliant and talented as you."

"Then maybe those people shouldn't be comin' with us."

"You can't tell me not to come," Ann said furiously. "Anton's the one really in control. I'll leave when he tells me to ... where is he?" She looked around.

"I think he's ridin' wit' Seth," Lieutenant said sharply. "So right now, I'm the second in command here."

"I'm as much a woman as you are, *Lieutenant*." Ann sneered.

"Then act like one, *Captain*," Lieutenant said.

They rode the rest of the way in silence.


Toni felt more and more tense at each and every 'family' dinner that Mrs. Carter held.

*I just fuckin' wish I didn't live with the woman. At least than I could just hate her like everyone else,* Toni raged inside.

Mrs. Carter fixed her daughter's hair with a soft smile.

*It's not as if I could ever like her,* Toni thought, watching her eat the potatoes. *But I just ... can't feel good about drugging her if it's gonna make her keel over.*

"Did you ever find that tape?" Mrs. Carter asked.

"No." Toni gulped.

Mrs. Carter sighed. "Well, I bought some more, but you can't borrow things next time unless you're more careful, yes?"

"Yes."

"Will you promise to be more careful?"

"Yes, Mrs. Carter."


*Elephant in the room. The phrase so does* not *do justice to the situation.*

*More like one elephant killed another, and its body is in the room.*

Joseph moved over to the sink and started on the dishes.

"And I didn't even have to yell." Ann smiled at him. Joseph just looked down.

"Okay, that was a bitchy comment," Ann groaned. "Come on Joseph, stop giving me the silent treatment. If something is on your mind, just *say* it."

Joseph put another dish in the dishwasher.

"You can say anything to me, remember?"

Joseph took another dish from the sink.

Ann snatched it away.

"Ann, put it back."

"No," she said sharply. "Not until you talk to me."

"Ann, we can't talk here," he warned, looking around.

"We've done it before," Ann reminded.

"So?" Joseph grabbed for the dish, and she pulled it away.

"So ...?" Ann asked, holding it above her head.

"So we ain't anymore, okay?" he snarled. "We ain't talkin' anymore, we ain't ... just give me the damn dish."

"Why not?" Ann demanded.

"Why *not*?" he yelled. "Oh let's see." He considered, hand on his chin. "Maybe its 'cause you never let me finish a damn sentence, or maybe it's 'cause you go off on me every day for no reason, or maybe, just *maybe,* it's 'cause *you fucked Gregg bare out by his woodpile!*"

"I would not fuck him without a condom!" Ann hissed.

"So you *did* fuck him!" Joseph yelled, throwing the dishtowel in her face.

"Hey, don't throw this at me!" Ann ordered, whipping it back at his face.

"Why not? Maybe you could use it to clean yourself off," Joseph suggested nastily.

"I *didn't* sleep with him!" Ann said.

"*You admitted to it! Just now!*" Joseph screeched.

"I'll admit to doing ... stuff with him, but not to sleeping with him," Ann said hurriedly.

"Oh, great," Joseph said sarcastically. "So you just suckin' his dick is supposed to make me feel so much better?"

"You don't know what I did with him, so don't act like you do!" Ann snapped.

"What? You gonna tell me?" Joseph hollered.

"Why? You want to know?"

"*No*! No, I don't fuckin' wanna know what you —" Joseph grabbed his head to ward off the images. "I just ate dinner, Ann. I'd rather not throw up now, thanks."

"Joseph, no." Ann blocked him from going out. "No, you have to listen to —"

"Why?" Joseph screamed. "So I can hear how good he was? How much better he was than me, so you just *had* to have some?"

"He *wasn't* better than you, baby, that's what I wanted to tell you I thought —"

"Oh, so you went and tried, and he wasn't as good as you thought, so you figured you'd come back to your safety boyfriend? Well no thanks, bitch," Joseph said to her.

"Hey *don't* call me a bitch, okay, asshole?" Ann said furiously. "I come here trying to apologize —"

"Well you suck at it!" Joseph declared. "I don't wanna hear you anyway. It don't matter."

"Why?" Ann shrieked. "'Cause I made one mistake?"

"One *mistake?*" Joseph screamed. "You —" He dropped his voice and came right up to her face. "You got any idea what it's like to hear from *Seth* 'Oh your girlfriend has blown over a hundred guys, and by the way one of them is Gregg, this past week?!' You have any idea how sick that made me?" Joseph admitted furiously. "You fuckin' tore me up, and you had to know it would get out and hurt me more you twisted — whore."

"I am *not* some prostitute out blowing guys for their amusement. I do what I do for me because it makes *me* feel free and powerful, but —"

"Yeah, that's right," Joseph said in a low voice. "Wild-cat, right? It's messed up when you gotta flaunt bein' a slut. You have fun fuckin' half the town?"

"The guys I was with before now have *nothing* to do with you, Joseph!" Ann said angrily. "I was single, they were single, and no I didn't get any diseases so don't even ask. And you didn't seem to mind it when I was practically dry humping you! I didn't see you calling me a slut then!"

"That was different!"

"How?"

"'Cause you was with me! It was us! I thought you wanted that, I thought you —" Joseph grimaced, turning away from her. He couldn't look at her. "I thought I was enough for you. Clearly, I ain't, so fuck it. It's done. Over."

"No," Ann said just as finally. "It isn't over until I say it's over, and I say no. Joseph, I made one mistake. I fucked up, okay? But we can work through this."

Joseph looked at her — at her tear-filled blue-green eyes, dragon's eyes, her hair falling in her face. He felt something yank inside his chest.

*Was this how she got all them other guys? This easily?*

"No — no," he said. "You ... I can't pretend you didn't do this. You can't just have your way 'cause you flutter your damn eyes and say sorry, Ann."

"You're gonna just walk away from me?" Ann asked, eyes widening.

*Shit, shit, shit, think of something Annabelle, think fast! You can get out of anything remember! Remember?*

"Yes — I am. Now get outta my way," Joseph ordered, looking away.

"What, you can't even look me in my eyes?" Ann demanded, getting angrier as the tears got harder to hold back. "I always knew you were a coward."

Joseph snapped. "Hey, fuck you — *cunt.*"

"Take that word back right now," Ann growled dangerously.

Joseph moved close to her face, his voice soft and cruel. "*No.*"

Ann saw red as she slapped him across the face hard and he stumbled back into the counter. Ann watched him pull himself up, saw the fury in his smoldering eyes. She drew her self up and challenged him back.

"Fuck you," he swore and pushed past her.

"Fine," Ann yelled. "Go run away, Joseph! See if your little brown-haired bimbo is so much better!"

"I will! At least she ain't a used up ho like you!" he yelled down before slamming the door.

"Good — a virgin like your sorry ass!"

"I hate you!"

"Good — we finally agree on something!"

Ann felt like going upstairs and ripping his room to shreds — she could do it too. Instead her eyes fell on the neatly stacked dishes.

One by one she snatched them up and hurled them at the wall, smiling with vicious delight as they shattered.

*One, two, three, four, five ...*

Her aim started strong — *that's one fuckin' talent I have at least* — but after each dish it weakened.

*Asshole, jerk, bastard, coward, liar, idiot ...*

Five, six, seven dishes broke before Sherry came hurtling into the room as Ann dissolved into tears on the floor.


*I hate him.*

"Now we just thread it —"

*He's the first person I have ever truly hated.*

"And our final bomb is done."

*He isn't to be trusted.*

Charlie watched Seth's handsome, Greek god-like face break into a smile. The bombs were done. It sounded so ominous, like they were terrorists, or school shooters, not righteous rebels.

*Well, it's all about what side you're on anyway, isn't it?*

"So what's our plan?" Gregg asked.

"Charlie, come over here," Lieutenant called, and Charlie moved hesitantly over to the group. "Where are Joseph and Ann?"

"Coming," Charlie said dazedly. "They're on their way now."

Gina stared at her. "How can you hear them?"

"They're angry and it's loud, like banging drums," Charlie said, and the girl nodded at her as if she was a speaking zebra. The sound of footsteps and heavy breathing turned their attention to the door.

"So what's the plan?" Joseph asked, walking in as if Ann wasn't behind him.

"That's what we're asking," Gregg said.

"I didn't ask you, did I?" Joseph spat at him.

"Don't start with me," Gregg said.

"I'll say or do whatever the fuck I want to you," Joseph said, raising his eyebrows.

Gregg stood up. "Look man, if this is about she-wolf over there, she came onto me first —"

Joseph lunged toward Gregg, and Ann grabbed for his arm.

"You wanna fight me now?" Gregg said, getting up in Joseph's face. "You think I can't handle you?"

"I will fuck you up so bad your mother won't know you." Joseph snarled. "Say another damn —"

"Both of you shut the *fuck* up!"

Everyone froze as Toni stalked in between the two boys.

"Before you start with your oh-so-manly fight, maybe you could stop and use these things called *brains* you have in your heads," Toni said.

"He —" Joseph began.

"He did naughty things with your girl — yes, we get it," Toni said flatly. "I know you're angry and beating his head to a pulp sounds real appealing right now, but it won't change a thing."

"Make me feel better," Joseph asserted.

"Yeah, and then our whole group falls apart, and he leaves and turns us all in," Toni said back. "Would that make you feel better?"

"I wouldn't turn us in," Gregg said virtuously. "No matter what I think of him —"

"Save it, Casanova." Toni cut him off. "You messed around with someone in a relationship. I understand why Joseph wants to crush you into many little pieces."

"She seduced me!" Gregg said.

"Did she tie you down and force feed you Viagra?" Toni asked.

"No —"

"Then you have no excuse," Toni said sharply. "Don't give me that 'she seduced me' crap. It takes two to do the horizontal mambo, and being seduced doesn't mean you couldn't say no."

"Thank you, Toni," Ann said.

"For what? You're the one who cheated," Toni said, turning on Ann. "You started this. It's your fault. Put that in your bed and sleep with it."

There was silence for a second then —

"Damn." Anton threw his head back and laughed. "That was a million times better than *Real Housewives*!" He clapped.

"Sad times," Lieutenant said, patting Ann on the back. "Okay, can we get back to work?"

"Did you get it?" Seth asked. Anton took out the wallet. "He lives on 24 Roster Street."

"And he works the night shift?" Seth asked. "You're sure he's the right one?"

"I always get my information right," Lieutenant said sharply.

"Okay." Seth nodded. "Here's what we do. When the guards inside the school come in for the night shift, they drive past the gates into the parking lot. Two nights from now, we're going to sneak into this guard — uh —"

"Steve Benson," Anton supplied.

"Yeah, whatever," Seth said. "We're gonna sneak into the back of his truck, and he'll drive us inside."

"How do we get inside the school?" Toni asked.

"I'll get us in," Joseph stated. "I can get in through one of the windows."

"How?" Gregg asked.

"I have some unique talents," Joseph drawled.

"Okay, okay," Lieutenant headed off another fight. "Once we're inside, we gotta plant the bombs."

"Will there be guards inside the school?" Charlie asked.

"Probably not," Seth shrugged.

"But what if there are?" Charlie persisted. "What if they get hurt?"

"They're *guards*," Seth emphasized. "They're the ones who've been shocking us and beating us up from the beginning."

"They're still people," Toni argued.

"So what, you're developing a conscience now?" Seth countered. "You've been drugging the fucking principal until she barely can stay on her feet, and now you care?"

Toni was silenced.

"So we need to place the bombs in different areas for maximum effect," Seth continued. "We —"

"That's easy," Anton said. "We just make teams and each take a floor. What about getting out?"

"We get out same way we got in," Seth said as if it were obvious. "The truck."

"But once the bombs go off, they'll check —"

"Yeah, that's good," Anton cut Charlie off. "We'll do that."

Charlie frowned, but Anton motioned for her to wait. Once Seth, Gregg and Gina got up to leave, Anton pulled her and the others into a corner.

"I don't trust him," Charlie said.

"Me either," Anton confirmed. "But that's okay. Last time we did this 'operation,' me, L, and Toni got out through one of the windows and jumpin' from the roof, to the truck, and over the wire. We can do that this time. Joseph —"

"I'll open the window," he attested.

"Good," Anton said. "As soon as y'all have planted the bombs, come up to the top floor, right side, where the window is. We won't tell our friend over there. He don't need to know about our escape."

"It's so close," Lieutenant whispered. "You sure Dana is waitin'?"

"Yes," Charlie confirmed. "She'll wait. She feels guilty enough for what she did. She'll want a way to fix it."

"To get away ..." Ann whispered. "God. I can't wait."

"*You* can't wait?" said the unusually silent Melvin. "Knowing we're getting the fuck outta here is the only thing keeping me alive."

"We're so close," Toni said. "If we can just pull this off, next week we'll all be miles away from J. Alter High."

"We just have to pull it off," Anton affirmed. "A'ight. Break."

# chapter nineteen red

## "Can't see anything."

"That's the idea, Joseph. That's why we chose dark of the moon."

"I'm not a complete idiot, Ann, I can —"

"Both of you shut up," Anton whispered. "Can anyone see the truck?"

"No, it's too dark," Melvin whispered.

"Ann, you take Gina round the back and see if it's in the garage."

"Yes, sir."

Ann jerked her head, and led the other girl over around the back of the house of Steve Benson, security guard at J. Alter Academy.

"What do we do if it's in the garage?" Lieutenant asked.

"Force open the door?" Seth offered.

Toni swallowed painfully. She was dying to shift but too terrified to move. Lying on her stomach on roots and shrubs outside of the man's house in pitch black night wasn't exactly comfortable.

*At least no one has to worry about the wires.* Everyone had torn off the wires, because since they were leaving afterwards, they didn't need to worry about getting caught. They were all dressed in black. It was nearly impossible to see anyone.

*Well maybe not impossible for Charlie,* Toni thought. The smaller girl was beside her, and Toni could feel her shaking.

Reaching out, Toni found her hand and squeezed.

"It'll be okay. We'll pull it off," Toni soothed.

"Maybe," Charlie answered. "Maybe."

"Shit," Ann swore. "It's locked."

"How do we get in?" Gina asked.

"Believe it or not I'm trying to figure that out, not just sitting on my ass," Ann said sarcastically.

"But you're not sitting: you're crouching," Gina pointed out.

Ann ignored her, instead going around the front of the garage and feeling at the bottom. There was a tiny stripe open, Ann felt with her hands. Not large enough for her to fit through.

*But I know someone who might.*


Lieutenant shifted when Ann touched her shoulder. "Seriously, Ann!" Lieutenant hissed. "Don't sneak up on black people. It's bad for your health."

"We need Charlie," Ann whispered to the group. "She might be able to fit under the garage."

"How does that help the rest of us?" Seth drawled.

"My mom has the same type of garage. There's a mechanism on the inside where if she presses it, it will open. It's safety against getting stuck inside."

"Charlie, can you fit?" Anton asked. Charlie shivered. "I'll ... try."

"Okay." Joseph nodded. "Let's go."

"Stay low," Anton reminded them. "And go one by one."

Once everyone was over by the garage door, Ann took Charlie's hand and led her over to the small area open at the bottom.

"Can you fit under?" Ann whispered.

Charlie felt the space. "It's really small."

"You're a really small person," Ann encouraged.

"If I get stuck," Charlie said, "don't let the gate come down on me."

"I promise," Ann swore.

Charlie steeled herself and lay down. Sliding herself with her hands, she moved under the gate.

"How's she doin'?" Melvin asked.

"I don't know. How you doin', Gnome?" Ann questioned.

"Um, I've been better." Charlie winced. "Oh!"

"What?" Toni questioned quickly.

"I'm — I can't move anymore," Charlie gasped. "I'm stuck."

"Okay, we're gonna pull you out," Ann said, kneeling down.

"No!" Seth pushed past them. "She goes under."

"She's *stuck,*" Ann explained harshly.

"If she doesn't get under, we won't be able to do anything," Seth said.

"We'll find another way in," Joseph argued.

"There isn't," Seth said brutally, and pushing Ann away roughly, he shoved Charlie.

"Ow! Hey!" Charlie whimpered.

"You're hurting her!" Ann grabbed at Seth's arm, but he shoved hard and Charlie rolled to the other side.

*"Charlie!"*

Charlie coughed into the dirty concrete floor. "I can't see."

"Are you okay?" she heard Toni say.

"Yeah." She coughed again, feeling with her hands. "I can't — can't see."

"Find the light," someone said.

"O — okay." Charlie closed her eyes. *I need to see ... focus ... think, focus on seeing ... I need to be able to —*

Charlie opened her eyes. She could see now, as if there were a dim light behind her eyes, almost as if she were wearing night vision goggles. "I can see."

"Do you see the switch?" Ann asked.

"Yes!" Charlie said, walking up to it. "There's two switches on the panel. Which one do I turn?"

"The right one!"

"The left one!"

"Just do them both!"

"Ah!" Charlie gave a soft shriek, covering her ears. "Confusing small freshman is not funny!" She closed her eyes and flipped up both.

"He'll see the lights!" Anton warned as he rolled under the opening door.

"Once everyone gets in, close the door again," Seth ordered, as he slithered under.

"Are you okay, Charlie?" Ann asked, glaring at Seth as she touched the smaller girl.

"I'm fine." Charlie nodded, lowering the door back down as Toni and Melvin finally passed under.

"You're bleeding," Toni noted, touching Charlie's ankle.

"Wrap it up. We can't have anything dripping in here," Seth said.

"Oh, don't apologize," Melvin said to him. "Not like it's your fault or anything."

"I got her under didn't I?" Seth said archly.

"Yo, how do we hide in the back of the truck if he looks?" asked Lieutenant. "Does he have a sheet or somethin'?"

"Lemme see," Joseph said, grabbing the side with one hand and launching himself into the back. "Whoa!" he said, falling over.

"Smooth, Valdez," Seth said snidely.

"You wanna know how to say 'fuck you' in Spanish?" Joseph said helpfully. "Of course you don't — so fuck you." He looked down at the cargo in the back of the truck. "Oh, fuck," he whispered softly.

"What is it?" Anton asked.

Joseph picked up one of the cargo and tossed it fluidly to Anton.

"Shit, it's a gun," Gregg swore.

"Really? I wouldn't a' realized," Joseph said. "We're so lucky we have your genius mind wit' us."

"It's weird looking," Ann said, coming over. "It doesn't look like a normal shotgun."

"Let your girl see," Lieutenant said, and Anton handed her the gun.

"How many are up there?" Melvin asked Joseph.

"About thirty," Joseph answered. "It's a whole shipment."

"I know what this is," Lieutenant said slowly. "It's a tranquilizer gun. I've seen this type before, but it's been modified."

"It's for hunting, right?" Gina said. "Like for taking down big animals, right?"

"Yeah," Lieutenant said in a low voice. "Big game. They use ones like these to take down polar bears so they can attach shit to them to monitor them."

"They're for us," Toni said softly. "We're the big game."

Charlie's head whipped to the side. "Footsteps," she whispered, her eyes wide. "He's coming."


Steve Benson frowned as he walked out to his garage, which had almost surely been lit a second ago. Maybe a raccoon had gotten in.

"Door's locked," he mumbled to himself.

Benson pressed the button on his key chain that opened the garage door and stepped inside.

Something crunched and he looked down. He reached down and picked up some kind of bracelet.

Eyes narrowing, he ran his hands over his truck, looking in the windows, opening his doors. There was nothing there.

Moving around back, Benson stuck his hand in the trunk and felt around. The guns were there, safe. But just to be sure, he grabbed the edge and pulled himself up into the back.

Benson shifted and moved through the guns, pushing aside the stacks to get to the very bottom. He kicked a few around, making sure to search every inch. All the guns were there and nothing else. He jumped back down and turned off the garage light.

"Wait until he starts the car," Joseph whispered.

"You mean until he rolls us over?" Melvin asked, clinging to the underside of the car. "I'm about to fall. I can't hold this if it starts moving!"

"No, but we need the engine so he don't hear us," Joseph reminded. The engine revved and everyone winced at the loudness of it.

"That's my cue," Joseph whispered, swiftly dropping down and rolling out from under the car. He jumped up into the trunk and maneuvered so he was in the rearview mirror's blind spot.

"C'mon," he urged, grabbing Toni's hand as Seth jumped up and laid flat.

"Quickly," Anton whispered, getting in as the car started moving. Once up, he helped pull Charlie on with one hand.

"Is everybody on?" Gregg asked, panting.

"Mel, Toni, Charlie, Gina —" Anton counted off. "Ann?"

"Wait!" Ann whisper-cried as the truck began moving. Anton grabbed her hand, and she held on as it started moving out.

"Jump up!" Anton ordered her.

"I'm trying!" Ann shrieked, feet running helplessly as she tried to jump up. The truck sped up as it left the driveway.

"I'm slipping — fuck!" Ann swore, trying to jump up.

"You gotta give me your other hand!" Anton groaned, using two hands to hold on.

"I can't —"

"He's gonna see us," Seth hissed. "If she can't get up let her go! Look —"

Seth moved toward Anton, reaching for their hands before Joseph shoved him roughly aside. Grabbing Ann's right hand, he leaned over the edge and clasped her left.

"Pull," he yelled over the exhaust, and Ann choked and nodded, finally getting her footing and climbing up and collapsing inside the truck.

"What the fuck was that?" Seth said disgustedly, as Ann panted into Joseph's shirt, and he closed his eyes as he caught his breath.

"What was — you woulda thrown her outta a moving vehicle!" Lieutenant spat.

"No," Seth corrected. "I would have had her jump off and wait for us at the house, rather than get her limbs ripped off by falling when the car went faster! I don't want anyone to die, here."

"Sure," Anton mumbled, as Joseph opened his eyes and Ann swallowed and rolled off embarrassedly. "Thank you," she said, meeting his eyes for a quick minute.

"No problem." Joseph nodded, glancing at her as she fixed her hair.

"Part one of mission — getting onto truck into Academy without getting caught/becoming road kill — down," Melvin said. "Now we just have to work on part two — getting out at the Academy without getting caught. Any ideas?"

Everyone else breathed, panted, and/or stared at Melvin.

"Good," Melvin said cheerily. "My turn."


"ID pass?"

"Come on man, you know who I am!"

"I can't open the gate without it," said the guard at the Academy gate. "Honestly, that's what activates it."

"Can't you give me a pass here?" Benson pleaded. "I can't find mine."

"Did you check your seat?" the other guard asked.

"Of course I checked my —"

Benson picked up the wallet lying on the seat. "How the —"

The other guard laughed. "Ah, Steve."

"It wasn't there before," Benson said earnestly. "Not just that. Someone stole it I swear, it wasn't here. They stole it, maybe they used it to sneak inside —"

"Steve, you gotta relax." The other guard shook his head as he opened the gate. "These are kids. Messed up kids, but they're kids, they're not the army."

"Okay, man." Benson nodded, driving inside. He whistled as he turned towards the parking lot and lined his car up against a white van. There was a series of thuds from the back, and he stopped short.

"What the hell?"

He jerked his truck to a stop, slammed the door, and moved over to the trunk.

Five dart guns were lying out on the ground. Benson frowned.

Something rolled past his feet and he jumped. "Freeze!"

He knelt down to see what it was.

"Just another gun," Benson sighed. "I'm getting too old for this."

Benson loaded them back inside and locked the car door before walking over to one of the school's side doors.


"Joseph?"

Lieutenant and Gregg moved apart as Joseph rolled from under the white van to meet the rest of the group behind it.

"That was your brilliant idea?" Joseph huffed, wiping dirt and gasoline stains off his face.

"It worked didn't it?" Melvin argued.

"Yeah. It worked great. Now how are we supposed to get over there?" Toni pointed at the school, about five feet away. "How are we supposed to get there without them seeing us? We're wearing black, but look at all the lights. They'll see our faces."

"Not everybody." Anton snorted, pointing to his own. "Some of us got built in camouflage, right L?"

Lieutenant was looking at Joseph. He raised his hand to wipe his face again and she caught it. "Hey!"

"How much of that stuff is there under the van?" she demanded.

"Exhaust, dirt, and gasoline?" Joseph asked, confused. "Tons, why?" He looked at her watching his black streaked face. "Oh. I get it." He nodded slowly, grinning. "Camouflage."


"Did you see that?"

Mr. Prime pointed to where he had seen movement for the guard beside him, and the guard turned his flashlight over to the side of the school.

It illuminated a few garbage cans through the blackness.

"Raccoons," the guard informed Mr. Prime. "We get them everywhere. If you follow me ..."

The two men turned away and did not notice the blackness shift. Shadows like figures moved down the side of the school, toward the classroom window.

"How is he gonna open it?"

"Shut up, Gregg," Gina ordered as Joseph took out his lighter.

"Everyone, let the man have some quiet," Anton whispered.

Joseph turned on his lighter and pressed it to the edge of the glass.

"He's gonna burn the window down?" Gregg said dubiously.

"Shh!" the rest of the group hissed.

Joseph closed his eyes, praying for focus, and crossed himself. He flicked on the lighter and pressed it to the edge of the glass.

"It — didn't really do anythin," Anton said, when Joseph had finished running the lighter around the edges.

"Is it on?" asked Lieutenant, as Joseph frowned at the lighter, the creases in his face deepening.

"Let him try it again," Charlie said.

Joseph's eyes narrowed as he ran the lighter determinedly around the edges again, melting nothing more than a thin line.

"Yo, we ... we can try and find another way in," Lieutenant fielded. Joseph leaned his forearms against the window and closed his eyes.

"What is this anyway?" Seth demanded. "He's trying to burn down a window with a *lighter?*"

"He thinks he's a mutant now." Gregg snorted.

"He's done it before," Ann said quietly.

"Well I guess he lost the touch." Gregg snickered.

"Will everyone," Joseph said, slowly opening his eyes, "just. Shut. The. *Fuck.* Up!"

Everyone stumbled back as the lighter blazed. Joseph himself covered his eyes as he fell back on the damp grass.

"Whoa," Gregg whispered.

Joseph blinked, his eyes still temporarily blinded. He pushed up on his hands and winced, feeling his forearms. He identified two long burns on either one. "What happened? Did I do it?"

"Oh, yeah." Ann nodded, voice flat. "You did it."

Joseph shaded his eyes and picked up his lighter. "Ow!" he gasped, almost dropping the still hot plastic. Slowly the flashing impressions cleared from his sight.

Melted glass dripped from the edges of a gaping hole in the window, wide enough for even Toni to fit through unharmed.

*Fuck me,* Joseph swallowed, staring at it.

"How did you do that?" Gregg asked.

"I have no idea," Joseph answered. "I've never done somethin' that big before."

"It's pretty amazin', yep," Anton acknowledged. "Now can we get on with this *Mission: Impossible* shit?"


"No — *you* go on the second floor, Anton."

"Who put you in charge?" Anton demanded of Seth.

"I'm just trying to get it all figured out," Seth explained. "If Charlie and Toni, Ann and Gina, Gregg and Melvin, and Anton and Lieutenant and you team off, that leaves Joseph to watch the escape route here, and I go to the library —"

"Why do you need to go to the library?" Joseph narrowed his eyes.

"To place some of these" — Seth held up the bag filled with pipe bombs — "inside it."

"I don't see what's so important about the library," Charlie spoke up.

"Why not?" Seth countered. "If we don't blow it, they'll just build the school up around it, and we won't have done shit."

"But —"

"Yeah — that makes sense," Anton cut Toni off. Toni frowned at him, and he caught her eye in the dim glare from the outside light posts and winked.

*Of course,* Toni thought. *If he's there then we can sneak out early and make it to Dana and her getaway car.*

*Wow.*

*I can't believe that in my first year of high school, I am about to become a fugitive. It all feels ... unreal.*

"That sounds like a plan," Joseph said. "One change though. Gregg should stay and guard the exit. I'll go with Seth."

"What?"

The question came from half the group. Toni frowned at Joseph, but Charlie was going back between Seth's darkened expression and Joseph's defiant one.

*Great. We're trying to get out, and they're still busy playing alpha male.* Toni groaned inwardly.

"I don't think that's a good idea," Ann enunciated pointedly.

"I second." Anton raised his hand. "And I think Seth —"

"Yeah," Seth said with a half-smile that made Toni think of a growling dog. "Me and *hombre* here will go to the library, while Anton and Lieutenant take the cafeteria, Ann and Gina take the lower levels, and Charlie and Toni and Gregg can stay —"

"I don't wanna be the watchdog," Gregg complained now.

"Fine, I'll stay." Melvin growled. "Can we just go and get it done with?"

"Okay," Anton said, looking at everyone in the group, his people last. "Break."

"Good luck," Gina began to say to Joseph as Seth moved away. "I hope —"

Ann pushed her aside and grabbed Joseph's arm. "What the hell do you think you're doing?" she asked.

"I know what I'm doin'," Joseph said abruptly, and Ann pulled back, stung.

"Trust me," he said softer, looking at her before turning and moving after Seth. Ann breathed in sharply, then turned and rushed out of the classroom, making Gina hurry to catch up.

"Charlie..."

Charlie tried to lift her feet, but they wouldn't move.

"Charlie," Toni whispered louder. "Come on."

"My feet won't move. They're stuck." Charlie heard herself breathe shakily.

"No, they aren't," Toni said, moving one for her. "Now let's go."

Charlie nodded and let Toni pull her away, as Melvin sank down and his shadow melded with others on the cold floor.


"This doesn't feel right."

"I know L, okay? But if we just get this shit done with —"

"What if the bombs are rigged?" Lieutenant questioned, as they moved through the dark hallways. "Ever think of that?"

"They ain't," Anton confirmed. "I checked. I made sure. Look, we plant the damn things, and if they don't go off, so what? We'll just run outta here."

"We can't just run out now 'cause Joseph decided to be an idiot and run off and have library fun wit' Seth," Lieutenant grumbled. "Tryna fuck up our plans."

"He ain't tryna fuck up our plans," Anton corrected, as they moved down the hall to the cafeteria. "He's tryna make sure Seth ain't up to anythin'. He ain't tryna play the idiot. He's tryna be the hero."

"That's a double-edged sword," Lieutenant argued. "Who cares if Seth is up to somethin'? As long as we get out, this whole school can go to hell."

"Then lets' stop talkin' and send it there," Anton said, pushing against the cafeteria door. "We'll have to — oh. It's open."

"Lucky for us," Lieutenant said dryly.


"Are you sure we're going —"

"I've been down here a lot okay?" Ann snapped, descending to the Discipline levels. "I should know."

"What's in there?" Gina looked in one window. Ann grabbed her and pulled her back. "Listen Daisy Head Mayzie, we have a job to do here —"

"I know, okay?" Gina said haughtily. "I was chosen for this as much as you. And don't try bullying me just because you feel threatened by me."

"Threatened by you?"

"Because your ex likes me that's not my fault, okay?" Gina said, going to open their sack of bombs. "He —"

Ann grabbed her ruthlessly and pinned her against the door. "You'll stay away from him and keep your delusions to yourself if you have any interest in looking as pretty getting outta here as you did coming in."

"Are you threatening to use these on me?" Gina asked, looking at their stash.

"Those?" Ann glanced down. "God no," Ann laughed lightly. "I wouldn't want to *waste* them."


"So you remember how we're supposed to set them?" Toni asked. "Can you help?"

"No," Charlie said, staring as Toni attached a bomb alongside one classroom door.

"What do you mean, 'no'?" Toni asked, looking up.

"I ... this doesn't feel right," Charlie insisted. "Planting bombs? We're not terrorists here. We should just run away and tell the rest of the world about this school. That way we look good, and they don't think we're the monsters."

"We're not killing anyone," Toni said sharply, trying not to consider the reasoning in what Charlie was saying, the same reasoning inside her own head. "This school deserves to be blown up."

"I agree," Charlie said. "But do we deserve to be the ones to do it?"


Joseph crouch-ran after Seth away from the main school, then rolled into the bushes around the smaller library building.

"So how we supposed to get in?" Joseph asked.

"Well *maybe* we could get in the way you did about oh, ten minutes ago?" Seth suggested condescendingly. "With your little lighter?"

"Maybe I could use it to light somethin' else on fire," Joseph mumbled. "You ever think that *maybe* if we do that they'll see the light?"

"I'll watch," Seth said brusquely. "Look, maybe one of the windows is open," he said, grabbing the sill to raise himself to one of the windows. "Look, they must not expect break-in's here. This one's open for air, I guess."

Seth shoved the half open window wider and forced himself through. "Got inside."

"Yeah," Joseph said slowly.

"Stay outside if you want," Seth drawled as he stood up. Joseph jumped up himself, pushing with his hands. Seth waved through the glass, and Joseph held on with one hand and flipped him off with the other.

Seth 'accidentally' let the pane drop on Joseph's fingers. Joseph bit his lip and cracked it, tasting blood and staring daggers at the handsome blonde. Nevertheless, he pulled himself inside and dropped quietly onto the library floor.

"Thanks for breakin' my hand you —"

"Shh," Seth cut Joseph off, with a finger to his lips. "We're in a library."


"How long do we have until they go off?"

Anton finished setting the last pipe bomb. "Supposed to be half an hour till fireworks time. Everybody knows, right?"

"Uh-huh," Lieutenant said, eyes fixed on the small homemade device. "Funny." She half-laughed uneasily. "Technically we pullin' a Columbine here. Actually, that ain't really funny."

"No," Anton said sternly. "Columbine was two kids massacrin' other kids in the school. We're tryna blow up the school to help the kids. We're not doin' wrong."

"Say that again?" Lieutenant asked.

"What?"

"That we're not doin' wrong," she repeated, eyes staring vacantly at the bomb.

Anton took her by the shoulders and turned her eyes to his. "We are not doin' anythin' wrong," he said, then smiled crookedly.

"Tell me it again when we get the fuck outta here," Lieutenant requested, and Anton breathed a laugh.

"Let's dip."

"Are we done yet?"

"Ask me it again."

"Are we — Ow!"

"Sure, now we're done," Ann said, looking up and smiling sweetly.

"You pinched me," Gina accused. Ann just rolled her eyes and stood up.

*Great, now how do I get rid of her so we can all meet up?*

*Maybe that's why Joseph went with Seth — to get rid of me.*

Ann's heart dropped into the soles of her sneakers. *Maybe he doesn't want to go now — no. No, he wants to get out. He just doesn't want to be around me.*

"They won't find out it's us right?"

"Huh?"

"I said," Gina repeated, irritated, "you don't think they'll find out it's us, right?"

"Hope not," Ann said nonchalantly. "If not, we have to hope women in jail are nicer than in high school."

"Jail?!"

"We are about to blow up our school," Ann reiterated as if to a child. "Granted, it's just pipe bombs, so it'll just break glass and burn whatever wood is in the school — but still."

"What — what do we do?" Gina asked, looking now as if she might cry.

"We? I don't know about you," Ann said. "But I plan on being far, far away by the time they figure out it's us."

"Well you should have said something before!"

"I tried! You didn't listen!" Charlie insisted. "And why should I tell you anything? You didn't tell me that Mrs. Carter was walking around like she'd had a heart attack."

Toni pulled back, guilt again rising in her stomach. "I — those are Katrina's pills, okay? I didn't know what they would do! I wasn't gonna tell anyone about that!"

"Then why did you tell Seth?" Charlie accused.

"I didn't tell him!" Toni said honestly.

"Then how did he know?" Charlie asked. "Katrina? If she told we're —"

"No, Katrina said she had only used them once, as an experiment, not more than once, and if she said she had made them she'd be in too much trouble," Toni explained.

"Then how could he know?" Charlie said slowly. "If you didn't tell him ... how would he know?" She watched Toni.

"Well he might be psychic like you," Toni offered. "Or he would have to know from Mrs. Carter, but then if she told him that —" Toni paused and felt her heart stop for an instant.

"She knows," Charlie whispered.


Joseph ran his fingers over one book title idly. "So why blow up the library? You got, like, a hatred of books?"

Seth placed one bomb against a chair leg. "You love reading or something?"

Joseph bit the inside of his cheek and pulled out the book and held it open. "I might," he said defensively. "I like stories, I just — the words," He swallowed, looking at the ones in the book. "Words are all mixed up and backwards." He snapped the book shut and shoved it back in, where it promptly fell out and landed spread open.

"Too bad," Seth said insincerely and placed another bomb by a chair. Joseph's eyes narrowed into slits. "I think you forgot somethin' there," he said.

"What?" Seth looked up.

"You didn't set it up all the way," Joseph said in a low voice.

"Oh. Yeah." Seth rearranged the bomb. "Thanks."

"Welcome," Joseph said, eyes still watching the senior as he stood up and walked casually away.

"So you still ain't said why we should come and blow up the library," Joseph said, hands behind his back as he moved over to the restricted section and touched the chain separating them from the rest of the books.

"I already told you," Seth began. "If we leave —"

"Yeah, you told me," Joseph said, taking the chain in one hand. "But see, I don't buy that story. It sounds like you made it up to me."

Joseph waited then frowned. "Seth?"

He turned around. Seth was not in the same room.

Joseph walked towards the librarian's desk, and touched the bag left there. The bag full of bombs.

"He left the bombs," Joseph whispered touching the sack, before letting his hand fall and touching the empty receiver on the desk. "He left the bombs and took the — phone." His line of sight followed the extension cord under the door to the librarians office. He leapt over the desk and slammed into the door, pulling at the handle.

*Locked.* "Fuckin' betrayin' son of a bitch." Joseph hissed, pulling harder. He smashed his fist furiously into the lock.

"*Ow!*"

From inside, he could hear laughter.

"Oh a'ight," Joseph said, taking out his lighter and putting it to the lock. "Now laugh, bitch!" He snarled as the locks holding the door shut melted. Joseph kicked the door open.

Seth looked up, the phone to his ear and smiled.

"There you are."

"Put the phone down," Joseph ordered.

"You caught me." Seth smiled, holding up the phone. "Now do something about it."

Seth moved and the penknife in his hand gleamed.


Toni was out of breath but her feet kept running. Charlie whipped past her and threw open the cafeteria doors. "Guys, we have to go, they know —"

The room was empty.

"Shit," Toni swore, hands on her knees as she tried to catch her breath. "Think they went to the window already?"

Charlie whirled around, eyes spinning with the room. "Two upstairs, two down. The boys — the boy's are one hall away."

"What?" Toni asked as Charlie took off again.

"I'm not a Kenyan here," Toni called after her, following the tiny girl streaking down the left hall. "I'm from Boston! I'm not a marathon runner!"

*And I should never have come here.*


"What was that?" Gina asked.

"Probably a squirrel or Jason or —" Ann stopped. There it was: the unmistakable sound of footsteps. But not booted footsteps. It was the clack of heels.

*High heels.*

"She's here." Ann gasped. "Here now."

"Who's here?" Gina asked loudly. "Is it —"

Her voice was muffled as Ann covered her mouth with both hands. "Shh," Ann whispered into her ears. "We have to get out and warn the other —"

"Down here!"

Both girls froze as a flashlight searched down the stairs. Ann moved them both slowly, inching to the only available other exit — the janitor's staircase.

"Stop!"

Two guards stepped down and pointed their flashlights in the girl's faces, partially blinding them. Through the light, Ann was able to make out the heels clacking down the steps as Mrs. Carter descended and nodded. "Good. Phone it in: we found our first two."

"Put your hands up," one of the guards ordered. "Where we can see them ... slowly..."

Ann pulled up Gina's, since the girl was frozen in terror, and showed them their empty palms as her eyes ran along the floor. There — if she could just inch a bit left ...

"Where are the others?" Mrs. Carter asked. "If you answer us —"

"We don't know!" Gina said hysterically, and Mrs. Carter snorted, unconvinced.

*Just a few inches more ...*

"If you can tell us where they are, we will be more inclined to —"

"Oh we know where they are," Ann said. Everyone, including Gina, stared at her. "We know," Ann continued, her foot right where it needed to be. "But tell you about them? Like hell."

She kicked the bombs hard and the guards and Mrs. Carter all jumped back. "Run!" Ann yelled. Gina screamed, and Ann groaned, grabbing the girl's shoulders and forcing her to the exit. "Run!" She forced Gina through the door. Slamming it shut she grabbed Gina's shoulder. "Next time I tell you to run," Ann said, "run."


"What is —"

"They know," Toni said swiftly to Gregg. "They know."

"Wait — who does? Like — the teachers —"

"Everyone," Charlie said eyes wide. "We have to get out. Find everyone. Out."

"Okay, we go to the window," Gregg said. "We —"

All four turned as the door banged open and Ann and Gina collapsed on the ground. "They're — they're —"

"Seth betrayed us, we already know," Toni said. "We have to sneak out before —"

"Too late." Ann coughed, pulling Gina up. "They're already in the school."

"So we need to make it to the window," Gregg said. "Get to Melvin."

"We'll never get out that way," Toni stated. "It's too close to the ground. They'll catch us."

"We can't leave Melvin!" Ann half-yelled. "Down there ..."

"They already have him," Charlie said, tilting her head.

"Shit," Ann swore. "Well — we ... we gotta rescue him!"

"No," Charlie said, eyes closed. "Not the Academy. Our people, Anton and Lieutenant." She looked up. "They're waiting at the top floor."


"We have to go back down!"

"No," Anton told Melvin sternly. "We told them to come up here — if we leave, they might come up and —"

"And what if they can't get up?" Lieutenant questioned. "What if they're caught?"

"How can we help?" Anton said.

"Doesn't matter," Melvin said, moving away from the window. A new pane had been installed to replace the one Anton had broken. "We still can't leave them."

"Okay, Melvin stays here, we try and go down," Lieutenant said.

"No, no, no!"

"Anton?"

"No," he said stubbornly. "Not Anton. Not Anton — Anthony. And no, we don't have to go, because they're coming."

Anthony looked up.

"They're all coming."


Joseph watched as Seth casually flipped the blade in his hand.

"I wondered if you would ever figure it out," Seth said, watching Joseph's eyes watch him. "I guess you're smarter than you look."

"How long you been sellin' us out?"

"Oh, I got the job a while ago from the woman in charge."

"Mrs. Carter — "

"No." Seth cut him off. "The woman in *charge*. The Headmistress. Mrs. Principal didn't know anything till two nights ago."

"You set us up," Joseph said, without question.

"Yep," Seth agreed. "Sorry about that." His eyes were watching Joseph, but he caught the blade effortlessly as he flipped it. "I bet by now all the Academy guards—our school has guards, how cool, right?—all of those aides and guards are swooping down on our friends."

*He's toying with me,* Joseph realized. *To buy time.*

Joseph backed away but Seth was faster, blocking the door.

"Ah, ah, ah." Seth stepped in front of him, blocking his view. "No, you need to be patient here," Seth drawled. "Take your time. That's why you get so much wrong and I get so much right. You're always rushing things. Take your time. It took time to set up your friends. It'll take time for you to —"

Joseph lunged for Seth so fast he nearly caught the taller boy off guard. Nearly. Joseph felt a stinging rip at his cheek before falling to the floor. Seth chuckled as he circled.

"Now I see I have some things to teach you," Seth said. "So I'm not gonna use this knife here too much if you impress me. Impress me a lot, live up to your mouth, and maybe I'll leave you in almost one piece." Seth circled Joseph who got up on all fours, blood rushing through his veins, hot and fast. Seth's foot connected with Joseph's rib. Joseph struck out blindly. Seth hurried back, laughing. He was enjoying this.

"Not fast man, not fast. I don't think you're —"

Joseph whipped his foot around, catching Seth's ankle. As he stumbled, Joseph grabbed the handle of the penknife in the other boy's hand and forced it away, punching Seth hard in the ribs. Like lighting, Seth found Joseph's arm and threw the smaller boy away from him.

"Oh, yeah!" Seth said, delighted. "This is what I'm talking about! You're almost fighting like a man —" Joseph leaped at Seth, feigning right and then moving in to kick for his chest. Seth caught his knee, and backhanded Joseph.

"Don't make me slap you like a bitch," Seth chastised. "You have to come at me fast and get out before I get to you, like this —" And he flew in at Joseph, elbowing him in the shoulder, and striking his stomach with the blade, leaving a shallow, painful slash. Seth pulled back, twice as fast.

"See?" Seth explained. "Every time you make a stupid move, I'm going to slash you, see? I —"

Joseph lunged, ducked, and grabbed the blade, holding it away from Seth as he slammed the boy into the wall and pounded into him with his fists. "Like that?" he yelled, hitting him hard. "Like that? You like —"

Seth used his legs to kick Joseph off him and onto the ground. This time the taller boy was breathing harder. Then he laughed. "Yeah!" He grinned. "That's what I'm talkin' about! Fight like a man, not a boy. Now we're having fun." He jumped toward Joseph, knocking him to the ground. Joseph kicked for Seth's balls to get the stronger boy off of him, scratching him with his nails. Seth pulled back spitting. "What the fuck?" he demanded. "Don't scratch me like some bitch or kick me in the balls!" He stood above Joseph, who panted.

*C'mon man,* Joseph thought. *For once just get up, fight, and win!* Joseph hadn't fought like this in a while though, and he could feel it. He was tiring, while Seth circled him.

"C'mon boy," Seth said. "You gotta be the man here. Men are supposed to protect their girls, not be outdone by them. *Your* girl fights back hard. I bet they'll have a hard time holding that wild-cat down. I mean, unless they use the easier way to get her down," he taunted. "If it was me, I'd just lay her flat out and take my time —"

Joseph didn't think, didn't plan. His body found energy he hadn't thought was there as he threw himself toward Seth, tackling the bigger boy to the ground. He felt the knife at his shoulder but didn't register it. He grabbed the blade in one hand, and wrestled with Seth. They rolled on the ground. Seth was bigger and stronger, but Joseph fought like a man possessed. The bigger boy's cocky smile was gone as they fought, both gaining the advantage only to roll over again. Joseph held Seth down and finally ripped the blade from his hand. Seth pushed Joseph off and stepped back, panting.

Just then there was a flash from the Academy and then a smash, like fireworks or—

"Our bombs," Joseph whispered. "They're goin' off."


"Was that another bomb?"

"Just keep moving."

"Stairs." Toni panted. "I swear to God, after this I never want to see stairs again."

"If there is an after to ... get ... to." Charlie huffed as the group of six rushed up the stairs.

"We —"

Gina screamed as they collided with Lieutenant and Anton coming down the stairs, Charlie tripping and sliding precariously close to the staircase edge. Ann grabbed her and yanked her to safety.

"They all comin' too?" Lieutenant asked, looking at Gregg and Gina.

"I knew this was too many for this operation," Anton grumbled. "Come on."

He led them up the stairs, where Melvin was waiting at the window.

"How is this a good getaway spot, again?" Ann asked.

"You gonna break through the window again?" Lieutenant asked.

"The glass is too damn thick. It's fuckin' bullet proof. I checked," Anton said, waving his hand at it.

"Where's Fire Boy?" Gregg put in. "Now we could use him."

"He is still with Seth," Charlie said, looking out the window. "He turned us in by the way."

"Fire Boy?"

"Seth!" Ann snapped then froze. "Oh God, what if they already caught him?"

"No," Charlie said absently. "He's fighting him though."

"Is he winning?" asked Gina and Ann simultaneously.

"Okay, you know that focus thing people do?" Melvin said. "Now would be a good time and —"

"We need something to break down the window," Anton stated, feeling it. "But I don't know how. We were supposed to have Joseph here to take this down."

"Wait, I thought the meeting place was at the window?" Gregg asked.

"They were gonna leave us to get caught!" Gina accused.

"No, we were gonna leave you to your lives," Anton countered. "We ain't got any here, but y'all do. We thought we was doin' you a favor."

"Leaving us here to be caught?" Gregg yelled. "How does that help us? There's no way they're gonna let us live this down —"

"Not our damn problem," Anton snapped. "We didn't want you in this in the first place. That was all Seth —"

"What are we supposed to do now?" Gina demanded.

"Does your family love you?" Charlie asked.

"The hell kind of question is that?" Gregg snapped.

"If they love you," Charlie said, head tilted, "they'll take your side."

"That's crazy-talking," Gina said.

"No, it's not," Toni said.

"I agree," Lieutenant said. "Look, you guys. When we get out over the fence, you run first. Run to your homes, your parents. Make up a lie, tell them we forced you here, you were doped, something, but make them understand how bad you'll get if you get taken by J. Alter Academy."

"Only works if we can get this damn window open," Melvin said, running his hands over it. "Wish we had one of those guns."

"We can't get through it, even if we had one of those guns," Anton growled. "I told y'all its bullet proof."

"Is it bomb proof?"

They turned to Lieutenant. "We still have two. Could we bomb it? I mean clearly —"

There was another sound of exploding, crashing, breaking. "Clearly," she resumed. "They work."

"I'll try anything now," Ann said, looking at Charlie. "I think our psychic hears footsteps."

"Do it fast," Charlie warned. "They're almost here."


"That door's locked. You won't get through."

"Back away from the window, Seth," Joseph ordered.

"No," Seth stated, eyes on the knife in Joseph's hand. "You're pathetic," Seth said, goading him. "Do you wanna know how easy it was to trick your friends? As easy as your girl, and she's hard to top —"

Joseph swerved in like lightning. He had been waiting, and he slashed, aiming for the larger boy's neck. Seth pulled back, and Joseph took off a bit of his ear instead.

"Yeah." Joseph panted, eyes glittering cruelly. "Not so fuckin' easy now, huh?"

Seth didn't bother responding. He just jumped for Joseph. Each boy caught the other's wrist and they tumbled to the ground, struggling to overpower each other.

Joseph felt cool metal at his throat and gritted his teeth, trying to stop the tiny penknife from ending his life. That would be too sad a way to die. He felt his hands weakening. Seth was stronger than him. There had to be another way out. *Think man,* Joseph thought. *You don't gotta fight fair. This is Seth, and he wants to kill you. That knife ain't no joke.*

Seth bore closer to Joseph's neck, thinking he was winning. Joseph put both of his feet on Seth's chest and kicked him off and over his head. Joseph rolled away and into a crouch. He looked up at Seth, who waved the knife at him.

Joseph turned down to look at his own empty hand. *Fucker.*

Seth cut at him, and Joseph was forced to twist and dodge, his eyes constantly on the little knife.

"Hey." Seth pulled back for a second, able to tease him. Seth stood on his toes. "I can do ballet too, see?"

Joseph leaped forward and grabbed the knife in his palm, ignoring the searing pain as he kicked Seth in the chest. Seth swept back, and for the next ten seconds the boys were a blur of clumsy, painful blows.

Seth grabbed Joseph by the neck, ignoring the blow the other boy landed to his cheek, and kicked him ferociously in the chest. Joseph tumbled roughly over the tables, thudding to the ground and banging his head on the bookshelves.

Gasping, Joseph tried to catch his breath and found that he had none. Reaching with one shaking hand to his nose, he smelled blood.

There was a sound Joseph couldn't identify as Seth walked slowly over to where he was, and then he heard something dragging.

"You cut up my face," Seth said, voice harsh. "You fuckin' son of a bitch!"

Joseph screamed and arched up as the chain used to block off the restricted section of the library hit his back.

"Yeah," Seth said, with vicious delight. "Deal with that." He smirked. The smirk faded when he realized Joseph was laughing.

"A whip?" Joseph said, laughing through his bloody nose as he looked over at Seth. "I said from the beginnin' man. I am not your boyfriend or your bitch, so put that shit away."

"Oh you're funny." Seth snarled. "You're funny." Seth snapped the chain at Joseph again, causing him to cry out. "And" — another hit — "you just ..."

Joseph ignored the words. His eyes focused on the penknife, and he grabbed it, pushing himself to his feet.

"You think you're tough now." Seth nodded then whipped the chain out, slicing into Joseph's cheek.

"Fuck," Joseph swore. Joseph tried to run at his opponent. Seth just gave another crack of the chain to Joseph's chest, burning a line of pain down it, knocking him backwards into the bookshelves.

"This is going to be short," Seth crowed.

Joseph pushed to his feet, adrenaline and anger the only things keeping him upright. He ran at his attacker again. This time the chain whipped at his leg, yanking him onto his back, to his opponent's great amusement.

"C'mon boy, is the fight gone? I actually feel bad, throwing you around like a doll."

Joseph shook the sweat out of his eyes, glaring at Seth. The boy dragged the piece of chain, circling. Joseph narrowed his eyes. Seth smiled, and Joseph jumped to his feet and moved towards him.

The chain cracked out again, but this time Joseph threw up his arm, so it snapped around it. Grabbing a hold of it in his hand and tugging hard, he pulled Seth's arm down just enough for him to get to Seth's body and slash with the penknife into his shoulder.

Seth screeched and grabbed for him but Joseph was too fast. He dodged back quickly, unraveling from the chain.

"Little fucker." Seth watched him now more warily. Joseph's mouth twitched.

The chain cracked again, but this time Joseph jumped, so that it thwacked the ground. He jumped and dodged while Seth became more and more agitated. When his opponent stopped to catch breath Joseph saw his chance, and threw the penknife at Seth's chest.

Seth gasped as he fell, and Joseph watched in adrenaline-blunted shock as Seth pulled it out of his left side.

*Finish it.*

Joseph strode towards Seth and yanked the knife out of the other boy's hand.

"Well go ahead then." Seth half-laughed, eyes cold and glittering. "Go ahead and get it over with if you're such a big man."

"Nope," Joseph said, picked up the chain. "I'm not gonna kill you. I'm fourteen. I don't care how fucked up this school is, they can't turn me into a murderer yet."

"Ow!" Seth moaned when Joseph tightened the chains around the senior, tying him solidly to a chair leg.

"Nope, no killin'," Joseph said, standing up and looking straight into Seth's ice blue eyes. "Not that I don't know you wouldn't a' killed me in a second. There's somethin' wrong wit'chu, way more than wit' me. But I don't hate you as much as I pity you."

"P — pity me?" Seth stuttered.

"Yeah," Joseph said, walking back over with the bag in his hands. "So you can contemplate that for a bit and if you get bored —" He dumped the contents of the bag into Seth's lap. "Play wit' your toys."

Joseph ran to the window of the library, wiggling his way out. He ran over to the main school. Suddenly his eyes were arrested by blaring flashlights.

"Stop! Freeze right there."


*This has all gone very, very wrong.*

Charlie swallowed, the lights in front of her going into varying points of distortion. Anton landed on the top of the van only to see the guards before them swarm around Joseph.

"Have they seen us?" Gina hissed.

"Of course they have, bimbo," Toni snapped.

"Let's just get over the fence before there's no chance," Charlie whimpered.

"First we get Joseph," Ann said, moving to jump off the van.

"No." Lieutenant blocked her, eyes running over the scene — down to Benson's truck beside them and its contents.

"Gina, Gregg, Charlie, get over now. We'll deal with this," Anton said, grabbing Gregg and half-helping, half-throwing him over the fence to the other side. "*Go!*"

"You up there—stop!" one of the guards yelled, moving towards the truck. Joseph ran at the guard and kicked him hard in the stomach. "Yo, you guys run!" he ordered everyone atop the van as Anton practically tossed Gregg over. "Run, I'll hold 'em—"

His words were strangled up as a guard grabbed him around the neck from behind with one arm and tried to cuff his hands with the other. Joseph choked as the man gained a hold of him. *He's stronger than me,* he recognized, *I should lose this fight.*

*But I won't 'cause I have this.*

Joseph closed his eyes and managed to get the penknife from his pocket. "Damn it!"

The guard stumbled back, yanking the little knife out of his thigh. Four more guards surrounded Joseph. One picked up a radio. "We need everyone to come down this end. Harris, you go to the trunk and get one of the —"

"*Guns?*"

Two of the guards looked up just in time to see a gun from the truck move — through the air — and find its way into the hands of the tall black girl atop the van.

"How the hell did she ... it just ... what was that?" demanded one guard.

"You mean this?" Lieutenant asked, before raising it and firing into the chest of the guard with the radio. He stumbled and fell, seizing a few times before lying still.

"Holy shit," one guard whispered.

"Sad times," Lieutenant said coolly, the gun still held at the ready in her hands. "Now back away."

"Okay, okay," one guard said, moving backwards. "We'll go."

"L," Charlie whispered. "That one, he —"

Swiftly the guard snatched the penknife from his fellow's knee and held it to Joseph's throat. "You don't want to do this," the guard said. "You put that gun down before you do something that will result in a criminal charge."

"Bullshit," Lieutenant said, raising the gun. "I ain't the one holdin' a knife to a minor's neck."

"You won't hit me," the guard warned. "You got lucky with that other shot."

"Bullshit too," Lieutenant snapped. "My uncle taught me how to shoot a gun before he left. I could put a dart in your head right this minute."

"I don't believe you want to do that. I believe you are at heart a good person and —"

"Yeah, keep talkin' that game while I aim in on your balls —"

"Stop, stop, stop!" Charlie screamed, making two guards cover their ears. "This is crazy. This is supposed to be a school. You're not supposed to be threatening your students, this is —" Charlie gasped. "No ... come on, this isn't a movie, this is a school. You can't do this. We're not criminals, minimal, sinful —"

"Get over the fence," Anton said in her ear, and he dragged her over to the edge.

"Stop moving," the guard with the penknife ordered. "Now everyone just calm down, and put your hands over your heads —"

"Mr. Rooney, get that knife away from my student."

Mrs. Carter's voice rang out over the grounds as she led two more guards and a number of teachers towards them. When Rooney lowered the penknife slightly, Joseph started to move and Rooney dropped the knife and twisted Joseph's hands behind his back, shoving a knee into his neck. Ann leaped off the van into the trucks trunk and grabbed up a stun gun and pointed it at Rooney. "Let him go."

Rooney snorted. "You don't know how to use that."

"You didn't ... even cock it," Joseph coughed out.

"Shut up, asshole," Ann ordered. *He's right, though. I don't know how to use this.*

"Look, you're gonna hurt yourself," Rooney said firmly. "Hand it to me —"

He moved forward, and still holding Joseph, grabbed Ann's leg and tripped her as she fumbled for the trigger. "Oh, fuck it." She growled, and flipping it around, jammed the butt of the gun in Rooney's face then smacked the side of his head, knocking him down.

"Let's go!" Anton said, as he started to push the babbling Charlie over the fence. "I can't fly without my glasses," she informed him.

"Right." He nodded, "Nah, you can fly. Just jump wit' me, see?"

Charlie found herself falling to the ground with the older boy, hitting it painfully and feeling something crack.

"Y'all hurry the fuck up!" Anton hollered before pushing Charlie to her feet. "Run," he croaked, grabbing his knee. "*Run!*"

Charlie took off into the dark.


Joseph stepped back as Ann and Lieutenant smashed the guns into the car window. Reaching in and unlocking the door, he ushered the three girls and Melvin inside.

"You can drive right?" he asked Ann.

"Sober?" she said uncertainly. "Um ... "

"Now, figuring out now would be good!" Melvin barked.

"Maybe Toni should drive. This was her idea," Lieutenant half-yelled, her eyes wide, almost hungry.

"Are you happy you just shot someone?" Melvin asked.

"He ain't gonna die. It's just a tranquilizer." Lieutenant brushed it off.

"Okay," Ann said. "But the key isn't —"

Joseph rammed the penknife into the ignition and forced it to turn. Outside the window the guards and teachers stepped back.

"I know I'm dreaming now," Toni said.

"Moving would be nice now!" Melvin said, agitated.

Ann put the car in drive and pressed on the gas, surging forward and almost running over one of the guards.

"Not murdering would be fine too!" Melvin said.

Ann made a worried sound as she whirled the wheel. "Just gotta get out the door, baby," Joseph said, not calmly at all.

Ann made the turn while bashing into another car, the van scraping painfully against the side.

"Just get to the gate!" Joseph yelled.

"I'm trying!" Ann screamed. She pressed on the gas hard and they hurtled to the gate.

With a smash they hit it — and didn't make it through.

"We have it half-open." Lieutenant pointed out the window, leaning out. "If we can get through —"

There wasn't even a sound as Lieutenant slumped over the seat. Ann screamed as Joseph pulled the dart out of her neck. "Shit, get down —"

He fell back into the seat and Ann pushed at him. "Joseph? Joseph get up —"

The dart hit her in the chest as the guards came around the side, and pointed the dart guns at them.

"Well, it sounded like a good pl—"

Melvin was cut off mid-sentence, and Toni didn't even try to fight it off when it came.

*Yes,* she thought going out. *It did seem like a good plan, didn't it?*

# chapter twenty queen

**"I can't believe I let this happen."**

"I wouldn't entirely blame yourself, Evelyn," the taller woman advised. "You did manage to stop them blowing up most of the school and captured them before they did considerable damage."

"Not enough," the principal said darkly. "They stabbed one man, knocked out another, drugged me, brutally beat up poor Seth who was brave enough to try and stop this, and there is still enough damage to much of the lowest levels that a number of those rooms will need weeks before they are operational again."

"Of course," the Headmistress said, hands behind her back as she observed the camera images of the school on the numerous screens in the room. "Hitting hardest the Discipline levels, the areas of their torment."

"Areas of their *torment*?" Mrs. Carter spat.

"I am merely trying to think like our vandals," the Headmistress clarified. "To catch a criminal you must understand why he does what he does — his line of reasoning. It is the same with teenagers, and teenagers are easier to understand than criminals."

"Normal teenagers, maybe," Mrs. Carter said, her fingers drumming on the desk. "Normal teenagers don't try to blow up their school."

"Normal teenagers are not brought to this school."

Mrs. Carter looked up as the Headmistress moved over to the computer. It was paused in the middle of a video. "How are we dealing with our vandals?"

"The ones we *have*," Mrs. Carter said with emphasis, "are still waiting out their punishment in separate forms. We have Mr. Levant and Ms. Jackson undergoing shocks and isolation. Ms. Cost's mother seemed to think food deprivation would affect her daughter. Mr. Valdez has been on sleep deprivation for nearly a week, and we are still contacting Ms. White's parents for a confirmation to use aversive outfitting."

"And Melvin Stavos is getting out today," the Headmistress supplied.

"Yes," Mrs. Carter confirmed. "He will be under constant supervision and on shun, no contact with anyone but teachers and family."

"Have you considered that by cutting them off from the student population you will only enforce their hatred of the school and nurture their closeness to each other as boarders?"

"I don't see how letting them make other friends will help," Mrs. Carter said sharply, voice rising. "Gregg's parents refuse to give him into our care, saying he was pushed into the whole thing, and that they won't have their child punished like a boarder. I have to meet with them again today, and we suspect that there was at least one other student involved. They made non-boarder friends, Headmistress. And look what they did."

"Still, you cannot effectively stop their rebellion by outside pressure," the Headmistress said, leaning one arm on the desk and typing into the computer. "That will only increase their feelings of self-righteousness."

"Then how do you propose to stop them?" Mrs. Carter snapped.

"Don't get angry, Evelyn," the Headmistress said evenly. "You must crack them from the inside. Once our passionate friends realize that it was not us who 'did them in', but they themselves, they will fall."

"They know you sent Seth," Mrs. Carter informed. "Joseph said so in one of his sessions."

"Seth would not have gotten in had not one of their own members supplied him with the location of their 'base'," the Headmistress said as she pulled up footage on one of the screens. "Seth would have gotten nowhere if he didn't have a man on the inside."

The Headmistress nodded to the screen, and Mrs. Carter's eyes widened as the faces of the Headmistress and one other student came into focus.

"I would not have ... God, not have even *suspected* ..." Mrs. Carter whispered. The Headmistress smiled.

"I would," she informed the principal. "I think they deserve to know the truth ... perhaps we should start by bringing in Mr. Stavos today?"

Mrs. Carter caught her breath. "I really never know what's going on inside your head, Sophia."

"Of course not," the Headmistress said. "If we —"

The phone on the desk rang, and Mrs. Carter picked it up swiftly. "Yes. Yes." Her face drained of color, then her cheeks surged red. "Yes, of course. Thank you very much, officer."

She hung up the phone and turned. "We found her."

"I'm afraid." Charlie laughed loudly. "I'm scared. Please, don't let them lock onto me. The walls can hear you here."

"You just need to stay calm," said the faceless guard who held her shoulder. Her wrists were cuffed behind her back, her feet cuffed with a chain in between so she could just shuffle enough to move. She had lost every inch of plumpness on her. Her body was covered with dirt, grass, leaves, and still-bleeding scratches. She looked every inch feral, every inch insane.

"Please, please." She tried to stop. "Please — no. Not in here. Here is death, here is pain, here are walls — *Oh God the walls!*" she shrieked.

Before her very eyes, the walls began to waver and shiver and then, like plastic in an overheated microwave, to melt. Charlie froze, eyes unnaturally open, pupils dilated like a cat's as the walls dripped into pools of white hot liquid that began flowing towards her.

"*No!*" she yelled, lifting her feet off the ground. "No, I can't touch the ground, the walls are too hot, they're melted, please, please I need to be outside in the sunshine, and the trees and animals not inside, it's too loud ..."

"Thank you, Officer Guillory," Mrs. Carter said, her heels clicking so loudly on the floor that Charlie wanted to rip out her own ears.

"Thank you for bringing her back." Mrs. Carter frowned. "But it must have been difficult to walk with her with those ... well on her feet ..."

"It took three of us to bring her back," said Officer Guillory. "You wouldn't think she's strong, as tiny as she is, but if she took a drug or something ... PCP can do that to you —"

"Because it induces a state of psychosis," said the tall woman who stepped in behind Mrs. Carter.

"Sophia Valentina, Headmistress," she announced, shaking Officer Guillory's hand.

"You."

The others turned to look at Charlie. "You — you...you started all of this ..."

"I suggest we take her to the lower rooms," Mrs. Carter stated. "If we can lay her down —"

"I can see through you, bitch." Charlie hissed at Mrs. Carter. "Can see inside of your rotten core, pore. Whore. I can see ... see ..."

The muscles in Charlie throat constricted as she stared at Mrs. Carter's face. To her utter horror, when the principal turned, only half of her face was pale skin. The other half looked as if the skin had been ripped away. Blood vessels, tissue, eyeball socket: as if the principal had been skinned, Charlie could see it all. Her stomach roiling, her eyes moved down as Mrs. Carter turned and the left side of her body was revealed to be as gapingly open as her face.

"Oh, God," Charlie whimpered, turning away. She looked to her side at Officer Guillory and screamed. His face was ripped open as well. Charlie looked down and moaned in disgust, her own arm also a gory plethora of veins and organs. She tried to reach for it to close it up.

"Can't close it up," Charlie heard.

"She's trying though, isn't she?" said someone else. "*Char-lie's try-ing.*"

"She must die — die, die, die."

"No, she must live, for she is Chosen."

"Little bitch — kill her ..."

"Save her ... save the Chosen ..."

"Bitch, bitch, bitch! Kill her, kill her, kill her!"

"What is she saying?" Mrs. Carter stopped the discussion.

"Who — the girl?" Officer Guillory turned to look at Charlie. "I didn't hear. What did she say?"

"She said," Charlie giggled, looking down, eyes glancing up. "She said, '*Kill her!*'"


"Mrs. Nearson, it will only be necessary until we can find separate places for them to stay, and if you find them anywhere near each other, the shocks are fully back on their —"

"Yeah, well they were on them before, and they still managed to sneak out," Sherry snapped at Ms. Donelle.

"We have all the camera's back up, and if they manage to sneak past them you will definitely hear them on your checks," Ms. Donelle explained.

"They managed to ... I never woke up, and ... well, they must have drugged me," Sherry said, raising her voice.

"How would they have managed to do that?" Ms. Donelle asked lightly.

Sherry bit her lip. "Fine. I'll take them. But I want them separated as soon as possible," Sherry stipulated. "I'll take one, but not both."

"If you could choose, which one would you take?" Ms. Donelle asked.

"The boy," Sherry said without hesitation. "You can almost trust the boy. He's not much of a liar. Not like Ann."

"Okay then." Ms. Donelle nodded, curtly, and began walking. "Follow me."

Ms. Donelle stopped at the third white door on the left and took one ID card from her belt. She ran it through the lock and the door opened just enough for them to both step through and close it again.

Sherry didn't quite jump, but the two golden eyes staring at her from underneath darkened lids were more than unnerving.

Joseph was sitting in a chair in the center of the small room, his pant legs and shirtsleeves pulled up enough to show that the wires and their silver coin points were now on his arms, chest, legs, and back. Sherry looked down at his wrists and ankles, bound to the chair with thick straps.

"Joseph?" Sherry called. He just looked at her through his burning eyes.

"He's wearing headphones," Ms. Donelle informed her as she walked over and removed them. "It's a form of sleep deprivation which we developed — mild, and not made by stress positions. The wires are just in case he nods off. It's been sixty hours now. That's the limit we have from the judge. Besides, I think the lesson has sunk in. Right, Joseph?"

"Sure," Joseph said, his voice heavy. "Yeah," he laughed weakly. "I'm the picture of health and sanity." He wet his cracked lips. "And I'm as sweet as a baby lamb."

"Ms. Nearson is going to remain your supervisor," Ms. Donelle informed him. "But after this week, Ann will be moved to another house, and you will be —"

"Ann's gettin' out too?" Joseph asked, for the first time looking awake.

"She is coming with you both today," Ms. Donelle said carefully. "But you will not be allowed to have any contact with her, and after this week, she will be moved to a different house."

"But not her parents', right?" Joseph asked.

"I ... am not sure why that is a concern of yours," Ms. Donelle stated, brow furrowing.

"Her parents kicked her out. They shouldn't have her back. They'll hurt her," Joseph said slowly, his exhaust evident.

Ms. Donelle raised her brow, glancing over at Sherry. "I think here the worry is that she will hurt herself. They put her into our care so we could help her stop hurting herself and others, so we could teach her to control her behavior."

Joseph seemed to be wheezing. It took both women a moment to notice he was laughing. "Good job." He snorted painfully.

"Here." Ms. Donelle handed Sherry the shock controller. "I am going to undo these restraints, then you are going to follow us out. If we have any trouble, we will call the guards, but we would like to see if you can walk to the bus without any event."

"Don't worry 'bout me, Ms. Donelle," Joseph said, eyes half-shut. "I don't hit unarmed women. I'ma gentleman like that."

Sherry watched as Ms. Donelle allowed Joseph to stand and walked him out of the room.

"Now," Ms. Donelle began. "If you are able to —"

"Joseph!"

All four whipped their heads around as Charlie's scream echoed down the hall. Sherry visibly shivered. The scream was like a wild animal, primal, and without a doubt —

"That's the most God-awful thing I've ever heard," Sherry pronounced.

Joseph moved a little forward to watch as police officers, the principal, and one other, taller woman walked along while two guards and two aides carried a writhing, screaming Charlie down the hall.

"Joseph!" Charlie screamed again, and Joseph heard it as if she was standing on both sides of him, screaming into his ear. "Joseph! Help! Please God, help, I didn't mean it! Tell them I didn't! I wouldn't hurt a fly, I don't want to die, lie, please — Oh, ow, oh..."

"Hey!" Joseph yelled, trying to move toward her. "You're hurting her! Yo, stop she's just a —"

*Fuck!*

Joseph fell to his knees as his sleep deprived body was hit with three shocks in a row.

"Careful," Ms. Donelle warned Sherry. "More than fifty and we have to inform the judge. Don't overdo it."

"I'll try not to," Sherry began, "but if I'm —"

"There they are."

Both women looked up as two aides escorted Ann down the hall toward them. "We've been looking for you."

Joseph looked up. Ann's face was almost gaunt, her body visibly thinner, and she looked about as tired as he felt. Her eyes stayed down as she was moved beside Sherry.

"She was some trouble coming down, but I think she's mellowed out a bit," said one aide. Joseph's eyes followed her.

*Yeah. Mellowed. Right. She looks like someone sapped all the ... all the 'Ann' out of Ann.*

"Well I'll leave them to you," said Ms. Donelle to Sherry. "We should have ..."

The words ran together in Joseph's mind. The short spark of adrenaline that getting out and seeing Charlie had released was wearing off, and the need to sleep was starting to overtake him.

Green-blue eyes shifted under her lashes, and Ann looked at him, down at her hands, and up again. Joseph frowned, as she repeated the motion. His brain working slower than usual, he finally looked down just enough to see the glimmer of a key in her hand before she slipped it under her tongue. She winked.

Joseph almost smiled.

*More than five days in a room with white walls should be considered torture.*

Toni swallowed and tried to move the straps on her wrists. They were chaffing her skin horribly.

"So sure, I'll just wait here until my parents give the call to let you all shock me stupid right?" Toni called, moving her head — the only part of her free — to stare at the cameras. "You can wait forever, 'cause my parent's aren't sick like you people. *Bitches.*"

*I mean — hopefully.*

"So," Toni said aloud. "I've been yelling, screaming, swearing, ranting, and even singing. But I haven't been talking have I?"

Toni glanced over at the recording device on the table near her. "And that's what you want isn't it?" she said softly. "You wanna know how we did it. Seth couldn't say everything, and we won't tell anything."

She watched the recorder. "Well, I won't tell either. So fuck you."

Toni closed her eyes. *God, if I wasn't crazy before, I am now.*

Toni's punishment, which she had laughed at at first, was isolation: a week so far of no human contact in a soundproof room. Her only way out was the same as any of the "vandals": offer information. Say where Charlie was, how they managed to get out of the school, or how she had drugged Mrs. Carter.

She had amused herself by singing Christmas carols and Gospel songs into the recorder until her voice gave out.

"Maybe," Toni offered. "When you stop feeding me crap, I'll tell —"

"*Toni!*"

"Charlie?"

Toni twisted her head as much as she could. She watched the door, waiting for Charlie to be brought in, but there was nothing.

"Charlie?" Toni called. "Where are you?"

"*Toni! You can hear me?*"

"Of course I can hear you. Stop screaming before you rupture my eardrums," Toni ordered.

*Of course I can hear her?*

*In a sound proof room, I can hear her?*

"Charlie where are you?" Toni asked hesitantly.

Toni waited.

"Charlie?"

"*I can see you.*"


"I can see everything!"

"Get her arms down — you get her legs —"

"She's fighting me —"

"She's a hundred pound girl. You can't —"

"I'll be good, just don't strap me down," Charlie yelled, eyes searching for the principal. "Don't shock me please, pretty please, I'll be good, please, it isn't necessary please ..."

"I've got her legs," yelled one aide.

"*Please!*"

"Charlie."

"Please! No, God, don't shock me —"

"Charlie Persan."

"Huh?" Charlie gasped, looking over at the tall woman who had spoken.

"I will not have them shock you if you lie down," said the woman.

"I don't want restraints. I don't need them," Charlie said, her eyes darting around.

"If you lie down, you may not need to be," the Headmistress stated calmly.

Charlie watched the Headmistress's face ... something was fogging up her eyes. "I can't see," she said.

"Just lie down. We just want to talk," the Headmistress said. Charlie breathed a sigh of relief and lay back.

They were on her before she could thrash out again, holding down her feet while they bound her in. Charlie screamed, but her own voice couldn't drown out the voices of the aides and the guards. It was the other voices which did that.

"She is sinful. She will be punished!"

"She is great, and Chosen, and she will be saved!"

"Bitch, bitch, you're a witch!"

"Doesn't the bunny look funny, lying down like that?"

One of the aides reached for the wires on the table near the four point board. "*Don't* do that," Charlie warned, staring at the woman. "If you do that, actions will be taken."

"She has made another threat. We should apply the wires," Mrs. Carter stated.

"No," the Headmistress overrode. "No, get the net and run it over her, then we leave for a while. Give her some time in here."

"No!" Charlie begged, eyes wide. "Please no. I can see everything, hear it all, I feel everything, I can see death and life and—"

"And a rest will do you good," the Headmistress said as a net was brought down on Charlie from the top of her head to the bottom of her ankles and pulled snug at four corners. "I can't breathe!"

"Yes, yes, you can breathe," the Headmistress said, her voice still utterly calm. "And that is what we need you to do, what you need. A little rest so you can try and go to sleep."

"No, I can't sleep, they're telling me to keep my eyes open," Charlie shrieked breathily. "They're telling me I have to see, that I have to see everything ..."

"No one is telling you anything," the Headmistress intoned.

"You can't fucking hear them. They are too talking to me!" Charlie yelled viciously. "I can hear them —"

"They aren't real," the Headmistress said.

"I can see you, all hanging out, and the walls all falling down..."

"It isn't real," she repeated.

Tears wet Charlie's face. Her eyes were red and swollen behind the net. "Please," she pleaded, whimpering. "I am so scared. Please, I'm so scared ..."

"It will be alright," the Headmistress said, as she began backing up. Charlie suddenly realized that everyone else had left the room.

"No!" Charlie screamed her throat hoarse. "No! Please God, don't leave me! They'll hurt me, *please!*"

"You will be fine," said the Headmistress as she locked the door.

"I want you to get Mrs. Waters and tell her to bring down the equipment for a full scan," the Headmistress stated to one of the guards once outside the room. "By the time we have everything ready she should be calmed down in there. If not, we'll put her under anyway."

"Should we monitor her?" asked one aide, looking through the small circular window into the room.

"No," the Headmistress said. "Just let her scream awhile."

Charlie *was* screaming but over the cacophony in her own head, she couldn't make out her own voice.

"Please," she cried helplessly, as the figures moved away. "Please don't leave me. I'll be a good girl, I'll —"

"*Charlie.*"

Charlie stopped. This voice didn't sound like the others. This one sounded like —

"*Toni?*"

*When did Toni become a voice in my head?*

"*Toni, is that you?*"

"*Yes,*" the voice answered. "*Everything's going to be okay. I can see you too.*"


"I don't believe you."

"We're not asking you to believe us Melvin," the Headmistress said evenly as Melvin watched the footage on the screen. "We're just asking you to believe your eyes."

"No, no, you messed with that tape. You made it look like ... no." Melvin shook his head, watching the interview on the screen. "That doesn't make any sense. No wait ... it makes perfect sense. You want to break us, so you fake this to get us to turn on each other."

"We would never have gotten in without it," the Headmistress said inexorably. "Seth would never have found out where you were had not your friend told us."

Melvin continued to shake his head. "No. I don't believe you. I don't."

"You just —" Mrs. Carter began, but the Headmistress cut her off with a hand motion. "That's fine Melvin. We just wanted you to see. We think you deserve the right to know."

Melvin turned away roughly as he was led out.

"He doesn't believe it." Mrs. Carter shook her head.

"Yes, he does," the Headmistress said surely.


"Wake up."

Joseph was sleeping deeply, without dreams.

"Wake *up*!"

Joseph frowned and burrowed deeper into his pillows. Sleep, peaceful, restful ...

"Ow!"

He sat up and felt a hand cover his mouth. "Quiet," Ann hissed. "If we move too much the cameras will pick it up, but they still suck in the dark."

"Wha' — this is su'pid," Joseph grumbled, grabbing some of his covers. "I'm goin' back to 'ed."

Ann shoved him, and Joseph whirled and caught her arms. "Don't do that again," he said dangerously.

"Or what?" Ann challenged. Joseph moved so he was inches from her face, and Ann realized with a rush that she could see his eyes even in the pitch black.

"We ... we have to go," Ann said, pulling back. "Look, I stole the key." She showed him. "We don't even need your window. We can walk right out the front door."

"And do what?" Joseph snapped.

"And find a way to free our friends!" Ann said as if obvious. "I know where Gregg and Gina live! If we get them out, we can find a way to —"

"*To what?* To get them as fucked up as us? So we can ruin their lives too? We're done, Ann. They found us out, they locked us up, they got fuckin' stun guns! We tried, and we failed. Game over."

Ann moved off his bed and stood up slowly. "I thought you said you would never give up on somethin' you wanted? Guess you lied."

"*I* lied?" Joseph exploded, standing up rapidly. "Okay, that's it. You get your ass outta my room, with your fuckin' bullshit and your — you know what you are, Ann? You're a liar."

"Great comeback," Ann taunted.

"Nuthin' but the truth, baby," Joseph drawled. "You're a liar and a pathetic cheap little drama queen who doesn't care who gets fucked over as long as she gets her thrill, and who doesn't care who she fucks or where she does it."

"Obviously, since I was stupid enough to think of fuckin' you. But thanks for correcting my mistake," Ann said. *Good, its dark he can't see my face get all ugly when I cry.*

"I thought you weren't a coward, Joseph Valdez," Ann said to him. "I guess you proved me wrong."

"I thought you had a heart, but you proved me wrong," Joseph said coolly. "I thought only guys let their dicks run their brains, but I guess women can let their —"

"Yeah, throw that in my face." Ann cut him off. "I barely cheated on you, and I tried to apologize to you, and —"

"You are *such* a liar." Joseph laughed angrily. "You should win an Oscar for that shit. You would never have told me if I didn't find out, admit it. Admit. It."

"Of course I wasn't gonna tell you!" Ann practically yelled. In the other room, Sherry made a small noise. "Because I knew you would act like this, be an asshole over something that was, you know —"

"What, an accident?" Joseph snorted.

"Basically!" Ann responded.

"Oh, please." Joseph scoffed nastily. "I ain't stupid. At least, not that dumb. Gimme some credit. You went out and found him because you wanted to see how easy you could play me. Well congratulations — you did it." He clapped. "You're a cold hard bitch, and I'm the stupid loser you played. Are we done here?"

"That's not why I did it!" Ann said shrilly. "But yeah," she said back cruelly. "You were easy to pull one over on. Does it make you feel good to be that gullible?"

"Good I found out this early," Joseph said bitterly. "So I wouldn't have to play along pretendin' to be your boyfriend. How many other guys you sleep with? Guess they were smarter, knew you never wanted anything more than dick."

"Fuck you." Ann choked. "You don't give a damn about me? Fine, I already knew that. But you don't have to keep throwing it back in my face that I'm worthless. If I wanted to be treated like that, I would go back with Gregg."

"Then maybe you should!" Joseph yelled.

"Maybe I will!" Ann said, turning on her heal.

Joseph's throat clenched. "He doesn't care about you. Why would you be with a guy who doesn't even give a fuck about you?"

"Oh, because you care so damn much?" Ann hollered back.

Joseph closed his eyes and took a deep breath.

"That's what I thought," Ann said, turning to open the door.

"I love you."

Joseph swallowed, tasting his mouth now that the words were out of them. He didn't like how he felt now — open, vulnerable. *I don't like the L word,* he thought, biting his tongue. *People always twist it to their own advantage.* He opened his eyes carefully, not sure what reaction he was going to get.

Ann just stood there, watching him, her mouth opening and closing. Joseph coughed a bitter laugh. "Yeah, that's what I thought," he muttered, turning away.

"Why did you say that?"

"What do you mean?" Joseph said, his back still to her.

"Why did you say that?" Ann repeated, voice rising unsteadily. "You wanna see me cry or something? You want sex? I thought we already established you don't have to lie to me to get sex since I'm so easy."

"I didn't —" Joseph started to yell, then with a quick glance at Sherry's room, lowered his voice. "I'm not tryna butter you up for sex, I'm not tryna make you cry I just ..." Joseph looked around, and Ann didn't need to see his face to know the look he wore when trying to collect his thoughts. "I just needed to get it outta me, I ..." Ann could just make out his face turn to her. "I just wanted you to know."

Ann heard wheezing. *Is he laughing at me?*

*No,* she realized. *No that's me. That's how I sound when my breath is going this fast. Oh God, I can't catch it, that's why it's so fast.*

"Ann?" Joseph asked slowly. *She didn't say it back,* he thought, his mood turning even blacker. *Well, fuck it,* he thought sorely. *But still —* "You okay?"

"Can't breathe," she rasped.

"Shit, wait." He hurried over to her, grabbing her arm. "Yo, we can call Sherr—"

It took Joseph a minute to react to her kiss — then he moaned and pulled her to him. He wondered for a second if this would end up on the cameras. *Whatever — I don't care. I don't care about anything now.*

He pulled her arms around his neck and she dug her nails into his shoulders. He shuddered, and Ann shivered when she felt it. She moved in closer, pushing against him. Joseph kissed her harder, and she opened her mouth for him so his tongue could steal inside and touch hers.

The kiss was deep, unsteady, and hungry. Ann swallowed, wondering if this was what having a heart attack felt like. *No, it feels like burning slowly,* she thought dazedly. The heat melted right down below her waist and spread through her stomach. This was more than nervous lust: this was need. She hadn't felt it before, and it petrified her.

"C'mere," Joseph mumbled against her mouth and pulled her over to the bed. They tripped onto it, half slipping off. Ann laughed, and it turned him on more.

"I love that," he whispered.

"What?" Ann asked breathlessly.

"Your laugh," Joseph clarified, swallowing when he realized she was on top of him. "Its just ... it's beautiful."

"Oh — yeah thanks," Ann managed.

*Yeah thanks? That's all you can manage Ann — 'yeah thanks'? I am utterly fuckin' hopeless.*

"Don't let me talk, just kiss me, please," Ann requested. Joseph kissed her, and she slipped her hands under his shirt to touch over his heart. Joseph took her hands and together they got his shirt off: it got stuck at his head and they had to yank. Then together they ripped off every coin metal piece and threw the wires over the side of the bed. Ann kissed over his neck and slowly down his chest. Joseph winced as she touched a bruise.

"Sorry," she said, looking up.

"No, no, don't stop," he pleaded, and she leaned down and let her mouth run all the way down to his belt-line, where she blew teasingly.

"Shit," he whispered, his eyes rolling up. He ran his hands up under her shirt, and fumbled with the buttons. "I ... I can't —"

"Having trouble?" Ann snorted. "I guess you've never done this before."

"Don't tease me woman, or I'll *rip* it off," he warned.

"Do it," she responded.

Joseph looked at her silhouette for a second then did as she said.

"Don't rip my bra though," Ann said, taking it off herself. She gasped when he ran his hands up over her breasts and bit her lip hard when she felt his tongue slide up her belly to take one nipple in his mouth. She whimpered, and Joseph half-grinned.

"Oh." He breathed into her ear while his fingers continued to rub one nipple gently, the other hand pulling off any wires she had missed. "I learn fast, see?"

Ann nodded and pulled his face to her hurriedly, kissing him rapidly. "I ..." she said, in between passes on his mouth. "I want you."

"Me too," he managed back. He felt her tugging at the jeans he had been too lazy to take off, trying to undo his belt. "I ... I can't." She frowned, and Joseph laughed nervously. "Yeah — I'll — I'll do it," he said, undoing the buckle and pulling off the belt and getting the zipper down. He felt Ann's hands, at first hesitant, then more boldly pulling his boxers down and he almost came when he felt them touch his skin. He reached for her, but she was already pulling off her pants. Ann looked up and felt her nose touch his as she slipped out of the last bit of her clothes, and realized that they were both completely naked.

"I'm scared," she said, voice cracking.

"I know," Joseph confessed. "Me too."

*So scared,* Ann thought. Moving closer to him she felt him reach down to touch her, and she moaned loudly when he slipped two fingers inside of her. It was too much to take and she reached down to touch him in return.

"Oh fuck ... Ann." He groaned when she wrapped her hand around him, and he pulled her closer. For a few minutes there was just the steady sound of their rising pants. "Please," he was able to say finally. His brain was no longer in any kind of control. "Please — please ..."

Ann moved over to him and kissed him, and heard the catch in his breath. Knowing he was as scared as her helped as she pulled him over to her and felt him pushing inside her.

"Oh, fuck," Joseph heard her whimper, and she clasped at his back, hard. "Am I ... am I hurting you?" Joseph asked, stopping as much as he could.

"I ... no. Well, yeah but — I think this is the part that hurts the most. I think it gets better after this. Don't ... don't stop," she begged, and he nodded and sunk down on her, bearing her onto the bed and kissing her as he pressed down. He felt her wrap her legs around his waist. "Better?" he asked.

"Uh-huh," was all she could say, and Joseph just nodded and smelled her hair, her skin, loving the sound of her gasps. Ann held onto him tightly, torn between pain and pleasure, terrified and elated.

It was either the drugs, a miracle, or both, that Sherry heard nothing and slept on.

Mrs. Carter glanced over at the Headmistress who continued watching the girl before them. "Amina?"

She didn't answer.

"Ms. Jackson?" Mrs. Carter asked again. Lieutenant turned imperiously to her principal. "Ya'll think I'm foolish enough to not see what you're tryna do? Bring me in here, bring us all in here, and show us some Photoshopped video of ... tryna make us turn on each other? Well you can give it up, cause we ain't stupid like that."

"You take photography and video art, don't you?" the Headmistress asked.

Lieutenant just nodded, eyes narrowing suspiciously.

"Then you should be able to see whether or not this tape has been played with," the Headmistress said. "You can see —"

"I don't know what you can do!" Lieutenant snapped. "Y'all have torture devices, and shock machines, and stun guns and — you could completely have arranged this tape for all I know."

"Even if we could," Mrs. Carter said, "how would we have been able to find out where you were hiding? Or what your plans were? Or certain details provided by —"

"You think you can fool me?" Lieutenant spat. "I know how these mind games go, and I'm not gonna fall for it. No way, end of story."

The Headmistress nodded as if considering, then said kindly. "Well we can give you as much time as you need to watch and verify for yourself the contents —"

"You can quit with the sweet approach, 'Mistress.'" Lieutenant cut her off coldly. "I don't need anymore time. I'm done here."

"I see," the Headmistress said, and Mrs. Carter couldn't quite tell if she was smiling. "Alright then. You can go."

"Oh, thank you," Lieutenant said snidely and turned to go out.

"That went well," Mrs. Carter said sarcastically.

"It did," the Headmistress said. "If you could excuse me for a few hours? I have something I need to oversee."


Blackness.

That was all Charlie knew: darkness. Silence.

*That's weird though, knowing that you know nothing? Maybe I just have my eyes closed. So if I just open them ...*

"Is everything working, Wendy?"

*I can't open my eyes.*

"Yes — someday you have to tell me how you build all this equipment so it can be moved, the scanners —"

*That's Mrs. Waters, the chemistry teacher.*

"Someday."

*That's her: the Headmistress. The mistress of the school, the woman behind the curtain.*

*But why can't I open my eyes?*

"I am a scientist," said the Headmistress, "but I'm not the expert here. Can you explain to me what it is about her brain that has you speechless?"

*My brain?*

"Her brain is different," Mrs. Waters said, almost whispering.

"I guessed that. May I ask you to elaborate?"

"Charlie has less grey matter in the temporal lobes and the frontal lobes. She also has increased glutamine and dopamine levels. This is normal."

"Normal?" asked the Headmistress.

*Normal?*

"Normal for paranoid schizophrenia," Mrs. Waters clarified.

*No!*

"But," Mrs. Waters continued, "she is forming new synapses at the rate of — my God, I cannot even calculate. It's almost as if to combat the schizophrenia, her brain has developed stronger, larger, better."

"What could she do?"

"Do?" Mrs. Waters asked confused.

"Yes. *Do,*" the Headmistress pressed. "You said her brain is better. How would that manifest?"

"Well — she might be smarter...she might have stronger senses and a better ability to comprehend, and ..."

"And what?" the Headmistress pressed.

"I don't know," Mrs. Waters confessed. "I don't know what she could do. She is new. Like the others, she is new."

"Like Amina Jackson? I read your report, but I understand you were — interrupted," the Headmistress posed.

"We had to put her under again," Mrs. Waters said, swallowing. "She was still manic, but we couldn't tell at first. She made herself look not manic, spoke slower, seemed calm, answered questions..."

"As if she could control it?" the Headmistress asked silkily.

"She tried," Mrs. Waters said. "But that would be hard. She was struggling. All that energy from the high of mania — it has to have somewhere to go, you cannot just bottle it up."

"She seemed calm when I talked to her," the Headmistress noted.

"She is now going to fall into depression," Mrs. Waters informed. "Probably one worse than any other."

"Even worse if she thinks her friend has betrayed her," the Headmistress mused softly.

"Betrayed?" Mrs. Waters asked.

"Nothing." The Headmistress shrugged. "Have you seen Mr. Levant yet?"

"I have his brain scans." Mrs. Waters nodded. "Nothing abnormal."

The Headmistress shook her head. "I suppose you didn't stay long enough."

"What do you mean?" Mrs. Waters asked.

"I had you do brain scans last year and you said that the first two at the beginning of the year were radically different from each other, and the last radically different from the one you did end of last year?"

"Yes but this one now was like the last one of —"

"Which one?" the Headmistress asked. Mrs. Waters frowned. "Have you seen his handwriting?" the Headmistress continued. "Here is a paragraph written by Anthony ..."

"Yes ...?"

"And here is the same paragraph written by Anton," the Headmistress continued, showing another sample. "And here ... is one by 'Ant.'."

"But they are all the —"

"No," the Headmistress whispered. "No, they aren't."

"You cannot tell me you think you have found," Mrs. Waters stuttered, "you think you found a —"

"A multiple, yes," the Headmistress asserted. "They are not as rare as you may think."

*Sweet Mother of Everything. I know what she is doing.*

*I have to tell them. Damn it move Charlie, move!*

"You did put her under, right?" the Headmistress asked.

"Yes," Mrs. Waters said, confused.

"How long ago did you put her under?" the Headmistress asked.

"Long enough," Mrs. Waters said, watching the Headmistress stare at the unmoving girl. "Why?"

"No reason," the Headmistress said, shaking herself a little. "No reason."


Sherry yawned and then sat bolt upright.

"I didn't check on the fucking kids," Sherry swore. She strode over to Ann's room. "Time to get up," she said roughly, poking the bundle of sheets. "Time to get up!"

The bundle didn't move.

Sherry sucked her teeth and whipped the sheet back. She stood still for a moment, going very white, then turned and thrust open the door to

Joseph's room.

The two teens were so deeply asleep, they didn't move when the door banged open.

There was a softness in Ann's sleeping face that made her look almost sweet. Joseph's arm was wrapped securely around her waist. The sheets didn't hide their nakedness, and the happiness still registered in their afterglow.

Ann made a small, puppy-like whimper, and Joseph sighed and buried his head more deeply into her neck, her hair tickling his face. Sherry's eyes fell on the wires on the ground.

"Dammit!"

Ann's eyes flew open when the hairbrush hit her head, and she gasped and shoved Joseph awake.

"Wha'?" he mumbled, eyes lazing open before he snapped upright as well.

"I am calling the school this minute," Sherry said. "You were given another chance, and you blew it. It would serve you right if you got pregnant from this, Ann," she said in a low voice and watched both of them stiffen. "Or are you both so stupid you didn't think that would happen? Both of you, both of you will pay for this, but luckily it won't be my problem because I want you both out of my house!"

"You're gonna turn us in for this?" Ann asked.

Sherry laughed. "Of course I am. Why wouldn't I?"

"Because if you do we might have to let slip how easy it was to drug you considerin' how many different pills you had in your closet," Joseph threatened.

"You — those are my business," Sherry hissed. "None of yours!"

"Oh, but it's the school's business," Ann said icily, "since the supervisors are supposed to be drug-free. I don't think they'll be happy to know you lied about your problems and hid them. In fact, they might just think you helped us all along."

"You bitch," Sherry whispered, then strode forward, whipping around her hand. "You ungrateful —"

"Hey!" Joseph snapped, and Sherry stumbled back, clutching her wrist. "Don't even try to touch her."

Sherry swallowed hard and then half-ran out of the room and quickly dialed the emergency number. "Yes, I need you to come right now. The students have ripped off their wires and been violent toward me."

*It's like a needle piercing your brain, like a migraine on steroids,* Toni decided, trying to keep her mind off the weird headache. *God, just stop!*

The door opened, and Toni bit her tongue painfully.

"Time to go," said one aide as two guards followed her into the white room.

"Go where?" Toni asked as the woman slowly undid her straps and then swiftly cuffed her hands.

"Don't know," the woman said curtly, standing her up and leading her silently down the hall.

*That's funny,* Toni thought, *my headache gets better the further I go away. Maybe it was from sitting in that room too long. Or maybe —*

The aide pushed open the door and indicated for Toni to go in. Toni frowned but did so, hearing the door snap shut behind her.

*I'm in a hall of cameras,* she thought, looking around at the walls. Video screens covered all three sides, along with computers, and chairs that she suspected were for the aides who monitored the schools. In each screen she could see a different part of the Academy.

"So this is how you watch us," Toni said aloud.

"It's one way."

Toni turned. Sitting at the desk was Mrs. Carter, but she wasn't the one who'd spoken. The tall woman behind the desk had, and she stepped around the principal to face Toni.

Grey eyes locked on Toni's hazel-green ones, and thin lips spread into a half smile. The woman was of indeterminate age and her suit was nondescript. In fact, there was nothing special about her appearance other than her height, and the hair that was as red as was possible without help from a dye.

"Hello, Toni," the woman said courteously. "I am Sophia Valentina. Would you like to sit down?"

"I'd prefer to stand," Toni said. "You're the Headmistress aren't you?"

"Yes, I am," Ms. Valentina chuckled. "Toni, I would like to show you something. I believe you are the last of your friends to see it."

"Did they like it?" Toni asked. The principal frowned. The Headmistress smiled.

"They had mixed feelings," Ms. Valentina answered. Her voice was open and easy, almost comforting. "I don't think they enjoyed it at first —"

"If they didn't want to see it I don't either, thank you," Toni said evenly. Ms. Valentina smiled more widely.

"That's fine," she said kindly. "But I do believe it is something you would like to see. I think you would feel you had the right to see it, if you knew what it was. Besides," she continued, watching the girl's expression closely, "it might change your opinion of whether you wish to stay or not."

"What do you mean?" Toni questioned.

"Your mother and father are a few minutes away," Mrs. Carter explained. "When they get here, it will be your decision on whether to stay or go."

"Go ..." Toni repeated. "You'd let me go?"

"If you so choose," Ms. Valentina stated, "you may. We will discuss your dismissal with your parents. But before they arrive, I would like to show you this footage."

"Okay," she said quietly. "I'll play along."

Ms. Valentina nodded and walked over to type something into the computer. "If you would watch this screen." She tapped the fourth screen up. Toni watched, as the Headmistress drew up a video labeled *November 20th, 2012*. Four weeks ago.

"I am very glad you decided to do the right thing Ant," the Headmistress said on the tape. "I think your parents would be very proud, and they want you to do well here."

"Yes ma'am," said —

"Anton," Toni whispered. "No."

Yes. It was him. The same body, same features, same face ... except that it wasn't. There was something different about him. The Anton Toni knew held himself high. This one looked as if he was trying to disappear into his chair. He blinked rapidly, twitched incessantly, and his voice was soft, stuttering, with a thick Southern accent.

"Well I—first I wanna say that ... that I neva, eva woulda thought 'bout doin' all this ... was my friends who got me into it, you know, the ones who tried ... tried to ... to my parents—"

"I know, Ant, I know," the Headmistress said soothingly. "We won't blame you for their choices. Just tell me what you said you told Seth."

"I — well I told him everythin'," Ant stated. "All about ... you know my friends, and their plans to ... well, to do all kinds of things to the school, things I neva woulda wanted to do, I swear! I —"

"I know, Ant," Ms. Valentina repeated calmingly. "What was it you said about where this group meets?"

"Oh, they meet out at this old house, run down, past the train tracks," he confessed. "And they meet after midnight, 'cause that's when the lights go down, you know? And, and they have ways of tellin' when a meeting is comin'."

"What ways, Ant?"

"Paper," Ant stated. "With invisible ink, they pass the scraps when no one's lookin'. Can't see it if you don't know how. I can't remember how right now, but you'll find out, I'm sure."

"Of course," the Headmistress said. "Now, you said there were plans?"

"Yes," Ant said. "But I don't know what. They don't tell me. They say they'll take care of everythin', but ... well I just don't know. I can't say."

"Would you be able to show Seth how to get there?" the Headmistress asked.

"Of course ... you — you ain't gonna tell my parents I was there, right?" Ant asked, eyes widening in open plea.

"Of course not," the Headmistress soothed. "There would be no reason to tell. You weren't even there."

The video ended. Toni stood still.

*I'm just a broke as fuck actor,' Anton said — or was that Anthony? God, it makes no sense!*

"It doesn't make any sense," Toni whispered. "He wouldn't betray us. Unless you — " She pointed accusingly at Mrs. Carter. "You threatened him. You and that two-faced skater boy wannabe blackmailed him until he turned us in."

"If you mean Seth," Mrs. Carter stated, "he was the only one to come forward and help us, and in doing so, save lives you would have —"

"The bombs were his idea!" Toni snapped. "He came up with them, not us! We were the ones who made sure we did it at night, so we wouldn't hurt any people, just this goddamn Guantanamo Bay school! We just wanted to get away!"

"You are only making yourself look bad here," Mrs. Carter said flatly. "Flying off the handle and throwing around foolish names —"

"Foolish names?" Toni spat. "Foolish — oh sweetie, God must have stepped on your brain with Her high heels before shoving it into your head. You shock us, and lock us up, and take away our rights, and —"

"And you try to blow up our school," the Headmistress cut in.

"Only because of what you do to us," Toni launched back. "You started this."

"No, Toni," Mrs. Carter said, opening a file. "You did. You and your friends were brought here because you harmed others, or yourselves, to the point where your parents had no other choice but to send you to a place where you could be restrained from your dangerous behavior. You had a choice, Toni," Mrs. Carter said earnestly. "We said from the beginning, if you had chosen to obey our rules, you would have had all the rights and privileges we could give you. You chose to take the path of harm, to yourself and others, and we were forced to enact consequences. We are trying to protect you — all of you," Mrs. Carter said. "Sometimes that means taking away your freedom to hurt yourself."

"How do you do that?" Toni whispered. "How do you convince yourself that shocking, starving, restraining is ... you know I thought Seth was real evil," Toni proclaimed. "Cruelty because he could, with no remorse ... I thought he was the worst. But he's a scorpion, he stings because it's in his nature. He can't care, he doesn't know how. But you." She pointed again at Mrs. Carter. "I've seen you with Becky and Katrina. You can care, you do love, and you choose to ignore that, and do this to us," Toni continued. "Would you give your daughter the same treatment we get, huh?"

"If she did the same behavior, if it was necessary," Mrs. Carter answered. "Yes. I would."

"Then you're sick," Toni said softly. "You're sick and you think we're crazy. This place is crazy. This place is worse than juvie, and if we were so bad we would be there."

"It is only because of this school that you escaped that," the Headmistress cut in. "These are brave words. Were you saying them when you watched Serena Osterman die?"

Toni went cold. "I didn't kill her."

"No," Ms. Valentina said, watching Toni breathe fast. "No, you just ran when you could have helped —"

"I did help!" Toni screamed. "I tried to grab her hand and pull her up, but she slipped and fell in. I couldn't get to her, it was pitch black, she didn't know how to swim, I ran to get help, I —"

"And why was Serena out in the woods, in the swamp in the middle of the night?" Ms. Valentina pressed. "Why was she found beaten up the next week, her clothes ripped half off Toni? Was it because she bullied you?"

"It wasn't just me," Toni said, eyes watering now, in anger, in fear, in shame. "It was everyone! She was like that to everyone. She almost made one of our friends *kill* herself —"

"Almost." Ms. Valentina raised a finger. "Instead, Serena died. Did you enjoy your revenge, Toni? Did you —"

"It wasn't my revenge," Toni said hoarsely, "I didn't want that. We were just supposed to take her clothes and make her run back, so she would know what it was like to be humiliated. But then Jenny got mad and hit her, and everyone else laughed —"

*Including me,* Toni thought.

"But it wasn't me who pushed her in!" Toni defended. "I tried to help her, when everyone else ran, I tried to help her, but her hand slipped and ..."

*And I ran.* Toni could see it all. They'd laughed at Serena. The girl was vicious, no one felt any pity for her. They hit her. Toni had hit her too, a hard slap for Hana who had cut her wrists after Serena outed her to the school and led the students in making Hana's life a living hell for months. Toni had felt no pity when Serena started to cry. No one had. They had laughed right up until they pushed her into the pond, and discovered it was deeper than anyone knew.

Then they ran.

Toni had climbed over onto the branch to try and grab Serena's hand. She had had it, she had held it right up until Serena's fingers slipped through.

Then Toni, too, ran.

"You didn't go to jail," the Headmistress whispered to Toni, who stared ahead. "You could have, all of you could have, if her parents had chosen to press charges."

"I tried to help her," Toni repeated.

"But you arranged it," the Headmistress stated.

"I didn't mean for it to go like that," Toni barely forced out.

"Well, that's the trouble with these things, isn't it?" Ms. Valentina said, straightening up.

"Sophia?" Mrs. Carter said, looking up from the phone. "Mr. and Mrs. White are here."

"Let them in," the Headmistress said, watching Toni sink into a chair.

"Toni!"

Toni felt her mother rush over and hug her. "Oh baby, why are you crying?"

"Am I?" Toni said absently, touching her face. The tears had soaked the top of her shirt. "Didn't notice."

"Honey." Her mother brushed aside a curl, but Toni turned away.

"While I understand you want to talk with Toni, I would like to get this over with as soon as possible," the Headmistress said, shaking her parent's hands and gesturing for them to sit. "This is an unusual case."

"Why?" asked Toni's handsome father. He resembled a shorter, older John Legend. "What's the big problem? She's being expelled?"

"We really don't have expulsion here." Mrs. Carter took over. "We take in the students no other schools will. We just aren't sure Toni fits with the J. Alter Academy community."

"Why is that?" asked Toni's mother, a heavy, pale woman with short hair and a pretty, dimpled face. "If you can fit anyone in, why not Toni?"

"Our curriculum is such that ..."

Toni ignored Mrs. Carter's empty words, and watched the Headmistresses face. *I could have gone to juvie ... so could have Katrina ... but the Headmistress chose to bring us here—chose ...*

"I'm the only one you're letting leave," Toni said.

"Just a moment, honey," her mom said. "Are —"

"Am I the only one you're sending away?" Toni demanded loudly. The others turned to her.

"Yes," Mrs. Carter answered.

"Why?" Toni said.s

"Ms. Valentina looked over the events, and decided that you might not fit here," Mrs. Carter said.

"Why me?"

"In a minute Toni," her mother said sharply. "Now ..."

*Why only me?* Toni thought. *I wasn't even that important in the whole plan. I'm no different from anyone else!*

*Different.*

"I'm not different," she whispered.

"What?" Her father looked over at her.

*Joseph can control fire,* Toni thought, *Lieutenant is telekinetic. Charlie is psychic, Anton — Anton, Anthony can mess with electricity, and I —*

"I can't do anything," she said aloud.

"You can do lots of things," her mother said, putting her hand on her knee. "Toni?"

"So I was a mistake." Toni looked up, straight at Ms. Valentina. "I was brought here as a mistake. And now you're just gonna let me go? Let me go out and tell everyone what happens here?"

"Well, here we have some stipulations," Mrs. Carter said. "You both recall how you signed the confidentiality clause. That clause still holds, even in a situation like this."

"But I don't see how that's proper," Toni's father argued, "seeing as how ..."

Toni again tuned them all out. *I can go,* she thought. *I can get away and never have to worry about this place again. I can be free. I don't have to be afraid of shocks, and wires, and white rooms. I can sleep in my own bed, and live my life, and say fuck it to this whole sick place.*

*I can leave my friends.*

Toni looked down at her wrists, chaffed from the straps. *What's happening to everyone else? I could get out, but they're all left here. I wouldn't be able to speak out for them. I would be like Anton, turning my back on all of them, running away and —*

"And leaving them to drown."

"Toni?"

Toni looked up and around at the circle. "We don't need all this."

"Um, well sweetie," her mother said, watching her hesitantly. "We have to consider carefully whether —"

"No, we don't," Toni corrected. "Because I wanna stay."

Mrs. Carter raised her eyebrows so high they seemed to go right into her hair. Toni's mother's mouth was still moving but emitted no sound. Her father just stared.

"Are you certain?"

Toni turned to the Headmistress and met her cloud grey eyes. "Yeah, I am. I want to stay."

# acknowledgments

Thank you to Kate Hayman, for giving me the basis of J. Alter Academy and Dana Lovejoy. I expect you to recommend this book to everyone you know!

Thanks to my bestest friend Maxine, who gave me the character of Toni, sharp tugs when I needed to be pulled back to earth, and back pats when I needed those too. Thank you to my other bestie, Anna, for undying support, love, and sass.

Thanks to my two incredibly skillful editors. First, to Good Cop Nina Terhune, for her ability to both to tell me when someone didn't quite "cut the mustard," and to put up with her excitable author roommate. (Also, for being a *Buffy* fan, because that always means one is a good person.) Then to Bad Cop Alec Kubas-Meyer, whose obscenity laced edits were always hilarious and on point. The book wouldn't be here without you.

Thanks to my amazing, wonderful, impossibly great designer, friend, and book savior Joshua Langman. Bloody Beluga, the book just wouldn't have happened without you!

Thanks to Njide, Nneka, Ari, Mitch, Korb, Sarah, Julia, Max, Kendall and all my friends back home.

Thanks to Tana, Emma, Ben, Bradley, Dominic, Evan and all my Westies. We don't need recreational drugs to be too cool for school!

Finally, thank you to my first and number one fan. You know who you are, and you know how much I love you. As Christina Aguilera would say, "Spread your wings and soar!"

# about the author

Born in Massachusetts in 1992, Aubrey Coletti is an American writer, dancer, choreographer, and song-writer who currently attends Sarah Lawrence College. She began work on *Altered* when she was fifteen and finished it before her senior year in high school. Now eighteen she is currently working on a sequel to the *Altered* series, which she intends to be either a trilogy or quartet.

www.ingramcontent.com/pod-product-compliance
Lightning Source LLC
Chambersburg PA
CBHW071130170626
46809CB00002B/560